KEEPERS OF THE FAITH

Keepers of the Faith

a novel

SHAUKAT AJMERI

MAWENZI
HOUSE

We acknowledge the support of the Canada Council for the Arts for our publishing program. We also acknowledge support from the Government of Canada through the Canada Book Fund, and Government of Ontario through the Ontario Arts Council.

Cover design by Kaamil Ajmeri
Cover photo by Aa Dil
Author photo by Sameera Tayabali

Epigraphs:

Excerpt from *The Rubais of Rumi, Insane with Love*, Translations and Commentary by Nevit O Ergin and Will Johnson (Inner Traditions).

Excerpt from *Gitanjali: Song Offerings*, by Rabindranath Tagore, Introduction by W B Yeats (Kessinger Publishing).

Library and Archives Canada Cataloguing in Publication

Title: Keepers of the faith : a novel / Shaukat Ajmeri.
Names: Ajmeri, Shaukat, 1961- author.
Identifiers: Canadiana (print) 20200161652 | Canadiana (ebook) 20200161679 | ISBN 9781988449968 (softcover) | ISBN 9781988449975 (HTML) | ISBN 9781988449982 (PDF)
Classification: LCC PS8601.J64 K44 2020 | DDC C813/.6—dc23

Printed and bound in Canada by Coach House Printing

Mawenzi House Publishers Ltd.
39 Woburn Avenue (B)
Toronto, Ontario M5M 1K5
Canada

www.mawenzihouse.com

For My Mother and My Sister

Not before the minarets and mosques
Come tumbling down
Will real peace enter into our lives
Not before faith becomes heresy
And heresy becomes faith
Will any man of God become truly Muslim

JALALUDDIN RUMI

Leave this chanting and singing and telling of beads!
Whom dost thou worship in this lonely dark corner of a temple
    with doors all shut?
Open thine eyes and see thy God is not before thee!
He is there where the tiller is tilling the hard ground
and where the pathmaker is breaking stones.
He is with them in sun and in shower,
and his garment is covered with dust.
Put off thy holy mantle and even like him come down on the
    dusty soil!

RABINDRANATH TAGORE

Foreword

——

It is no easy task to survey and present a comprehensive view of the recent history of a close-knit Shia Muslim community to a broad public audience without compromising on the rigor demanded by the subtle nuances of that history. In an ambitious endeavor to do precisely that, Shaukat Ajmeri masterfully executes just such a task in his debut novel *Keepers of the Faith*, setting an exemplary standard that ought to be followed by aspiring writers in the genre of historical fiction. However, it should be noted that the term "fiction" as employed here ought to be understood in a restricted sense, since parts of the novel are anchored in the heartrending events that took place in Udaipur during the early seventies of the last century, the repercussions of which survive to this day.

The novel commences with an innocent love story between Akbar and Rukhsana from Udaipur, proceeding through strange twists and turns in their fortunes, moving to Bombay and finally culminating in the United States. It depicts in vivid detail a tale of separation and sorrow, not only for this young couple but also their extended families and numerous other members of their community, who are now scattered throughout the seven continents, a function of the draconian weapon of excommunication wielded mercilessly by the high priest. The latter's vast powers, as critically analyzed by modern scholars, arise from the lethal combination of religious and economic influence, which creates a huge problem not merely for the Momins (as the members of the community are here called) but also for the state as well.

Keepers of the Faith is an inspiring and provocative novel. Ajmeri deserves full credit for his lucid style and thoughtful and philosophical reflections over the bewildering events that unfold. The scenes are vividly depicted and come alive before the reader's eyes like a beautiful tableau painted by a master painter. In my view, *Keepers of the Faith* should be read by all Momins conversant with English. It is hoped that soon the novel will be translated into Urdu, Gujarati, Hindi, and other languages, so that inquisitive readers all around the globe can also enjoy this masterpiece.

ISMAIL K POONAWALA

Professor Emeritus of Arabic and Islamic Studies,

University of California, Los Angeles

Prologue

KHATUN, WITH ONE EYE ON the clock, was unable to concentrate on her book. Rukhsana had not come, as she always did late afternoons. When it was past suppertime, Khatun stood up and started pacing. Rukhsana might have taken ill, she thought. She had not come the day before, and the day before that. Worry began to quicken Khatun's pulse. Although the girl's house was just up the street, Khatun thought it prudent to wait out another day. The next day at sundown again she waited—her anticipation layered with prayer—for the sound of familiar footfalls, for that sweet knock on the door. None came.

Khatun decided to pay a visit. *I hope the girl is all right.* For the past eight months, ever since Akbar left for Bombay, hardly a day had passed without Rukhsana coming over and the two of them sitting down chatting quietly over a cup of tea. Not showing up for four straight days was odd. Something was wrong. After cooking supper, Khatun changed into decent clothes and walked to Rukhsana's house. The stench of garlic still languished in her fingers. No matter how many times she washed her hands with soap, she could not get rid of it. She must ask Zubaida, Rukhsana's mother, for a tip to erase the odour. It was a cold February evening, the sun was about to turn in for the night, and the street was bathed in the mellow light that signals the winding-down of humans and their affairs. She opened the front door of the house, climbed the unlit stairs, and saw that Rukhsana's room was bolted; a brass lock hung from the latch. *Where could the girl have gone at this time?* She knocked on

Zubaida's door. It was slightly ajar.

"Who is it?" Zubaida asked.

"It's me, Khatun."

Silence. *Why is Zubaida not saying anything?* Without waiting another second, Khatun removed her slippers and entered the room. Zubaida was sitting at her customary spot on the divan, stiff as a statue, face taut with tension. She did not reply when Khatun greeted her, nor did she smile or look up to meet her eyes.

"Is everything all right?" Khatun asked.

Zubaida did not speak a word.

"What is it with you? And where is Rukhsana?"

"She is not here." The words came out cold and curt.

"What do you mean, not here—where is she?"

"How does it matter to you?"

Khatun was shocked. She had never seen Zubaida so rude before. Had she offended her in any way? She couldn't recall. But even if she had, so what? There was no need to be so hostile.

"It matters, she's been coming to see me every day, and now for the past four days she's disappeared. Obviously, I'm concerned."

"Well, she's not coming to your house anymore."

"What are you saying, Zubaida? Why won't Rukhsana come to my house? She's now my daughter, too!"

Zubaida's eyes welled up. And Khatun, who had been standing all this while, went down on her knees and hugged her.

"What's wrong, Zubaida?"

"I was expecting you'd come. What took you so long? Remember how when we were girls we made a pact that if we had son and daughter, we would marry them to each other? Who would have thought it would come true? It *was* coming true. How happy it made me. But it was not to be . . . " Zubaida wiped her tears with a small handkerchief. "It's all over," she said. "My poor girl's heart is broken. She has not stopped crying ever since she was told to end this relationship."

"End this relationship, why, what are you talking about?"

"You know why. Mowlana's fatwa, decreeing that we break relations with all you radicals. You have challenged his authority as our spiritual father. That's what my husband says. You know what a fanatic Qamar is, he will do anything Mowlana says. When Qamar found out that Rukhsana was visiting you, and especially of her love for Akbar, he had a fit. You should have seen his rage. It was as if I had sold my girl into prostitution. He even raised his hand to her. If not for me he would have killed her. He said, 'You better take care of that girl, and next time if I see any of you near those infidels I will wring your necks.'"

Khatun was speechless. She couldn't imagine a father saying such a thing.

"Zubaida, how can this be?" she said. "Please don't let this happen. Rukhsana and Akbar have nothing to do with this quarrel. Please, do something. The sin is not that they love each other, the sin is to tear them apart. How will we face God when the day comes?"

"You think I did not protest?" Zubaida replied. "I told him the exact same thing. You know what he said? 'Allah will be pleased that we remained loyal to our Mowlana. If Mowlana is unhappy, Allah is unhappy. Consorting with the enemies of Mowlana is a greater sin.'"

"Oh God, what madness is this?" Khatun cried, more angry than sad now. "What will I tell Akbar? That he can't marry the love of his life because Mowlana says so? And what about

Rukhsana, how is she taking it? Where is she, anyway?"

Zubaida burst into a fresh bout of tears.

"You know what is the greatest tragedy for a mother?" she said at length, her voice heavy with pain. "The death of her child. And you know what is the next worst thing? The death of the child's dream. I would not wish such calamity upon any mother . . . And here we are—what kismet."

They both fell silent, enveloped by a sorrow they thought they would never know.

The sun had gone down. Zubaida had missed her *maghrib* prayer and hadn't even realized that. The power went out, and in the partial darkness Zubaida lit a candle. "This ugly-faced electricity goes out every other minute," she cursed. The flickering flame of the candle was reflected in the mirror of the steel cupboard, and the objects close to the candle threw large, eerie shadows on the wall.

"Where is Rukhsana?" Khatun asked again.

"The day it happened, she was hysterical and refused to eat for a whole day," Zubaida replied. "Qamar packed her off to his sister's place. He has threatened to keep her there until she comes to her senses. But you know Rukhsana, she will break but will not bend. May God help my poor darling. I went to see her this morning. She speaks only to me. Her aunt is considerate and understands, but refuses to sympathize with her cause. The whole family is hung up on Mowlana. I wish I could break free from this madness, but you know it's not possible. I've got to think of my two girls and their future."

"But what kind of future do you see for them? They are robbing Rukhsana of her happiness."

"I know. But what can I do? It's not that we women get to decide our futures. Qamar will throw me out on the street if I try anything smart. And even if I leave, who will take care of me and my girls? I've no money nor the education to go out and find a job. I'm not like you."

"I know it's not easy."

"And you know what," Zubaida said, "it is not just this—the two of us can't even meet. If Qamar were to see you here, God knows what he will do."

"Are you serious?"

"That is what excommunication means, all radicals become untouchables. We should have expected this. My in-laws are bigots; they follow Mowlana like shadows. And Qamar . . . the devil has taken hold of him," Zubaida said, fretting with her handkerchief. After a pause, she said, brightly, "But we can meet secretly. We can always find a way."

Khatun nodded, but they both knew it was a vain hope. Mowlana had declared war on a section of the community, dubbed them as Radicals because they did not obey him on a simple secular matter; because they insisted on expressing their civil, democratic right. Then, as a consequence, there had been the atrocity at the shrine in Sadikot, when the women were attacked by the Mowlana's goons. Khatun was one of the victims. That should have forewarned her. She had heard rumblings of how relationships would be torn apart, but she could not have imagined that it would come so close to home, affect her so personally, so viscerally. It was as though Sadikot had come to torment her all over again. She felt a heaviness in her heart. Wiping a tear, she took an envelope from her purse and gave it to Zubaida.

"This letter is for Rukhsana, from Akbar. It came by post."

1

WHEN EXACTLY RUKHSANA TIPTOED INTO his heart, Akbar could never tell. But when the first consciousness about girls dawned upon him, she was already there, nourishing his hon-eyed dreams. He was a lanky boy of twelve, with a shock of thick black hair and a face that did not invite a second look. He was by no means handsome, but had a disarming vulnerabil-ity about him that held a certain charm. Socially awkward and always unsure of himself, he spent most of his time alone. He would often climb up to the "tower top" of his family's home to steal a glimpse of Rukhsana. To show off. To let her know of his love for her, of which she did not have a hint and per-haps would not even care if she knew. He could see her bal-cony down the road from his vantage position and would wait for her to emerge there. Often she never came. But there was always tomorrow. He had learned to live in hope, a young hope unsullied by a corrupting world.

It started to drizzle. How he loved the scent of the first rain—the hot, thirsty earth emitting a damp sigh of relief. Monsoon came to Udaipur reluctantly, as if obliged to pay a visit to a poor country cousin. And when it did come, it usually arrived late, in July or sometimes even August, having already showered its bounty elsewhere. It sprinkled this beautiful southern nook of Rajasthan with the remainder of its wares. People had learned not to expect much of the miserly monsoon; they were happy as long as Fateh Sagar Lake filled up. The level of water in the lake seemed to mark the quotient of happiness of the people.

That year the water level in the lake had hit rock bottom. All of summer, the westerly wind bore the arid feel of the Thaar desert up north. The sun unleashed its fire without respite. Even a whiff of cloud in the sky would get the hopes of the city soaring. Humans and cows and dogs huddled together in every slice of shade they could find, seeking refuge from the merciless sun. Fans and coolers were ineffective inside stone and brick houses. Just a couple of hours into the morning, the city's homes would begin to feel like furnaces. Hibiscus and dandelions and other flora that spring had coaxed out of the ground wilted; green grass was scorched into straw; only neem and peepal and the native khejri had any chance of surviving the summer.

The "tower top" that Akbar had clambered up to was the topmost terrace of their house. Of the six storeys, the bottom three floors of the building were the living quarters, open in the middle to let air and light through. The top three were terraced rooftops, each smaller than the one below. His grandfather had overseen the construction of the building and lavished attention and money on it to make it the best and the tallest in the neighbourhood. The "tower top" was small, no more than six feet by four. A low one-foot barrier of cement grille ran around it; not much of a protection. This adjunct had no obvious purpose, and was almost inaccessible as it had no stairs. One could only reach it from the terrace below by jumping and catching hold of its plinth, hanging by the fingers and vaulting oneself up with brute muscle power.

The light rain petered off and the clouds were driven away by a sudden wind. The sun had begun to hide behind Sajjan Garh, the Monsoon Palace that stood up on a hill in the distance. Akbar moved to the edge of the railing to look down. A crow flew overhead, shrieking. *If I were to fall down, that would be the end.* He stepped back and turned his gaze to the balcony at the other end of the street, with its parrot-green doors. She was not there, but her mother sat there as usual, knitting and keeping an eye on the goings-on in the street below.

From the street, the first-floor balcony didn't seem far. Most evenings Rukhsana would spend her time there. He would pass her house on his bicycle a number of times, even when he had no errand to run in that direction, taking the longer route just for an off chance that he'd be noticed. He could never gather the nerve to look up towards her balcony, but he hoped she would see him. He increased his odds by making as many trips as he could. If not Rukhsana, at least her mother Zubaida's eagle-eye would catch him. Zubaida Auntie was a friend of his mother's, and their families met often.

Earlier that evening he had been flying his kite from the middle terrace, but in a battle with other kites, his was cut loose. He was disappointed by the loss. On top of that, his forefinger had been lacerated by the sharp kite string. In the morning he had given a red abrasive coating to the string and laced it with glass powder, a ritual every authentic kite-lover performed in order to ace it in the battle of the skies. His string had not been good enough, after all. And he had used all his pocket money of the past three weeks for the materials. His family was well-off, but his daily allowance was limited to a quarter rupee, which didn't go far. His father, Zahid Ali, was frugal and wanted his only son to appreciate the value of money.

Akbar sat down at the edge of the tower top, looking down at the terrace below, dejected, his legs hanging down. The floor, baked by the sun all day, felt warm under him. As he thought of his lost kite, wondering where it might have landed, he saw a sudden movement in the distance. He looked towards it. It was Rukhsana at her balcony. Excited, he almost waved at her. She was looking out on to the street apparently talking to someone. Even from this distance he could make out her smile, the contours of her face, the flushed cheeks. He imagined the impish glint in her eyes. She wore a pale-yellow dress, sleeveless, her arms resting on the balustrade. A mauve ribbon held her shoulder-length hair into a jaunty ponytail. He could have sworn she saw him when she turned to go inside.

It was beginning to get dark, and the moon like a giant alabaster lamp was emerging from the eastern sky. The neem tree a few houses away to his left hosted a parliament of birds. He could smell food, the aroma of burned masala wafting up from the neighbourhood kitchens. He jumped down from his perch, almost twisting his ankle as he landed. He brushed the seat of his shorts and went down to the main terrace. He filled a watering jug from a tap and watered the drooping, thirsty plants. Grandfather was fond of his little garden. He had cement planters built into the walls on either side of the terrace and had them painted crimson red. Earthen pots in different shapes and sizes were scattered around the periphery. A gardener came to tend the plants once every fortnight, and Akbar was charged with watering them in the evenings. While at it, he confided to them his heart's secrets. He was particularly fond of the jasmine vine that grew in the far corner, its small white blossoms sweetening the nights. His mind somehow associated the fragrance with Rukhsana.

Akbar went downstairs, where his mother was in their room, engrossed in a magazine. Akbar and his parents were part of a joint family. His father's two brothers, their wives and children, and the widow of the fourth brother and her children all lived in the same house. His room, which he shared with his parents, was on the first floor overlooking the street. In the common kitchen on the ground floor at the back, the women took turns cooking food. All the meals were eaten in the kitchen from a thaal, a large platter around which everyone sat.

———

When they'd finished supper, Akbar picked up the clothspread on which they had eaten, took it to the front door, and shook off the crumbs with two quick jerks over the street.

"Don't do it right in front of the door, you fool, do it on the side," said Farzana, his cousin.

After supper every day, Farzana and Akbar's other cousin, Zainab, would stand at the front door to chat and pass time, or so it seemed. They were attractive girls of eighteen and a magnet for the neighbourhood boys. As if on cue, the boys would appear from nowhere, passing back and forth in front of the house. The girls pretended not to pay attention and kept on chatting, occasionally giggling for no apparent reason. They were obviously enjoying the attention, though they would never cast a second glance at those "loafers." A gaping social and economic chasm separated them. The girls had been brought up to consider themselves superior, well beyond the dreams of these street Romeos. But the latter persisted, it was a free country. Some of them would park themselves on the stoop of the house across the street and talk loudly to make themselves heard.

Bherulal, who lived two houses down, spotted Akbar and called out to him.

"Hey, Akbaria, come over tomorrow. We will play kabbadi," he said, while looking at the girls, a smirk on his face.

"Okay," Akbar said. Fearing Bherulal would want to strike

up a conversation, Akbar quickly retreated inside the house, winking at his cousins on the way, indicating to them that he was on to their game.

"Hey, what was that about?" Farzana said after him. "This little runt is getting too big for his boots."

Back in his room, Akbar picked up a book, sat down near the window and started to read. The windows, shut during the day to keep out the noise and dust, were opened at night to let in the cool air. The boys had gone and it was quiet outside. The night had finally come as a respite from the scorching heat. Soon a pack of dogs would let out a paroxysm of barks. All night long they would punctuate the silence maddened by ghostly visions.

When he could concentrate no more, Akbar got up and went up the stairs to the main terrace to lie down on the cool bedding that he'd laid out earlier. Moiz, his older cousin, came and lay beside him, on his own bedroll, and started teasing him about Rukhsana. Akbar turned his back to him, pulled the sheet over his head, and closed his eyes.

2

A MONTH LATER, RETURNING FROM an errand one afternoon, Akbar saw his grandfather's grey Ambassador parked in front of the house. His casual saunter turned into a sprint. He arrived breathless at the car, found it empty and locked, and ran straight into the house and upstairs to his grandfather's room. Sajjad Ali, a slim, spindly man with a white goatee and a balding pate, was putting on a bush shirt. He had presently come out of the bathroom after a shower. Akbar sneaked in quietly, grabbed him around the waist, and yelled, "Dadaji!"

"Hey, my child, I was looking for you," Sajjad Ali said, trying to lift Akbar up in his arms. "Uff! You've grown so tall."

"What did you bring for me?"

"Hmm, arré, how could I forget your gift? I'm so sorry, beta."

"Dadaji, I know you're joking."

Sajjad Ali walked over to his duffel bag that lay near a table and pretended to look for his wallet.

"Where has it gone?" he said, rummaging in the bag, his back towards Akbar.

Akbar looked on, sitting on the bed, his head resting on the bedpost.

"Here it is," Sajjad Ali said as he sharply turned around, with a book and a bar of chocolate in his hand.

"Oh, Dadaji, thank you." Akbar stood up on the edge of the bed and hugged his grandfather, leaning on his back.

Moiz walked in and said salam to Sajjad Ali, who gave him his gift, a chocolate bar and a set of watercolours. The boys sat on the bed and ate their chocolates. The sun was still too sharp for them to go upstairs to fly their kites.

Sajjad Ali took his clothes out from his suitcase and carefully arranged them in the armoire built into one wall. His wife of forty years had died two years ago. He was a self-made man, and hard times in his youth had taught him to manage his personal affairs. Unlike other men, he was not clueless without a wife. Yet he missed her as a companion, the gentle guide who ordered his life in ways he did not realize until she was gone. Their arranged marriage had evolved into mutual care and affection that mere love, often too transient, could not aspire to.

When they married, he did not have a steady income. Born in British India, he graduated from the Bombay Presidency College and was well educated by the standards of those days. If he wanted to, he could have found an office job, but working for others was looked down upon in the culture he grew up in. Sajjad Ali possessed entrepreneurial smarts and ambition that only a city like Bombay could fulfill. Udaipur was too small and provincial for him.

In those days he would visit Bombay for months on end, leaving his wife and children behind in Udaipur. After ten years of struggle he had established a hardware business—one shop in Bombay and another in Udaipur. Nazir, the younger son, lived with Sajjad Ali in Bombay. The other two sons ran the Udaipur branch and got to spend time in Bombay on a six-month rotation. Akbar visited the city during summer vacations whenever his father happened to be there. Bombay never failed to excite him; its cosmopolitan energy overwhelmed him. Boys his age were smarter, they knew more about the world, they spoke English fluently. The sea, the roaring waves, and the undulating coastline that, seen from Marine Drive, bright and lit up at night, looked as though a constellation had descended on the sea. Ice cream came in so many colours and flavours that he ran out of fingers to count them. English movies attracted him the most. For a small-town boy, they opened up a window to a world he had not before imagined.

"Are you taking care of my plants?" Sajjad Ali asked, turning to Akbar.

"Yes, Dadaji, they are doing well. The roses and marigolds are blooming."

"Dadaji, you know?" Moiz suddenly butted in, feeling jealous.

"Know what?"

Moiz looked at Akbar, averted his guilty look, and spoke to their grandfather with a straight face, "You know, Akbar climbed up to the tower top."

Akbar glared at Moiz at this sudden betrayal.

"Did you go up there?" asked Dadaji.

Akbar did not answer.

Sajjad Ali's tone was stern. "If you do that ever again you will get no more presents from me."

"I promise I'll not, Dadaji."

I should have the access to it blocked, Sajjad Ali said to himself. It was a mistake to build it.

Akbar struck Moiz on his thigh. "You snitch."

Moiz slapped him back. "Hey, don't touch me!"

They went at each other before Sajjad Ali could realize what was happening. "Stop it! Enough now!" he said.

———

The next day was a Sunday and the house was a hive of activity.

The men were home and got in everyone's way. There was a touch of anticipation in the air. Grandfather was dressed up.

"Where are you going, Dadaji?" Akbar asked.

"Don't you know, Mowlana is in town?" Dadaji said, surprised.

Akbar recalled his mother and aunts discussing over supper the procession that was to take place. They sounded excited and wondered where to station themselves to catch the best view of their spiritual leader. Akbar hadn't paid much heed to their talk as he was having it out with Moiz over his treachery.

Mowlana was the high priest of the Momins, the small Shia sect to which they belonged. In Udaipur, Momins lived in a collection of neighbourhoods called Mominwadi—"the locality of the believers." Akbar's house was on the outskirts of Mominwadi, along the stretch of road where a stone wall with ramparts had once protected the old town. Udaipur was a historic city and had been capital of the kingdom of Mewar. It was a princely state under the British Raj.

The Momins in Udaipur were probably converted from the local trader class of Baniyas, although if you were to ask Akbar's father, he would proudly insist, "We are Rajputs." But that was a vain boast. Being a Rajput carried the prestige of a martial race famous for its valour. Momins in Udaipur showed none of those traits. Their ways and mores were typical of Baniyas: traders and shopkeepers, frugal and trustworthy, given to simple living and setting much in store by the ethic of saving for a rainy day. Although most of India's top industrialists were Baniyas, Momins by ambition and by acumen never rose beyond shopkeeping.

Mowlana was their supreme leader, filling in for their Imams or Caliphs—the last of whom was believed to have gone into hiding. In the absence of the living Imam, the Mowlanas had not only arrogated to themselves the Imam's spiritual power but also wantonly gone beyond their calling and started dictating the destinies of their flock.

"I'm going to see the parade," Sajjad Ali said.

"I want to come too," Akbar pleaded, tugging at Dadaji's sherwani.

Sajjad Ali hesitated, then said, "Go, run, get ready."

In Mominwadi the streets were festive. People hurried along to go catch a glimpse of their beloved Mowlana, their children tagging along behind them. Women wore colourful lehnga-blouses and odhnis—the head-and-shoulder wraps. Older women had donned full-on hijabs. Men were dressed in pants and shirts, some in white kurta-pyjamas, their heads covered with topi, the knitted skullcaps. At every street corner, arches of bamboo had been set up and adorned with fruits, flowers, and currency notes. Everywhere hung streamers and bright buntings. Akbar and his grandfather walked at a leisurely pace, giving way to people who rushed past them. Akbar bombarded Dadaji with questions—How old is Mowlana? Why is he visiting? Why must everyone see him?—which he answered patiently, gesticulating with his stick. On one occasion, he prodded a stray mongrel out of his way.

In the centre of Mominwadi, at the intersection of the main street and a side lane was the house of Dadaji's sister, Kulsum Auntie. She was a widow, and her only son worked in Kuwait. Her unshakeable faith in Mowlana more than made up for her brother's heresies. A corner room offered a clear, unobstructed view of the streets on both sides. Anticipating Sajjad Ali's visit, Kulsum Auntie had placed a chair at the corner window. The room had been dusted up and tidied; windows were open, through which the morning sun flooded in, and the thin gauze curtains fluttered in the breeze.

Akbar stood at the window, holding on to the chest-high brass bars, leaning his head out, anxious to get a better view of the street. Dadaji had settled into the chair and was also leaning forward. Kulsum Auntie brought him a cup of tea and Akbar a glass of Tang, the much-prized imported orange drink. There was nary a Momin man working in Kuwait who did not pack a tin of Tang when he came home. Akbar loved its tarty, zingy taste and knew that Auntie had a tin stashed away in the steel cupboard, under lock and key.

There came a shriek of horns. On the street below, four motorbikes in a formation of twos appeared, leading a procession. Behind them marched the community band, consisting of local boys in smart white uniform playing a military march on drums, trumpets, and bugles. An oversized bass drum brought up the rear. The band-leader in the vanguard impressively twirled his mace, threw it up in the air, and caught it deftly each time. Behind the band crawled a white Ambassador decked in flowers. The faithful on both sides, especially the women, lunged towards the open rear windows, thrusting their hands inside in supplication, shouting, "Khamma Mowlana, khamma Mowlana!"

Akbar caught a glimpse of a disembodied hand holding a tasbih. He had heard of Mowlana but had no idea that people could get hysterical upon seeing him. He asked Dadaji, "Is he our God?"

"No, but the next best thing, I suppose, from the look of things."

Akbar was puzzled, not quite sure what Dadaji meant.

"Amma was telling me he lives in a palace in Bombay."

"Yes, a stolen palace."

"Mowlana steals?"

"He doesn't have to. He can just claim what he wants to."

"That must make him more important than Prophet Muhammad and Mowla Ali?"

"Of course not, but for Momins, maybe . . . "

"Amma was reading me the stories of the Prophet and Mowla Ali. Their lives were simple. They didn't live in palaces. They were so poor that sometimes they didn't have enough to eat."

"Yes, times have changed. Our Mowlana is well-fed, but there are many Momins who are very poor."

"We are Muslims, aren't we?" Akbar asked.

"Of course, we are."

"Then why don't other Muslims have a Mowlana?"

"Let's put it this way, they are the lucky ones."

"Who is Mowlana, tell me," Akbar begged.

"It's complicated," Dadaji murmured, as he got up and studied two framed black-and-white photographs that hung on the wall. Two men swaddled in reams of starched white cloth, bearded and bespectacled, peered down imperiously. The one on the left was older, the face stern, the eyes piercing, and the lips pursed tight as though holding back a sharp tongue. "This is Shatir Kaifudin. He is dead. He was the previous Mowlana. And this," Dadaji said, pointing to the younger one, who looked unhappy like a man burdened with greatness, "is Noman Noorudin, the son, the one who was in the car. We have Mowlanas because we used to have Imams. We believe that Imams were the direct descendants of the Prophet. Our last Imam disappeared—about a thousand years ago, he went into hiding and never returned. Ever since then, Mowlanas have taken over."

Kulsum Auntie brought another cup of tea for Sajjad Ali, and sat on the bed, wiping her brow with her dupatta. The morning breeze had given way to the waves of stolid midday heat. "What *Ramayan* have you opened up here?" she asked.

"I'm telling Akbar the story of our Mowlanas," Sajjad Ali said.

"Don't listen to him, Akbar, he will poison your mind," she said.

Sajjad Ali ignored her jibe and strode to the window. The street had almost cleared. Only a few stragglers hung around, and women stood chatting in the doorways. Turning to Akbar, Sajjad Ali continued, "Our ancestors were actually Hindus who, in a fit of madness, what else could it be, converted to the Momin faith, and in doing so hitched our fate to the whims of the Mowlanas. And here we are today." He put his hand on Akbar's head, and ruffled his hair. "Let's go."

"Why did the Imam go into hiding, Dadaji?"

"Because his life was in danger—rival Muslim groups wanted to kill him."

"Do they still want to kill him?"

"Of course not. We have become tolerant of each other. And we live in a secular country where everybody has the right to worship their God and practice their faith."

"So why is our Imam still hiding?"

"That is the question that keeps me awake at night," Sajjad Ali said as he made for the door. Akbar noted a twinkle in his eye.

It was past lunchtime, and they headed home, Dadaji holding an umbrella over their heads to shield them from the sun. On the way, Akbar looked up at his grandfather and said, "I want to live in Bombay."

3

As they walked home, Akbar spotted her walking towards them with her mother and little sister. She was wearing a printed pinafore, her two side braids tied with red ribbons. He nervously adjusted his hair. *Hope I don't look like a buffoon.* He was ready with a smile in case their eyes met. But when she passed him, she was looking straight ahead, ignoring him on purpose. The taste of Tang in his mouth had suddenly turned sour. He swallowed. Her indifference felt like a stab.

Like what he had felt on their last encounter, which was on Eid day, two months before. His father had got him fitted with a new suit for the occasion, and he had felt like a prince, though also terribly self-conscious. After the morning prayers at the mosque and having had their Eid treat of sheer-khurma, the men and children of the house were ready to set off to visit relatives and friends. The kids would receive gifts of cash and were eager with anticipation.

Akbar asked if they would call on Zubaida Auntie; seeing Rukhsana would be the best Eid gift he could imagine. His father said no, because they must visit relatives first, and there were so many of them. There was not enough time for Zubaida Auntie. Akbar was disappointed, but then he had an idea: why not go and visit Zubaida Auntie on his own first, before he left with his father? He thought up an excuse.

"Amma, Zubaida Auntie was asking me about my Eid clothes."

"What about them?" his mother asked.

"Nothing, just that she wanted to see what I was wearing for Eid."

"Hmm . . . "

"Can I go and show off my suit to her? I'll also get Eidie."

"All right, be quick about it," Khatun muttered, not entirely convinced.

Akbar was out of sight in a flash before she could change her mind. He walked the short distance to Zubaida's house in quick steps, trussed up in his tailored suit, his new black leather shoes biting his ankles. By the time he was climbing the stairs to the first-floor home, his throat was dry and his starched white collar soaked in sweat. *This is not a good idea.* His ruse had been so dumb, he wondered how Amma had swallowed it. What would Zubaida Auntie think? He had not yet thought of an explanation. Whatever he said would surely sound foolish. It was not too late to turn back. But the urge to see Rukhsana demolished all other concerns. Especially today, on Eid day, she would be looking her best.

He went in. Visitors were greeting each other, in various stages of arriving and departing, all of them in new clothes, bright and crisp and pressed. Quietly, he slid into a chair by the door, his eyes searching for Rukhsana. Zubaida Auntie soon noticed him. She was sitting at one end of the divan, resting her back against a cushion. Rukhsana was nowhere in sight.

"Akbar, when did you come?"

He could only manage a smile.

"Has your mother sent you for something?"

"Yes." But he could not for the life of him think of what to say.

"What is it?"

"She said salam, Eid Mubarak," he blurted out, looking away from her.

"Oh, Eid Mubarak." She looked puzzled. "Will you have something to eat?"

"No, thank you."

"Come on, don't be shy. Try my sheer-khurma, it's better than your mother's," she said with a chuckle.

Akbar smiled, relieved that she did not pursue the cross-examination. She called out to Rukhsana to bring the sheer-khurma. His heart thrummed on hearing her name. He waited, letting his eyes wander around the room. It was rather sparsely furnished. A flowery fabric sofa next to the divan and three wooden chairs with padded cushions on the opposite side. Framed photos of two relatives—Rukhsana's grandparents, he assumed—on the wall seemed to stare at him with suspicion. He looked away. Just then Rukhsana entered, carrying a bowl on a tray.

She looked lovely in a knee-length dress, her loose hair secured at the temples with butterfly hairpins, talcum powder on the face, eyes smoky with kajal, a dagger-like mark of kohl elegantly extended at the corners of her eyes.

He broke into a smile. Their eyes met and she favoured him one in return: a faint parting of the lips. He looked for a hint of pleasure, a hesitant self-conscious shyness that his presence might have evoked, but he found none.

"Give it to Akbar," Zubaida said. "He is looking dashing in his suit, don't you think?"

Embarrassed, feeling all eyes in the room upon him, he shifted in his chair.

"Eid Mubarak," he said in a barely audible voice.

"Eid Mubarak," she replied, put the tray on the side table, and went and sat down next to her mother. He ate quietly, trying not to slurp, as his mother had taught him, and threw sidelong glances at her when she was not looking. She caught him a couple of times eyeing her. He detected a smirk on her face. *Was she laughing at him?* He felt like an idiot, coming here on a lame excuse. He finished the sheer-khurma quickly, told Zubaida Auntie that it tasted nice, then took her permission and left. At the door, when he turned to say goodbye, Rukhsana wasn't even looking at him.

———

Akbar's extended family, like most Momins, mistook rituals for religious faith. The Quran, the Prophet, and the oneness of God were accepted as given truths. The five pillars of Islam, however, were not firmly grounded in their house, though the women were more particular in their observances. At namaz time, when the muezzin called out, they unrolled their prayer rugs at home and prostrated before Allah. During the month of Ramzan they fasted from dawn to dusk, and then went to the mosque for the evening prayers. The men too went, whether they were fasting or not, and at iftar time, when the fast was broken, they all ravenously consumed crispy mutton samosas with tea, then came home and ate dinner. During Moharrum, the women attended majlises—gatherings where elegies were recited to commemorate the martyrs of Karbala. Haj was still out of bounds. Nobody had gone to Mecca yet. Not even Dadaji.

For Momins, their religion was more a community affair, a social glue. The Mowlana never allowed them to suspect that there might be a spiritual aspect to the faith. He had tightly leashed the community to ritual and routine. The less they learned about the faith, the easier it was for him to keep them corralled. He forbade them to read the Quran and draw their own meanings from it. All meaning had to come from him.

Although Dadaji was not a believer, he insisted that the children learn to read the Holy Book and pray namaz and understand the basics of their faith. When they were older they could do as they wished, find their own God. When Akbar was ten he and his cousins were sent every Sunday morning to a mullah's lair two streets behind their house. He was Sheikh Idris Dhamal, the local priest handpicked by Mowlana to manage and control the community. The mullah's two daughters, Amina and Fatima, in their early twenties and both dull and bored, would teach two groups of children side by side in the same room. They encouraged everyone to recite loudly and the children took the instruction with unabashed gusto. The sessions ended up being free-for-all shouting matches on the verge of breaking the sound barrier. After weeks of tuition, Khatun noticed that Akbar could not even recite Surah Al Fatiha, the first verse of the Quran. What he had learned instead was how to make farts by joining his two palms.

She pulled the kids out and hired a personal tutor, Sagheer Ali, to come and teach at home—under her supervision. Sagheer Ali, a middle-aged soft-spoken mullah, was told to keep the children's noses to the grindstone, especially Akbar and Moiz's. For the first few weeks Akbar was on good behaviour, testing the waters. Then, whenever his mother was out of earshot, he began to ask questions. Why was the Quran in Arabic, a language they did not know? *Because it originated in Arabia.* Why can't we read it in Urdu or Hindi? *Because translations are no good.* Does Allah only know Arabic? *Hmm . . .* The teacher lost his cool and told him not to ask stupid questions. Just learn to read, he was ordered. Akbar applied himself and began to decipher the letters, started connecting them into words and then full sentences, but they made no sense to him. He asked for their meaning. Sagheer Ali patiently explained what little he knew. Akbar remained dissatisfied. He said he would not study until he understood what the Surahs meant. The teacher insisted on the superfluity of meaning, explaining that there was merit in just reciting. Akbar remained unconvinced. Khatun intervened but could do little more than exert her authority. To Akbar's insistence on understanding what he was reading, she had no credible argument. Moiz was no better. Fascinated by the Arabic letters he spent most of the time calligraphing them rather than learning them.

Over the course of three summers Akbar willy-nilly managed to perform the basic prayer and gained a modicum of proficiency in reading the Arabic script. When he reached high school, the demands of secular study and exams kept him busy. And by then he was too old to bother with religious instruction anyway. Khatun gave up on him reluctantly, but was satisfied that he had at least learned the rudiments of the faith.

4

—

A FOUR-WHEEL-DRIVE SPED DOWN A narrow two-lane road heading south. It was an old CJ3B Mahindra, packed to over-capacity, passengers spilling out. Travelling in comfort was an unknown concept in these parts; there was always room for one more person. The family had invited relatives to join them, making sure every available space was filled up. The rear flap door was opened out to accommodate more people.

Akbar sat on the edge of the extension, one hand clutching the iron chain that held it up, the other grabbing his mother's arm; his legs dangled down. He watched mesmerized as the road sped past under him, dust flying into his face, wind storming his hair. Moiz was sitting beside him, shouting to make himself heard. He was telling a joke about an old man who had dreamed of a beautiful woman, but unfortunately her image was blurry, he could not see her properly. When asked why, the old man said because he went to sleep without his glasses. Moiz roared with laughter at his own joke. Akbar laughed too, but more because he was just happy. He would see Rukhsana, and the world was a nice place after all. Even silly jokes were funny.

The party, comprising women and children, was heading to Sadikot, two hundred miles south of Udaipur. If not for one Shaheed Babji, a Momin divine who was killed there by bandits in the eleventh century, the dusty little town would have remained obscure to the world. Every year on his death anniversary, Momins converged on Sadikot to say the prayer of ziyarat and pay their respects. This year was special because Mowlana would attend the occasion, and Momins were descending in droves upon Sadikot. It was nearly five years since Akbar last saw Mowlana, or rather his hand, from Kulsum Auntie's window in Udaipur.

They reached Sadikot in the late afternoon. The path leading to the mausoleum was unpaved and crowded with people and street vendors selling snacks, fruits and juices, mementoes, and toys. Driving through the throng was impossible, so the driver pulled up at a distance from the great wooden gate of the mausoleum complex. Akbar and Moiz jumped out and went straight to a vendor selling mango brittle. Akbar's widowed aunt, Fizza Chachi, fretted about getting a room at the complex. The women and children in the family deferred to her wishes, since she was the eldest aunt. People often mistook her candour and booming voice for authority, and she used it to advantage. She asked Khatun to run to the office and book a room. She yelled at Akbar and Moiz to stop wasting time and help carry their beddings, bags, and supplies. They had come prepared for a ten-day stay.

The gate was large enough for an elephant to pass through. Carved in front and arched on top, it was studded with shiny brass spikes. It was firmly closed, but there was a doorway in its right wing that was manned by a sentry. They followed the crowds and entered. The guesthouses were a series of rooms on the left and at the far end, each with a verandah out front. On the right was a two-storey building comprising the administration offices on the ground floor and Mowlana's residence on the first, with a balcony running across its length. The mausoleum, a white, domed structure inlaid with stained-glass arabesques, was in the middle of the grounds, surrounded by a vast courtyard paved with hexagonal marble tiles interspersed with black square stones—a pattern typical of Islamic design.

Khatun had secured a room on the right side of the guest-house across from the shrine. The three women with their four children would live there, and cook inside when necessary. The relatives who had come along would have to fend for themselves. The children would sleep outside on the verandah after the nightfall stories had been told. During the day they would play in the courtyard, while the women would visit the mausoleum multiple times and socialize and gossip without having to worry about their men and their daily cares and chores. This type of quasi-religious pilgrimage was the only vacation most Momins had known or could afford. Khatun had already run into her friend Zubaida and other women from Udaipur.

Once they had settled in their room, Fizza Chachi started pumping the kerosene Primus stove to prepare tea. Water was put to boil, and tea leaves were added, but when she looked for the sugar jar, she couldn't find it.

"Didn't we get sugar?" she said, raising her voice, indignant that such an essential ingredient was forgotten. Seeing Akbar lolling around, she snapped, "Go borrow some sugar from Zubaida."

Akbar could have kissed her. What luck. He was not counting on meeting Rukhsana so soon upon arrival. Their room was at the end of the verandah. He sprinted and stopped in their doorway, panting.

"Auntie," he said catching his breath, "Fizza Chachi wants to borrow some sugar."

Rukhsana and her sister Rehana were playing cards by the window. She looked up and allowed a smile. Akbar shot back a blast of sunshine. Emboldened, he ventured, "What are you playing?"

"Mungis, can't you see?" she said, brushing off his overfamiliarity.

"That's so boring," he said, unfazed.

The two girls made faces. Rukhsana was almost fifteen and had begun to notice Akbar's attention towards her. Although she enjoyed it, she pretended nonchalance. Whenever the two families met, he would gravitate to her and make small talk, but she would give him the cold shoulder. Her indifference would hurt him, but he knew he would win her over one day. It was only a matter of time.

He hung around while Zubaida Auntie rummaged through her things to find a cup for him. He hoped she would never find it.

Back in the room, Rukhsana's smile stayed in his mind. Absentmindedly, he traced an *R* on the floor with his finger as he waited for his tea. Cups and saucers were limited, so they took turns. Women went first, followed by the children. They poured tea into a saucer, blew on it to cool it, and slurped it up noisily. Khatun sipped directly from her cup, and in order not to stand out or be seen as uppity, she had announced that she liked her tea hot.

In the evening the moon was out, three-quarters full. The mausoleum shone resplendently in the lunar glow. It was a square marble structure with a large onion dome capped with a golden finial. Slim minarets shot up from the four corners. Islamic motifs and floral designs in blue and ruby-stained glass covered the walls. It was a beautiful, unassuming monument, dedicated to a Momin saint whose life was steeped in legend and myth.

Akbar slept on the verandah that night with Moiz and other cousins. Rukhsana, he guessed, wouldn't be far away down the corridor. Breathing the same air as he, looking at the same moon. *What good fortune.* The next ten days in Sadikot with her around had suddenly made life worth living. He began to scheme ways to get to talk to her, know her better. He ached to move beyond the casual encounter, beyond the shy nods and tacit smiles.

In the morning, before sunrise, the muezzin's call to prayer woke them up, and soon after morning prayer the comings and goings of people forced them out of their bedrolls. The courtyard was already abuzz with activity by the time they finished their breakfast of tea and rusk-toast. It was a bright, hot morning, the day of Urs, the death anniversary of Shaheed Babji. For a Sufi, death is a wedding, when the soul meets its beloved, God. But for the worldly Momins, Urs was just a religious event, with a community meal and a routine ziyarat, prayer for the dead. But today's Urs was special, because Mowlana was expected to attend the ziyarat that morning.

The boys came out dressed in white kurta-pyjamas and topis on their heads. The topi for men was *de rigueur*, the beard optional. Most men were clean-shaven. Women were in traditional lehnga-blouse, young girls wore salwar-kameez. The dupatta, covering head and shoulders, was a must.

Presently, members of the Noorani Guard, Mowlana's volunteer security force, emerged from behind the office building in their khaki military-style uniforms, caps on their heads and batons in their hands, and tore through the crowd, parting it like a sea as though Moses had arrived. The guards quickly formed a chain on both sides of the cleared path to keep the crowds at bay. The Mowlana appeared on the balcony above and the throng erupted into shouts of "Mowlana!" "Mowlana!" "Khamma Mowlana!" joining their hands with respect and love.

When he came down the steps and stood on the edge of verandah, the hubbub reached a crescendo, slogans rent the air. Mowlana was dressed in pure white. Yards of thin starched muslin draped his body and shoulders, a tipped gold-threaded headpiece crowned his head like that of a sultan. He was fair in complexion and sported a thin white beard. Slowly, regally, he started walking towards the shrine, his right arm raised to bless the restless crowd, a tasbih woven around his index finger and thumb. He looked constantly from side to side, moving his raised hand, acknowledging the crowd with a smile. When he came closer, Akbar wanted to catch his eye, lock his gaze. But Mowlana did not look at him; he was not looking at anyone in particular.

Mowlana's sons, the shahzadas, or princes, followed him, all dressed in white, the red and green accents in their headgears peeking through. But for their bushy beards it was easy to mistake them for a flock of swans gliding by.

Mowlana, followed by his entourage, entered the mausoleum while some of his Guard stood by the door to keep out the riff-raff, baking in the sun. It took one hour for Mowlana to finish ziyarat and emerge. Once again the congregation broke into a tumult. He walked towards his residence, though this time his steps were quicker. The Noorani Guards moved away, breaking the chain, and the human sea collapsed on itself, erasing the parting.

As Akbar began to search for his family members, he saw a group of men rampaging through the crowd, shoving and hitting anyone they could. Suddenly they turned towards a woman, and before she became aware, the men rushed towards her and started pommelling her with their fists. She cried out. Another gang of thugs had descended upon a small group of women. Some of the men were from Udaipur and the others were strangers whom Akbar had never seen. He was horrified. A large, bearded man pushed a woman to the ground and kicked her in the thigh; another one pulled at her dupatta. Someone shouted, "Yes, she is the one, the wife of the radical leader!"

All around him, women were being kicked and pushed, their clothes ripped. The Udaipur women were the target; even children with their mothers were being shoved and attacked.

Akbar feared for his mother and aunts, and Rukhsana and her family. Where were they? Where was Moiz? People were fleeing towards the gate and the guesthouses, tripping over each other. Children were bawling. Women were crying out, "Save us, save us!" Mowlana had appeared on his balcony; seeing him, some of the women cried out, "Mowlana, save us, Mowlana, save us!" Mowlana did not move; he said nothing. Akbar would remember him as smiling. Filled with rage, he ran and butted a man who was kicking a woman on the ground. She got up and ran. Akbar dashed towards another clump of bullies attacking Zubaida Auntie. He lunged at the perpetrators. Bystanders joined him to chase away the goons. Rukhsana appeared from nowhere, crying out, "Amma, Amma!"

Zubaida Auntie got up and brushed off her clothes. "I'm all right, Akbar came in the nick of time."

Rukhsana took her mother to their room, and when the two had left safely, Akbar began to look around for his mother. Whoops went up every now and then. He saw women, many of whom he knew by face, bruised and bleeding, their clothes in tatters; some of them were with their children. Then the pandemonium eased, as suddenly as it had started. The thugs melted into the crowd. Finally Akbar saw Moiz attending to a woman who was lying on the ground. As he approached, he saw that the woman was his mother. Blood trickled from the side of Khatun's head, and her cheek was swollen. The two boys helped her get up and they hurried towards the guesthouse.

Khatun's dupatta was lost, one sleeve of her blouse was ripped. She felt naked, ashamed, and shaken. They had pulled at her hair and her head was hurting. The verandah of their guesthouse was abandoned, and their room was locked from inside. Akbar knocked on the door. "It's me," he said. Farzana opened the door quietly and let them in.

There were cries of horror as Khatun staggered in, groaning, assisted by the boys. She was helped onto her bedroll. Someone got her a glass of water.

"They were men from Udaipur," Akbar explained, "they were pointing out the women, and the thugs fell upon them."

The assaulters were roundly cursed.

"What kind of animals are these that attack women," Fizza Chachi said. "We were standing by the verandah when it all began. We ran into the room and closed the door tight."

She started attending to Khatun, making a turmeric paste and placing the salve on the wound. Then she nursed Akbar and Moiz's wounds. The three victims were given hot milk with turmeric. "This will heal your internal injuries," she said.

Akbar went to the window, held it slightly ajar, and peeped outside into the verandah. It was early afternoon, and things had quietened down. People were going about their business; children were out playing as usual. Normalcy had returned giving a lie to the violent mayhem of just half an hour ago. Zubaida Auntie came by and smiled upon seeing Akbar. "How's your mother? I heard she's injured," she said.

"She is all right, sleeping now, I think," he said, his eyes searching for Rukhsana.

"The girls are in the room. I have told them to latch the door from inside," Zubaida said, then whispered, "Now let me in."

Akbar shut the window and opened the door, just enough for her to come in.

She went straight to where Khatun was sleeping and softly put a hand on her forehead. She said nothing, but tears had welled up in her eyes. Wiping them with a small handkerchief, she turned to Fizza Chachi.

"Many of our women have already left," she said.

"First tell us, how are you? Akbar says they attacked you also?" Fizza Chachi said.

"I'm fine, just a nasty push. But it could have been worse if my hero had not arrived in time." She affectionately patted Akbar on the head.

Akbar blushed. "I don't know where I found the courage," he said.

"God gives us courage," Zubaida said. "Especially when cowards attack women. So many of our women have run away, leaving behind their belongings. Others are cooped up in their rooms like us, waiting for things to calm down. Some are planning to leave tonight. What are your plans?"

"We had arranged for the driver to come next week," Fizza Chachi said, "but we can't wait that long, I suppose."

"Right, you can't. I'm going to the market to call home, and I've come to ask the boys to accompany me," she said, eyeing Akbar and Moiz. Akbar nodded. As an unlikely saviour of her mother he hoped he had taken on a new shine in Rukhsana's eyes.

"I can ask my husband to inform your men to send your jeep tomorrow," Zubaida added.

"Please do that, God bless you," Fizza Chachi said. "And also tell them that everything is fine here. And can you please not mention about Khatun?"

Tea was served all around. With the door and windows shut it was hot and stuffy in the room. Sounds of people could be heard outside. Soon it would be dark; going to the mosque for prayers or for communal supper was out of the question. Sleeping outside in the verandah was also out of the question.

"What's going on, why did they attack us?" Akbar asked.

Zubaida Auntie replied. "Mowlana's people did not like it that the Youth Association candidates won the municipal elections and their handpicked candidates lost. I had suspected that there might be trouble, but not this, this is qayamat. It's hell."

Akbar and Moiz accompanied Zubaida Auntie to the market.

The next morning they began to pack. Khatun felt much better, having taken a tablet the previous night. Her head had stopped throbbing, though her body still felt sore. She couldn't believe what had happened. If not for her injuries, she would have discounted her own memory of it. How was it even possible that women and children were assaulted while Mowlana looked on? She washed her face, carefully avoiding the sore parts, and changed to get ready for the trip back home. Zubaida had informed them that the driver should be there by noon.

Khatun looked in her hand mirror to examine her injury. The side of her head was still slightly swollen. The hair around her wound was matted with congealed blood and flakes of dried turmeric. A bruise inflamed her left cheek like rouge gone rogue. She was hardly able to recognize herself. The spark had gone from those black almond-shaped eyes; the arching brows, the long eyelashes, her small nose, a mouth set to a fixed smile—something was askew. But her translucent pale brown skin was aglow, in defiance of the harrowing ordeal. Silently, she thanked God for not making things worse.

At noon their driver arrived and they left Sadikot.

———

They reached Udaipur late at night. Zahid Ali was shocked to see the state Khatun was in. The news of the disturbance had reached him already and, his wife being a women's activist, he was half-fearing that she might be targeted. "I was hoping and praying you would be safe." he said.

"After Mowlana finished ziyarat on Urs day, men started attacking our women. I was pushed to the ground in an instant and they kicked me and pulled at my clothes," Khatun said.

"Do you know who the men were?"

"I know some of the men were from Udaipur," Moiz interjected. "Don't know their names but I have seen them around. Can't forget their faces." Zahid Ali sat there thinking. He asked Moiz about his injured nose and how he was feeling. Moiz said he was all right. Addressing the boys, Zahid Ali said, "You boys were brave. Thank you for taking care of the women. You have become men now."

Akbar beamed with pride. Moiz was indifferent to the praise. He didn't need anyone to endorse his manhood, even if it was his uncle, whom he respected. He was all of twenty-one, strong and handsome, comfortable in his own skin. He had an artistic bent but was also practical, a doer. He had no patience for people who hemmed and hawed over important matters. The urgency of decisive action had never been greater to him than at that moment.

"What are we going to do now?" he demanded.

"I don't know, it's not up to us," Zahid Ali replied.

"Not us then who? I want to break the legs of these people."

"You think I'm not angry, I don't want to get even? But let's wait. The Youth Association has called a meeting tomorrow. Let's see what they decide."

Moiz shook his head in disapproval. "I know what they will say—maintain calm, do nothing."

"So what are you planning, a riot?"

"No, not a riot. It doesn't matter what it is. But we want justice. They beat up Chachi, they could have killed her. They attacked many other women, and children, too. Do you think we should let them get away with it?"

"We can't take the law into our own hands."

"So what are we going to do, go to the courts, file cases? Who will you call as witness? Mowlana?"

"Yes, Mowlana was a witness," Akbar jumped in. "I saw him standing there watching the whole thing."

"Stupid, I was being sarcastic," Moiz said. "Do you think Mowlana will testify against his own goons? From what I can see, he approved of the attack, if not actually ordered it."

"You can't say that for sure," Zahid Ali admonished.

"What do you mean, 'for sure'?" Khatun shot back, her tone bordering on anger. "I am certain. He is our Mowlana, Zahid. He claims to be our spiritual father. We almost worship him. He calls us his children. How could he stand there calmly and watch his children being beaten? That's what he did. I saw it."

Zahid Ali felt the tectonic plates of his faith shifting under him. His peace-loving, Mowlana-obsessed community was beginning to show cracks. He lay awake in bed, his wife beside him violated and humiliated, and he felt helpless and impotent. The thought that he should do something gnawed at him. But what? Moiz was right, those bastards could not be allowed to get away with it. One part of him was seething to take revenge, another tried to reason, to assess the consequences. Finally he fell asleep, lulled by his wife's gentle snoring.

———

The next morning, as Zahid Ali was about to leave for his hardware store, his nephew Moiz came running with the news that the Youth Association had asked all its supporters to close shop for the day.

"So there is a public meeting? But why close shops?" Zahid Ali asked.

"We're protesting against the atrocity in Sadikot. Sending a message to the authorities."

Earlier that morning a clandestine con-fab had taken place at Moiz's friend Iqbal's house. Recently it had become a hangout for the young men who had become fed up with the docility of their elders. Gone were the days, they said, when anyone could heckle them or their womenfolk with impunity. They were ready to defend the honour and safety of their mothers and sisters, and the events of Sadikot had now spurred them into action. They were raring to take revenge. A lesson had to be taught.

"Dogs that attack women cannot belong to our community," Luqman said. "In fact, they cannot belong to any human community," he added with a flourish. Luqman was the gang's *de facto* leader. He wore rings on all four fingers of his right hand, and a talisman hung around his neck from a black thread. He clenched his fist as he spoke and would have certainly banged it on a table if there were one.

The room they had gathered in was fondly called the White House, and it was here that they planned how to confront the local priest, Sheikh Dhamal, and his lackeys. The room was large, with windows and two doors, one of which opened onto the street. A cot, a few chairs, and a writing desk in one corner were the only furniture. A carom board stood on its side along the wall. The cot was in the centre, and they sat on it and on the chairs. The lime plaster on the walls was peeling off in places, creating maps of countries yet to be discovered. An old ceiling fan whirred lazily overhead.

"So what should we do now?" asked Iqbal.

"We know what to do. We'll break their bloody bones," Moiz said with anger.

"Right, but don't say it in so many words," Luqman said. "Do we have any names?"

"I know who they are," Moiz said. "But I don't think any of them is back in town yet."

"We will wait, then."

One of the boys lit a cigarette and passed it around. Smoking was forbidden among Momins, though chewing tobacco and eating paan were acceptable. The censure against smoking was strong, because apparently it took tobacco abuse to the next level as it had an element of exhibitionism, of defiance and chutzpah. Momins chose their vices wisely, keeping them low-key.

Moiz took a deep puff and emitted three consecutive volutes, to Akbar's utter amazement. The latter had tagged along with Moiz to the meeting. He had never seen him smoke before. And Moiz, engrossed in the issue at hand, was unmindful of Akbar's presence. When their eyes met, and seeing the look of shock on Akbar's face, he winked at him nonchalantly.

A knock on the door startled them. The partly smoked cigarette was instantly crushed underfoot, and everyone flailed their hands to clear the air. Iqbal's mother came in with a tray of assorted cups and a kettle of tea. She sniffed suspiciously.

"I don't know how many of you are here, but here's some tea. I hope it's enough for all of you," she said.

As they sipped their tea, Luqman looked at Akbar and smiled. "So how is it going?"

"Good."

"I've heard of your heroic feats on the battleground. That earns you an honorary membership in our gang."

Everybody chuckled.

Akbar was in awe of Luqman who was an athletic young man with round eyes, chiseled face, thick, lush hair swept back, and an incongruously thin voice. Fearless and bold, he possessed qualities rare among Momins and he had friends in other communities. But the company he kept was not always considered respectable, and he was often dismissed as a ruffian. But he defied the stereotype of the namby-pamby cowardly Momin who trembled at the sight of the Sunni Muslim boys. The young men he gathered at the White House were a new breed, brave and brash, on the ready to defend the community.

———

The Momin Youth Association had been formed some years before to promote education among young Momins. It was an offshoot of a welfare organization that helped poor people, especially those affected by the sectarian Hindu-Muslim violence. But it was not liked by the clergy, because it was formed without their permission and was outside their control.

In recent years, the Mowlana, who was based in Bombay, had begun to tighten his grip over his followers. This process had begun with his authoritarian father, Mowlana Kaifudin, who in a fit of arrogance had declared himself the sole owner of all community property. Mosques, mausoleums, and community centres in every village and town in India—and across the globe wherever Momins lived—now belonged to him. He shut down or took over private charities and schools, claiming that philanthropy was Mowlana's exclusive preserve, not of his followers, no matter how rich. He began to run the community like a business—religion was the product and an obedient, abject following was his captive client base.

Mowlana Noorudin, the son, had built on his father's legacy. An elaborate system of *ijazat* (permissions) had been set up, catching Momins every step of the way. With it came a cradle-to-grave tax regime—an annual, arbitrary fee imposed on every Momin for the privilege of being a member of the community. For weddings and feasts, births and burials, and any other occasion, social or religious, money was demanded. Those who could not pay were denied permission and harassed until they relented. The only life event that the priesthood did not make money from was female circumcision. Imposed as a mandatory canon on seven-year old girls, it was done in complete secrecy by old crones using crude implements.

Dissent was punished by total ostracism, when no one in the community, including any family member, was allowed any dealings with the "rebel." The priests and their flunkies threw their weight about, claiming to act on behalf of the Mowlana; people had generally believed that he knew nothing about the abuses inflicted in his name, until that fateful day in Sadikot.

Khatun had been especially targeted because she was a rebel.

Sheikh Idris Dhamal, Udaipur's local priest, was furious when women had started their own organization, the Zanana Wing, threatening them with dire consequences.

Khatun was the secretary of the Zanana Wing. "Do what you want, but you cannot stop us," she had said.

For some time the tension between the priest and the nonconformists like Khatun had been low-key, simmering on a slow fire. It came to a boil when four members of the Youth Association stood for elections to the Udaipur municipal government. The priesthood commanded them to stand down, saying they had no permission to do so. The Youth candidates would not budge, insisting that it was a secular, civil matter and the clergy had no business telling them what to do. Sheikh Dhamal, a stout, sadistic man with close ties to the Mowlana's "royal family" and as such prone to exaggerated self-importance, fielded his own four loyalist candidates. They should have won, by holy writ, as they had the blessings of the Mowlana, but they lost. The defeat exposed the Mowlana as a hollow, fallible figure, his prestige as a divine interlocutor in the mud. Udaipur Momins were divided by rancour. Sadikot was the revenge and punishment.

The much-ballyhooed community meeting on the morning of the strike ended in commotion. It was held at the community mosque and people came in great numbers, excited and angry. The wounds were fresh and emotions on edge; seeing how quickly the situation could get out of hand, the Association leaders called for caution. Moiz, Luqman, and their gang demanded action, they hungered for revenge. But there was no appetite for it. The elders quoted Gandhi, "An eye for an eye will make the world blind." The gang trooped out in disgust.

Akbar followed them to the White House. The carom board was set up, and they started playing. The others stood around. Doors and windows were open but the air did not move, it was thick with rage and frustration. Ideas flew around on what to do next. Moiz and his partner pocketed the pieces in quick succession. Presently he placed the striker on the baseline and was concentrating on pocketing the last white piece. Everybody fell quiet. Moiz sprinkled some more powder on the board, and as he focused, Iqbal, the prankster, shouted "go for it." Moiz missed. He cursed Iqbal.

"We'll need a donkey," Luqman said suddenly.

"A donkey?" Moiz asked in surprise, slapping the red queen piece back in the centre of the board.

"We will need it soon."

"Why not take him," Moiz said, pointing to Iqbal.

Everyone laughed, and in an instant Moiz was on the floor, Iqbal's knee on his neck.

5

INSIDE EVERY MOMIN HOME IN Udaipur, the Sadikot incident and its causes were endlessly discussed and analyzed. People were disillusioned with the Mowlana. Many among the devout lost faith in him overnight. His photos, which people had lovingly hung up in their homes and shops, were taken down and trashed. A false god had fallen, and people felt free but also anxious. A void had opened up for them. A people tethered to the whims of a leader were suddenly free to act according to their consciences.

On the third morning after the Sadikot incident, Akbar was on an errand on his bicycle when, as he entered a side street, he was greeted by loud noises from up ahead. A kind of procession was advancing in his direction. Akbar slowed down and waited with anticipation. There seemed to be some kind of trouble, and he knew instinctively that Luqman and his crew were behind it. Boys were wielding sticks, banging on tin cans, and yelling at the tops of their voices. In the middle of the crowd were two donkeys, walking in tandem. A boy rode the first one, shouting with gusto, "Inqalab Zindabad!" (Long live the Revolution!) Behind him on the second donkey was a large man, facing backward. His face was smeared with black shoe polish, and a garland of shoes hung around his neck. He looked stunned and helpless, his head bent, eyes downcast. Rather large for the animal, his feet dragged on the ground. When he came up close, Akbar recognized him. He was one of the men who were directing the thugs in Sadikot. The boys jeered at him, and men slapped him as he passed by them. The women, without exception, shouted "Shame, shame!" Some spat at him.

Akbar watched, overwhelmed, as the chaotic cavalcade passed by. He did not see Luqman or Moiz or any of their gang. Trust them to orchestrate this production and leave it to the crowd to execute it.

———

In the lanes and bylanes of Mominwadi trouble brewed. Daily there were disturbances, incidents of harassment and skirmishes. Anger was still raw and tempers ran high. Rumours were rife. Pelting stones at people's houses had become common, and in a few weeks every window pane in Mominwadi had been shattered and replaced with cardboard and newspaper. The White House gang roamed the streets, as did other bands, Loyalist and Radical. The slightest provocation from either side would result in blows and fisticuffs. Neighbours set upon neighbours, friends upon friends. The once peaceful Momin community was now riven with distrust and violence.

One Saturday afternoon, when Akbar reached home after school, he heard loud noises coming from Vastiram, a neighbourhood behind his house. He saw people hurrying in that direction. He put his books down and rushed to join the crowd, ignoring his cousin Farzana's shouts to stay put. Moiz and Luqman and the rest of the boys, he assumed, would be there already. When he arrived at the scene, a full-blown riot was in progress. Men were throwing rocks at Sheikh Dhamal's house while cursing and shouting at him. It was the same ochre building where Akbar had gone to learn the Quran some years ago. The sheikh was holed up inside with his family; the windows were tightly shut. Caught up in the frenzy around him, Akbar picked up a couple of rocks and aimed at the window, recalling the violence in Sadikot and the attack on his mother.

Presently he saw Moiz and a dozen other youths carrying a hefty log towards the house; as they neared it, they gathered speed and crashed it into the door. It shuddered but did not give. The attackers attempted again, charging with greater speed and force. The door shook but stayed in place. Upon the third attempt it came crashing down, bringing bits of broken mortar with it.

Before the crowd could rush into the building, the police came charging, swinging batons, hitting people on their backs and legs. Somebody threw a fireball through the broken door. A collective gasp went up. People started running in all directions. Some were lucky to escape the police batons, others not. Akbar received a nasty blow on his bum and yelped with pain. The next instant he was dragged by his collar towards a police van. Frightened and nervous, he pleaded that he had done nothing, he was innocent. The cop slapped him and shoved him into the van. Moiz and Luqman were already inside, towards the front. They looked roughed-up and disheveled, but seemed carefree, chatting casually, peering through the window, surveying the chaos that probably was their handiwork. Their faces darkened when they saw Akbar stumble into the van.

"What the hell are you doing here?" Moiz hissed.

"I was only watching," Akbar said.

"You had no business being here."

He hollered at someone outside to inform Akbar's mother that he was with him and safe.

The van filled up quickly and was soon on its way, crushing stones and sticks under its tires. Outside, the crowd had thinned. Boys had sought refuge behind some buildings, others on the rooftops were launching stone missiles at the priest's house and the police. A fire was raging at the entrance to Sheikh Dhamal's house, people were rushing towards it with buckets of water.

The van entered the police station outside Hathipole, not far from the scene of the riot. Soon two more vans arrived and unloaded more familiar faces, youths as well as older men. There were about forty of them and were all locked up inside a large holding cell that was dark and stank of urine and sweat. The walls were black and sticky to the touch. Normally law-abiding to a fault, the very idea of being in police custody was unimaginable to Momin men.

Luqman looked at Akbar, who was leaning against a wall, fear writ large on his face. He went up to him and smiled. "Don't worry, everything will be all right," he said.

"I don't want to be here," Akbar said, thinking how heartbroken his mother would be. And Rukhsana, he had no idea what she would make of it. As her mother's defender in Sadikot, he thought he must have risen in her esteem, now this would put paid to that.

"I'll do something, I know the inspector, I'll tell him you are still a minor and he will probably let you go."

Moiz, who was standing beside him, wrapped his arm around Akbar's shoulders and pulled him close. Akbar couldn't hold back his tears. The two cousins hardly ever found tenderness between them, given their pranks and fights and rivalries in the past. But now Moiz felt protective towards him. The mess they were in was serious. At that moment Moiz's heart melted with affection for his kid cousin.

"It is already late afternoon," Luqman announced. "The

officers have finished for the day. I'm afraid we'll have to spend the night here."

People grumbled at the news. Some were still nursing the wounds they had received from police sticks. Luqman asked the guard for medical help, and soon received a first-aid box. Then two guards arrived carrying battered aluminum plates containing two thick, dry chapattis and watery daal.

"Who can eat this kind of food? Motherfuckers," a man complained.

"Can you ask them to bring a hammer? I want to break my chapatti!"

6

ASIF HUSSAIN WAS A FLAMBOYANT personality. He was swarthy, with soft features and keen eyes, magnified by round Gandhi glasses, and a first trimester paunch; his hair was oiled and slicked back. Although short of temper and brusque of manners, he was the voice of reason which found expression in his eloquent oratory. When he spoke on matters of importance, his tone was sharp and urgent. He was one of the radical candidates who had won the municipal election. An engineer by profession, he volunteered his time for community service. After Sadikot when the nerves were shot he tried to keep the tempers in check. He explicitly warned against violent retribution. As a leader and now a city councilor, he appealed for calm. But young hotheads were in no mood to heed his counsel.

Sporadic skirmishes continued daily despite his best efforts. But with the riot the situations had completely gone out of control. Things came to a head when an old man called Hashim Kanchwala died. According to Islamic custom, the dead should be buried quickly. The old man's son, Zafar, went to Sheikh Dhamal to get permission for the burial ceremonies to proceed. Only with a written permit could these rituals be performed—the digging of the grave, bathing of the body, a mullah to say the prayers, the fatiha meal, and so on. Permissions were granted routinely before, but after the debacle in municipal elections, the priest had turned hostile. First the women were attacked in Sadikot. Then began the harassment of the Radicals.

Zafar and his father belonged to the Radical faction. So

when he went to seek permission for the burial, he was not even allowed to enter the priest's residence. He was told at the door that Sheikh Dhamal would not give his consent until certain conditions were met: Zafar should denounce the Radicals, condemn and curse his father, apologize, and, finally, renew his allegiance to the Mowlana. He should say lanat on his father, which meant invoke the wrath of Allah upon him.

Zafar refused to accept the conditions. He approached Councilor Asif Hussain for advice. The councilor gathered a few people and marched to the priest's residence with Zafar. They were not allowed in. Tempers rose, yelling began, and a few men forced their way in.

Never before had Sheikh Dhamal been confronted this way. There was a time when he walked the streets of Mominwadi like a peacock in heat. Not anymore. These days he sneaked in and out in his little Fiat with windows rolled up, knowing that if he stepped out into the street, the women would lynch him. Upon seeing the intruders the priest, red in the face and frightened, demanded, "How dare you come in like this?"

"Because you won't allow us in any other way," Zafar replied. "All I want is permission to bury my father."

"You will have it," Sheikh Dhamal said. "Just accept the conditions."

"Conditions? You're asking me to curse my father!"

"So what? He was only your worldly father. Mowlana is your spiritual father. You people have hurt him by disobeying him, by going against his wishes. You know how much he loves you. He loves all his children. But you must earn his love back. The only way to do that is to curse everyone and everything that comes between you and his love for you."

"But my father has done no wrong."

"I have explained to you his sin. Now go, don't waste my time."

"Janab, please do not test me at this time, in this hour of sorrow. Whatever misunderstandings there are, we can discuss them later. Don't make my father's death an issue. Don't deny a dead man the dignity of a proper burial. Allah will not be pleased."

"You rascal, you will teach me about Allah? If Mowlana is angry, Allah is angry. Now get out of here."

The dead man's elder son, Zoeb, happened to be on the Loyalist side. His wife and her family were staunch supporters of Mowlana and were close to Sheikh Dhamal. His father's death put him in a dilemma. He had the filial obligation to attend his father's funeral but only at the risk of upsetting the priest and his wife's family.

Sheikh Dhamal suspected Zoeb would succumb and run to lend his shoulder to his father's bier. In order to preempt him, he summoned Zoeb.

"Our Mowlana's love has saved you. Now the choice is yours. Either you throw soil on your father's grave or choose to remain on the side of haq. The truth."

The priest, clad in white robes, sat on a white padded divan in a large alcove at the far end of the room. Windows behind him opened up on to the street. A squat mahogany writing desk sat in front of him, on which a notebook lay open. He held a fountain pen in his right hand. An open ink bottle was perched on the edge of the desk. The room had a coat of tan oil paint, was clean, with only floor seating. A smell of incense sticks lingered. Bookshelves and a steel cupboard stood on one side, and an antique-looking chest of drawers on the other.

From this room and with his pen he issued the edicts that were rocking the community. Zoeb had no idea that his younger brother Zafar had been dismissed from here half an hour ago.

The late afternoon sun filtered through stained glass windows, throwing shafts of coloured light across the room. Zoeb squatted on his knees, bowing low, hands joined.

"You know the haq, the truth, I'm talking about?" Sheikh Dhamal asked. "It is the truth of Mowlana, of Allah. It is Mowlana who is going to save you here in this world and in aakhirat, the hereafter. If you want to hold on to the rope of Allah, hold on to Mowlana. Do you understand?"

"I understand, janab, but he is my father. Can't Mowlana forgive him?"

"Even Allah can't forgive him."

"But, janab . . . " Zoeb mumbled, smouldering inside. His beloved father was dead, and this man was not only forbidding him from going to his funeral but calling him names. For one fleeting instant, he was tempted to pick up the ink bottle and splatter the bastard's smug face.

"I told you already, if you go to the funeral you better prepare one for yourself, too, because you will be dead to your wife and your children. Now go and stop wasting my time."

Zoeb got up, stepped backward, and retreated, bending down.

"Spineless idiot," Sheikh Dhamal muttered.

The news of Sheikh Dhamal's high-handedness spread among the Radicals. Not allowing a dead man a timely burial was the last thing they needed to hear. The next day they took to the streets and marched towards the priest's house. Word spread about the great injustice of the priest and hundreds of people joined the demonstration. They shouted slogans denouncing Sheikh Dhamal and the clergy. They were angry and impatient, ready to explode. As they reached the sheikh's residence, rocks began to fly from the crowd towards the house. In a matter of minutes the peaceful protest turned into a rampage. By the time the police arrived on the scene and dispersed the protesters the priest's front door was on fire and the streets were littered with sticks and brickbats and slippers and shoes. A handful of Radicals were in jail and a peaceful community was divided and in upheaval.

That day Zafar's father was buried before sundown, without priestly consent. The caretaker at the cemetery would not allow his workers to dig the grave without the official permit, so outside help was hired. On the third day after the death, the fatiha meal was held for the community, also without permission. Somehow, priestly assent seemed not to matter anymore. The Radicals suddenly felt freer, less encumbered. This newfound freedom did not compromise their faith in any way, all they had done was to sever the mental chain that tied them to the clergy. Some among them with a scholastic bent of mind dusted the Momin scriptures and studied them afresh. They discovered that the system of permission was not mentioned anywhere in the text. It was an elaborate hoax cooked up by the clergy. They also discovered that the oath of allegiance was due only to the Imam (who was in seclusion) and not to the Mowlana. The oath was a rite of passage. Its purpose was to initiate Momins into the faith, and not to enlist them into the slavery of Mowlana which is what the clergy had cleverly turned it into.

———

Upon hearing the news of the arrests, Councilor Asif Hussain had rushed to the police headquarters at Surajpole and asked to see the police chief, Superintendent Surinder Sharma. He explained to the chief the reason behind the violence and asked for the men to be released for it was not their fault. Instead, he demanded that the priest be arrested for causing the riot. "People were angry," he said. They had been provoked. When men are not allowed to bury the dead they lose their cool. Couldn't the Superintendent show some leniency? But the police chief was unsympathetic. He could not understand why anybody would need permission for burial. In any case, he said that cases had been filed against the rioters, and the law had to take its course. His hands were tied.

Meanwhile, in the prison the arrival of a home-cooked meal at supper time was greeted with joy. With the food came news that Hashim Kanchwala was interred that evening, and the entire community had turned out for the funeral, except the dead man's older son, Zoeb. They could not comprehend how a son would not attend his father's funeral. They condemned Zoeb, calling him weak and henpecked, until an elder spoke up in his defence.

"It's easy to pass judgement on others," he said with irritation. "My problem is not with the choice he made; my problem is with the priest who foisted the choice on him. Zoeb's marriage, his children, his entire future were at stake. He couldn't have renounced it all in a rush of sentimentality. He had to choose between his family and his dead father. He chose his family. Will you fault him for that? The fault is of those who inflict such cruel choices. They are the evil ones."

"Okay, agreed," Moiz said, "but that does not absolve Zoeb of his responsibility. When we accept those choices, we are accepting the clergy's authority. We are strengthening their hand. Today one man succumbs, tomorrow another, and in no time the whole community will have a rope around its neck."

"But we are already strung up, don't you know?" said the old man, looking around, and seeing nodding heads. "When we gave our oath of allegiance to the Mowlana, we mortgaged our minds, bodies, and souls to him. Why, we have to renounce our wives if we disobey him. How ridiculous is that! We are called the slaves of Mowlana, not the slaves of Allah. That's a blasphemy, if you ask me. Only a charlatan would want his followers as slaves. Did our beloved Prophet call the believers his slaves?"

The old man grunted in disgust and fell silent.

Tired and aching, the men slowly began to doze off. Some were stretched out on the bare, grimy floor, others were squatting with their backs against the wall. Akbar sat next to Moiz in a corner, half asleep, his head leaning on Moiz's shoulder. Moiz and Luqman were speaking in whispers. Akbar awoke suddenly as the small iron door of the cell opened with a tortuous slide of the rusted latch and the screech of the door hinges. An officer entered with two policemen in tow, bearing flashlights.

"Who's Luqman?" the officer asked sternly, sweeping his beam across the jumble of sleepy faces. "And Moiz." He named three others, all of them from the White House gang, and ordered them all to go out. Luqman asked where they were being taken, but the officer just shoved him out with his hand.

The flashlight beams receded down the corridor, fading into an unforgiving darkness into which the five boys disappeared. Those who remained wondered where they had been taken in the dead of the night. The timing of the visit and the officer's manner did not bode well for them. Not a leaf stirred outside; the air was still and dense. Even the crickets had fallen silent. The men's eyes shone in the dark cell like disembodied, floating lamps.

A sharp cry tore through the night. Then another, then another. Blood-curdling shrieks echoed across the courtyard. Akbar's heart stopped beating, and he wiped his tears with his sleeve. No one spoke. Would they suffer a similar fate? After a while the shrieks died down, and they heard what they surmised was the thudding of wood striking flesh. For a long time afterward, Akbar could hear distant moans. Sitting in the corner with his hands embracing his legs, his head on his knees, he felt helpless, alone, and broken.

When he awoke, the gentle light of dawn had spread like a soft silk scarf over the courtyard. The birds were singing and the leaves of the neem tree danced to the caresses of a zephyr. This idyll belied the terror of the night.

Akbar's throat was parched and he eagerly drank the tea when it arrived; the brew had only a drop of milk and was sweet as a syrup. Later, Momin Youth volunteers brought better tea and breakfast. But he had no appetite. He wished somebody would tell him where Moiz and the others were. When the sun was up and the shadow from the eastern wall fell across the courtyard, Councilor Asif Hussain arrived to see them. On being told of the nocturnal thrashing meted out to the five boys, a dark cloud swept over his face. He had come with the good news that all of them would be released later that day. He became thoughtful, then without wasting any time, he strode straight to the resident inspector's office. He asked the inspector about the beatings. The inspector told him someone else had been on duty the previous night. He showed no concern, but opened a log book to check if anything had been recorded. There was nothing.

"Probably it was an order from the higher-ups," he said.

"But I met the higher-ups this morning, and they made no mention of it," Asif Hussain said.

"They are not obliged to tell you anything," the inspector shot back.

Asif Hussain arose, thanked the inspector, and left, feeling naïve and foolish.

By midday the heat in the cell was unbearable. The accused were paraded out into the courtyard and made to stand facing each other in two rows. The inspector sat on a chair in the shade of a neem tree. He called out the names of those being released on bail, but added that they would have to wait. Those who were not called out were free to go.

When he reached home, Akbar was greeted with hugs and kisses. His mother cried at seeing his sorry state. When Asma Chachi, Moiz's mother, asked him about her son, Akbar gave her a sketchy account, omitting the beating and the shrieks. The news would reach her eventually, and he did not want to be the bearer of the grim tidings.

Moiz returned home a week later and would not talk much. The family had already learned of his ordeal at the police station. He was bruised all over, but he was back and his mother could not stop thanking Allah for returning him to her. Asif Hussain had come to see them a few times to show support, and Asma Chachi accused him bitterly of abandoning her son. Asif Hussain aplogised for the nasty turn of events and said that the police had been bribed to beat the boys. There was nothing anyone could do.

7

THREE MONTHS LATER MOIZ BROKE his ankle in another fracas and became housebound. Akbar spent all his free time by his bedside, and they chatted about studies, the Momin issues, and how the court cases against Moiz would affect his future. Moiz was not worried, he had full faith in the lethargy of the Indian judicial system. He had one more year of college, and then he would decide what he wanted to do. A college education was a modern, secular requirement, and the family insisted that he complete it. They talked about everything but that dreadful night. Akbar did not have the heart to ask, and Moiz could not bring himself to talk about it. Whenever he found the conversation veering off towards that painful episode, he would change the subject.

He needled Akbar about Rukhsana.

"What's her name, yeah, Rukhsana," he said. "Are you making any moves or still being coy?"

Akbar smiled and said nothing.

"Come on, man, you've got to do something. She's a nice girl, pretty, and bright, too, from what I hear. Go talk to her before some other idiot does."

Akbar nodded.

"You know, I'll let you in on a secret. The girls too are crazy about the boys, only they have more tact. They know how to hide their feelings. Look into their eyes, they tell all. The girls want the boys to talk to them, but when you approach them they feign indifference. Don't get put off by that. It's their guile.

You have to persist, and once you break their resistance, they fall like a ripe mango into your hands."

Akbar listened, not sure if Moiz was pulling his leg.

"It's hard to get them to love you, but once they do, they will cling to you for life. They are more sincere and loyal than us boys. But you know what the tragedy is?" Moiz asked.

Akbar shook his head, but was all ears.

"The tragedy is that these hotties, these mangoes, always fall into the hands of idiots."

Akbar wanted to tell Moiz that things with Rukhsana were progressing quite well. It was only a matter of time. Did that make him an idiot?

Akbar's silent overtures over the years had not escaped Rukhsana's notice. He had sought her out at every possible occasion, and yet whenever they met, their encounter would last no more than a few seconds. Akbar's shyness had been one hurdle, the other was her complete apathy. It was like a wall, high and solid. There seemed no way he could go past it.

After the Sadikot incident, however, when they met at the Momin library she approached him directly and started chatting. He could hardly conceal his surprise and joy. She asked about his studies and after his mother, and Akbar answered her unhurriedly. He kept the conversation going with small talk, his shyness for once not holding him back. When she asked him about his prison experience, he was taken aback, wondering how she knew. He told her of the dreadful night, omitting the details, for he was not sure what she would make of them.

Some days later she and her mother came visiting, to show their sympathy. Zubaida Auntie launched instantly into a tirade against Sheikh Dhamal, calling him a vile, slimey man who lost control of his eyes and hands in the presence of women. She thanked God that Akbar was spared rough treatment in the prison. Then in sotto voce she confided that her husband Qamar had been making noises against the Radicals. "He doesn't like the way you people are defying Mowlana."

Akbar only half-listened to her; his attention was on Rukhsana. Her attitude had softened towards him. The way she looked at him. There was a gleam in her eyes whose meaning was hard to dispute. The eyes hold the secret. Moiz was right on that score. If jail was the price of her love, he was willing to spend a hundred nights in custody. But how could he be sure it was love and not his wishful thinking? Oh the dilemma. If only there was a telltale sign, like the colour of hair turning green when there is mutual attraction. It would save so much heartache and agony.

They began to meet in the library. He spent most of his evenings there waiting for her, and noted the days and the time she came. She maintained the pattern of her visits. Sometimes she would borrow a book and leave, other times she would pick up a magazine and sit at a table to read. Then he would be quick to accost her, for there was no knowing when she would condescend to stay back and read the next time. Soon the halting conversations, the awkward silences gave way to more easy chitchat. They discovered that they both liked novels. They began to exchange books and discuss them. Premchand, Tolstoy, Kamleshwar, Austin, Dickens became their accomplices, forging a bond between them as they debated their stories and characters. Akbar often took a contrarian stand, which made her the more passionate about her point of view. He enjoyed riling her up. The argument and the sparring, he hoped, would break barriers, bring them closer.

Akbar was not the only one craving for her attention. There was always a lad or two in the library hovering in her vicinity, trying to talk to her. Akbar would feel a pang of jealousy whenever she smiled and talked to them in a friendly way. Rukhsana was aware how the boys eyed her when she passed them. She could have had any of them eating out of her hand, but she had begun to develop a soft spot for Akbar. She found his shyness and vulnerability endearing. He was not bad looking either, and he was smart. There was something about him, something ineffable, that pulled at her heartstrings. She found that she had begun to feel his presence when he was not around. He was on her mind all the time. She could not wait for tomorrow to see him again. She concluded that this feeling must be something special. One evening, when she came to the library she walked over straight to him instead of going to her customary place. She said salams and sat down across from him, and started talking casually pretending like this was all normal. She saw a look of muted, puzzled glee on his face, and secretly exulted in his confusion. *If this does not send a clear signal to him then I do not know what will.*

He remained clueless. As days passed, he dithered and Rukhsana's frustration mounted. She had played her gambit, now it was his turn. She could see in his eyes the look of affection, the smile when they met, the shadow on his face when they parted—all the symptoms of a guy upside-down in love. But when it came to doing something about it, saying it, he seemed to be strangely constrained. She began to lose patience with him and his shyness didn't seem that cute anymore.

They continued to meet as usual and he talked about everything in the world but that one thing, the invisible monkey that was jumping between them, bawling for attention. Left to him, he would dilly-dally for the rest of his life, she concluded. She made the next move. She wrote a note to him and put it inside the book she had brought for him.

Salams,

I'm writing this after much thought, so don't take it lightly. And don't take it the wrong way. I'm taking the initiative because you would not. You are all talk and no action. I want to know what's on your mind. What's with all our meetings and talks and exchanging books. Does it mean what it appears to be? I know you will say, "What are you talking about?" But you know what I'm talking about, so please do not pretend. And stop this charade. Speak your mind. I will be waiting.

R.

When Akbar read the note, he closed his eyes, looked skyward, and thanked God. He took a deep breath. How ardently he had wished for this moment, and here it was for real, within his grasp. In response to her note, he wrote,

Salams,

I really don't know what you are talking about.

A.

He put the slip of paper inside the book that he returned to her when they met at the library the next day. He had a naughty glint in his eyes. Rukhsana eagerly opened the book to look for the note. She read it. Her face went blank. Without even looking at him, she threw the book back at him and turned to go.

"Rukhsana, please stop," he said. He had only meant to tease her. How stupid of him. And he thought he was being clever. She was heading briskly towards the exit and he feared she would walk straight out of his life. Frantically he ran after her and blocked her path. She stopped, breathing heavily and not looking at him. He could see her face going red, her lips quivering, tears pooling in her eyes.

"I love you," he said.

She tried to push him away, "Don't talk to me."

He caught both her hands and kissed them.

They were still between bookshelves, and nobody saw them. To kiss a girl's hand in public would be scandalous. And such an open declaration of love was as uncommon in their town as an empty Fateh Sagar. Young people mostly lived out their romantic fantasies vicariously through Hindi cinema and its suggestive songs. These things didn't happen in real life. He walked home with her, contrite, begging her forgiveness. She did not speak the entire way, but when they parted, she said, "You have any idea how much courage it takes for a girl to confess her love?" He was never to trifle with her feelings again.

8

THAT NIGHT AKBAR COULD NOT sleep. A song was playing in his head. He wanted to dance. He was in a daze. He could literally explode with joy. He wanted to climb to the "tower top" and announce it to the world. He wanted to go and tell Moiz that the mango had fallen, and no he was not an idiot. That Rukhsana was no fruit, she was an intelligent girl who knew her mind and was by far more decisive than him.

He tossed and turned, the night seemed too long and he could not wait to see her again. He began to think of ways to meet her in a secluded place, away from prying eyes. The library offered no privacy, and he suspected that people might already be talking about them. He didn't want to give them more fodder for their gossip.

In the narrow lane behind his building there was an old abandoned house, where nobody ever went. People thought it was haunted. One wing of its front door was missing, and the remaining one tilted precariously, ready to fall on anyone who might enter. Maybe that's the place for us, he thought. It's rundown and derelict but at least nobody will bother us there.

When he broached the idea, Rukhsana brushed it off. "There's no way I will enter that place," she said.

"Fine, if you can live without seeing me, then have your way."

"If that is the choice, then I'd rather not see you," she said.

Akbar was hurt and confused, for he could tell that she was serious. Other people in the library were watching them. He said nothing and left, hot and bothered.

For the whole of next week, Akbar did not go to the library and sat at home, miserable. He kept himself busy with school work, but not for a moment could he keep Rukhsana out of his thoughts. *What a stubborn girl.*

Over the weekend he met her at a wedding. He sighed. *How can anyone be so beautiful?* She came up to him and whispered, "Where the hell have you been?"

"In hell, where else? But what is it to you?" he muttered and slipped a piece of paper into her hand.

His note said: *I will wait for you at the haunted house from six to seven every evening. If you wish to see me you know where to find me.* If she was stubborn, he was no less.

If she really loves me, she will come, he thought. The next day he waited behind the crumbling walls of the dusty, dilapidated front courtyard of the house. Resting against a pillar, he tried to read a book but only stared at it. The narrow lane was not frequented by many, and any sound of footsteps set his heart racing. The courtyard was open to the sky, and a soft evening light poured in. The house was not as scary as he had imagined. It was going to pieces all the same, and there were no cobwebs he had to tear his way through. This meant that other people came here too. The rooms, which were around the courtyard, were locked, but it seemed to him that the lightest shove would bring the doors crashing down. On one side of the courtyard a narrow staircase without banisters ran up to the first floor and from there to the rooftop. Akbar decided to check it out one of these days when it got dark. When Rukhsana came, *if* she came, he would like to lie down up there next to her and watch the stars.

For two days Akbar waited in the courtyard and went home dejected. Maybe he had set an impossible condition for her, he shouldn't have held her to ransom like that. It was not a way to treat someone you loved. On the third day, when he had almost given up, she appeared at the doorway. She must have approached cautiously, for he did not hear her steps. She stood there hesitantly to check before stepping inside. Akbar rose to greet her and in that rising he felt a relief like waking from a nightmare.

"Don't be scared. No ghosts here," he said, a prayer of gratitude inflecting his voice.

Rukhsana took a few steps and then ran and hugged him, taking him by utter surprise. She held him tightly, breathing heavily. Her hair gave off a faint aroma of coconut oil, as his hands stroked her back. They held each other close for a long while, without moving, without a word. He could hear her heart beating. *I could spend the rest of my life like this.*

When she stirred and looked at him, there were tears in her eyes. He felt like holding her face in his hands and drinking them off. Instead he asked, "What happened?"

She showed him her hands. Her pretty hands with henna designs, into which he had placed his note the other day, were swollen and bruised.

"Who did this?"

"Sister Amelia. I wanted to come on Monday, but . . . "

Sister Amelia, the matron of St Mary's Catholic School, had a fiendish reputation. Under her tutelage the nuns, imbued with missionary zeal, held a few hundred heathens in their thrall. Sister Amelia ran the school like a seminary and imposed a joyless discipline. No jewellery, no make-up, no vain smiles. Hair had to be braided, with blue ribbons to secure it in prescribed fashion. White shirt, blue skirt, white socks, and black shoes. No exceptions.

Once in the past, Muslim parents had petitioned to the school that their religion required girls to cover their legs after a certain age, therefore skirts were not suitable for them. Could they wear slacks instead? Amelia could not believe that backward heathens would have the temerity to make such a request. She told them to take their daughters to a madrassa. Hindu girls were not permitted to wear bindis on their foreheads. If there was a wedding in the family, a St Mary's girl was not allowed to decorate her hands with henna. Hennaed hands were a frivolity that had no place in an institution of learning, Amelia ruled.

That was Rukhsana's crime, for there had been a wedding in her family and she decided to apply henna. It was wintertime and she hoped to conceal the infraction under her woolen gloves. A classmate told on her to the teacher, who reported the matter to Sister Amelia, and the tigress, as she was sometimes called, promptly arrived, scenting blood. Rukhsana was beaten ten times on each palm with the edge of a ruler.

"I will kill that bitch," Akbar said with passion, holding both her hands tenderly.

She smiled. "Don't do anything crazy, my hero. I want you with me, not in jail."

———

They kept their tryst at the haunted house every other day from six to seven in the evening. It was their time, scooped out of mundane living. It was their space, a sanctuary from the upheaval that was shaking the foundation of their community. They had given a name to that time and space: Piece of Heaven. They found peace amid the ruins, stability among broken things. They explored the house, venturing a little farther each time, holding hands and chatting, laughing. She would do most of the talking, telling him about her school, her friends, her fears, her joys; all that was happening in her life. How happy she was about them being together, and how she dreaded if anything bad were to happen to them.

They talked about religion and their community and how it was coming apart and how Mowlana was allowing it to happen. They agreed that Mowlana was rigid and uncaring, and misusing his position. She told him how Mowlana had changed her name on a whim, that officially she was Sakina and the new name was causing so much confusion—the teachers called her Sakina and the friends Rukhsana. She preferred the latter and had told everyone to call her by that name.

"It's an odd way for Mowlana to exert his authority," Akbar said. "So arbitrary, so random. He should have better things to do. Allah is rahim, Allah is karim. Mowlana is neither. He goes around changing people's names and sends out thugs to beat up women."

She said her father would beg to differ, because according to him all divine authority was vested in Mowlana, and he could do no wrong. Then her father was blind, Akbar said, hadn't her own mother been a victim in Sadikot?

Akbar and Rukhsana at their haunt remained innocently above the fray, as if the vortex of acrimony swirling around them would not suck them in. As if they were impervious to the hatred Mowlana's edicts had unleashed. As if their love was a solitude unaffected by the chaos. As if their piece of heaven would not be swept away by the rising tide of ostracism and witch-hunt.

Akbar would invariably arrive at the haunted house before

Rukhsana. One day when he was late, he spied on her from the door. He couldn't believe this lovely human being was actually and finally his. He couldn't bear to think how he would leave her behind. Rukhsana sat at her usual place, hands clasped on her knees, eyes darting around, surveying the place, occasionally landing on the door. Then she saw him, and complained why he was late.

"There is something I have to tell you, please don't get mad," he said as he sat down beside her and took her hands in his.

"What is it?"

"I never got a chance to tell you this before. For a long time I've dreamt of going to college in Bombay."

"Still dreaming or actually going?" she asked, her tone suddenly rough.

"Going."

"Hmm, for three years! Then what about us?" She pulled her hands away from his grasp, her body tensing.

"Nothing will happen to us. I will write to you every day. The colleges there are better, it's a big city, there is so much to do, there are so many opportunities. After graduation, I want to find a job there, and I want *us* to settle down there, make it *our* city. Of course, Udaipur is nice, it will always be our home. We'll come back here to retire," he said with a chuckle.

Rukhsana was on the verge of crying.

"So you have decided everything then."

"I've decided nothing. I'm dreaming, for *both* of us."

She got up to leave. "That is all fine. But I am worried about the three years in between. You know how things are. And my father, you know . . . "

"Nothing will happen jaana, we won't allow anything to happen. Besides, I will be here during summer vacations."

She turned and started towards the door.

"Please don't walk away," he said. "I'll not go if you don't want me to." He smiled and drew her closer and tried to kiss her.

"Stop it," she said. "It is Ramzan."

Ramzan is the month of fasting, when even your deeds have to be pure, and you abstain from material pleasures including sexual intimacy. Akbar rarely fasted during Ramzan. At his home the practice was enforced half-heartedly. He did not like the idea of Rukhsana fasting, the ordeal was punishing. But she said she felt good and found a certain peace when she fasted. The Iftar time, the end of the fast, she said, was so spiritually satisfying that she could not describe it in words.

"The day after tomorrow is Laylatul Qadr, the Night of Power," Akbar said. "Everybody will be at the mosque. Why don't you come here? I have to show you something."

"Hmm, what?"

"It's a surprise. I'll meet you at the end of this lane at ten, okay?"

It was the night in which Muhammad received his first message from the angel Gabriel, who commanded him to read in the name of Allah. "Read, read," the angel exhorted and then asked the Prophet to recite a verse. The Momins spent the whole night in worship, remembering Allah, in the belief that angels descended and heard their prayers. For the boys and girls, however, it was the night to preen and show off, check each other out, and stuff their pockets with nuts and chocolates. It was the time to gallivant around and have fun.

Akbar awaited Rukhsana at the end of the alley outside their hideout. The winter months had passed, at last, and the air was warm. He heard a dog barking and feared it might scare her away. Then he saw her, emerging into the dim street light like a dream coming to life. She wore a mauve satin salwar-kameez, an organza dupatta wrapped around her head, and an array of glass and gold bangles that tinkled when she moved her hands. When she came closer, he smelled the sweet scent of rose attar.

"I told Mother I'm out with friends; but I can't be away long."

"Okay, come with me."

Akbar took Rukhsana by the hand and led her up the stairs into the haunted house. He had brought a small flashlight with him. "Watch your step," he said. They had come up to the upper floors before, but never to the terrace, for fear of being seen.

"I wonder whose house it was, and why it was abandoned," Rukhsana said.

"Ownership dispute, I think. Brothers fighting over possession. Typical, isn't it?"

"Good for us."

"Yes. Okay, here we are. Help me with this." He took out a white counterpane from a cloth bag and spread it on the floor.

"What's this for?"

"You will see, hold your horses, madam."

He lay down on his back and invited her to join him.

"I'm not doing that. This is not right."

"It's not what you think, just come," he said and caught her by the hand. "Trust me."

Rukhsana sat down beside him, still hesitant. Her bangles jingled as she secured the dupatta around her shoulders.

Akbar said, "You know, it is very freeing to lie down in places other than your bed. Come, I will show you something. Look at the sky."

Rukhsana lay down and looked up. Akbar took her right

hand, caressing it with his thumb, feeling its soft, supple texture. With his other hand he pointed up. The sky lay unfurled above them in panoramic splendour. He had read about the morning and evening stars, and the constellations. He scanned the sky for the Big Dipper, for Orion but there were too many stars for his untrained eyes to tell one from the other. He lay there mesmerised by the cosmic spectacle. Rukhsana beside him completed his joy. How many times had he wished for this moment.

"Let's look for a falling star and make a wish," he said.

"What will you wish for?"

"Do you have to ask?"

She looked at him and smiled. He wanted to kiss her but didn't want to startle her. Besides, it was Laylatul Qadr, and it might not go down well with her religious sensibilities. Or the angels.

"Imagine our life together like this," he said, turning to look at her.

"In Bombay?" she teased and pressed his hand. Her teeth gleamed in the dark.

"Yes, let these stars be witness," he said.

They lay there in silence, dreaming of nights to come that would stretch endlessly like the heavens above them. It had been six months since they first came here; apart from their appointed meetings they had come here even at other times, driven simply by the urge to be with each other. Akbar never ventured beyond kissing her on her lips and neck. His favourite turn-on was her nape; he would hug her from behind and gently caress it with his lips. She would melt in his arms. Once, emboldened, his hand encroached on her breast, but she pushed it away. He never went that far again. Mostly, they would sit and talk, he never letting go of her hands. For a long time afterwards she could feel the sensation of his touch, the warmth of his skin. When she spoke, he would look into her eyes, matching her words with the changing hues there. Sometimes the words just fell away, and he would lose himself in those translucent pools in which he could see nothing but openness and innocence.

Akbar had been writing poems for some time. In some he poured his love for her, in others his dissatisfaction with the world found an angry and urgent reproach. When he told her about the poems she asked him to bring them to their rendez-vous and she would read them aloud. The repertoire was soon exhausted, she urged him to write more and would recite them with great affection. When she liked a verse she would read it over and over. She told him he had a talent and should never stop writing. Poems, like the books they read and discussed, became their literary signposts by which they mapped each other's feelings and thoughts.

But for the haunted house, he would have never known what it was to come so close to another person; what it was for two lives to completely immerse into each other. The house became a shrine to their love, and Akbar developed a reverence for old and abandoned places. Among their ruins, in the detritus of times past, haunted by the shadows of broken dreams and forgotten lives, there still was, and perhaps always would be, he came to believe, a place for renewal, a chance for rebirth. Surrounded by its crumbling plaster, in its dark silences the two of them became one, imagining a life together. Their dreams and promises to each other would echo within these walls for years to come. They hoped that the house would always remain in this state, providing sanctuary to other lovers at other times.

But they couldn't keep their love a secret. Although a gang of boys had chanced upon them once, it was Moiz who trumpeted the relationship. Akbar had confided in him, of course. He was in love and wanted to tell the whole world. He never knew that telling it to Moiz would amount to the same thing. Moiz took to teasing Akbar about Rukhsana in front of his crew, then Luqman started needling him too, and thus word got out. Among the young crowd in Radical circles their affair became an open secret. Akbar, a loverboy! *Silent waters truly run deep!* But as long as their parents didn't know, neither Akbar nor Rukhsana was worried. It was the adult world that was dangerous.

9

RUMOURS ULTIMATELY FOUND THEIR WAY to Khatun's ears. She had suspected something of the sort all along. All those meetings and visits to the library and exchanging of books had not remained hidden from her. She liked Rukhsana and approved of the relationship. Rukhsana had flowered into a fine young lady. Khatun could scarcely believe how full the girl had become. When she was born, Khatun had joked with Zubaida that Akbar's wife had come into the world. The two of them made a tacit pact, hoping their son and daughter would find each other when they grew up. And how they had. When she broke the news to Zubaida, she hugged her in delight.

"Oh Khatun, I can't tell you how happy I am. When I see them together my heart spills with joy. God bless them," Zubaida said, eyes moist, and lips mouthing "thu thu thu" to ward off the evil eye. Then she cautioned, "I'll not tell Qamar about it yet. You know how he is, and how things are. I'll wait for the right moment. Insha'allah all will be well."

Akbar's father, Zahid Ali, greeted the news with far less enthusiasm. He was not opposed to the match but expressed concern about Qamar. The man was odd, he said. In any case, the kids were still young. Akbar should focus on his studies and career first. He had no idea what he wanted to do with his life, but had already decided whom to spend it with? Where were his priorities?

Akbar, however, had made it clear that he would not sit at their hardware shop. He could not imagine himself selling nuts and bolts, hinges and door knobs all his life. He wanted to study journalism in Bombay. His father had flatly refused at first, urging him to join the family business. And if he really wanted to do something else, why journalism? Instead, he advised, do medicine or engineering. There's money and high status in those professions. But Akbar had his mother's backing. She persuaded her husband to accept their son's decision. Zahid Ali had agreed reluctantly, but he could not see how one could make a decent living working for a newspaper.

Grandfather Sajjad Ali too was ill-disposed to Akbar's choice of career. His businessman's instinct militated against the idea of working for a salary. He tried to talk Akbar out of it, and enumerated to him the virtues of owning a business, being his own boss. Hardware is where the hard cash is, he said. Akbar would not be persuaded. Sajjad Ali grudgingly accepted that the young generation was different, education was opening up their minds and a hardware shop was hardly the hook that would keep Akbar anchored.

Akbar had visited Bombay many times on short trips, and from a young age he had been pestering his father to let him live there, with Dadaji and Chacha, his father's younger brother. But his mother said he was too young: "Who would take care of you there? Maybe after you finish high school."

Now that time had come. What was pulling him to the big city, he could not tell. This much he knew—he had to study and live in the city. And prepare grounds for a future in which Rukhsana would be by his side. In the interim, though, he would have to live away from her. On her part, Rukhsana had gradually accepted the idea. She understood his love of the big city, and his determination to study there. She began to see that

Bombay had a lot more to offer, and although she had never visited the city she had begun to weave conjugal dreams about it.

Akbar had applied at Elphinstone College in the arts programme and planned to major in journalism. Formerly the Bombay Presidency College, this throwback to the British Raj was the alma mater of his grandfather. Weeks before his departure, Khatun began to get anxious. She knew that once he was gone, he would come back only as a visitor. He was just out of high school. How could she give him up already?

Two days prior to departure, he had told Khatun about Rukhsana.

"Amma, you know Zubaida Auntie's daughter, Rukhsana?"

"Yes, what about her?"

"Well, you know we're friends . . . I mean more than friends."

"Hmm, what does that mean?" she said, half-teasing him. There was a shyness in his eyes, and he very nearly blushed.

When he said nothing, she continued, "You really thought I had no idea what was going on? Zubaida and I had long wished for this, you know. Your father is also in agreement. But for now, we want you to focus on your studies."

Akbar's blush broke into a big smile and he hugged his mother. He could not wait to inform Rukhsana about it, and when they met at the haunted house the day before his departure they could not contain their joy.

"You know, my mother likes you," Rukhsana said. "But with my father I can never be sure."

Akbar sounded hopeful and told her everything would be all right. Their valedictory meeting ended on a cautious note. Rukhsana cried as she hugged him. He promised to write her every day.

———

After his departure, Khatun took to Rukhsana with renewed affection. She invited her to spend evenings at her house. "Now that Akbar is gone, I could use some company," she said. And so Rukhsana often dropped by before supper, sometimes just to say salams and check if Akbar's letter had arrived. He wrote to her at his parents' address to keep the correspondence out of her father's prying eyes. Rukhsana admired Khatun, who was educated, well-read, and fun to talk to. And she was Akbar's mother, she needed no other qualification to be liked and loved.

Rukhsana dropped by every day, hoping for a letter from him, even if she had received one only a few days back. There was an off chance, she hoped, that he might have penned an extra missive in a burst of ecstatic love. This did not happen, and her heart would sink a little, but whenever she received his regular letter, she would be delirious with joy and read it in bed, over and over.

When it arrived by post, Khatun would place it on the table by the window. Later, in the evening, Rukhsana would come, and upon seeing the letter her eyes would light up. Khatun would observe her from where she sat, and seeing the jubilation on her face, she would feel fuzzy inside, though outwardly she would pretend to be calm. She herself would not hear a word from Akbar for weeks. She would ask Rukhsana after him, and tease her, partly out of envy, partly out of concern. "The boy has stopped writing to me," she would say. Rukhsana, embarrassed, would allow a shy smile.

The two of them, like mother and daughter, were relaxed in each other's company, often talking about Akbar, whose absence they felt acutely and pulled them closer.

"Once we were in Bombay during summer holidays," Khatun said one day, "and we drove through Kamatipura, the city's famous, or rather infamous red light district. You know what I'm talking about? Akbar's Nazeer Chacha for some reason drove through this shady area lined with chawls and tenement buildings. Outside every other window hung a red lamp. It was a sign that the lady of the evening was open for business. We adults kept our embarrassed silence, but Akbar was about ten then, and inquisitive as he is, he asked in all innocence, 'Why are there red lights outside these windows?' For a moment, nobody said a thing.

"Then came Nazeer's reply. 'It's Diwali, they celebrate it every night.' Akbar, who was sitting in my lap said, 'Nice, so where are the fireworks?' To which Nazeer promptly said, 'The fireworks happen inside.' Of course, it doesn't sound funny in the telling, but how we all burst out laughing! Akbar gave me a puzzled look; he knew his question had not been answered but had the good sense not to pursue it."

Rukhsana smiled, picturing Akbar's boyish bewilderment. "For me," she offered, "what I found amusing, and, of course, endearing, were his utterly lame excuses to see me and talk to me."

"Yes, I know. One Eid day he said he was going to visit your house, just like that, out of the blue. Only now I realize what his motivation was."

"Yes, I remember, and I feel so bad that I wasn't too kind to him . . ."

Khatun said, wistfully, "I wonder how he is doing in Bombay. He will have to start his life over . . . everything will be new for him. Make new friends, adjust to a different lifestyle. They say it's a city of dreams, but dreams are not cheap. They don't tell you that every dream rides on a thousand nightmares."

"Not to worry, Auntie, he will be all right. I know it."

"Can you please not call me Auntie? I'm your Amma now."

Rukhsana smiled, and reached for the letter on the table and put it in her purse. On the way out before she closed the door behind her, she turned around and said, "See you tomorrow, Amma."

10

In Bombay, Akbar lived in Noorani Manzil, which consisted of two buildings side by side enclosed by a compound. Out front was a long ribbon of yard where boys often played cricket. Only Momins lived in these buildings. The boys here spoke Gujarati and English fluently. Akbar could speak Hindustani and was too embarrassed to utter anything in English. Even though the missionary school he attended in Udaipur employed English as a medium of instruction, he could not speak it well. The English teacher Mr Vaz was a sadistic sourpuss who taunted and humiliated students for being provincial heathens, and killed whatever passion they had for learning the language. In the end, Mr Vaz imparted wounds in place of learning. In Bombay, the boys were confident; Mr Vaz had not happened to them.

Akbar would take the bus to college and often sit in the upper deck by a window. The traffic, the bustle, the sea of people riveted his attention. Eagerly, hungrily he devoured the vignettes of life unfolding below him. Taken together as a whole, the city seemed like an organism, a variegated animal on the move, restless and insatiable, with a mind of its own. He wondered where he and Rukhsana would fit in this chaos that was forbidding and enchanting at the same time.

He enjoyed the freedom that college offered. Unlike school, there was nobody to discipline you, nobody to tether you to a timetable. But with freedom came responsibility—he alone was responsible for his education. The college building was a colonial-era, gothic structure with large dank classrooms with high ceilings. He applied himself to his studies, and in a matter of a few weeks his days fell into a rhythm. At home, Dadaji became his companion and confidant. He looked forward to sitting with him in the balcony in the evenings and talk about college, current affairs, and the developments in Udaipur, the news of which he got from Rukhsana and his mother. He wrote to Khatun sporadically, and to Rukhsana every day, as he had promised. On his yellow, lined notepad he would journal his thoughts every night before going to bed and by the end of the week when he had totted up enough pages written on both sides, he would post her a fat letter.

He learned from his mother that the situation in Udaipur was getting worse. Mowlana's fatwa of excommunication, let loose like a virus, was slowly eating away at relationships, creating rifts and divisions. There was confusion over the meaning of the edict, for the Loyalists did not know how much and to what extent they should boycott their friends and relations. The boundaries were not neatly drawn. How does one wrench away completely from loved ones, not to speak with them at all? How do lifelong friends become enemies just like that? Or husbands and wives become strangers overnight? How do fathers shun their daughters? Or sons discard their mothers?

When the British broke the Indian subcontinent into two, people at least had a chance to migrate and swap places. In Udaipur, people had nowhere to go. In the same house, in the same family, under the same roof fences went up, barriers were built. Hearts turned to stone. Blood ran cold. The Loyalists were forced to systematically weed out loved ones from their lives. Zealots, officious and vengeful, started spying and squealing on people. It seemed as though walls had sprouted eyes and ears.

Nobody could be trusted anymore. If a Loyalist mother were caught speaking to her Radical son, she would be summoned by Sheikh Dhamal and reprimanded and, moreover, made to denounce her son as illegitimate and to reaffirm her allegiance to the Mowlana. Nine months after Sadikot, the fatwa had turned a large swath of Momins—the Radicals—into enemies. Where there once were simple folks living out their ordinary lives, there were now people divided by hatred and blind faith.

But here was the conundrum: the Radicals were steeped in their religious beliefs and their rituals. For generations, their daily life had been tied to customs and ceremonies tightly controlled by the priesthood. Now they had defied the Mowlana, the head priest, due to the abuses and systematic extortion, but this did not mean that they were renouncing their faith. Excommunication meant exclusion from their community, not from their beliefs. They still wanted to continue to be part of their Shia faith as defined by their scriptures. And so they were sometimes caught in contradictions.

In most cases, the Radicals flouted the requirement of ijazat, or permission. They no longer had to pay every step of the way. For matters that needed urgent attention such as burial, childbirth, etc., they could not wait for Sheikh Dhamal's acquiescence. But for a marriage ceremony they could wait. Mowlana's blessing, their faith had decreed, would make matrimony holy. They wanted to do it the proper way—with proper religious sanction.

Nobody had suspected that the Momin Youth Association's foray into a municipal election might balloon into a full-blown rebellion against the clergy. Despite the bedlam in Udaipur and the bad blood that had come to pass, the Radicals still hoped that things would be resolved amicably. Soon after the Sadikot incident, a number of them trooped to the nearby town where Mowlana was sojourning and sought his audience, with a desire to settle the matter. They sent him their grievances: the terms of the oath of allegiance were too harsh; the need to seek a priest's permission for every little thing was unnecessary; millions of rupees were collected from Momins, that money be spent on the welfare of the community; local centres should have the autonomy to elect committees to run their own affairs, instead of being harassed by appointed bullies like Shiekh Dhamal.

Mowlana dismissed their demands and declined to meet them. Instead, he demanded unconditional submission to his authority and the renewal of their oaths of allegiance. Weeks and months passed, and the Radicals stuck to their demands, but the supposedly infallible, divinely-appointed Mowlana would not bow to what he considered a ragtag band of infidels. Slowly, a formal and organized resistance began to coalesce around the agenda the Radicals had put forward. The spontaneous rebellion of a year ago grew into a radical movement.

The Radicals began to exercise their freedom. They now felt free to think, to act, and to live their lives in accordance with their consciences, while practicing the tenets of their faith. They were still a tiny minority, however, compared to the vast numbers of Momins in India, Pakistan, Africa and elsewhere who all swore loyalty to the Mowlana. The Radicals were declared infidels. They were no match for the prestige and power that the Mowlana had inherited and commanded. Even as they were demonized by the Mowlana, the Radicals drew inspiration from the Battle of Karbala, where Imam Hussain chose to martyr himself rather than submit to the debauched and despicable usurper, Yazid. They saw their struggle, like Imam Hussain's, as one of truth and justice against oppression.

Being a majority in Udaipur, the Radicals came to control the mosques, community centres, and other properties. The Loyalists effectively "boycotted" themselves out of the community. The Radicals opened their mosques to everyone but the Loyalists would not come because the Radical imam—the prayer leader—did not have the Mowlana's sanction and therefore, they were told, prayers under him were unacceptable to Allah. Rukhsana's father, Qamar, became one of Sheikh Dhamal's minions and was tasked with keeping his flock in line. He of course started with his home.

———

Akbar did not receive Rukhsana's letter three weeks running. In her last missive she had sounded worried. She said things were not looking good, that her father was pressuring them to cut off relations with the Radicals. And although he, the father, did not know about their affair yet, it was only a matter of time before he found out. Her mother, she wrote, was not very hopeful, given her father's devotion to Mowlana. She had no idea what to do and was feeling lost. Akbar saw the letter was stained with tears, the words smudged. But he still hoped that things would turn out fine. How bad could it get?

When Rukhsana's letters stopped coming altogether, he knew the worst had happened. He wrote to his mother to find out. Khatun replied saying that the curse of excommunication had fallen upon them; Zubaida Auntie, under pressure from her husband, had severed all relations with them. She had visited Zubaida when Rukhsana did not come to see her for four straight days. She found out that Rukhsana had been exiled to an aunt's place because she refused to break her relationship with Akbar. Her father, Qamar, was adamant and his writ would prevail. There was nothing she could do. The letter read like a death sentence to Akbar. A darkness spread before his eyes. He knew exactly how Rukhsana would have felt. He wanted to howl in pain and anger.

Later, at tea, he told Dadaji the news. Dadaji looked at Akbar for a long moment. At length he said, "My dear boy, I do not want to give you false hope. Let me be frank. These mullahs are the biggest enemies of freedom and love and everything that is good in between. Your girl and her mother are like trapped rabbits; they can do nothing. Neither can you. I'm sorry, but this is the reality."

Akbar had hoped that Dadaji, always an ally, would understand his pain and comfort him, offer a solution. He was deeply disappointed. He did not want to accept the reality, as Dadaji called it. There was no way he was going to give up. He phoned his mother that night. When he was finally connected through a telecom service, the line was bad and the conversation brief. Khatun's voice came mixed with static, as if she were speaking from outer space. He pleaded with his mother to do something. "There has to be a way, Amma," he urged.

She said, "Rukhsana's father won't allow even our shadows to fall upon her, let alone allow us to talk to her or Zubaida. I understand how you feel, jaana, but you must forget her." After a pause she added, "It breaks my heart to say it, you know that, don't you?"

Akbar felt crushed and at that moment hated his mother for being so blunt. *No matter, nothing is over until I talk to Rukhsana, I must talk to her.*

He called her home. The line was again bad and the conversation briefer. Zubaida Auntie answered the phone. On hearing Akbar's name her response was gruff.

"What do you want?" she demanded.

"Auntie, I want to speak to Rukhsana."

"No, she can't speak to you."

"Auntie, please."

"It's best you don't, and if you really care for her, don't ever call again."

"Auntie . . . "

She hung up and he stood there holding the receiver. It felt heavy, like a rock.

———

At Noorani Manzil, all Momins were loyal to the Mowlana and his administration, and so Akbar and his family had to appear loyal. The people at Noorani, knowing about their family connections, remained largely indifferent but there were a couple of zealots who made it their business to meddle. Sooner or later they would come sniffing.

At dinner one evening Dadaji expressed his fears. Everybody agreed that things might get tricky. Nazeer Chacha had lived in Bombay all his life and had nothing but contempt for the clergy. He was a practical man with a dour sense of humour. When he laughed his whole body shook. For him religion was an opium minus the pleasure, hence only meant for fools. He loved life and was given to enjoying it. His friends were liberals like him. "What matters," he said, "is not to give the dogs a bone to chew on."

"You're right," Sajjad Ali said. "Let's be as discreet as possible."

———

Zubaida pleaded with Qamar to bring their daughter home, but he wanted Rukhsana to pledge that she would not meet the infidel boy again. It was Sunday and it had been a week since she was banished. While Qamar was reading the newspaper, Zubaida got dressed and went out without bothering to inform him. She headed straight to his sister's house. Enough was enough, she had decided. She would bring her daughter home. It was a cold, sunny morning, a few people were about on the street. The radio was playing listeners' choices of Hindi film music. One of her favourites, "Go, fly away little bird," sung by Mohammed Rafi, was on. Every home or shop she passed was tuned to it and Zubaida didn't miss a single beat of the song till she reached her sister-in-law's house.

On hearing her mother's voice, Rukhsana came out running from inside and hugged her.

"Enough of this," Zubaida said. "Gather your stuff, let's go home." Her sister-in-law was happy that Zubaida had taken a stand, though she dared not show it.

"Does Qamar know about this?" she asked as a formality, so as not to appear to approve Zubaida's intervention.

"No, but he will know pretty soon," Zubaida said firmly.

On the way back, mother and daughter walked in silence, their nerves taut in anticipation and their ears oblivious to the tunes playing on the radio. When they entered the house, Qamar lowered his newspaper and peered through his glasses. Upon seeing Rukhsana, he threw the paper aside and shot up as on a spring.

"What is she doing here?" he yelled.

"This is her home," Zubaida said calmly.

"I told you she can't stay here until she . . . you know what."

"No, I don't know, and I don't care," Zubaida said, each word fortifying her defiance. "This is her house, and she doesn't need to pledge anything to live here."

"You, woman, don't you dare talk to me like that. I'll not accept this."

"And I will not accept my daughter being exiled from her home. I cannot live without my daughter. If you want her out, then I'm out, too."

Qamar backed down. "Be warned, both of you," he said. "Know your limits."

Over at her aunt's place Rukhsana had missed Akbar more than ever and desperately wanted to talk to him. Her eyes were puffed from lack of sleep, there were dark shadows beneath them. She had lost her appetite, and her aunt had warned that if she didn't eat she would die. That would not be such a bad outcome, she had thought. Without Akbar there was nothing to live for anyway.

Now at home she found it hard to believe that the man was her father. *What is it that makes my father so cold, so cruel. Surely, it can't be the love of God. Akbar was right, Mowlana is to be blamed.* She felt sorry for her father. She could never respect him. In one week the distance of ages had grown between them. Not that she was ever close to him. His affection for her and her little sister had always been grudging. She could not recall a moment when he had held her in his arms, hugged her, played with her. *What was wrong about us? That we were not sons?*

————

Qamar Kapdawala was a successful cloth merchant, a business he had inherited from his father and increased manifold. But he gave the credit for his accomplishment not to his own talent and hard work but to the blessings of Mowlana. He believed that he was indebted to Mowlana and lost no opportunity to show his gratitude. The last time Mowlana visited Udaipur, before the incident at Sadikot, Qamar had offered to hold a banquet in his honour and even, if Mowlana condescended, to host him at his humble farmhouse.

Upon receiving the offer, Sheikh Dhamal arranged a meeting with Qamar. Qamar was elated. On the morning of the meeting, he shaved, trimmed his moustache, and put on his newest white kurta-pyjama. He dabbed some attar behind his ears. He stuffed two hundred-rupee notes into a lifafa—envelope—to take with him. One did not go to meet the priest empty handed, one carried *salam*. The greeting, salam alaikum—peace be upon you—was not enough. Salam in Momin parlance had come to mean money. The higher the rank of the priest, the greater the amount. This was precisely why Qamar had been summoned—to discuss the heft of the lifafas for the Mowlana and his family.

With the priest in his living room sat four other men in pristine white. Sheikh Dhamal himself, who was a distant relative of Mowlana, wore a white starched stole around his shoulders. His headgear was a neatly-wrapped white pagdi. On entering the room, Qamar got down on his knees before the priest, who stretched out his right hand to him. Qamar accepted it with both his hands and pressed the lifafa in it, and then took the hand to his right eye, then his left eye, and finally to his forehead and lips. Then as he proceeded to kiss his knees, Sheikh Dhamal deftly shoved the gift under a cushion beside him. Qamar then stood up, stepped back a few paces, and squatted on his knees, hands joined in supplication.

The priest smiled contemptuously. He came straight to the point. "Do you have any idea how fortunate you are that

Mowlana has accepted to break bread with you and stay in your house? When his holy feet cross your threshold, you and your family will be blessed for generations to come. Know that the angel of Allah will be visiting your house."

"Please, janab, I cannot describe how blessed I am," Qamar said.

"There are two things. First, Mowlana has agreed to stay at your farmhouse. But this bhai," Sheikh Dhamal pointed to the man sitting on his right, "has seen your farmhouse. It will need to be renovated, so make it worthy of Mowlana."

Qamar bowed in agreement.

"Second, Mowlana has generously accepted the invitation to a banquet in your house—which will also have to be renovated."

Qamar bowed again.

"Now we must discuss the salam. Mowlana does not travel alone; his princes and princesses and other dignitaries will accompany him. Every member of your family must present salams to all royal guests. I'll specify the amount for each of them when the time comes."

"Whatever you say, janab."

"And one more thing, Mowlana's cook travels with him, so keep your women out of the kitchen. You can go now."

A jubilant Qamar went home and announced, "Mowlana has accepted to come to our house for a banquet."

Zubaida frowned.

"And guess what? Mowlana will also stay at our farmhouse."

Zubaida grunted audibly. Well, well, misfortunes never come singly, she wanted to say. Instead, she asked, "How much will it cost?"

"Oh, this woman, always so cynical. 'How much will it cost?'

Can you even hear yourself? Aren't you ashamed? Mowlana's blessings are boundless. All this wealth, this prosperity, this very breath I take is because of him, do you realize that? How crude can you get? How much it will cost, ugh?"

Over the next weeks Zubaida saw with rising frustration her house being transformed. The stone steps at the front door were replaced by white marble; the inside staircase was widened and supplanted with black granite. The kitchen was expanded by encroaching into the adjoining room, which was Rukhsana's. At that time Rukhsana could not have imagined that it was only a precursor to the bigger tragedy to come. Mowlana was not just shrinking her room but would also one day crush her heart. The dining area where royal mouths would be fed was refurnished, and the whole house was repainted.

Mowlana was received with much fanfare and fawning and scraping. Qamar introduced his daughters to him; upon hearing Rukhsana's name Mowlana said the name was not appropriate; her name is Sakina, he declared. Qamar bowed. But Zubaida was opposed to the new name and they had a big row. Rukhsana said she liked her name and did not want be called by any other. Qamar almost slapped her for her insolence but Zubaida intercepted the blow. "Aren't you ashamed to raise your hand to your daughter?" Qamar hissed and pushed her away. Mowlana's bidding had to be done, and no earthly power could stop him from doing that. He hired an agent to run the bureaucratic gamut and got the name altered in her birth certificate, in her school and in the municipal records. Officially she became Sakina and he insisted on calling her by that moniker, and with pride; to her mother and sister and others she remained Rukhsana.

All things considered, Qamar must have spent two million

rupees for hosting Mowlana. His prestige in the community rose several notches. This was some years before the revolt engulfed Udaipur, when Mowlana was still revered by one and all.

Upon hearing about the extravagance, Akbar's father, Zahid Ali, felt compelled to speak with Qamar. They were not the best of friends but knew each other well, the way men know each other in a small community. So one morning when he ran into Qamar at the paan shop in Mominwadi, he greeted him and ventured, "If you don't mind, may I ask you a question?"

"Sure," Qamar said. "What is it?"

"I'm hearing that you spent twenty lakhs on Mowlana's visit."

"Yes, that's about right. Why do you ask?"

"My dear friend, don't you think that's a lot of money?"

Qamar was taken aback for a moment. Then he said, "Now don't you lecture me on this. It's my business, what I give. What is it to you?"

They picked up their paans—their quota for the day—and started walking.

"Qamar Bhai, I'm not lecturing you. I know you can afford to spend that kind of money, and it makes me happy that some of us are so blessed." Zahid Ali paused, choosing his words, knowing he was on thin ground. He spat out betel juice at the side of the street and said, "What I'm saying is that your money would have been well spent if you had done something for the needy. I'm speaking as a friend. You know how many poor people we have in our community. Those twenty lakhs would have gone a long way to feed and educate them."

"Oh please, stop it. The poor don't need my money. They need Mowlana's blessings, and he showers us all with it all the time. You won't understand. It's a matter of faith. You don't know what faith is."

"Qamar Bhai, maybe I don't understand faith, but what I understand is that the money you gave to Mowlana is not coming back here. You were not the only one; there were others too who gave. Some gave willingly, like you, and some not so willingly. All in all, a huge fortune was taken from us, from our small community here. We need that money here, our economy needs that money. If nothing, at least you could have re-invested that sum into your business."

"Wow, that's rich. A flop merchant telling me how to run my business. Some gumption you have," Qamar said with disdain and turned into a side street and headed for his shop.

Zahid Ali watched his friend walking away. "What a fool," he muttered.

———

At that time Zahid Ali had no idea that Qamar's idiocy ran so deep and would one day destroy the love of two young people. So when Khatun reported to Zahid Ali about the fate of Akbar and Rukhsana's romance, he took a philosophic view.

"It is better not to have any relations with fanatics," he said. "If Akbar were to marry into that house, there would be pressure on us to conform. We would have to compromise our position, make adjustments for the sake of Akbar's in-laws. I don't think we want to be in that situation. And anyway, that idiot Qamar would never marry his daughter into a Radical family. I feel sorry for the kids, but in the long run it is best for both parties that this match has not come to pass."

11

AKBAR SAT BY THE SEA, at Nariman Point on Marine Drive, watching the waves arrive and smash upon huge boulders at the shore. He came here for a walk every day after supper, and had just strolled all the way to the tip of the promenade, which ended abruptly, like an unfinished sentence. He liked the sound of the waves and puzzled over their wasted effort—how they rushed to meet land, full of passion, and then dissipated into white spume. He could see where they ended up, but from which distant shores did they arrive?

The setting sun was a fuzzy orange orb sinking slowly into the Arabian Sea before him. The salty humid sea air clung to his skin and soothed him. A strange silence lurked beneath the constant rumble of the sea. He looked at the horizon as the last of the sun was swallowed up. As the dusk fused the water and the sky and as the tireless waves pounded against the rocks he felt a tide of melancholy rising in his gut.

The previous day he had watched two young lovers seated not far from him. The breeze carried their muffled voices, but he could not decipher anything meaningful. He was envious and silently prayed for them. He had been reminded of Rukhsana. Her memory had frozen into a dull constant ache. At least once a day he read the last letter she had written:

Oh my dear Akbar, how I miss you, how I wish you were here. I don't know what to do. I feel alone and helpless. How can it be that we have to end our love? And why and for what? Nothing makes sense to me. I tried talking to my mother but she feels helpless, afraid to go against the wishes of my father. Usually I do not speak to him, I'm scared of his temper. But for my sake, for our sake, I picked up the courage and talked to him, wanted to tell him that what he was doing was wrong. He became very angry and raised his hand to me but mother intervened.

I hope by now you must have got the news about what has happened here. Your last letter was so full of love, I read it again and again and cried. The words "last letter" give me goose bumps. And perhaps this might be the "last" from me too. Oh Akbar, I can't believe this! I have not been able to meet your mother also for so many weeks. I miss her too.

Things are really bad here, nobody is even allowed to look at the Radicals. Everybody is spying on each other, can you believe it? I am hoping things will calm down, that people will come to their senses. Let us stay positive. In the meantime, please do not write, my father will kill me if he finds out.

Let's pray that this madness ends soon. Love you so.

R

Akbar had received it soon after he called her home and Zubaida Auntie had rudely hung up on him. The letter was fraying at the creases; in the last two years he must have opened and folded it a thousand times. He had clung to it like a drowning man at a straw.

He had last seen Rukhsana at the hideout when he departed for college; he had been to Udaipur twice during summer vacations but didn't catch even a glimpse of her. There was no question of her coming to the community library, it had become the preserve of the Radicals. Through a friend of a friend he had sent her a note, asking if she could meet him at the haunted house, and waited for her there. She never came.

Zubaida Auntie had cut all ties with Akbar's mother and

though they lived on the same street she refused to acknowledge her when they passed each other. Khatun understood why. Were Zubaida to be seen speaking to Khatun, she would be ostracized and in order to be reinstated—made pure again—would have to go through the rigmarole of apology and oath of allegiance; not to mention face Qamar's opprobrium. They could have met clandestinely, but Zubaida showed no interest.

Hundreds of people were affected this way. Relationships had ended abruptly, as if interrupted by death. No goodbyes, no farewells. If an end of a relationship could be labelled as murder, then what happened in Udaipur was a massacre. No blood was spilled—it just turned white. Akbar still could not believe how quickly the fortunes of his community had changed, and how quickly he had lost Rukhsana. If this were not enough, Dadaji passed away after a heart surgery that went awry. And not long after, Akbar was driven out of Noorani Manzil.

———

On the morning of his death, Sajjad Ali awoke early when the nurse came in to give him his medicine and clean his bedpan. It was dark outside, and he could see the headlight from the occasional cars on the road. He lay wide awake, breathing heavily, feeling a throbbing pain in his chest, but otherwise he was in full control of his senses. The day he was brought to the hospital following a sudden cardiac arrest, he had had an inkling that he would not be going back home. The prospect of death frightened him at first, but as days slid by he made peace with himself. Surgery, medicine, doctors and nurses fussing over him, the comings and goings of relatives seemed like the vestiges of a life that seemed distant and tenuous. The world looked different from the deathbed. All those struggles, those travels, the quest for wealth and knowledge and a million sundry things—what had come of them?

When the nurse left, he stared at the ceiling fan, and his mind wandered to the cherished memory of his childhood . . . He was sitting on the mud floor of his house with an Urdu reader on his lap; an oil lamp was burning by his side, and his mother was making him repeat aleph, bey, tey, pointing out the letters. Her face glowed in the warm lamplight, and a strand of hair had strayed loose from her dupatta . . .

A tear trickled from the corner of Sajjad Ali's eye and burned its way down his cheek.

———

Sajjad Ali was buried at the Jafalwadi Momin cemetery. Prior to the funeral, his son Nazeer Ali had gone to the priest's house to seek permission for burial. The priest's secretary checked his account to make sure no dues were outstanding. That done, Nazeer Ali had to pay for the burial plot, and the preparation of the grave. He had also to purchase the *billet-doux*, the note of intercession by Mowlana, addressed to Allah, requesting the Almighty to admit the deceased into Heaven. The missive would be placed in the shroud and buried with the body. The secretary said, "Without this letter, without this passport to paradise, every soul wanders in infinite wilderness." Then he looked Nazeer Ali directly in the eye and taunted, "In your Udaipur these days I hear that the dead are going to their graves without this letter. What a shame. Without Mowlana's help they will burn in hell, and before that, in the grave, their punishment will be relentless."

Nazeer Ali said nothing. He was sympathetic to the Radicals

but had kept his distance from them for he knew that theirs was a lost cause. He saw the clergy as a mafia running a protection racket. "You throw money at them and buy your peace," he had said when the topic came up at a soiree at a friend's house. "Can you fight the mafia? You can't. And these people in white robes, they are worse. They use religion as a cover and make the whole con game look legitimate. They have got the community by the balls. The moment you act smart, they tighten the grip, and you howl and scream and go running back to them with a fat lifafa in one hand and aching nuts in the other."

His friend with close connections to the clergy listened amusedly and smiled at Nazeer's colourful description. "The bottom line is," the friend said, swirling ice cubes in his single-malt imported Scotch whiskey, "pay up and shut up. Go with the flow, become a part of the spectacle, or they will make a spectacle out of you."

"Never a truer word has been spoken," Nazeer Ali said and raised his glass. "To our collective impotence."

———

At Sajjad Ali's funeral, only a few friends and neighbours from Noorani Manzil had turned up. Akbar's parents and other family members in Udaipur did not. Nazeer Ali had advised them not to, for he was not sure how their presence would be received by the Loyalist circles in Bombay.

Nazeer Ali's counsel proved prescient. When he and Akbar returned to Noorani Manzil from the cemetery, two gentlemen drew Nazeer Ali aside, saying they wanted a word with him in private. Nazeer Ali invited them over. He sat with them in the living room, while Shama Chachi made tea for them in the kitchen, her blood boiling. Akbar followed her into the kitchen and whispered, "Why are they here?"

"I know why," she said. "But let's wait." She served the three men tea with nankatai biscuits and returned to the kitchen, where she and Akbar listened in.

Hussain, the sharper and more cunning of the two visitors, said, "Nazeer Bhai, may your father's soul rest in peace, Mowlana's blessings are with him. The dead have found their peace, but we who are still alive must deal with issues of faith. We've come to talk to you about something important."

Nazeer Ali nodded.

"It's about Udaipur, your hometown. The Radicals have gone astray, they have challenged Mowlana. We know your brothers and sisters and their families have been excommunicated." He paused and rubbed his nose with the back of his hand, eyed Nazeer Ali, then looked away. "It is a good thing that they did not attend the funeral. You know what happens to people who ride two horses at the same time?"

Nazeer Ali seethed in silence.

"You're part of a bigger family—the family of Mowlana. Let us preserve the harmony of this family. For the intelligent a hint is sufficient."

Nazeer Ali's body was tense, sinews taut, blood rushing to his head.

Ismail, the other man, who was slurping his tea, loudly munching the biscuits, returned the empty cup to the saucer on the coffee table and concurred, "Nazeer Bhai, please do not misunderstand. We mean well."

At the door, Ismail saw Shama in the kitchen by the stove. "Thank you for the tea, Bhabhi," he said, leering at her from top to bottom, and closed the door behind him.

"Motherfuckers," Nazeer Ali muttered. "Did you see their

gall? They come into my house and threaten me, warn me not to meet my family?" He rolled up the *Times of India* and whacked it hard on the coffee table. Akbar looked crestfallen as he recalled Dadaji's fears. Nazeer Ali walked up to him and patted him on his shoulders. "You don't have to worry."

When Akbar thought about the issue, he saw little reason for alarm. This was his last year in college with just a few months to go, and he was not planning to visit Udaipur before the exams anyway. But a month later, when his parents visited Bombay, the hounds returned baying for his blood.

Nazeer Ali had written to his brother explaining the circumstances at Noorani Manzil and how his stay there might jeopardize their situation. Akbar's father understood, he had seen enough of the havoc that excommunication was wreaking. So, a few weeks after the funeral, when he and his wife came to Bombay, they stayed in a hotel. In the evening when Akbar came to see them after college, they all snuck into the cemetery to pay their respects to Dadaji. This was important for Zahid Ali, as he had not seen his father in months and was unable to visit him in the hospital.

The hotel was on a busy street in Bombay Central, a cheap joint where the white bed sheets had yellowed with age and neglect; cockroaches darted in the bathroom, water dripped from a leaky tap. The Formica laminate on the bedside table was peeling off. Two wooden chairs with frayed plastic netting belonged by rights to a junkyard and were most likely infested with bedbugs. Akbar felt depressed.

A waiter knocked on the door and entered with their order of teas, bhajias, and samosas. He placed the tray on the bed. It occurred to Akbar that had they stayed at Noorani Manzil, his parents wouldn't have had to pay for all of this.

They discussed Akbar's plans for a while. It was clear that he could not stay with Nazeer Uncle after he finished college. Akbar reassured them that something would turn up for him. The talk inevitably veered towards Udaipur, and how the community had split into two distinct camps. Zahid Ali informed him that a mass wedding had taken place and been a grand success. Since the Sadikot incident, nobody had married among the Radicals, because despite the bitter opposition to the clergy they still hoped that a reconciliation was possible. The Mowlana was their spiritual head, his exalted position being an indelible part of their belief system. Although they had rebelled against his high-handedness and had been ostracized because of it, they could not deny his centrality to their faith.

The Radicals had done away with many small and quasi-religious controls the clergy had been tripping them with, but marriage was different. They still held on to the notion that matrimony without Mowlana's blessings would be incomplete. They still hoped Mowlana would relent, accept his "children" back into the fold, redress their grievances. The Radicals sent petitions to him for a dialogue, and a delegation of "the brides in waiting" travelled to New Delhi to meet with the prime minister and the president to present their case, urging them to intercede with Mowlana. But Mowlana remained stubbornly unresponsive.

The Radicals had shown remarkable patience, had waited for more than two years. When all their pleas and petitions failed they decided enough was enough. Life cannot come to a standstill because a leader refused to budge, to show compassion. A mass wedding was then organized for one hundred and seven couples. The Momin Youth enlisted Muslim qazis to perform the nikah ceremony and thus overthrew the last vestige of Mowlana's ritual authority over their lives. They continued to practice the faith of their ancestors and to demand reforms, but for their workaday affairs, they had freed themselves from the clergy's stranglehold.

Udaipur's Mominwadi had been decked out with buntings, streamers, and lights; the festivities lasted for several days. A hundred and seven grooms dressed in sherwanis and golden phetas, and weighed down by garlands and the sense of occasion, led a procession with brass bands and thousands of excited and joyous people. They reached the sports ground, where large marquees had been set up and a hundred and seven brides dressed in traditional red saris and adorned with jewellery awaited their grooms. The marriages were solemnized in the presence of priests from different faiths. Politicians, scholars, and community leaders from various parts of India were in attendance. The event made the news nationally and internationally. "Even BBC covered it," Zahid Ali enthused.

Khatun related the work that Zanana Wing was doing, teaching the Quran and namaz to girls. They had also started coaching widows and other poor women in skills to help them earn a living. "The Radicals have also founded a bank, the Udaipur Mercantile Cooperative, it is doing well," she said. Moiz was working for it. Then she added, "He remembers you a lot, and Luqman, too."

Akbar smiled.

But Moiz, restless as ever, was planning to go to Kuwait.

"Why Kuwait, what will he do there?"

"He wants to get away from here, to avoid the court cases against him. He wants to get away from the mess. Aren't you two in touch?"

"Not really. He's not the type who writes letters."

Rukhsana was not mentioned. It had been almost three years since they separated and his parents considered the matter closed.

They went downstairs to the restaurant to have supper. They ordered keema, nihari, and tandoori naan. The food when it arrived seemed to be floating in oil. The naans were hot and aromatic, fresh off the tandoor. Zahid Ali broke a piece of naan, dipped it in the nihari, and with oil still dripping from it, put it into his mouth and exclaimed how incredibly tasty Bombay food was.

Akbar and Khatun exchanged looks. "If you add a ton of oil to it, of course it's going to taste good," Khatun said.

"No, these cooks are the masters. That reminds me, tomorrow for breakfast we must have paya. It's been ages since I had paya."

Again, mother and son exchanged smiles.

And so for the next three days Akbar had breakfast with his parents. He would meet them at the hotel and then the three of them would take a taxi to the paya shop on the corner of Baingan Bazaar that served goat trotters. It was a takeout joint where people lined up with their steel bowls and tumblers. In the shop next door, a clutch of men squatted around a tandoor making naan. At the back of the paya shop were two tables and chairs for those who wanted to eat at the premises. Akbar and his parents sat down there, watching the line of eager customers waiting to be helped.

"Paya and khameer naan is a combination invented by God," Zahid Ali said when the food arrived. He tore his naan into small pieces and mixed them with his fingers into his bowl of paya curry and began eating with a delight bordering on ecstasy. After each mouthful he licked his fingers. He turned to the owner and said, "Chacha, what magic do you stir in this, why is it *so* good?"

The man grinned.

After breakfast, they walked around the streets. The Baingan Bazaar was a largely Momin neighbourhood. The former Mowlana, Shatir Kaifudin, father of the present one, was buried here in a grand mausoleum that matched Kaifudin's domineering personality. He was the chief architect of modern Momin destiny and had laid the foundation of the current troubles.

Khatun had not seen the mausoleum from inside, and although her heart had hardened towards the clergy, when Zahid Ali suggested that they pay a visit she agreed to go with them. They were dressed like other Momins, pants-shirts for men and lehnga-odhni for women, and there was little chance of them being identified as Radicals and being thrown out. Nobody knew them in Bombay.

Inside, in the middle of a large hall Kaifudin's grave was covered with a bright maroon velvet cloth, rose and jasmine petals strewn over it. An outsize, ornate chandelier hung from the dome. On the white marble walls the entire Quran was engraved in gold. The shuffle of feet and the rustle of clothes suffused the silence. Muffled voices echoed in the high-ceiling chamber. Momins circumambulated around the grave and kissed it on all sides. Large framed portraits of the two Mowlanas hung on the wall, people kissed them and some stood before them with hands joined, as though in prayer.

"What an irony," Zahid Ali muttered, "don't they know that the verses on the wall condemn idolatry."

"This is new to me. When did we start *worshipping* Mowlana," Khatun said, unable to contain her disgust.

When they came out, a white Rolls-Royce pulled up in the middle of the road at the entrance to the monument. People rushed towards it with joined hands crying, "Mowlana! Mowlana!" The guards kept them back. Mowlana got out of the car and made his way inside, blessing the crowd with a raised hand.

"Here arrives our god, in flesh and blood," Zahid Ali said, shaking his head.

They walked down the street and stopped at Kaifee Sweets. Zahid Ali, as expected, bought his favourite habshi halwa and anjeer paak. He asked Akbar if he wanted some. Akbar declined. Then it was time to say goodbye. He embraced Akbar and said, "Okay, jaana, you take care. We have a busy day today, and in the evening we catch the train back home."

Khatun hugged Akbar tightly, with the inevitable tears in her eyes, and they parted.

Akbar walked to the main road and stood at a crowded stop to take the bus to college. When the Number 5 arrived, he lunged forward, propelled by the throng behind him. He went and sat on the upper deck as usual. Seeing the Mowlana again stirred in him the memory of Sadikot, of Rukhsana playing cards with her sister. A sad, melancholic longing washed over him.

———

Two days later, after breakfast, he sat in the balcony reading the morning paper. The monsoon season was on its last legs, the air was hot and humid. Soon he would leave for college. The doorbell rang, and he got up irritably, wondering who would call so early in the day. Through the peephole he saw the same two harbingers of doom.

He opened the door and let them in, then went to call his uncle, who was taking a shower. Shama Chachi, mumbling a curse, came out to greet the visitors and asked them to wait.

"Would you like tea?" she asked for form's sake.

"No, we are fine, thank you," Ismail said, ogling her.

Shama excused herself and slipped into the kitchen. Akbar hung around, but the two men did not acknowledge his presence and were busy talking softly to each other. He went to the kitchen and had a glass of water.

"Chachi, I hope it's not about my parents."

She said. "Whatever it is, we'll take care of it. You go on now, you'll miss your bus."

Nazeer Ali came out and greeted the men. He did not apologize for keeping them waiting; in fact, when Akbar told him who had come, he deliberately took his time getting dressed. Now he sat down across from them.

"Well, sorry to bother you at this early hour, but since we were heading out we thought we would drop by," Hussain said. "We won't take too much of your time."

Nazeer Ali said nothing.

"The thing is . . . you know we had a talk last time. But it seems you did not understand what we had to say. We have reports that your brother and his wife were visiting Bombay."

"You seem to know everything."

"Well, such are the times, Nazeer Bhai, such are the times. We've got to be vigilant. More to the point, though, your nephew Akbar was seen with them."

"They are his parents, why wouldn't he meet them?"

"Sure, he can, but not while he lives in this building."

"This is his house. Where else will he live?"

"That is not for us to say, Nazeer Bhai. His parents are

munafiq, infidels, they are excommunicated. We true believers cannot associate with them." Hussain paused and rubbed his nose with the forefinger. "And those who do so also become munafiq, they break their covenant with Mowlana."

"Akbar has nowhere to go, it is his house," Nazeer Ali managed through gritted teeth.

The two men looked at each other, and Ismail grimaced, looking frustrated, as though dealing with a recalcitrant child who simply refused to understand.

"Nazeer Bhai," he said, impatiently sucking his teeth, "you understand that if he lives here, you cannot live here either. We warned you last time, precisely because we wanted to avoid this situation. But there is a way out." He took out a crumpled handkerchief from his pocket and started cleaning his glasses. "Advise your nephew to renew the oath of allegiance to Mowlana . . . but," he affected a cough, "before that he will be required to condemn his parents and renounce them. There is no other way. We can arrange it, let us know."

They both got up. Ismail, putting the handkerchief back into his pocket, said finally, "I hope you will do what is best for your family. You have a few days to decide."

Nazeer Ali banged the door after them. Back on the couch he held his head in his hands. Shama put a cup of tea on the table beside him, and sat down.

"Drink your tea, it's getting cold," Shama said.

He lifted the cup and took a sip. It scalded his tongue. He cursed loudly. "Covenant, my arse," he said. "To hell with this religion, to hell with this community. Motherfuckers! They have a problem with a son meeting his parents. What is this, the Dark Age?"

Nazeer Ali finished his tea in silence, while his wife packed his lunch. When it was ready, he picked the lunch box and briefcase and left. A second later he knocked on the door. "I forgot my hand towel." Shama went inside and came back with a set of two. "This community or this humidity, I don't know which will kill me first," he grunted.

When Akbar came home, he was eager to know what had transpired in his absence. He went to the kitchen to turn on the stove to warm his tea, which always sat there in the pot for him. The reheated tea tasted like brew made of sawdust, but he did not mind. He would usually have his tea in the kitchen, but today he took it to his uncle and aunt's room and knocked on the door. Shama had just woken up from her afternoon nap.

"Chachi, what did those troublemakers have to say?"

"I'll be with you in a minute," she said.

Akbar went back to the living room and waited, perusing the morning papers that lay on the coffee table. When Chachi came in, he sat up straight. From the look on her face, he could tell it was not good news.

"They spotted you with your parents," she said. "I don't understand. Why can't people mind their own business?"

"So now what? What do they want?"

"The same stupidity . . . oath of allegiance and denounce your parents. Otherwise you can't live here. But let's not worry too much about it. Your chacha is going to talk to the committee and see if there is a way out."

"Denounce my parents?"

"You know how it is. It's nothing for them. They will denounce their own mothers if it profits them. And that's what they do. I've heard that Mowlana never talks about his mother, never goes to her grave to pay respects. Nobody knows why, it's a big secret. You see, they don't even spare their own mothers.

Where would we figure in their heartless scheme of things?"

That was hardly consolation for Akbar; imminent homelessness was staring him in the face.

"Don't worry, we'll work something out," Shama said.

"Chachi, you know there is no way out—except that I move out."

"Move out where?"

"Tomorrow I'll find out at the college hostel."

"But beta, we can't let you. This is not acceptable."

"But my living here is not acceptable to them. And as you said, they won't even spare their mothers."

Shama could not argue with that. She herself had sacrificed her relations with her family, which was Radical and lived in Udaipur. She hadn't seen them in two years and couldn't be by her mother's side when her father died. Daily she had lived with that guilt.

Akbar was out of Noorani Manzil in two days, lucky to have found a room to share at the hostel. He would stroll the shores of the Arabian Sea every evening feeling like an orphan in the city he loved. First Rukhsana, then Dadaji and now a home—his losses were mounting. He felt depressed not knowing what more tragedies were to come.

12

A WEEK INTO HIS THIRD and final year in college, India experienced what would be seen later as a calamity. The prime minister, Indira Gandhi, declared a state of emergency in the nation. Overnight, people's basic freedoms were abolished. Police repression increased, newspapers were censored, editors were dismissed, opposition leaders were put behind bars. Protest marches were violently suppressed, unions smashed, and strikes busted. For the next twenty-one months Indira Gandhi ruled India by decree, like a demagogue.

Akbar did not realize the significance of what had happened until two weeks later, when he attended his first political science lecture. The professor, Gopal Deshpande, began his class by declaring, "These are the darkest days for India since Independence." He was a thin, intense man with unkempt, long hair who wore a khadi kurta and jeans. His thick bifocals rested halfway down the bridge of his long sharp nose. "Speaking of independence," he said in his deep, sonorous voice, "how many of you think India is independent?" The question was rhetorical, but it made Akbar think. "Do you think," the professor continued, "that holding elections every five years makes for independence? The only difference between now and the British Raj is that instead of Gora Sahibs, we have Brown Sahibs. Faces have changed, but the facts on the ground have not changed. The power elite," the professor paused and wiped the sweat from his forehead with a white handkerchief and nudged the glasses up with his forefinger, "the power elite—those who own factories and land, and what comes out of those factories and land—control our destinies, yours and mine. And these jokers in Delhi, in Parliament, they are the paid servants of the rich. This democracy, this so-called democracy, is a charade. You've been had, my friends, you have been had."

Professor Deshpande turned around and wrote on the blackboard in neat capital letters, POLITICAL SCIENCE. "To tell you the truth," he resumed, "there is no science in politics. Politics is a big shell game, my friends. There is nothing you will study here in this class, from this book," he held up the thick textbook, "which will make sense outside this ivory tower, in real life, where power is the real deal. And that power resides not in Parliament and legislatures—but in corporate boardrooms. All these political theories about forms of government and all these isms will not make you any wiser. Politics, when stripped to its basics, is nothing but a struggle between the haves and the have-nots. Everything else is window-dressing. Democracy such as we have here is the prettiest of them all, but it is decoration all the same. When people rise in protest against inequalities, when resistance gets too hot for the haves, for the power elite, they order their domestic helps, their kaamwali bais, to clean up the mess. In the present case, Indira Gandhi duly obliged and suspended this lovely little pretence we call democracy. This is the stark, naked truth. This book won't teach you that. I may be arrested and beaten up for sticking my head out, but look at me, do you think I care?"

The professor paused, as if to consider the import of what he just said. "As your teacher, my job is not to feed you platitudes. You may think I'm a cynical, frustrated loser, and perhaps there is some truth in it, but trust me, I know. I know what I'm talking about. What I'm asking you to do, in plain words, is to unlearn everything you have learned. Question everything. When I say everything, I mean everything, including what I'm saying now."

Akbar listened to this harangue, hanging on to the professor's every word. He didn't want him to stop. Akbar had not heard anyone speak with such flair and such conviction before. And his ideas! He never imagined such thoughts were even possible. That someone could be so intrepid. What he had learned and valued in his life thus far seemed of little consequence.

"Why should we question everything?" a student asked.

"Because unless you do, how would you know any better?" the professor replied. "Things are never as they seem. The appearance and reality are two different things. We live in a make-believe world. Remember the Romans? They got the masses busy with bread and circuses. They threw people to the lions and called it entertainment. Well, cricket and movies are our circuses. Our masters invent all kinds of distractions to hide the truth. The purpose of real education, in the Socratic sense, is to refuse to be distracted, to question the stories they tell us."

Professor Deshpande paced back and forth in front of his desk, oblivious of the sixty-odd pairs of eyes staring at him. He stopped abruptly, looked up, and said, "Okay, enough of my rant. Starting next week, I will teach the course proper. But don't expect me to spoon-feed you. I am, as you may have concluded, a contrarian jerk. Every idea in this textbook will be questioned. The class is dismissed."

The following week, for Deshpande's lecture the room was filled to the rafters. Word had got around that the professor was a firebrand with a talent to set minds on fire. They wanted to check him out. But Deshpande never showed up. A substitute lecturer came instead and said she was taking over the course.

Akbar did not attend her class again. Deshpande had lit a spark in him, and now he was gone. Had someone reported him to the police? Was he now paying the price for speaking out? After Deshpande's disappearance, Akbar totted up one more loss to his list. The college was now devoid of that thrill that comes from breaching boundaries. There was no one around like Deshpande to expand one's horizons, to slaughter the sacred cows.

Akbar suddenly lost his motivation to study. He neglected classes, pottered around listlessly, hung out with friends at a tea stall behind the college and went to the movies. While the boys flirted with the girls and smoked joints, he kept clear of such frivolities. Nothing seemed to hold his interest. Then one day a fifty-rupee note was stolen from his desk at the hostel. Already living on a tight budget, the theft jolted him out of his complacency. He had become lazy and careless, and realized that that was no way to live. He did not have the luxury to wallow in self-pity and rue about life's meaninglessness. That was for the vain rich kids to do. He had to make something of his life, even if Rukhsana was not a part of it anymore. His parents were spending money on him. Hadn't he wanted to study in Bombay, become a journalist? And here he was.

13

THE NEWSROOM AT *INDIA WEEKLY* buzzed with activity: the constant rattle of typewriters, reporters shouting on the phones, endless rounds of tea and the clatter of cups and saucers, peons scurrying around on errands. Cigarette smoke hung in the room like a fog. Akbar sat at the copy desk editing a feature article for the upcoming issue. A year ago, after finishing college, he had applied for the job and was hired as an intern. The work was not very interesting and the salary paltry, but this being his first stint, he did not mind it, for it gave him a toe-hold in the industry and allowed him to live in Bombay.

With his meagre earnings, the only affordable place to board that he could find was a Muslim men's hostel on Mohammed Ali Road. The newsroom and his residence were worlds apart. The *Weekly* was the outpost of a liberal, modern India where men and women gabbed in English and judged one another on how well one spoke and wrote the language. For them English was the best of the colonial legacies. It was still the currency of power and prestige in metropolitan India, long after the British had departed. The sense of superiority and the advantages that came with knowing the language were taken for granted.

From his desk, he was a witness to a world that was unfamiliar and strange, and sometimes shocking. Men and women swore easily; they bragged about their sources. Women were self-possessed and smoked unselfconsciously, and would come and sit on your desk and touch you on the shoulder in a friendly, spontaneous manner.

Akbar, a mere provincial, was shy and kept mostly in the background. But he had his views. He believed that the beauty of a written piece was of little consequence if it did not help to make life a little less ugly. Around him the staff were not burdened with such idealism. Their preoccupation was not to inform and enlighten but to turn out good copy. He could not say much, a lowly copy editor correcting their typos and shifting their commas. But he was determined not to stay in this position for long.

At the hostel, on the other hand, he was in a closed world. This experience was also new and strange to him. Being in a Muslim hostel, one's allegiance to Islam and its commandments were taken for granted. At every call to prayer, volunteers would come knocking on doors to draw believers out to the mosque for namaz. Akbar was not averse to praying but had always been cagey about public displays of faith. He had a healthy distrust of organized religion and the clergy's misdeeds had only confirmed his disbelief.

Once, when he said he couldn't come out to pray, an overzealous volunteer retorted, "Why, are you having periods?"

Akbar ignored the jibe. He often took comfort in the words of the poet Muhammad Iqbal:

Whenever I prostrated there came a voice from the ground
Your heart is immersed in God, what will you gain in prayer?

But he knew these people would quote the Quran and the Hadith and counter the poet's philosophic mysticism with the crude theology of the mullahs. It was best to remain silent. And over time, they gave up on him, calling him a kaffir. But when they learned he was a Momin, they dismissed him as an idol-worshipper. Akbar was happy with that.

Moiz came to Bombay on his way to Kuwait. They had a rollicking time together, and now that Akbar was also a young adult, they could talk and banter on equal terms. Every evening they visited Mehfil, a bar on Grant Road, where they enjoyed beers. Over drinks, they opened up to each other; Akbar shared his pain at losing Rukhsana; Moiz finally confided in him the recurring nightmares he still had, following that night in jail, the trauma of the beatings, the humiliation. Was all that struggle, the sacrifice worth it?—he wondered aloud. He seemed disillusioned.

The White House gang had disbanded, the fire of those early days had died down. The boys were getting on with their lives. A couple of them did not even finish college, distracted as they were by the conflict. Iqbal had joined the family business, and Luqman worked as a clerk in an accounting firm. Even so, the Radicals were still strong, sticking to their demands for reforms and learning to live independently of the clergy.

From Mehfil the two would walk to Delhi Darbar for a tandoori chicken dinner. Moiz was flush with cash, and had wanted to spend the Indian currency before he started earning Kuwaiti dinars. They would return to the hostel a little before midnight and, reeking of alcohol, they would disturb and infuriate his roommates, who threatened to report them to the management. But they never did for Moiz mocked them as snitching girls and it seems they took the insult to heart.

One evening at Mehfil, Akbar asked Moiz why he was going to Kuwait? Moiz replied that the bank job didn't appeal to him much and he didn't see any other prospects for himself.

"You are an artist, you have talent. I'm sure you can find something to do," Akbar said.

"No, man, I'm no artist, just an amateur. And in India, an

artist's life is a dog's life."

"But why Kuwait?"

"So many of our people have gone there and made good. I want to try my luck."

"You will become a big shot," Akbar joked, taking a sip. "The next time I see you, you will be reeking of perfume, looking dandy and all, a fat gold chain around your neck and a shiny Japanese watch on your wrist."

"Well, we shall see. You must come visit me someday."

"Hmm, will see. Don't much care for the Arabs."

"Oh fuck you, you self-righteous prick."

Akbar laughed. He liked riling up Moiz, partly because he enjoyed the barrage of invective that followed, which seared his prudish sensibilities and which he rather welcomed. With Moiz he was free, no pretences, no reputation to protect.

———

One Monday morning his editor gave him some copy to edit. It was an article by Kaiser Ali Mistri. Akbar had heard the name before. In the article, Kaiser Ali talked about the Momin clergy and how it operated as a government unto itself; how it imposed a slew of taxes on the community, which was kept on a tight leash. He mentioned Udaipur, the attack on the women in Sadikot, and the resulting revolt against the Mowlana's oppressive regime. Kaiser Ali wrote about the cruelty of excommunication; how it had created havoc in their lives; how the Loyalists were compelled to renounce their fathers and mothers, sisters and brothers. Even if they lived in the same house they behaved like strangers. Those who flouted the fatwa faced humiliation and shaming. Kaiser Ali explained that the clergy's tyranny was based on distortion of religion. Islam and the Momin scriptures did not give such powers to Mowlana. He argued that there was, in fact, no concept of priesthood in Islam, and the Momin priesthood in its current vile form was an invention, an imposition. Akbar read the article with breathless excitement. Somebody had at last dared to disrobe the clergy in public.

The following week, the article was featured as a cover story. It created a furor in the Momin world, and overnight Kaiser Ali Mistri was branded the devil incarnate. Letters of protest to the editor poured in; irate callers phoned and pelted the editor with choicest abuse. The clergy and its propaganda machinery went into damage control and denounced the article as an attack upon Islam. Momins were forbidden from reading the magazine.

———

"This is Akbar, our copy editor. He is a Momin from Udaipur, and a Radical." Thus Akbar's editor, Pramod Mehta, introduced him to Kaiser Ali Mistri when he visited the office. Akbar noticed how Kaiser Ali's eyes dilated progressively as the editor disclosed Akbar's credentials: Momin, Udaipur, Radical. Kaiser Ali beamed a smile and grabbed Akbar's hand with both hands. Evidently he was happy to see a young Momin man in a magazine office.

"I'm so pleased to meet you," he said.

"It is my honour," Akbar said shyly.

Kaiser Ali was already a hero in his eyes for having so boldly exposed the Momin clergy. He was dressed simply in a cotton kurta and loose white pants. A khadi bag slung from his shoulder. He looked to be in his early forties, Akbar guessed. A man of average build, just shy of being plump, he wore bifocals that magnified his already large eyes with a look of kind intensity. When he smiled, his face lit up like somebody had turned on the light. When they shook hands, Akbar felt a slight roughness on his palms and the cold touch of his ring, which was studded with a deep brown stone. Kaiser Ali spoke with calm authority, and his voice had a faint rasp.

"I was in Udaipur last month," he said. "The people of Udaipur have shown remarkable courage, especially the women."

Akbar nodded, thinking of his mother.

"Please come over to my house when you have free time."

"Yes, sure, I would love to come," Akbar said and took down his phone number and address. Kaiser Ali left with the editor, and Akbar stood staring for a long time at what he had scribbled, as though it contained a secret code that foretold his future.

———

A fortnight later, Akbar set off for Kaiser Ali's house in the suburbs of Bombay. It was a Sunday morning, sunny and humid; people were already up and about. Idlers as usual had monopolized the portions of sidewalks left over by shopkeepers and footpath dwellers. There was no place for people to walk, and if you were adamant, which Akbar sometimes was, you had to pick your way carefully among people and dogs, potholes and garbage.

The poverty he had witnessed in Bombay had always disturbed him. Even after having lived in the city for several years now, he was still perturbed anew every time he saw a beggar or a roadside shack. If it were just poverty, it wouldn't have troubled him so much. What bothered him were the extremes, that plenitude and privation exist side by side, and that those who had it all remained so indifferent and callous, and those who had nothing were so meek.

At Victoria Terminus while waiting for the train, he saw a young boy of barely five. His hair was matted down with grime and sweat, his body was covered in layers of dust. He wore no clothes except for old shorts that revealed more than they concealed. As he stretched his hand out to beg, Akbar noticed that dirt had settled into the lines of his palm, his fate buried under the sediments of misfortune. What struck Akbar was the boy's eyes. They were big and clear, the whites limpid. Akbar tried to read something in them. Perhaps self-pity. A hint of defeat and hopelessness. But he found none of that. The look touched him deep inside. He took out a five-rupee note and gave it to him.

14

HE TOOK THE HARBOUR LINE to Bandra. As he neared Kaiser Ali Mistri's house his excitement mounted. He had no idea how the visit would go, but he was eager to know about the man's work, his writings, and what had made him take up cudgels against Mowlana.

Kaiser Ali's wife, Farida, answered the door and showed him in. She was a kind-faced woman looking pale and tired, her hair tied in a bun. She was wearing a house gown and dupatta over her head, and held a cloth duster in one hand. The house was a two-bedroom flat, ordinarily appointed with all the accoutrements of a middle-class lifestyle. Kaiser Ali was in his study, which also doubled as his personal bedroom—a single bed took up one corner, at its foot was a desk weighted down by a typewriter and a scattering of books and papers. Across from the bed was a wall of books. The window overlooked the street, framing the sunlight that streamed in. A ceiling fan churned lazily overhead. Kaiser Ali was sitting on the bed writing on a notepad on his lap. On seeing Akbar, he smiled warmly and asked him to come in and sit down.

"How are you doing?" he asked, and without waiting for an answer, he continued, "Please give me five minutes, let me finish this before I lose my train of thought."

"Yes, of course, take your time," Akbar said. He started browsing the titles, a great variety of them on religion, philosophy and politics, mostly in English and a few in Arabic and Urdu and Hindi. *Why I Am Not a Christian* by Bertrand Russell caught his eye. He picked it up and started leafing through it. He had already read Bertrand Russell's autobiography with fascination.

"Yes, Akbar, tell me, how are you?" Kaiser Ali said after a while, startling Akbar.

"I'm fine, thank you," Akbar replied, closing the book and replacing it on the shelf.

"What were you looking at?"

"Bertrand Russell's *Why I Am Not a Christian*."

"That's a great book. Have you read it?"

"No."

"You must. Take it. Take other books also, if there's anything that catches your fancy."

"Thank you. I'd love to."

Kaiser Ali tore the page he had been writing from the notepad, folded it, and put it in an envelope. As he licked the glue on the flap, Akbar said, "Kaiser Saheb, you said you were in Udaipur recently. How are things there?"

Kaiser Ali began looking for a stamp in his drawer. "You know, Udaipur is the best thing that has happened to us Momins in a long time." Having stuck the stamp on the envelope, he continued, "Our community had been sleepwalking. Udaipur has given it a jolt. What do you people eat there?" he smiled. "Momins have risen against the clergy's tyranny before, but never in such large numbers, not in the history of our community. The Momin Youth is doing good work. I'm amazed at the energy and enthusiasm of the people. And the women, by God, they are something. They are in no mood to take any nonsense, not even from their men. I have great hopes for the future of our community. I know the clergy is digging its heels in and will do its utmost to suppress the calls for reform. But if a couple more cities follow Udaipur's example, this revolt will spread."

He moved his hands constantly as he spoke, and every now and then he would pause to take a breath and pull up the sleeves of his kurta. Akbar found Kaiser Ali's endorsement of Udaipur heartwarming. The episodes of Sadikot, riot, jail flashed through his mind. He recalled the suffering and pain, the fear and the excommunications; the sacrifices; how he himself became a victim. So did Kaiser Ali, as he found out.

"My whole family is on the other side. My mother, my sisters do not talk to me. But that's the way things are. The clergy is powerful, and you know what makes them powerful?"

"They have the money."

"Right, but more than the money?"

Akbar waited for the answer.

"Religion. Religion is a powerful ideology, and they have been misusing it to build an empire of deceit. Don't you think it ironic that the Islam that Allah sent to liberate people, to empower people, is being used to enslave people, chain their minds?"

Suddenly he got up and apologized, "Oh, I didn't even offer you water. Please come to the kitchen. Have some water." Akbar followed him. Kaiser Ali handed him a steel glass and filled it from a chilled bottle from the fridge. "Nothing like cold water. The fridge is man's best invention, if you ask me," he said and downed his glass in quick, lusty gulps.

"I'm making tea, would you like some?"

Akbar nodded.

Kaiser Ali filled the kettle with water and turned on the stove.

"So where were we?"

"Religion."

"Yes. Give a man a beautiful thing and he will find a way to make it ugly. Our species is fundamentally flawed." He smiled. Then he glanced at the kettle, which was about to come to a boil. He added two teaspoons of leaves to it, and milk, and turned down the heat to let it simmer. "Never boil tea too much. You know George Orwell once wrote an article on the art of making tea. What a man!" He turned off the stove, and let the kettle sit for a few minutes and then poured the brew into two cups through a strainer.

"You can sweeten your tea. I've diabetes, I avoid sugar."

Kaiser Ali reached for a jar of biscuits on the shelf beside the refrigerator. He took out a few and put them on a quarter plate. "I can't have tea by itself, have to nibble something with it," he said with disarming simplicity, his forehead collecting beads of sweat.

Akbar followed him back to the study, where he sat at his desk and Akbar took the chair by the window. The noise from the street made it hard for him to hear, so he moved his chair closer to where Kaiser Ali was sitting. In the next room he could hear Farida shouting instructions to a house help; they were moving furniture.

Kaiser Ali dipped a biscuit into his tea and caught the soggy portion in his mouth quickly before it could fall. As he sipped he talked about the women's rights in Islam, the difficulties of interpreting the Quran, the meaning of Revelation, about the Prophet and his mission. He had a completely novel take on these topics. Of course, Akbar had discussed these issues with his parents and friends, and had listened to some discourses of mullahs but he had not learned from them anything that offered a new perspective. Their Islam remained tightly shackled to the five pillars. Kaiser Ali did not even mention them. He said the central message of the Quran was justice; it urged the believers to establish a fair and egalitarian society. He said that literalist scholars had reduced Islam to a caricature. Akbar listened in rapt attention. He had read the English translation of the Quran and wasn't exactly bowled over by it. He had found the repetition of biblical stories, the dire warning of hellfire and the reward of houris rather tiresome. But with Kaiser Ali's erudite exposition, he began to see the book in a new light. Kaiser Ali held forth with such conviction that he nearly called the Quran a manifesto for revolution.

Kaiser Ali leaned forward, put away his cup. His voice assumed an earnest timbre of a man about to confide a profound secret.

"Look, there is a simple way to separate the historical from the eternal. You must be familiar with the phrase 'What would Jesus do?' We can pose a similar question, 'What would Muhammad do?' Suppose the Quran were revealed today, would it still be exactly the same as it was revealed fourteen hundred years ago?

"The Quran solved the problems people faced in those days. The problems of today's world are different. Do you think if the Quran were to be written today, it would prescribe chopping off hands? Of course not. However, will its core message have changed? The message of justice, egalitarianism, and charity? Of course not. Now you understand the pitfalls inherent in taking the text literally. What is open to interpretation is that which is prescriptive and historically specific. What is absolute is that which is eternal, the Oneness of God and the principles of justice and equality."

Kaiser Ali glanced at the clock on the opposite wall. "We

could talk about this till the camels come home," he said with a mock guffaw. "It's time for lunch." He went out.

Akbar overheard him talking to Farida. He got up and looked outside the window. His head was a whirlpool of thoughts. He looked down in the street but noticed nothing. It was all a blur and a murmur. For a split second he was in a fugue state, losing himself in a fog. He closed his eyes and leaned far out the window, then jerked his head back, trying to shake off the mental mist. When he turned around, he saw Kaiser Ali smiling.

"Looks like I've fried your brain with all that talk," he said. "We should eat now. Farida is getting the food ready."

Presently, she called out. They went into the kitchen, washed their hands, and sat at the table. "I've eaten already," Farida said. "You two help yourselves. There's keema, chapatti, and rice. And here's some pickle to help you along if the food is not tasty." She gave a self-effacing smile.

"Thank you, Auntie. I'm sure it is good," Akbar said.

"She is teasing you," Kaiser Ali said.

As they ate, Kaiser Ali told Akbar his own story.

"My father was a mullah. I had no shop to inherit. His life was hard; in fact, it was downright miserable. He was well versed in religious knowledge but he was no more than a cog in the Byzantine system that the Momin clergy has established. In their world, knowledge counts for nothing; on the contrary, you could be persecuted for knowing too much. I've seen priests scold and humiliate my father. One time a shahzada— a so-called prince from Mowlana's family—was visiting our town, Kapadvanj. I accompanied my father when he went to see this shahzada at the residence of the local priest.

"Protocol required that everybody prostrate before him.

They had no choice. It was ingrained in them to kiss the feet of the dignitary. My father complied, but I found the whole thing revolting, even at that age. I was fifteen or so. I refused. My father whispered to me, beseeching me to bow. I was stubborn, I simply stood there. The shahzada looked on, angry and baffled. I doubt he had encountered such defiance before. I saw him signaling his minder. This man came striding towards me, grabbed me by the arm, dragged me forward, and shoved my head towards the shahzada's feet. All this happened in an instant. I had no time to resist. I had tears in my eyes, and my father looked on helplessly, shame and pain written all over his face."

Kaiser Ali momentarily stopped eating. Akbar shifted uncomfortably in his seat, wanting to urge him to continue eating but feeling it might be impolite to do so.

"But this is not all," Kaiser Ali resumed. "The shahzada barked at my father. 'What is your name? Are you sure this thing, this pilla—this puppy—is your son? Haven't you taught him the ways of our faith? Now get out of here and don't come back until you have taught him some manners.'

"We left and walked home in silence. My father's steps were heavy, he was a man defeated. I felt sorry for him—and guilty for bringing this upon him. But my father said nothing to me about it, never blamed me. The incident was never mentioned again. And so I knew he supported my position, although he would not say it. These 'royals' were not worth bowing to; actually, no human being is worth bowing to. Prostration is due to Allah and Allah alone. After that incident, I swore I would have nothing to do with these vile people. My father slowly became withdrawn. He performed his official duties, but his heart was no longer into it.

"But the good thing that came out of that incident was

that my father became serious about teaching me Arabic, the Quran, and our Momin literature. He said, 'It is important that you know your religion, and know it well. This is the only way to confront people who abuse it. Knowledge is power.' And I tied those three words into a knot in my mind. That was the beginning of my foray into Islam, its history, and our own Momin tradition."

Kaiser Ali resumed eating, and now more relaxed, he continued. "That incident affected me deeply for a long time. But the dark mood lifted. It always does. But you know, remnants of darkness linger like shadows in your soul. I still feel a pang of anguish when I think about it.

"My father insisted that I also get a proper secular education. I'm trained as an architect, but, you see, life had other designs for me. One thing led to another, and here I am today, full-time activist."

They finished eating; Akbar thought he had stuffed himself and was ready to go. Before he left, he asked, "What has been the reaction to your article in our magazine?"

"As expected. I'm being cursed all the way to Hell and back," Kaiser Ali said with a chuckle. "Death threats are flooding in. They come by phone and by post. If they were made good, I would be dead a thousand times over."

On his way back, Akbar carried half a dozen books with him. His mind was reeling with the surfeit of knowledge it had received. He had not imagined Kaiser Ali to be so down-to-earth, so easy to talk to. He had a refreshing way of looking at the world. Islam in his hands was not some antiquated system of rituals but a tool for positive, constructive change.

When he reached the hostel, a telegram awaited him. It read: URGENT. FATHER SICK. COME HOME.

15

AKBAR TOSSED AND TURNED IN bed in his Bombay flat, unable to sleep the whole night. He had known for over a year that Rukhsana was engaged to be married and had thought he had come to terms with that bitter reality. Yesterday had been her wedding day, and he could not get her out of his mind. The memories came flooding back and with them the regret, the sense of helplessness. He wondered if things could have turned out differently. Maybe he gave up too easily. He could have gone to Udaipur and sorted it out face-to-face. Could Rukhsana have done anything on her part? But how could she have defied her father? We couldn't even write letters. Girls just have to obey. Now with the marriage, the last lingering hope he may have had was put to rest. He wondered if she had had any say in the choosing of her husband—lucky bastard! Would she be happy? His heart convulsed.

After five years of grind at *India Weekly*, he had joined the publishing firm Alfaz Books as a senior copy editor. When time and mood permitted, he wrote, not without considerable persuasion from Kaiser Ali, articles for magazines and newspapers. He had rented a flat in Prabhadevi, south-central Bombay. A ten-minute walk south was his office, and a ten-minute walk north was the beach on Mahim Bay, spitting into the Arabian Sea. On Sunday mornings he went to the beach for walks. Yesterday he had gone earlier than usual and walked the length of the beach, back and forth, a hundred times it seemed. When he was tired, he went to a restaurant round the corner from the beach and had a drink of water, and ordered two cups of tea, one after the other, and then went back to the beach with a packet of cigarettes. He sat resting against a wall, which shielded him from the strong October sun, and smoked. The sea was grey and muddy; the waves were lethargic, in no hurry to meet the land; the air was humid, smelling of the usual admixture of brine and muck so pervasive on Bombay's coastline.

To his left in the distance the narrow peninsula curved into the bay. The land rose gently from the sea into a squat hill and was dotted with fishermen's dwellings, a motley collection of huts threatening to become a slum soon. When night fell, lights in the huts came on and shone like yellow stars floating upon the sea; it looked beautiful then, the darkness masking the daytime squalor. His throat felt scratchy from his continuous smoking. He walked back to the restaurant and ate chicken curry and rice desultorily, then walked home and crashed into his bed. But he could not sleep. It had been ten years since the Sadikot incident, and five since he last saw her, when his father died.

He had rushed to Udaipur upon receiving the telegram, arriving early morning by the overnight bus. A cold December fog blanketed the city. He took an auto-rickshaw home. On the way he saw the early risers going about their business. On the sides of the streets, men sat by wood fires, hands stretched out, warming themselves. The morning air was acrid with smoke. Akbar sat staring ahead, his heart filled with trepidation. He had hardly had a wink of sleep. He ardently prayed for his father's recovery.

When he arrived, the front door was open. As he entered, he

was met by Moiz, who embraced him tightly, and choking on his tears, told him, "Your father is no more." Stunned, Akbar dropped his bag as his legs gave way. He heard women wailing in his parents' room. Moiz held him by the arm and took him inside. "Amma . . . ," he thought.

Inside he saw her sitting against the wall, flanked by two chachis, her face buried in her handkerchief. Akbar went and sat on his knees before her. He freed her hand from her face, and she looked at him. In the fleeting instant as their eyes met, they felt the sorrow of the world between them. She pulled him in and hugged him.

"Your father has left us, jaana, your father has left us."

Fizza Chachi tried to separate them, "Okay, enough Bhabhi, have sabr, have patience," she said.

Moiz, who was visiting from Kuwait, tapped Akbar on his shoulder and he stood up. Moiz explained how his father had suffered a heart attack two days before; he had been recovering well, but yesterday in the early hours he suffered another attack and succumbed to it.

Later that evening, when his father's body was brought home from the hospital and placed on the ground in the sitting room, Khatun threw herself on it and sobbed uncontrollably. Akbar sat by her side consoling her while the other women of the household quietly wept. The men took charge of the practical matters. Someone was dispatched to inform the town crier to make the announcement in the mohallas. The people who washed and prepared the body for burial were informed, and someone went to the community office to book the hall for the fatiha ceremony.

After the prayers at the mosque, the casket was carried on the shoulders of men to the cemetery. At every step—as the body was washed, covered in a shroud, taken to the mosque, over prayer, and now being hoisted to the cemetery, Akbar could not believe that all this was being done for his father—the man who was alive at one moment and dead the next. How could this be? Akbar almost buckled under the weight of the casket, and other men, eager to lend their shoulders, pushed him out of the way.

In the years since Sadikot, Radical Momins had begun to live free of the oppressive control of the clergy. Sheikh Hamid Ali, a learned mullah, took care of religious matters and officiated at marriages and burials. Excommunication had become a physical feature, like a wall, keeping families and friends apart. The Radicals enjoyed the freedom and self-dignity that came with managing their own affairs. The Loyalists remained beholden to the edicts of an indifferent Mowlana in Bombay and to the rude dispensations of his local priest, Sheikh Dhamal. None of Zahid Ali's friends from the Loyalist side came to his funeral.

On entering the cemetery, the men reciting the shahada—There is no God but Allah—the women still not part of the burial ceremony—the bier was carried to the gravesite. An unseasonal shower had drenched the earth the previous night, turning it muddy. The leaves on the grass and bushes along the narrow path brushed water against their legs. The sky was overcast and a mild breeze serenaded the dead. A calm like a solemn hymn hung in the air, each man suddenly aware of his mortality. What a beautiful place to lie in rest, Akbar thought.

Somebody asked him to get down into the pit and four men then lowered the body into it. Moiz was already in there. As the men above released the body, Akbar fumbled, not expecting it to be so heavy. He could barely hold his end, the head, and he was not sure how he was going to lower it gently. As he tried easing it down, it slipped from his grasp and hit the ground with a thud. The fall was not more than ten inches, he felt bad for being clumsy. Two men then helped him up, from where he threw the first clods of earth upon the shrouded body. Others followed suit, and as the grave filled up his heart sank deeper. The finality of death had never struck him as so absolute. For days the sound of the thud haunted him.

On the third day Khatun went into official mourning, the iddat, a period of four months and ten days during which, according to custom, the widow must remain secluded from the outside world. The windows of her room were tightly shut and covered, the curtains drawn shut. All the mirrors in the room were draped with white sheets, and an extra curtain was hung outside the door to prevent any accidental exposure. When Akbar came home in the evening, he saw his mother sitting in the corner of her room dressed in all white, reading the Surah Yasin from the Quran. A few other women were sitting around, some reading the Yasin and others chatting softly. He went and sat by his mother and put his hand on her knee. "Amma, you shouldn't be doing this?" he whispered, pointing to white sheets and the covered windows and doors and mirrors. She said nothing and continued reading.

Fizza Chachi, sitting beside her, answered, "These are the rules of iddat."

"I know that, Chachi, but we're reformers, and we still follow this?"

"Reform has nothing to do with religion. Our tradition dictates that your mother cannot go outside this room for four months. She cannot meet, in fact cannot even lay her eyes on any man other that those related to her by blood. She must wear white at all times, she can't look in the mirror, she can't use makeup, and she must eat simple food and live a simple life."

"This looks more like punishment to me."

"Shhhh, Akbar, don't say that," Khatun admonished.

"But Amma, this is not fair. Why must they imprison you in this cold, dark room? This is no way to mourn."

"This is not just about mourning, Akbar," Chachi said. "This is also about determining whether she is pregnant."

"What is wrong with you, Chachi, my mother pregnant?"

"These are the rules. The Quran has prescribed this."

"I know what the Quran has prescribed, but this—" he gestured around the room "—this is not part of it. This is torture. As for pregnancy, a medical test can determine that in no time. You don't have to wait for four months to find out."

"Akbar, you hold it there," Khatun admonished again.

"Every widow has to do it, I had to do it," Chachi said.

"But Chachi, this is all so unnecessary. This is no way to grieve. What my mother needs is distraction, not a constant reminder of her loss. The point is we should be comforting her not punishing her!"

"Akbar, we did not make these rules. This is the way things have always been."

"But it's not right, Chachi. Don't you see?"

"Hmm."

Seeing her mother tongue-tied, Farzana, Akbar's cousin, who was listening to the conversation, spoke up.

"Akbar is right. I don't see any point in this practice. And as for mourning, why are only women supposed to do it? When wives die, why don't husbands also sit in a corner and mope?"

"Now, you don't start it, girl!" her mother, Fizza Chachi, warned.

"But Amma, this is primitive. And none of this has to do

with the Quran. We call ourselves reformers, why can't we change this?"

"This is the way it is, things can't change overnight."

"Somebody has to start," Farzana said. "These are cruel rules made by frustrated men who don't like women. And Khatun Chachi, you are a leader of the Zanana Wing. You're educated. If you submit to this, what can we expect of others?"

Every morning for the next ten days Akbar went to the cemetery with other men to pay respects at his father's grave. On the tenth day the women of the house joined them for the first time, but not his mother. She would visit the grave on completion of the mourning period. On the way back from the cemetery, Akbar drew Farzana aside and told her he was not happy with the arrangement of iddat. As a woman, he said, she carried more weight in this matter and he solicited her support.

They thought of a plan and Akbar told his mother about it. Khatun agreed that the iddat as practiced by Momins was an archaic custom, a holdover from their Hindu past. Yes, it seemed like punishment, to keep women in their place, to show the widow that without her man, without her husband, she is nothing. Zahid Ali would not have approved of it either; he would not want his wife to mourn for him like this. She said she would like to free herself of restrictions but was afraid especially of what the other women might say. Tradition is like a stone around our neck and often it's the women who keep other women down. Akbar said the fear of "what people will say" feeds on itself. It perpetuates oppression. "I don't want you to suffer, not on any account other than the loss of my father."

With Khatun on their side, he and Farzana proceeded to remove the covers from the mirrors and windows, drew the curtains apart, and flung open the windows. The winter sun poured in and so did the noise of life from the street below. Khatun took a deep breath and almost smiled. Farzana then dismantled the second curtain outside the door. Her mother caught her in the act.

"What in God's name are you doing?" Fizza Chachi exclaimed.

"Getting rid of this thing."

"How can you do that?"

"Like this," Farzana said and yanked the drape down, and smiled. Her mother grunted her disapproval.

Khatun gradually started living a normal life and moved around in the house as before, though she made sure not to look out the window and withdrew to her room when male relatives came. She stopped wearing white clothes, ate meals with everybody, and looked in the mirror and took care of herself. The aunts had come around and supported her decision. But tongues clacked, as expected. Many women found it scandalous that a widow should enjoy so much freedom and comfort. One elderly woman, Gutti Bai, a crotchety crone known for her foul tongue, flew off the handle when she saw Khatun and the room transformed.

"Are you people having a picnic here?" she sneered.

Khatun and the chachis had expected this, and had appointed Farzana to deal with her. "We as a family have decided to do away with this production."

"And who are *you* to decide that?"

"Who's going to decide then, you or sheikh saheb?"

"You chit of a girl," Gutti Bai snapped, "this is how you speak to your elders." She got up trembling with fury and started to leave. Nobody stopped her, as politeness required. As she hobbled down the stairs, she mumbled under her breath, "The end times are surely near."

At the front door, noticing her scowl, Moiz teased her, "Gutti Bai, do come again."

"Shut up, you rascal," she hissed.

Some days later, Akbar was called to the community office. He asked Moiz to go with him. Councillor Asif Hussain, the leader of the Momin Youth Association, and Sheikh Hamid Ali, the priest of the Radicals, sat on a divan propped by white bolsters chatting in whispers. The sheikh was well versed in Momin literature and a conservative. On seeing him Akbar knew what was coming.

Asif Hussain got directly to the point, telling Akbar that his mother was flouting the rules of mourning. Akbar explained. The sheikh listened to him quietly at first, then the rosary in his hand started turning furiously.

"What do you think, Shariat is a plaything?" he bellowed.

"Sheikh saheb, please do not confuse Shariat with custom," Akbar said.

"This will not be allowed. Shariat is not your father's property that you treat it the way you please."

"Sheikh saheb, I have a lot of respect for you," Akbar said, getting up. "This kind of language doesn't suit you."

"You rascal, you will teach me manners?"

"No Sheikh saheb, who am I to teach you anything. I just want to remind you that we Radicals defied the Mowlana when he started throwing his weight about, do you think we will tolerate your tantrums? Come Moiz, let's go."

The two cousins left abruptly. Sheikh Hamid Ali muttered

curses. A minute later Akbar poked his head into the door and said, "Asif saheb, are we Radicals in name only?" He did not wait for the reply.

———

Not long after, one late evening Akbar sat by his mother on the floor in her room. The floor was covered with a neat handloom sheet and their backs were cushioned by pillows. Akbar did not share the room with his mother anymore, he had taken a spare one upstairs. He was reading a book and Khatun was folding laundry, the clothes giving off a pleasant whiff of the sun's warmth. There was a knock on the door. It was unusual for anyone to visit at this hour. Mother and son exchanged looks. Akbar got up to get the door. As he opened it, he couldn't believe his eyes. In the dim glow of the corridor stood Rukhsana, her face bright as if giving off its own light. She looked at him, lowered her gaze, and said, "Salam."

He moved the curtain to let her in.

Rukhsana stepped inside and went towards Khatun, whose eyes were already welling up. Rukhsana sat down and embraced Khatun and started weeping.

"I'm so sorry, Auntie," she said. Khatun patted her on the back and said, "It's all right, jaana, it's all right. God willed it."

"Amma has sent you her salams and condolences. Please know that she is thinking about you. She will visit you soon. She is just waiting for a chance when father will be away."

"Tell your mother not to worry. So, how have you been?"

"I'm all right, I suppose."

She sat down facing Khatun, and Akbar sat beside his mother. She had wanted to avoid meeting him altogether, for it would only revive old wounds. But this was the only suitable time she could come; her father was away and dusk would provide the cover. She had heard that Akbar was in town for the funeral and might be home, but she had to take the risk. The awkwardness of meeting him and Khatun after such a long time had made her hesitant, and at one point she almost decided not to come.

Now that she was here, she felt more at ease. She was glad that she came. She recalled the last letter she had written to him after the "breakup". She had penned it secretly when everyone in the house slept, and when she dropped it in the letterbox she had noted the soft rustle of the envelope landing on other letters. The sound had seemed so innocuous, so innocent of the message it contained. She had not known then that that would be it. The memory of it wrenched her heart. She had not heard from or seen Akbar since. She turned to him and said softly, "I'm sorry for your loss," and wiped the tears from her eyes.

"Thank you for coming," he said.

Akbar watched her. She seemed such a stranger, he couldn't believe she was not his anymore. He should spirit her away, before she was married off to some orthodox schmuck. He wanted to tell her he would love her till the end of time; he would make her happy at all cost.

Rukhsana looked at him from the corner of her eye as she chatted with Khatun. Then they sat in silence for some minutes. Five years of excommunication had created a void between them. There was so much to say and yet nobody knew what to say, where to begin. To break the silence, Khatun made small talk. Finally, Rukhsana took her leave. Akbar accompanied her downstairs to the front door. In the darkness of the stairwell, he suddenly took her in his arms and hugged her tight. "Don't go," he said.

Rukhsana gently pushed him away. "Please don't, this is not right," she said.

"Rukhsana, please, there's still time. Say no to your father."

"You don't know my father. If I could, I would have done that long back. Please let me go."

They stood in silence for a long moment, Akbar holding her hands, helpless, defeated. "Just one thing," he said. "Tell me this, do you still love me?"

She said nothing, released her hands from his grasp, and ran down the stairs. On the street, alone, she burst into sobs. *Yes, yes, I still love you, you fool.*

Before he went back to Bombay, Akbar visited the haunted house every day and waited for her hoping she would come.

———

Khatun's flouting of the mourning regimen was soon forgotten, and nobody dared to follow her example. Akbar was disheartened that the Radicals, who had the audacity to challenge the clergy, had been too timid to bring real reforms. But the good thing that resulted from Khatun's defiance was that women started talking about it. Despite the loud opposition led by Gutti Bai and the Sheikh, the issue was out in the open and everybody had an opinion about it.

What was hidden and pernicious and beyond debate was the practice of female circumcision. Every Momin girl, when she turned seven, had her clitoral hood excised. It was done clandestinely, unlike the boys' circumcisions which were celebrated with gaiety and distribution of sweets. Like other ancient customs the practice had a long history and had become a part of Momin culture. Mowlana imposed it as an article of faith. The Radicals continued to cut their girls out of habit deeming it as an important rite of passage. The conservatives, like Sheikh Hamid Ali among them, swore by its religious sanctity.

The act was a hush-hush affair. And as with iddat, the sanction came from the men, and women were the willing executioners. The girl's mother and a few women relatives would agree to have "the thing" done quietly. Through their secret channels the woman specialist would be contacted and she would come armed with a blade and candies. Akbar had had a vague idea of this practice but he did know of the pain it entailed until one evening when Rukhsana had come to the haunted house all upset.

Her young cousin Sabiha that morning had been rushed to the hospital because the bleeding between her legs wouldn't stop. The doctor said she had developed an infection, and couldn't believe how badly the sensitive part was mutilated. Akbar was aghast at the brutality of it. Rukhsana too had been a victim, as he had expected, and her experience she said was no less traumatic.

It was a bright Sunday morning, schools were closed for vacation, and she was playing hopscotch outside her house with her little sister Rehana. She noticed an old woman whom she had never seen before enter the house. Moments later her mother, Zubaida, called her inside. A floral quarter-folded bedsheet was spread on the floor in her mother's room. Zubaida's face was white as a sheet. The old matron whom Zubaida introduced as Masi Bai, "Auntie," was sitting by the bedsheet, digging into an old plastic handbag. She removed cotton swabs, some rags, and a straight razor and placed them neatly on the edge of the sheet. She asked Rukhsana to lie down and immediately launched into a story about a young village girl who grows up to be a beautiful woman. A prince finds her in the forest and falls in love with her, and wants to marry her. The village belle agrees but has two conditions. Masi Bai was dark with a stubby nose and flinty eyes. When she started talking she was transformed. Her voice became deep as though rising from her gut, and her eyes opened wide, pupils dancing, her face distorted with affectation. Rukhsana was mesmerized. When her mother held her hands down she did not know, or when Masi Bai, continuing with her fantastic tale, pushed Rukhsana's legs apart and pinned them under her knees she was not aware. But then suddenly she stopped listening. Maddened by pain, all she could see was Masi Bai's fierce cartoonish face yapping on. Rukhsana cried with shock and pain, "Amma, Amma what is she doing to me?"

"It's over, it's over," Masi Bai said gently, smiling, and pressed a swab of cotton between her legs. Then she took out pink and purple candies from her purse and gave it to Rukhsana. "The village girl married the prince and they lived happily ever after," she finished, smiling, revealing gaps in her teeth.

Rukhsana cried for hours afterwards. The sweets or her mother's blandishments would not console her. She resented the suddenness of it and the way she was fooled into it. She was too young to understand what had been done to her, but somehow she felt robbed. The pain persisted for several days, and was unbearable when she walked or peed. She asked her mother what had happened. Her mother replied that she had been made clean; she herself, and her mother, and her mother's mother had all been cleaned. Rukhsana was confused, how was she dirty before. She feared Rehana would be "cleaned" too. Some years later when she was returning home one Sunday afternoon from a friend's place she saw Masi Bai leaving the house. She had glared at her and wanted to snatch her filthy plastic purse and throw it into the open sewer that ran along the street.

Years later, Akbar wrote an article in *India Weekly* on the subject of female circumcision, noting that Momins were the only Muslim sect in India who circumcised their girls. Although not illegal, the practice was shrouded in secrecy and shame. Kaiser Ali Mistri told him that the practice, called *khatna* or *khafz*, was recommended only indirectly in Momin scriptures but was not made binding. More importantly, there was no mention of it in the Quran nor was it prevalent in the Prophet's time. The practice, he said, originated in North Africa—where it is now a major social concern—when Momin Imams ruled that part of the world in the middle ages and the converts to the Momin faith probably brought it with them. How it came to India was a mystery. The purpose of female circumcision, he believed, was primarily to control women's sexuality. Because of the clandestine nature of the practice, Akbar wrote in his article, it was not clear how many Radicals still practiced it. But given the lukewarm response to his mother's path-breaking stand on mourning, he concluded that the practice must be common still. Sheikh Hamid Ali, when asked, was emphatic that a woman was not complete until that offending "slice of meat" was cut. Akbar found it ironic that the sheikh could talk of cutting and completeness in the same breath.

16

Two years after her husband's death, Khatun went to live with Akbar in Bombay. In Udaipur she had adjusted to a life without Zahid; the extended family and the sisters-in-law were supportive, and she had her own mother and brothers to fall back on. She had continued to work with the Zanana Wing and quietly, with like-minded friends, she had campaigned to end the strictures of mourning on new widows. A few young members of the Zanana Wing raised the issue of female circumcision and Khatun joined them in their drive to end the practice. But on both fronts their efforts found little success. The Radicals were still too steeped in tradition to let go of certain customs.

What pained her most was to see women keeping other women down; doing the men's job for them. This will only change with education, she was convinced, when new blood will replace the old guard. She was happy that the Radical girls were keen on going to university and making something of their lives. And they seemed to be doing so well that they were overtaking the boys most of whom ended up sitting at family shops after high school.

Khatun hoped that the young women of tomorrow would not allow Masi Bais to touch their daughters; that they would tell their mothers to discard the oppressive rules of mourning. The future gave her hope, but the present made her feel alone and sometimes she was overcome with loneliness. Without her husband the evenings had become quiet and empty. For months on end, Akbar had been urging her to come and live with him in Bombay. She had been hesitant initially, reluctant to leave her familiar routine and her work behind. But finally she agreed to visit him for a couple of months and see if she liked it in Bombay.

For the first few days she felt out of sorts confined to Akbar's flat. The daily chores occupied only a slice for her day, the rest of the time she read magazines and books and watched TV. Sometimes she went for walks on the beach. After a few weeks, she said she wanted to go back but Akbar asked her to give it some more time. Being close to her son was the main attraction for her to stay back. She loved cooking for him. How he had grown and become a fine young man while being away from home, being away from her care. His liberal outlook on life, his innate sense of fairness, gave her immense satisfaction. His heart and mind were in the right places. Zahid would have been so proud of him. But she detected a sadness in him. The breakup with Rukhsana had hit him hard and she had hoped he would come around, but she could see that he hadn't gotten over her yet. He should get married, she thought, that would settle him.

One Sunday, Akbar invited Kaiser Ali over for lunch. They had been in touch regularly and had had many long and animated discussions about Islam and about the Momins and the troubles in Udaipur. Kaiser Ali was especially interested in the spiritual aspect of religion, and how superficial and ritualistic obsessions had robbed all faiths of their true essence, of their radical promise.

He could quote the Quran chapter and verse. Religion, particularly Islam, for him was just another story to explain human existence, to elucidate the human condition. What Islam lacked, he argued, was transformative potential. It was a decent guide for living in the world but did not provide the tools of transformation, of transcendence. Islam in his estimation fell short of guiding the believer to inner knowledge. He said that every human soul needed to be awakened, find its own revelation. To follow the revelations of others was like wearing other people's clothes. They can't fit you right and can never be your own. Even so, Kaiser Ali revered the Prophet of Islam and held out his life as an ideal to be followed, but he rejected the cult of sunnah that Sunnis were fixated upon. Similarly, he did not glorify the Imams, as the Shia did. He treaded the middle path along the great Islamic divide. Sunni and Shia mullahs hated him and denounced him as an infidel, and worse, a communist in Muslim clothing.

Khatun, like her son, was in awe of Kaiser Ali. Inviting him over for lunch was her idea. She had met him once in Udaipur at a conference and found him aloof and a bit dismissive. She put that down to his arrogance as an intellectual. It was a year since Kaiser Ali's wife had died of cancer, and Khatun never had a chance to pay her condolences. This was another reason to invite him over.

Since coming to Bombay, it was the first time she was entertaining. The Bombay standards were high and as someone from a small town she was eager to make a good impression. She told Akbar to buy a tender cut of the shoulder for mutton roast; she made vegetable pulao, daal makhani, and yoghurt salad, and, of course, soft, ghee-smeared fresh parathas. By twelve o'clock that Sunday the food was ready and she had taken a shower and dressed nicely, her hair tied at the back in a limp ponytail. The white dupatta around her head accentuated her face. It was past twelve o'clock and Kaiser Ali had not come. It was raining hard and they hoped he would take a taxi. Finally, the doorbell rang.

Kaiser Ali looked like he had been washed up on the shore in a storm. Water cascaded on all sides from him, forming a pool where he stood; his umbrella apparently had not been much of a defence against the wind-swept rain. The three of them exchanged a flurry of confused greetings amid smiles. Akbar took the guest's umbrella and left it out in the corridor to dry.

"I'm sorry to arrive in this state," Kaiser Ali mumbled.

"Don't worry. The rain is merciless," Khatun said. "Let me get you a towel. Perhaps you need a change of clothes. Akbar's clothes might fit you."

"No, no that is not necessary, this will dry out soon."

"You will catch a cold."

He followed Akbar to his room to change. By the time he came out, in dry clothes with his hair combed, Akbar and Khatun had laid out the table and were waiting for him. On seeing him, she put her hand on her mouth and stifled a laugh. Akbar let out a guffaw. They had never seen him in anything other than his trademark kurta-pyjama. The shirt was tight around his chest, buttons straining. He looked embarrassed and awkward. "Excuse me, if I look uptight in this," he said. All three laughed.

He ate ravenously. "Now I know where to go when gluttony strikes," he said.

"You're most welcome, Kaiser Saheb," Khatun said. She found that she liked him—he was gracious and modest. She did not see the hauteur she had sensed before in Udaipur. He talked of things scholarly but without pretensions. She interrupted the conversation when she suddenly remembered about his bereavement.

"I'm so sorry about your wife. Please forgive me for not having called before," she said.

"Thank you. It's been a shock. The loss of a partner is so paralyzing."

She nodded and looked away.

The rain was still falling and it had gotten darker. Kaiser Ali had no pressing engagements for the rest of the day, so he took his customary nap in Akbar's bed, unmindful of the clatter the downpour was making outside. By tea time the rain had not abated. Khatun asked him to stay until dinner. "Hopefully the rain will ease by then and the flood water will recede," she said. He agreed and retired to the desk in Akbar's room to do some work.

———

Kaiser Ali became a frequent visitor to Akbar's flat. Apart from public engagements and trips to conferences most of his time was spent in research and writing. It made him lonely sometimes. He was cut off from his extended family who had excommunicated him. On random Sundays when he was in town, he would come and spend the day with them. They would eat and drink tea and talk. Kaiser Ali would relate tales from his travels and would invariably end up talking about Islam, its essential message of justice—a quality which was starkly absent in the so-called Islamic countries he had visited. He said that the Quran had pioneered women's rights at a time when the world was still treating them as chattels, and Khatun would agree but then counter that by stating that archaic traditions were keeping Muslim women from progressing. Akbar looked forward to these visits and felt happy for his mother, who had begun to feel comfortable in Kaiser Ali's company.

Still, they missed his father. Zahid Ali had taken a dim view of his career in journalism, but would have changed his mind if he were here, Akbar thought. Once in a while on Sunday mornings the mother and son would go to Baingan Bazaar to have a meal of paya and naan, recalling how his father would eat them with relish. "This is a dish invented by God," Akbar said on one occasion, paying homage to his father. Khatun smiled, fighting back tears.

Khatun had not considered marrying again, although the thought would cross her mind now and then. She would feel a pang of guilt at the thought. Would Zahid Ali approve of it, she wondered. There was the question of finding the right man. Now that she had come to know Kaiser Ali better, she began to entertain the notion that perhaps here was the person she might consider. But he seemed remote—his status and prestige made him seem out of reach. He was a man on a mission—lectures, seminars and books consumed all his waking hours. She could not imagine a place for herself in his life.

Akbar had been quietly watching the incipient, unspoken pull between the two. Whenever Kaiser Ali visited, he would find one excuse or the other to leave the two of them alone. It had been nearly three years since his father died. Khatun had endured his loss with quiet stoicism. Recently she had found a job as a nursery teacher in a neighbourhood school. She had done well to keep herself occupied during the day, but she had no social life. Most evenings he came home late. Seeing her lonely made him uneasy. He wished he could spend all his free time with her, but that seemed unrealistic and he hardly had time to spare. His mother was still relatively young and would eventually need a partner, a companion. Kaiser Ali seemed to be just the right man.

It had been a year since Khatun came to Bombay, and she had not again mentioned about going back to Udaipur. Akbar understood why. He teased her, "Amma, at one time you hated the thought of living in Bombay, and now you don't even talk about going back. What happened?"

"It's not me, jaana, it's Bombay. The hold of this place grows on you. Besides, now I've things to do, I'm not wasting my time watching TV," she replied, smiling.

"Amma, can I tell you something?"

"What?"

"Have you considered . . . hmm, marrying again."

Khatun closed the book she was reading, put it aside and did not speak for a long while. "Now that you ask me, yes I've considered it, in passing. But something stops me from thinking about it seriously."

"I understand, Amma. But life is long and you can't live it alone. Of course, I'll always be there, but you know what I mean."

"Don't you think it's too soon? It's not easy to forget your father and move on. Then there is the question of finding the right person. At this age, you cannot have what you want."

Akbar rose from the dining table and came and sat down beside his mother on the couch. "Amma, I think father would want you to be happy, to have a companion. As for the right person, I've someone in mind."

"I know who you are hinting at, jaana," Khatun said with a candor that surprised Akbar. "But don't you see, we're worlds apart. He's a busy man, married to his causes, he doesn't need a wife."

"He's quite down-to-earth, Amma, we've seen that. And I have a feeling he likes you."

"Well," Khatun smiled. "It's not me we should be talking about! What about you? When are you going to settle down? People in Udaipur are approaching me and I'm tired of making excuses to them. It's getting awkward, you know."

"Oh, Amma, not again. My time will come. In good time."

Akbar wanted to broach the subject with Kaiser Ali also but could not gather the nerve to do so. Although they had come close and their relationship had acquired a certain ease and openness, they rarely encroached into each other's personal space. And he found it unseemly to talk to him about *his* mother. And so he helped things along where he could and left the rest to fate.

One Sunday evening, Khatun and Kaiser Ali were alone at home. Akbar had made himself scarce, saying he had a meeting with a writer. They no longer felt awkward in each other's company. After a while they drifted towards the window, sipping tea, contemplating. The noise from the street below reached them in a constant hum. The fading sunlight fell across their faces in a golden glow.

"Remember the first time you came here?" she said.

"Yes, how can I forget it?"

"You were quite a sight."

"I felt terrible. But you know I love the rain. What I find strange is how people go for the umbrella even if it is a light drizzle. A few drops is not going to kill you, will it?"

"Well, not everybody is free like you to enjoy the rain."

"You mean to say I am free?"

"You're not tied down to a job like other people."

"Maybe, but that is not the problem. I think it is to do with attitude. It's a matter of enjoying the simple pleasures of life."

"When people are rushing to work, you think they care

about simple pleasures?"

"It's a pity, isn't it? How we overlook happiness in pursuit of happiness."

They both fell silent. He gazed blankly into the distance. Dusk was creeping in, and the night would soon claim the day. Dust and vapour rose up from the street. Kaiser Ali tapped his fingers nervously on the windowsill. Then, turning abruptly to Khatun, he said, "I have to tell you something."

"Yes."

"I'm so socially inept, and I don't know how to put it delicately. I've never been in this situation before," he said as he placed his cup on the side table next to him.

Khatun waited.

"When I got married, I had no regular income and didn't have much in the way of a career. Then came writing and books, and the Momin cause, and then the travels. All of that kept me busy and away from home most of the time. It took a toll on my marriage. Farida was not happy the way things were going. She valued my attainments, such as they are, I suppose, but it was not the life *she* wanted. There was nothing in it for her. Although she never complained about it, I could see she was deeply disappointed in me, in how I had failed as a family man, as a husband who would come home to her every evening. Add to that the absence of children. Despair and boredom consumed her. It is possible that the cancer that took her life was the result of the stress she had bottled up inside. Sometimes I feel responsible for her early end."

He had a faraway look in his eyes. Khatun had no soothing words to offer, instead she felt the urge to take his hand and comfort him.

"I'm telling you all this for a reason," he said, turning to her.

Khatun looked at him.

"I wish to marry again. Will you marry me?"

Khatun was taken aback by the suddenness of the proposal and did not know what to say or where to look.

"I don't know whether you are ready to settle down again," Kaiser Ali continued, "but the thing is, I cannot offer much of settling-down. My life is that of a roaming dervish, as you know. It would not be a conventional married life. I need a companion, a friend more than a wife."

For a long moment Khatun said nothing. "You know, I find it very flattering that you should consider me. I want to say yes, but I do need time to think, if you don't mind."

Kaiser Ali nodded. "Yes, please do. I want you to know that I won't be offended if you say no."

17

RUKHSANA CLOSED HER EYES AS the plane lifted off, holding tightly on to the armrests, and prayed. She was nervous about trusting her life to a technology that would make her airborne with no guarantee of bringing her back to the ground. As the aircraft climbed higher, she wondered if she would see her home again. It was mid-1992, and India was in political upheaval. The passions of Hindus and Muslims were being squandered on the issue of the Babri Mosque in Ayodhya. Right-wing Hindu parties were threatening to take it down claiming that it had been built on Lord Ram's birthplace by a Muslim ruler four hundred years ago. If they succeeded, many people thought, they would take the country down with it. India as a secular republic was on the cusp of a major transformation. Rukhsana felt relieved to be going away, but she feared for the safety of her mother and sister. And Akbar. When did she last see him? Eight or nine years ago, right after his father's death. His memory had become a private mnemonic jewel she kept close to her heart. There was never a day she did not think of him. All that she loved and cared for she was leaving behind. Her grip on the armrests tightened.

Two hours before, at the departure gate at Bombay airport, she had bid goodbye to her parents and sister. They had arrived by bus from Udaipur the day before and stayed the night at a hotel near the airport. At the restaurant where they had breakfast that morning, only her father, Qamar, could find the voice to talk. The three women were lost in thought, impending separation weighing heavily on them. Rukhsana felt tremors in the pit of her stomach; she feared she might not see them again. Qamar talked of trivial things with complete disregard for the women's sadness at this moment of parting. He was just happy that Rukhsana had found a suitable match to his liking and now was flying to the USA to join her husband.

Qamar had planned that, after seeing Rukhsana off, they would visit the mausoleum in Baingan Bazaar, and he hoped to catch a glimpse of Mowlana. Zubaida and Rehana were not enthused. "Is it not bad enough that Rukhsana is leaving, and on top of that we have to go there?" Rehana grumbled. She was in salwar-kameez and dreaded the prospect of donning the hijab, which the Loyalist women were now required to do.

The Momin version of the hijab was similar to a nun's habit. It covered the head and shoulders, and was worn over a long ankle-length dress—both pieces usually cut from the same cloth. For the Momin men, the skullcap had become mandatory, and so was the untrimmed beard, a white kurta over white pants, and a white outer tunic open from the front and reaching well below the knees. If the men's clothes were bland, the women's were wildly colourful. When Momins gathered, especially when they lined up on the streets to greet the Mowlana, men on one side and women on the other, they made an impressive spectacle. Viewed from above, it might give the impression of a white surf of sea chafing against a horde of multicoloured penguins.

Momin men and women were mandated to wear this community attire in public. Qamar had insisted that the women of his house wear the hijab everywhere, even to the market or to college. But they had learned to put their collective foot down

and declared that they would wear the hijab only at religious
ceremonies. Rehana, the youngest and boldest, had a greater
latitude with her father. She often took up the battle on behalf
of the other two. Rukhsana, on the other hand, remained on
the sidelines, quietly supporting her sister. After the Akbar episode, her previously sunny disposition had been overcast by a
bitterness towards her father. She saw his Mowlana-obsession
as a malady. She hardly ever spoke to him.

Zubaida would often badger her husband: "You have found
your Mowlana but lost your daughter; that must make you
happy." In response, Qamar would yell at her to shut up. "It
is not the fault of Mowlana, you stupid woman!" He blamed
Akbar's family for being on the wrong side of the faith. And he
counted on Mowlana's blessings to find a suitable mate for his
daughter. So when a proposal came for her from a rich family,
he taunted Zubaida, "Saw Mowlana's miracle?"

Shabbir Panerwala was a software engineer who had settled
in Boston. His family was rich and, as important to Qamar,
staunch devotees of Mowlana. Shabbir's father was a sheikh, a
title conferred on him by Mowlana. It had cost him a fortune to
acquire it. In olden times, when knowledge was valued, these
titles were earned by deserving men who had distinguished
themselves in religious knowledge. A dignity was attached to
the position. In recent times, though, any wealthy man could
buy the title, mostly as a matter of prestige. There were different ranks of sheikhhoods, and each had a price tag. One could
shop around. It mattered little to Mowlana if the person on
whom he was conferring the honour was an illiterate, a thief,
or a smuggler.

Shabbir's father, Sheikh Fida Hussain, was semiliterate but

a self-made man who had built his business empire in Kuwait through a combination of hard work and good luck. But if asked about the secret of his success, he would without hesitation attribute it to Mowlana. From a lowly samosa-seller he had become the king of the hardware market in Kuwait. Sheikh Fida Hussain had everything money could buy, including respect. In Qamar's estimation, he could not have done better.

Rukhsana was indifferent to the match. Zubaida consented, too, seeing no particular reason to object. The family was rich and had a good standing in society; if nothing else, Rukhsana would at least have material comforts. That Fida Hussain was fanatical did not perturb her. She had one bigot in the house; Fida Hussain couldn't be worse. The only small reservation she felt was about Shabbir's family situation. Fida Hussain was divorced, and the children had been kept away from their mother, who had later died prematurely. He had married again. Rumours had also reached her that he had a mistress in Kuwait. But nobody would dare to call out a rich man on his transgressions. Qamar could hardly have been unaware of all this. But devotion to Mowlana and wealth, in that order, were qualities enough for respectability in his eyes.

For the wedding Shabbir flew down to India on a two-week vacation and met Rukhsana twice before they tied the knot. His family had been invited to Rukhsana's house for the "threshold climbing" ceremony—when the boy formally enters the girl's house for the first time. He came with a battalion of friends all dressed in community attire. He was a tall, baby-faced young man with a ready smile and serious eyes. He wore his cap slightly pushed back and the widow's peak peeked through. He carried himself with poise and there was something about him that seemed to declare that he had figured it all out. Rukhsana found him cute but for his beard, which was black and lustrous and untamed. She tried to imagine him without it. That day they hardly got to talk; they only managed to exchange a few glances amid the general chatter and the fawning the guests received. It was incumbent upon the girl's side to pamper the boy's family, and especially his friends. Qamar, wanting to do the best, had catered food from the most expensive chef, sweets were ordered from Bombay, and Shabbir was given a gift package neatly wrapped in cellophane and tied with a crimson ribbon that finished with a dainty bow.

The package contained Japanese cloth for a three-piece suit, a flashy wristwatch, a bespoke skullcap with elaborate golden threadwork, a pair of merino wool socks, a muslin handkerchief, a tasbih with sandalwood beads, and a framed photograph of Mowlana. The "American" boy, scion of a wealthy man loaded with Kuwaiti petro-dollars, deserved nothing less. Rehana had spent hours neatly packing the gift, making sure that all the items were not only visible but also secure and the package sturdy enough to survive the scrutiny it would receive from everybody present. Since it contained Mowlana's photo, it would be kissed reverentially and passed respectfully from hand to hand as though it were the Holy Book itself.

The guests left in the late afternoon, satiated and dulled by the rich and plentiful food they had consumed. When Zubaida found a moment alone with Rukhsana, she asked her what she thought of Shabbir. Rukhsana said nothing. As long as she lived under her father's roof and authority, she had told herself, she would accept everything without complaining. Shabbir did not seem a bad sort. But who could tell what was inside a man's heart? And mind? What demons animated his life? When she knew him better, perhaps she'd be able to negotiate her freedom and space. Thinking about this prospect filled her with a mellow dread. So much unfamiliar territory, so much emotional effort required to map out one's place in it. With Akbar everything was familiar, charted out. Her heart ached in anguish.

Back in her room to rest, she sat down at the dresser and regarded her reflection pensively in the mirror. She was wearing lehnga and odhni specially tailored for the occasion. The odhni slipped from her head as she leaned forward to examine a zit on her chin. The gold jewellery—the classical jhumka earrings and matching necklace and ring—were family heirlooms. The sun peeking through the parting in the curtains picked up a facet of the garnet in her necklace. Her beauty shone in that transient scintilla of light. Her long black hair was done in a rope braid, held with a fancy hairpin at the nape.

"You look lovely, aapa," Rehana said, coming in. "What has that guy done to deserve you?" Rukhsana looked at her sister and smiled the saddest smile.

———

Two days later in the evening, Shabbir came by on a scooter and took Rukhsana out. She sat sideways on pillion and held on to his seat for support, too embarrassed to hold him by the shoulder. They went to Fateh Sagar and sat on the railing at a secluded spot. He was wearing a dress shirt and pants and the mandatory skullcap. She was in white salwar-kameez with a red silk dupatta around her shoulders. The lake before them was calm, a light breeze playing on the surface. In the distance a boat was ferrying passengers to Nehru Park, the island garden in the middle of the lake. He told her about his job, his life in America. "Except for the bitter cold winter and taxes," he said, "life is good." People had freedom there, perhaps too much of it in his opinion, and they were individualistic and self-centred. "You can't relate to their culture," he said. "We have to seek our own kind to get a sense of belonging. Our traditional values are much better."

Rukhsana wanted to ask him what traditional values he was talking about, but did not want to sound confrontational. He asked her about her studies and what she wanted to do after marriage. "Would you like to work?" She said yes, it was important for her to work. They went to Shilpi Restaurant for a meal and sat out in the verandah overlooking the open courtyard that was paved with pressed earth. Dusk had fallen and the moon shimmered teasingly in the clear sky. Fire torches placed sparingly highlighted the distorted shadows of waiters flitting about. The aroma of burnt meat and smoke wafted out from the kitchen. As Shabbir's eyes followed the darting fireflies in the distance, Rukhsana stole glances at him.

"Something's been bothering me," Shabbir broke the silence.

"What?"

"Why are you not wearing the hijab?" his tone was stiff.

Rukhsana had anticipated the question and was surprised that it took him so long to ask. Marriage would be a new chapter in her life, and she had decided that she would not completely cede control of the script. The sudden eviction of Akbar from her life had put her in a funk, and she had been unable to act decisively. That mistake ended here. The first few weeks and months of this new relationship were crucial. How she responded to her husband would mark her territory. She had to make sure that she was not walked all over.

"Why are you not wearing your kurta-pyjama?" she asked politely.

"It's different for men."

"How so?"

"Because we are different. We don't have to hide our bodies," he said, irritated.

"And my body is exposed?"

He looked away and said nothing.

When the food arrived, they ate in silence, Shabbir swallowing his pride. Rukhsana made no attempt to talk. She couldn't believe that this guy who lived in the West, who had been out and about, who had seen the world, could be so chauvinistic.

"The butter chicken is delicious," he said.

She shrugged, happy to have drawn a line.

———

Rukhsana recalled this conversation forty thousand feet above sea level. The seatbelt signs were turned off, and flight attendants had started serving drinks. She looked out the window. A blinding sun blazed against the blue sky; a seamless stretch of clouds below her lay like a vast, rucked carpet. She was awestruck by the view. Floating in space with no frame of reference, ungrounded and rootless. She had a fleeting sense of anxiety. *What feats of human ingenuity have made this possible! This flying machine will take me halfway around the world in a matter of hours. And come to think of it, I will be in a different world.*

She hadn't tried to imagine what her married life would be like, or what America had in store for her. The whole time leading up to the marriage, and even until she found herself alone at the airport, the idea of living in a foreign country had seemed distant to her. Something far off on the horizon that she would have to deal with someday, but not at the moment.

She had in fact welcomed the idea of going away. That seemed to be the only way to put her past behind her. A new landscape of experience would create new memories, and this time, she hoped, they wouldn't come back to haunt her and hurt her. She was not starry-eyed about a happy or peaceful marriage, but she knew she was on surer ground.

The wedding had been a grand affair. Qamar did not spare any expense. To his credit, Shabbir's father did not demand any extravagance, although they did try to get Mowlana to perform the nikah, but he was traveling in London at that time. His son Mukammal Fakerudin came instead, demanding a fortune for his troubles, with which Fida Hussain parted happily. The grandee's every whim was satisfied and every fancy fulfilled. "Who does he think he is?" Zubaida grumbled. "He is hogging all the attention. The wedding itself has become a sideshow." Qamar and Fida Hussain, on the other hand, could not have felt more blessed. They walked around with their chests puffed, bursting with pride.

The reception was held at an open ground near Rukhsana's house. Tents were set up, and the venue was decorated with a million dancing lights. A stage had been constructed, its floor carpeted, with two plush chairs in the centre, and a plywood cutout of a palace facade with Mughal filigree design forming the backdrop. Shabbir wore a cream-coloured Nehru jacket and pants and a pheta with a white feather pinned askew to the front with a nifty broach. Rukhsana liked what she saw. *But I will have to do something about that beard.*

She was elegantly wrapped in a fuchsia-red brocade sari awash with sequins and paisley zardori motifs. Her jewellery of gold and emerald, light and elegant, complemented the sari. Her hair was tied back in a stylish chignon, and the small pendant of the headpiece encrusted with rubies rested on her forehead like a third eye. The makeup was a touch over-done. Zubaida took a wad of currency notes and made circu-lar motions over Rukhsana's head seven times and gave away the money to be distributed to the poor. Then she cradled Rukhsana's face in her hands and cracked her knuckles to ward off the evil eye. "May God always keep you in His protection," she whispered.

After the reception, when the guests had departed, only close family and friends remained. The time Zubaida had been dreading had arrived. Rukhsana now belonged to her husband. She hugged her daughter, and both wept, tears smudging the kohl around Rukhsana's eyes. An aunt stepped forward and separated them. Then the two sisters said goodbye, unable to staunch the tears. Each knew she was losing her best friend. Perhaps forever. Finally, Qamar hugged her and mumbled that she should keep her husband happy. *What about my happiness, papa?* Wiping her eyes, she looked at her mother and sister, quickly turned, and got into the waiting car. In the back seat Shabbir took her bejewelled hand and patted it.

Earlier that evening, Shabbir's friends had gone to his house and decorated the bridal bed. Long strands of roses and jas-mine hung from three sides. A canopy of flowers rose to the ceiling. A fragrant sanctuary of blossoms had been created for the bride to be deflowered.

Rukhsana's friends and cousins and aunts came later to offi-cially hand her over, to bestow her on the conjugal bed. They advised her to act demure but tough, not to give in to him easily. "Let him work for it," one said. They left amid giggles and jokes, shutting the door behind them, their voices trailing off.

Rukhsana was alone at last, and she wanted to cry. Her eyes welled up. Moments later, the door flung open with a jolt and Shabbir stumbled in, pushed by his friends. It was their turn to tease him. They counselled him to kill the cat on the first night (a reference to establishing his dominion over her). Someone told him not to drink the glass of milk when offered, because it might be spiked to put him to sleep. He smiled stupidly and closed the door behind him. He parted the curtain of flowers and sat down beside her. "You look lovely," he said. She did not respond. "You know, Mowlana has personally approved of this marriage, I consult him for all important decisions in my life. Why I do that, I'll tell you someday." He gave her a peck on the cheek.

Rukhsana flinched and suddenly felt exhausted and wanted to sleep. It was two in the morning. "I'm tired too," he said. She changed, and fell asleep as soon as she hit the pillow. He lay beside her, spooning her, his face buried in her hair, breathing its mellow scent, feeling her soft, warm body.

When he awoke dawn had broken. The heavy curtains blocked out the light, and the room was still partly dark. The scent of jasmines filled the room. Rukhsana was soundly asleep, snoring softly, her face turned toward him. He looked at her for a long time. Then he moved closer and kissed her on the lips. She opened her eyes. He slid his hand under her nightie, caressed her silken skin, and was pleasantly surprised that she wasn't wearing panties. His hands moved up and unclasped the bra. With the other hand he cupped the breast and massaged it tenderly, drew her closer. She turned her face away, shy and unsure. He waited and let his hands do the talking. She moved his hand away, again and then again. He persisted, gently. She squirmed, unable to reciprocate. It was not just her shyness.

Something was holding her back. Something which could not be named, something which she had pledged to someone else. This silent, subtle struggle went on for some time. She knew resistance was pointless. Finally, she relented. She moaned, alternating between pleasure and pain.

He plucked a red rose from the hanging garland and touched it on her lips, cheeks, and down the neck and traced the curves of her naked form all the way down to the toes. She closed her eyes and followed the soft subliminal caress of the petals. When she opened her eyes, he was smelling the rose.

"I don't know what's more exquisite, this rose or you."

"You think you are romantic, uh?"

He nodded.

"You know what is not romantic?"

He shook his head.

"Your beard."

His smile vanished.

"You can keep your beard if you have to, but at least trim it, give it a shape."

He said nothing and stared at her, eyes cold, expression leaden.

She reached out, and stroked his whiskers. "This makes you look . . . like . . . old," she said, eschewing the word "Taliban" that was about to slip off her tongue.

18

AKBAR WAS OVERJOYED TO LEARN that Kaiser Ali had proposed to his mother. Khatun had received the overture with some gratification but there was still a nagging doubt in her mind. Akbar tried to allay her reservations. She had to move on with her life, he told her. The memory of his father would always be there, and nobody could take his place. His father would have wanted her to be happy. By spurning this chance, she was depriving herself of a partner, a companion who would care for her. For weeks Khatun could not make up her mind, and Akbar, not understanding his mother's brooding uncertainty, stopped talking about it. Then one evening over dinner, she broached the subject on her own. She said she had given much thought to the matter, had consulted her family and the chachis in Udaipur and everybody had given their nod to the arrangement.

Kaiser Ali did not visit their house in the interim. When he came, finally, it was for the wedding. They married in a quiet ceremony performed by a qazi at a mosque in Mahim attended by a few of Kaiser Ali's friends. None of his family came, all being on the Loyalist side. Khatun had invited Nazeer and Shama but they excused themselves for the same reason. The fact that she was marrying the clergy's "number one enemy" was bad enough, and if they were to be seen hobnobbing with him and his new wife they would be instantly booted from Noorani Manzil and the community.

After the wedding, Khatun went to live in Kaiser Ali's house in upscale Bandra. They asked Akbar to move in with them, but he declined, preferring his independence. Khatun was mortified to leave him alone; she remarked how she had come to Bombay to be with him and now it seemed odd that she should abandon him. "Yes, how people change with time," he joked. Khatun smiled. It is time you also find a girl and settle down, she said.

———

Two months later Khatun came to visit Akbar in his flat in Prabhadevi. At the dinner table as they ate, she removed a photograph from an envelope and pushed it towards him.

"This is Naseem. Isn't she pretty?"

Akbar looked at the photo and quickly put it face down. "Amma, please not again. I told you I'm not interested right now."

"Right now is the right time. You are not getting any younger. You are twenty-eight."

"Amma, I cannot marry someone I do not know, do not love."

"So you're waiting for love to happen to you? And when will that be?"

"I don't know, Amma. I don't go around looking for it."

"But I know this much, jaana, the longer you wait, the harder it will be to find good girls. Parents are eager to marry off their daughters."

"Well, that is not a good thing, is it? Parents should not treat their daughters as disposable goods."

"Now don't be flippant. You will realize when you become a parent, when you have a daughter. All I'm asking you is to meet this girl once, talk to her, see if you like her. There's no obligation. There's no harm in meeting. They are Radicals like us. She is a good girl, pretty and educated. Hers is one of the established families in Udaipur. Old money, you know."

"Amma, these things don't impress me."

"I'm just stating the facts. And stop being judgmental about everything. The world doesn't turn on the axis of your ideals."

Akbar raised his eyebrows.

"No more argument. I will write to her family, saying we will pay them a visit when we are in Udaipur in August."

Akbar, defeated, spooned another heap of rice on his plate and began to listen to the news on television. Two years ago, in 1990, L K Advani, a senior leader of the Hindu nationalist party, the BJP, had led a chariot procession from Somnath in Gujarat to Ayodhya in Uttar Pradesh, a tortuous route starting from the west in Gujarat, dipping south, and then looping back north and then east in Bihar. An old, dilapidated mosque in Ayodhya called Babri Masjid was at the centre of the dispute. The Hindutava (Hindu nationalist) brigade claimed that the Mughal Emperor Babur had torn down the temple at the site of Lord Rama's birth and built the mosque in its place. Advani's procession, which traversed across the Hindu heartland of north India, whipped up the hysteria of revenge. The call to destroy the defunct mosque and rebuild the temple in its stead was presented as the righting of a historic travesty. For Muslims, the very idea was an outrage.

Advani's procession, dubbed the Journey of Faith, passed through scores of cities and villages, leaving a trail of blood in its wake. By the time it wound down, about forty cities were rocked by sectarian riots. Hundreds died, overwhelmingly Muslims. The Ayodhya issue was yet another episode in the long and never-ending saga of rancour between the two communities. Akbar bristled at the position the Muslims had taken.

He wrote articles arguing that Muslim resistance was misplaced and was only provoking extremism on both sides. The mosque was in a state of disrepair and hardly being used. He pleaded with Muslims to let go of the mosque, which had no historic or architectural significance. He urged that the situation be looked at dispassionately and not be allowed to become a point of religious pride for either community. But his articles were met with derision and anger from Muslims and applauded as a voice of reason by the Hindus. Muslims accused him of selling out and denounced him as an apostate.

He had long discussions with Kaiser Ali and the latter agreed with Akbar in principle. But from the point of view of Muslims, the issue was not as clear-cut, Kaiser Ali said. "Being a minority, they suffer from a siege mentality," he explained. "They feel that they are under attack. The matter is in the courts, so let the courts decide, let the rule of law prevail. But the Hindutva forces have no patience for that, and there are no votes in waiting for a legal solution. The votes are in the drama of confrontation, in working up people's emotions, in making one community the enemy of the other. The classic divide and rule. It's so easy to subvert democracy, such as it is."

By the end of 1992, Hindu kar sevaks, volunteers, were galvanizing across the towns and cities of north India for a march to Ayodhya. Hindu hordes gripped by hysteria would not be placated until their destructive fury found its catharsis. Babri Masjid's time had come. Meanwhile, the Congress government, under Prime Minister Narasimha Rao, twiddled its thumbs in New Delhi. Although Akbar was critical of the Muslim stance on the issue, it seemed bizarre that the Hindutva goons were allowed a free rein. Death and fear stalked in the by-lanes of India. All levels of government were complicit, letting things happen. Advani had sown a whirlwind two years ago, and the time had come to reap the bitter harvest.

———

In August, they had gone to Udaipur, and a meeting was arranged with Naseem, as Khatun had promised. The mother and son and other close family members were invited for lunch at Naseem's grand, multistorey house in Saheli Nagar. Her grandfather was a rich merchant who had made his fortune supplying diamonds and jewels to the palace. He had been on first-name terms with the former Maharajah of Udaipur and under his beneficence had come to acquire large tracts of land and property. Wealth and respectability cleaved to their family name: the Zariwalas. The patriarch, Ismail Seth, had long been critical of the clergy and its domineering ways. At a time when the rest of the Momins in Udaipur were licking the dust off Mowlana's feet, he was one of the few who openly defied the Mowlanas and called out their excesses. Momins used to call him muddai, infidel. After the revolt, he and his family had assumed a natural and moral leadership of the radical movement. Akbar didn't much care about affluence or influence, his measure for people was the position they took on issues close to his heart. Naseem's family passed muster.

Khatun was proud that such a reputable family had considered her son worthy of a match. She looked on the young couple with joy, remembering Zahid. He would have been so happy. The Zariwala house was posh and the guests were suitably awed. As soon as they arrived they were taken to Ismail Seth's room where he sat upright on a bed propped up by pillows. At a prim ninety-five he was a little hard of hearing, but all the same he regaled the guests with tales of the Mowlanas, Noman and his father Shatir. The father was quite a piece of work—sharp and ruthless, he said. Shatir's vindictiveness had no limits, he would have the graves of his detractors dug up; he ordered the Momins to pay fealty and tithe to him; he declared himself God on earth in a colonial court causing the presiding British judge to flip off his chair in utter shock; he claimed that the Imam visited him in the mirhab for a private behind-the-curtain tête-à-tête. "The son Noman," Ismail Seth said with a chuckle, "compared to the father is a mewling lamb." The old man had so many stories and Akbar suggested he should record them somewhere.

After lunch, everyone sat around in the drawing room making polite conversation. The guests praised the food and the hospitality. Tea was served and soon after the guests left but Khatun and Akbar stayed back so they could spend some more time with Naseem's family. Then, after a sufficient while, prompted by a well-established but unspoken protocol one by one they began to slip away leaving Akbar and Naseem alone in the room.

Akbar cast his eyes around, looking for a gambit to break the silence. The air hung heavy weighed down by afternoon heat. He looked at Naseem. She had natural, effortless good looks with high cheek-bones, small nose and thin lips. Her thick black hair with a blunt cut fell to her shoulders and a few loose strands carelessly clouded her face. She wore a teal and magenta salwar-kameez with a matching dupatta around her shoulders. They sat at the corner of sofas placed at a right angle to each other. Their eyes met, hers were animated and intelligent. They smiled. Rukhsana's face flashed in his mind.

He spotted a framed painting of Fateh Sagar on the opposite wall. It was a bit out of true, and he was tempted to go adjust it. It depicted a scene of a sunset, which he had so often seen and admired. What piqued his interest, though, was the stormy waters of the lake, which was unusual. "That's a nice painting," he said, finally finding an opening.

"Really?" she said, surprised.

"Yes. The waves, though, are unfamiliar to me. The lake is normally placid."

"Hmmm, true. Maybe it reflects the artist's state of mind."

"Interesting, who is the artist?"

Naseem hesitated. "I'm guilty of that travesty."

"Wow! You are far too modest. It is good. You *are* good."

"Thank you."

Akbar walked to the painting and adjusted it. Stepping back, he looked at it, satisfied. He asked what prompted her to paint a stormy lake. She said she was working on it when her grandmother died. That was also the time when Indira Gandhi was assassinated and a massacre of Sikhs had followed. Everything seemed bleak, men had lost their minds. And souls. Fateh Sagar, cradled by the hills all around, was like a haven of tranquility. "It is our emblem of what the world should be, beautiful and peaceful," she said. "But the reality of our world is different. So I tried to stir up that symbol a little."

Akbar fell silent and considered her interpretation. "I like it."

He asked her about her interests. She said she was a teacher by profession and painting and yoga were her passions. She taught yoga most evenings at a studio near Fateh Sagar, from where one could get a clear view of the lake. He told her about his editing job, his modest means, and wondered whether she would be able adjust to a life in a flat which was probably smaller than the room they were sitting in. She said she was aware how the big city was stingy about living spaces, and added in mock-seriousness, that although it would be a come-down for her, happiness could not be measured by the size of real estate.

Three months later on December 6, 1992 they got married. Earlier that morning, when Khatun showed Akbar the ruby-studded 22-carat wedding ring, he took it in his hand and was pleased by its chunky ornate beauty. "My mother gave it to me when I got married, and she got it from her mother," Khatun said. "It has felt the pulse of your ancestors. I hope it carries their blessings." Akbar smiled. It didn't bring much luck to you, he thought, remembering his father's premature death.

On that cold December morning, as they were slipping gold rings onto each other's fingers, Hindu mobs were tearing down the Babri Masjid in Ayodhya. The sensible, secular India watched in horror. The Prime Minister, Narasimha Rao, looked on helplessly. Sectarian riots broke out across the country, and once again innocent blood was spilled, of Muslims mostly. Udaipur was tense, and the administration deployed police throughout the city to keep the peace. The wedding reception scheduled for that evening was cancelled. Khatun did not see this disruption as a good augury. A pall of gloom settled on the two households, the festive gaiety of the occasion curdled into anxiety. The larger anger over the destruction of Babri Masjid, and what it represented, subsumed the inconvenience over a cancelled reception.

Akbar was hardly upset by the cancellation. It seemed a triv-ial setback considering what was happening in the country. He had found all the fuss attending to wedding ceremonies a bit too fastidious; he didn't like being the focus of attention and all the fawning and fuss that came with it. A few days later, a small function was held, but it was tempered by a despondency of the kind that lingers in the aftermath of a great calamity.

By the end of December 1992, the newlyweds were in Bombay. On New Year's Eve, Naseem fried pomfret, a fish she had never tasted before, to go with a side of grilled vegetables, daal, and rice. With the dulcet strains of Jagjit Singh's ghazals filling the room, the two of them enjoyed a quiet, candle-lit dinner. At the stroke of midnight, they stood and kissed by the window as fireworks lit up the sky in the distance. She said she loved fireworks, their ephemeral sparkle. How like a fountain of light they brighten our dark world, and then in an instant they are gone. She asked why beautiful things lasted only briefly while ugliness persisted. He pulled her closer, and caressing her back, whispered "Happy New Year" in her ear. There was apprehension in his voice. The state the country was in didn't allow for a confident joy. Any hope for personal contentment amid such chaos seemed foolish. The frailty of human happiness, indeed of human life, had become all too stark. What tomorrow would bring was impossible to say.

And it only brought more tragedy. A few days later, Bombay erupted in a wave of riots that continued for days. Aggrieved Muslims were provoked into violence when some extremist Hindus celebrated the destruction of Babri Masjid. In retaliation, the militant, right-wing, sectarian outfit Shiv Sena—Army of Shivaji—named after the seventeenth century Maratha hero Shivaji—pressed its hordes into a systematic massacre of Muslims. By the time their fury was spent, a thousand people were slain. The Shiv Sena supremo, Bal Thackeray, incited the mobs through pamphleteering. He presided over the mayhem in Bombay for days in what seemed to be a clear collusion with the police and the administration.

Akbar had come to love Bombay, but his very presence in the city was now an affront to Bal Thackeray and his ilk, who through their vile brand of Maratha chauvinism had created an atmosphere of hatred against outsiders, especially of the Muslim variety. The Shiv Sena goons had lists of Muslim names and homes, and they went about attacking, maiming, and killing. The gangs roamed the streets, trashing the city; the city that hummed with commerce and was forever high on finance; the city that attracted the dreamers and the desperate in equal measure; the city where squalid slums allowed high-rises to stand in their midst; the city whose Hindi films churned out a syrupy message of unity and love (to little avail); the city whose contradictions went to bed with its hypocrisies; the city whose diversity was being steamrolled into a collective funk, hammered by the dull banality of evil.

Such violent meanness cannot come from such a magnanimous land, Akbar thought. The men who were claiming to be the true sons of the soil had hardly understood the true nature of their heritage—its capacity for acceptance. Akbar was saddened to see that everything he loved about the city was falling apart. He knew that hate was not an answer to hate, that darkness cannot be dispersed by darkness, but how he resented Bal Thackeray. He was aghast how one man could hold the megacity to ransom and how he could whip up such murderous frenzy and get away with it. He wrote an open letter—dripping with sarcasm—addressed to Bal Thackeray and sent it for publication to *India Weekly*, his former employer. The editor, Pramod Mehta, refused to publish it, saying it was too provocative. "We do not want to further aggravate the tension; it is like adding fuel to the fire," he said. Akbar protested that

Thackeray could not go unchallenged, that he must know that the conscience of the city was not dead, that we had not lost our humanity—yet. But Mehta would not be convinced.

He called up Kaiser Ali to vent his frustration. "Can nobody touch Thackeray?"

"I don't know," Kaiser Ali said. "Thackeray, like Hitler with the Germans, has manipulated the Maratha sentiment to rally people to his cause. He cannot offer his people a secure future, but what he has given them instead is an enemy at whom they can target their ire. And the enemy as always is the 'other,' the outsider. Muslims bore the brunt of that rage this time because of Hindutva's anti-Muslim propaganda. In the past the Shiv Sena has attacked other communities, too—Marwaris, Sindhis, Parsis, South Indians—the people who nurtured Bombay with their sweat and genius and enterprise."

"So that means the government will allow him to have his way."

"Unfortunately, yes. I hear the police are culpable, too. There are reports of them aiding and abetting. Even if they did not, they did nothing to stop the mobs. For now, the man is having his way, for sure. And don't forget, criminal gangs are also in the game here; they are using the riots to settle scores."

Akbar's article never saw the light of day. He had sent it to many publications, some of them avowedly secular, but none had the gumption to bell the Tiger of Bombay (the tiger being the mascot of Bal Thackeray's Shiv Sena).

A fortnight after the riots, when the blood stains had been washed off the streets and the dead buried, Bombay was back on its feet, busy and energized, as though the bloodbath had never happened. Akbar pored over the morning papers at breakfast, and then suddenly he got up, went to his study and brought out his unpublished article. In the kitchen he torched it with a gas lighter and threw it into the sink. The flame leapt hungrily and devoured the three sheets of paper. The smoke rose from the sink and wafted towards the living room. "So this is how truth smells when it burns," he said as he came out.

Naseem, who had been watching him with curiosity, was amused. "That's very filmy, if you ask me," she said.

"Yup, right. But not as dramatic as when lives go up in smoke."

"Oh, come on. What's the point of this melodrama. There is nothing you could have done. Men had become monsters, and you think your words would have stopped them?"

"That is not the point, Naseem. It is the silence and lack of protest that is creating a space for more terror, more fear. Look at the *Times of India*—even for its mild criticism it has earned the nickname *Times of Pakistan*."

———

Five years after the Bombay riots, the Srikrishna Commission published its report. The press and the political class paid little heed to it. Not a single person was convicted. Akbar learned through the grapevine that Mowlana might have struck a secret deal with Bal Thackeray to spare Momins. The supremo was believed to have instructed his goons not to attack Mumtaz Manzil—a Momin residential building in Andheri—saying, "they are our people." The cozy relationship between Mowlana and Thackeray had been in the making for a long time. The clergy threw money at powerful politicians to buy protection. And sucking up to Thackeray seemed the obvious thing to do. But it never really worked as intended. The goons on the ground were too ignorant and too enraged to distinguish between Momins and other Muslims.

Years earlier, when Mowlana publicly cursed the first three Khalifas of Islam (whom the Sunnis revere and the Shias detest) and caused a riot, it was said that Thackeray's men came to the defence of Momins. But by the time help arrived most of the damage was done. The Momin Masjid in Baingan Bazaar, the neighbourhood from which Mowlana promulgated the imprecations, was also inhabited by Sunnis. The two communities had lived cheek by jowl peacefully for decades. But Mowlana's ill-advised diatribe that August day touched a raw nerve with fellow Muslims. Sunnis went on a rampage; Momin shops were trashed and set to fire. The infallible Mowlana, the protector and guide of his flock, fled the scene. Later he made a public apology for his *faux pas* on television.

———

At Alfaz Books, as senior editor, Akbar had the opportunity to work with writers and academics. Some had become his friends. One of them, Farid Alvie, had been persuading him to write a book. He suggested that he apply to American universities for research grants; they are generous and facilities are excellent. Akbar brushed off the idea as preposterous. He found ready excuses to dissuade himself—that everything that needed to be said had been said already; that he didn't have the stamina to flog a topic over hundreds of pages; that it was hard, arduous work. What a bunch of tortured wrecks writers were. Also, writing demanded time and commitment, which he could not afford. Naseem's teacher's income was not enough to help sustain even their frugal lifestyle if he stopped working. As it is she had to adapt to a far humbler lifestyle than she was used to. And to her credit, she had adjusted quite nicely without ever complaining. Akbar admired her maturity and high-mindedness.

Despite all the excuses he conjured up to put off writing a book, the thought kept nagging him. He enjoyed using words; he thought he could savour them, touch them, feel their materiality, as though they were tactile bits he could hurl into the air like coloured balls and juggle with them, and as with dance partners—sometimes sedate, sometimes sprightly—he could waltz and tango with. He found it amazing how words could be strung together to make a sentence, to make meaning. Add to those words a human voice and the magic was complete. We live, we breathe, and we speak. How extraordinary was that.

Can we think without language? he wondered. Language separates us. It gives us names, it makes Hindus, Christians, Muslims out of us. It robs us of our essence. When we strip away language, peel away words, what is left is innately human. Maybe that is what being human is. Language creates noise. Maybe that is why in silence we find our true self. Then the question hounded him: why human life is bedeviled by identities, which are assumed, accidental, acquired; which like detritus of belief and culture settle on our souls, effacing what is true and pure? Is this what is meant by losing one's humanity—that one forgets one's intrinsic human nature and submits to made-up ideologies? How astonishing was the power of ideas, and how they enslave the human mind! And if those ideas come from a scripture, a prophet, a megalomaniac, a Mowlana, there's no telling what havoc they might unleash.

In his little cloistered Momin world, he had seen enough wreckage caused by the power of ideology. It was not as horrific as the recent riots, there was no actual blood-letting, but the fissures of pain and suffering ran deep. Oppression was psychological, slavery was mental. The Momin clergy, like all charlatans, had doctrinal tricks in their bag, bon mots wrapped in shiny paper of dogma and held together by florid ribbons of fear and tradition. The Momin high priest promised paradise with a promissory note, but was not obliged to provide proof of the efficacy of his claim. Nor did anyone dare demand one.

In India, awash with gurus and godmen, religious hocus-pocus was common currency. In the Momin context, though, it seemed astounding. Islam was clear about one thing: only your amaal, your deeds, will determine your final abode in the here-after. The Mowlana touting his passport to heaven blatantly contradicted the Quran and didn't just get away with it but was celebrated for it. That was some chutzpah. Either Momins were too ignorant to know any better or too meek to call his bluff. Either way, it was the Mowlana who was having the last smirk behind his scraggy beard.

Akbar and Naseem often thanked their parents for having rebelled against the clergy. From childhood she had witnessed irreverence for Mowlana in her home and was weaned on the healthy skepticism for all things that issued from the mouths of the mullahs; Akbar had arrived at that position by circum-stance and temperament. They often discussed the state of their small community and why Momins were so beholden to Mowlana. The desire to belong and the fear of being ostracised, they agreed, had made Momins weak and compliant.

It had been ten years of marriage with Naseem. A new millen-nium had dawned, and the Y2K fear had proven to be a grand hoax. Over the years, Rukhsana had become a memory with a trace of receding regret. Distance, time, and the push and pull of daily life had been fraying the slender thread that still connected them. *Some things are not meant to be.* Akbar had come to have a deep affection for Naseem, and it was not the result of just having lived together for so long. She was lovely and intelligent and down-to-earth, despite her silver-spoon-in-the-mouth upbringing. Akbar had developed a grudging admiration for her positive, outgoing personality; for her gravitas when required and her profound insights which she wore lightly. She had a ready smile, was extremely well-read, and could give Akbar a run for his money, book for book, author for author. And unlike him, she made friends easily.

The blossoming of love in arranged marriages is an overwhelming Indian reality. There is a certain charm in discovering your partner, Akbar admitted. The wedlock accorded perfect legitimacy to the project, an exercise shot through with sexual desire and adventure. He unearthed Naseem's idiosyncrasies as he mined her sensuality from under the layers of her clothing, as he explored her uncharted body and discovered sweet erogenous spots. Her peculiarities, her pet peeves, her particular way of smiling, her harmless hypocrisies, what made her mad, ideas that excited her, emotions that wrenched her heart, the way she looked at him in surprise, curled her lips in disappointment, and a million other things. It was like an expedition of mutual discovery, only that they were not rushed. They were thrown together for life and had a lifetime to hone their relationship, adjust to each other's likes and dislikes, smooth the rough edges. Not everything was agreeable. Even so, there was more in common between them than he had imagined. The birth of their daughter, Farah, two years after the marriage had made him proud and humble at the same time, and turned him into a protective father. The past was now truly another country.

———

One humid Sunday evening in April, Akbar had just returned home with Farah from the playground downstairs. While Farah went to the bathroom to freshen up, he turned on the TV. Doordarshan was showing the old classic *Sholay*, yet again. The seventies blockbuster had captured the imagination of a generation and still tugged at its collective heart. Like the *Ramayana* and *Mahabharata* TV shows, *Sholay* had seeped into national consciousness, its dialogues and scenes becoming common lore. Akbar caught the scene where the villain Gabbar Singh is pacing back and forth at his rocky, barren hideout. Dragging his bandolier in one hand and letting it scrape the rock as he moves, with a doleful violin playing in the background, Gabbar Singh is angry that his men were made to skedaddle from the village by hired guns. His smile menacing, his teeth tarnished by tobacco, he is haranguing the men for being pussies. Then he sneers, "How many men were there?" Akbar knew what would come next and mouthed the dialogue before Gabbar could speak it. When Farah came into the room, Akbar was riveted to the screen. He had obviously forgotten that he had to warm the leftover food from last night and lay the table.

Naseem would be home soon from her yoga class. She taught ashtanga yoga on weekend evenings at the Nirvana Yoga Studio in the neighbourhood. In her day job as a teacher she taught mathematics and science to class five kids at a private school in Parel. She had made friends with another teacher and yoga enthusiast, Bela Nadkarni. Bela was doe-eyed and pleasant looking, her hair long and braided, topped with a jasmine wreath, her saris always impeccably worn. The two had hit it off right from the first day. Bela, who had had little interaction with Muslims, was pleasantly surprised to learn that Naseem, a Muslim, should be interested in yoga. Bela's family, having emigrated from Rajpur, a town in southern Maharashtra, was settled in Bombay for past two generations. She had lived in Prabhadevi all her life. Not many Muslims lived in the area. She did not have an opinion about them one way or the other, except what was generally thought and said about them: that they butchered cows, were cantankerous by nature, treacherous to the core, could not be trusted, bred like rabbits, behaved like dogs, and cheered for Pakistan in cricket matches. When they became close and began to share confidences, she told Naseem how she did not fit the image she had of Muslims, how far off the mark all the stereotypes were.

Bela learned about Shias, Sunnis, and Momins. She was surprised that Muslims also had so many "castes." She was a Saraswati Brahmin married to Prashant Nadkarni, belonging to an upper-caste sect from the Konkan region. She said she had heard of Mowlana, who had been in the news regarding his public apology over the Baingan Bazaar riots. She had also seen his picture with Bal Thackeray in the papers. Beyond that she had no idea who Momins were and what made their world go round. Naseem opened a whole new cultural vista for her. Bela never cooked meat at home, but her husband was fond of it. Whenever Prashant had a yen for meat, they would go to a Mughlai or Punjabi restaurant and order chicken tandoori and mutton biryani. Of late, his carnivore cravings were being satisfied in Naseem's kitchen.

The previous evening they had come over for dinner. Naseem had made vegetarian dishes for Bela. Prashant was floored by the mutton samosas Naseem made for starters. She served white akni soup with it. He couldn't get enough of the crisp, deep-fried delicacy. Then there was biryani and rogan josh with naan for the main course. A culinary treasure trove lay before him, his eyes and taste buds agog. The rogan josh Naseem made was based on an authentic Kashmiri recipe she had found on the Internet. The aroma of cardamom reluctantly disclosed a whiff of saffron. The meat was tender and melted obligingly in the mouth. The taste of the thick gravy, pungent and tangy, garnished with fresh coriander sprigs, teased the palate in phases. Prashant had never tasted a meat dish so delicious. When he asked from which culinary vault this had come, Naseem said it was Kashmiri Rogan Josh.

"Well, for that reason alone, India should never let go of Kashmir." He chuckled.

They all laughed. Akbar chimed in, "Yes, for that reason. But," his voice became grave, "there are other more important reasons to let it go."

Naseem gave him a look.

Prashant looked at Bela, his mouth full, caught midway into a chomp, his smile quickly fading.

Akbar, sensing the darkening mood, changed tack. "Relax." He smiled. "Wouldn't you want to know what those reasons are?"

Prashant allowed a smile, resumed chewing, and nodded.

"For one, it is extremely cold there. Imagine the energy India needs to produce to keep the Kashmiris warm. Second, Kashmir is good only for tourism, and thanks to Hindi movies they have done it to death, reduced it to a cliché. Who wants to go and spend good money on clichés. Kashmir, if you ask me, is a liability."

Prashant once again stopped chewing. He looked at Bela, who was staring at her plate, then at Akbar, whose poker face showed no clue as to whether he was joking or serious.

Naseem, irritated, finally said, "Seriously, Akbar?"

Akbar looked around the table. Farah and Rahul, Bela and Prashant's five-year-old son, were distracted by a toy car he was showing off. Bela reprimanded Rahul to finish his food. Everybody avoided looking at Akbar, except for Naseem, who was giving him the look again, eyebrows raised, urging him to shut up.

"You know these samosas, they are an Udaipur specialty." Akbar broke the silence. "Nobody makes them like we do. And I have eaten samosas in many homes, but I can bet nobody makes them better than my nani. But she is long dead now. May her soul rest in peace."

Prashant shifted his weight in the chair, and digging into his biryani he said, addressing Akbar, "My reference to Kashmir was meant as a joke, you know that, don't you?"

"Yes, no worries, Prashant, forget it."

"But I would like to know the real reasons, really. I hadn't imagined that you would have strong opinions on Kashmir. See, we can talk openly."

"Well, of course we should. I'm sorry for the way I reacted."

Prashant smiled. "Do tell us."

"Well, we should let Kashmir go because that's what the people of Kashmir want."

"But Kashmir is an integral part of India. How can we allow it to separate?"

"That is a misconception. At the time of independence, Kashmir's accession to India was conditional. A plebiscite was promised to let Kashmiris decide their future, but that never happened."

"There was so much political confusion at the time, and then the Pakistani insurgents launched an attack, and the Indian army repulsed them."

"And the Indian army has stayed put ever since."

"That is because of militancy and terrorism."

"Was Bhagat Singh a terrorist when he fought for freedom against the British?"

"No. I know where you're going with this, but it's not the same thing."

"It is the same thing, Prashant. The only difference is that we are now on the other side of the fence. India is to Kashmiris what Israel is to Palestinians. We are the occupier, the oppressor."

"Occupier. Oppressor. Really? I think you are getting carried away. What about Kashmiri Pandits, the Hindus who were killed and driven away and dispossessed?"

"Agreed, that was wrong. Kashmir belongs to the Pandits as much as it does to anyone else who calls it home. But please, let's not view it as a Hindu-Muslim issue, although it serves the purposes of realpolitik for both India and Pakistan to do so. It helps them keep the blood boiling on both sides."

Naseem looked at Bela and shook her head in dismay. "Prashant, your plate is empty," she said. "Why don't you take some more biryani."

"Yes, yes I will. Don't worry, I won't let anything come between me and biryani . . . not the least politics." He gave an empty laugh. Turning to Akbar, he said, "But you can't keep religion out of it."

"Of course, we can't, but religion is not the main issue. Azadi is. Freedom is. The majority of Kashmiris in the Valley happen to be Muslims. And my stand would still be the same if they were Hindus."

Akbar got up from the table, put his plate in the sink, and ran water over it. He came back and stood next to the counter with a glass of water in hand. "Come to think of it," he said, "this beautiful green blue Earth was given to us as one whole and wholesome gift. And what did we do with it? Drew lines on it and carved it into pieces. Countries, nation states, how artificial, how arbitrary is all this."

"But how could it have been otherwise?"

"I don't know, but it strikes me as a stupid way to live. These are not the dark ages you know. You just can't take other people's land by force and . . . "

"Well, Akbar, all this philosophical idealism sounds great. But . . . "

"There is no but, Prashant, no but. Why is idealism such a bad thing? Why this obsession with being practical? Perhaps we are where we are because we have shunned idealism from our lives. We are too busy genuflecting at the altar of practicality. Our culture teaches us to be realistic. And what does that mean? It means accept the conventions of life, accept its ethos, its structures, its divisions. Accept this fractured earth, accept this exploited land and its divided, miserable people who have forgotten how to dream. Accept everything as it is, because that is a practical thing to do. Idealists make trouble. Practical people become successful."

"Nice speech, but I would hate to burst your bubble. It is realism that's enabling us to enjoy this exquisite meal."

"But they are not mutually exclusive. Each has its place. The problem is it's all lopsided."

"Yup, and wanting balance itself is idealistic," Prashant chuckled, cleaning his plate of the last grains of rice. "The food was super-duper delicious, Naseem, thank you. And I can vouch Akbar had no hand in it. I didn't taste any idealism in there." He laughed.

Akbar affected to punch Prashant in the belly as he got up from the chair. "You son of a gun," he said, smiling. "Seriously, though, what would you do if you were a Kashmiri Muslim?"

"Enough, Akbar," Naseem snapped. "Now give it a rest." Looking at the others, she announced, "It's time for dessert. Guess what it is?"

The children shouted, "Ice cream!"

19

RUKHSANA BEGAN HER MARRIED LIFE in Boston with trepidation. She knew little about Shabbir except for his devotion to Mowlana which only increased with time. She had thought she could curb his zealotry with reason and dialogue, but he yielded to none. Her attempts to get him to trim his beard had fallen on deaf ears. He had ready answers to all her doubts and questions, and whenever he found himself cornered he invoked Mowlana as the ultimate source of truth. No further explanation was needed. She soon came to understand that Mowlana was the bedrock of his faith and he guarded him with a sensitivity bordering on paranoia. Even the slightest hint of disrespect for his idol would disturb him greatly.

As a software engineer Shabbir made good money and his skills were much in demand. They lived in a rented townhouse in Woburn, a twenty-minute drive from downtown Boston. He never attempted to own a house because that would require taking a mortgage and mortgage would entail interest and interest was forbidden by Mowlana.

Rukhsana had found America cold and aloof; she missed home. Shabbir was considerate and kind and, to dispel her loneliness, would take her for long drives in the evenings. On weekends, they would go downtown and walk around the city. They would often talk about India—she nostalgically about Mother and Sister, recalling the joys and the warmth of a small-town life; he critically of chaos and corruption back home, reminding her how lucky they had been to have escaped all that. He assured her that she would come to love America, she just needed to give it some time.

One evening when they were out on a drive, he casually mentioned that he had been aware of her liaison with Akbar, and that she was tainted already for having loved an infidel; that she should be thankful to him, and to Mowlana, for rescuing her from a life of heresy. She was shocked by the suddenness and the gratuitousness of his attack. She did not know what to say. What shocked her more was his tone of voice. There was the arrogance, the hubris of having done her a great favour and behind it was a thinly-veiled assertion of authority, as if he was warning her, laying down the law. He had not mentioned Akbar by name; he said "that infidel" contemptuously. It felt like someone had turned a knife into her heart. In that moment, she realized that there was a distance between them which could never be bridged. A sadness settled in her gut like a stone. Akbar's memory had been blurring with every passing year. How time had dulled the desire, and the pain of separation. It was because of Mowlana that she had lost him, and it was Mowlana again who was looming darkly on her marriage.

In Boston there was a thriving Loyalist Momin community. Shabbir introduced Rukhsana to his Momin friends and families and she had found them friendly; the women advised her where to shop for halal meat and told her where to go for discount groceries. Shabbir was well-regarded in the community, and although they all seemed to be besotted with all things Mowlana, Shabbir shone among them for the clarity and sincerity of his belief.

"Mowlana gave me a lifeline when the boat of my life was adrift," he told Rukhsana during one of their trips to the city. Rukhsana was new to the country, new to the orthodox Momin world by which she found herself surrounded, new to the marriage, new to Shabbir's zealotry of which she had only seen a glimpse, new to being called Sakina by everyone, and new to his demand for nightly sex.

One Saturday morning on a sunny spring day, they had taken a cruise on the Charles River and later strolled through Quincy Market in downtown Boston. For lunch he looked for a quaint New England restaurant that served halal food, which was like searching for a pork ribs joint in Jeddah. He settled for an Afghani restaurant called Darul Kabab. Over a sumptuous lunch of chicken tikka and Kabuli pulao, he laid his heart bare.

"The fact is, I wouldn't be here if not for Mowlana," he said earnestly. "When my parents divorced I was eight years old, my mother left my father. I later learned that she suspected him of infidelity; in fact he kept a woman in Kuwait.

"Mother took ill and died following a botched-up surgery. She was only forty. I had finished high school then, and father was visiting us from Kuwait when she passed away. I accused him of killing Mother; we had a big row. He told me get out of his house.

"That night I went to sleep swearing revenge, crying, and praying—pleading with God to help me. Then the unthinkable happened. Mowlana appeared in my dream. In his pristine white clothes, surrounded by angelic light, he spoke to me tenderly, with such love as I had never seen before. Or since."

Rukhsana felt a surge of sympathy for him and reached out for his hand.

Mowlana urged Shabbir to run away to Bombay and find refuge in his Zehra Auntie's house. When he awoke, he felt a strange calm. He had not cared much for the Mowlana before. He would pray only to God. The next day he escaped to

Bombay and began to live with Zehra Auntie, and enrolled in a technical college. Three years into the engineering programme Udaipur erupted into a revolt. Zehra Auntie sided with the Radicals, which was unacceptable to him, so during his last year of college he moved out of her house and lived as a paying guest with a Hindu family.

Rukhsana looked away, losing sympathy for him. She was all too familiar with the ugly business of renunciation. *Don't you guys have any shame? How can you disown your own family?* But she kept her thoughts to herself.

After graduation, Shabbir went to see Mowlana and related to him his story, how he came into his dream and how he had saved his life. Mowlana placed his hand on Shabbir's head and blessed him. Shabbir asked him what he should do next. Mowlana said, "Go to Amrika."

"And here I am," Shabbir said. "Life is good. Mowlana has been guiding me ever since. I went to see him before our marriage, to make sure I was marrying the right person."

"And?" Rukhsana asked in surprise.

"He blessed me and told me to be patient."

Rukhsana was not sure what that meant and didn't much care. She was perturbed by the way he had treated his aunt.

"So Mowlana is all important . . . he comes before family?" she asked out of irritation, even though she knew what he was going say.

"Yes," he said curtly. "Because of him I forgave my father. His love for Mowlana is pure, only later did I realize that. As for my mother, much that I loved her, she did not care about Mowlana and would have certainly become a Radical if she had lived. Being disloyal to a spouse in my eyes is a lesser crime. In my moral world, my father is a better person despite his indiscretions. I can no longer recall Mother's memory with the fondness I used to have for her. Ignorance makes you do stupid things. In a way, I'm glad she is no more."

"That's a terrible thing to say," Rukhsana couldn't hold herself back. "She was your mother, she brought you into this world."

"You won't understand," Shabbir said and gave her a flinty look. He left a ten-dollar tip in the check folder, grabbed the receipt, put it in his wallet, and made for the door.

That night for the first time Rukhsana faced his wrath in bed. He smacked her hard on her back and buttocks. She protested as she moaned in pain, not understanding what had suddenly gotten into him. He said it was just play, to perk things up. In the morning, he brought her tea in bed. Later that morning when Shabbir was at work, she called her mother.

"I want to come home, Amma," Rukhsana said on the phone. There was fear and sadness in her voice.

"What is the problem, jaana?" Zubaida asked.

Rukhsana said she was missing home, she was feeling lonely.

"It's a new country, you'll get used to it. Give it some time?" Zubaida said.

"No Amma, I don't think I can adjust to this place."

"Now don't be silly. It's been only a few months since you have gone. These things take time."

"You don't understand, Amma."

"Why, what is the matter, tell me? Is Shabbir not treating you well?" Zubaida asked.

Rukhsana did not answer. Then after a long pause she said, "Amma, I don't like it here."

She was ashamed. Her body felt sore and was still smarting from the beating. How could she tell her mother what had happened? She herself was grappling with the weirdness of it, the horridness of it. Her mother had so often saved her from her father's slaps, but now there was nobody to protect her. She felt scared and helpless and wanted to go back home, to her mother's lap. Zubaida told her that everything would be fine, that she had to be patient, that marriages require compromises.

Whenever she called home, her mother would advise her to hang in there. There is nothing that forbearance hasn't solved, she would say. Once you have children, you will have a reason to like the place. Months and years passed and Shabbir's abuses continued as retribution to her defiance, and he took care to camouflage it as a sexual game. She would protest and plead and beg him to stop not understanding how violence could ever be part of lovemaking. The very idea was unthinkable. He was strong and aggressive and would smother her with force and she would eventually submit, exhausted, defeated like a gazelle surrendering to the cheetah. The mornings after, he would be extra nice to her, and some evenings he would even bring her flowers.

Rukhsana was perplexed by his strange behaviour, by his duplicity, by his shifting attitude, by his unpredictability. She couldn't find a way to be tender with him in bed and absolutely dreaded having sex with him. There was no knowing when he would turn violent as part of the "play."

Rukhsana had a miscarriage in the first year of their marriage and Shabbir blamed her for not taking care of herself. Then when she got pregnant with Taha two years later she told him to keep away from her, and he had surprisingly complied. The pregnancy and the postpartum phase had been free of his sexual demands. Then when she was pregnant again with Taher, two years later, she made sure he made himself scarce again. Both the boys were named by Mowlana and Rukhsana had no say in the matter. She wanted to give them modern names but did not have the energy to pick up a quarrel with him.

Around that time, one morning she had been nursing the one-year-old Taher and thinking of nothing in particular. Then suddenly the penny dropped: Shabbir beat her whenever she challenged him or said something ill about Mowlana. She recalled all the incidents starting with the first one—the night following their trip to the city when he had told her his story. Everything fell into place. The flashback ran like a movie in her head. She was relieved and dismayed by the revelation. She kept herself occupied with the boys and on account of them kept Shabbir and his demands at bay. Now that she understood the motive of his violence, she had a better handle on him. She would ration sexual favours to him, making him at times desperate and restless. And on days when she called him out on his bigotry she would take refuge in her sons' bedroom and spend the night there. With the children around he did not have as much of a free hand as before, and Rukhsana learned to take advantage of it.

The Boston Momins organized Sunday madrassa for their children at a local community centre. About sixty Momin families lived in and around the county. At the madrassa, children were tutored to read the Quran, to pray namaz, and trained in the Momin way of life, the focus of which was the Mowlana. Every lesson began and ended with him. The Prophet Muhammad, his descendants, and the Imams were relegated to the background. The six-hour madrassa exhausted the kids. They came home drained of energy, in no mood to play or read a book; all they wished to do then was watch TV and go to sleep.

Rukhsana would often grill the boys about what they were taught. When asked who the greatest personality of Islam was, they replied, "Mowlana." And the second greatest? "Mowlana's father." They knew almost nothing about the Prophet of Islam. One Sunday Rukhsana woke up her boys with, "Come on, sweeties, go brush your teeth and wash your faces, it's brainwashing time." Shabbir was within earshot. The remark stung him. That night the sex was rough.

While the boys attended madrassa, Shabbir went to a religious class for adults. The classes were called halqa, into which a select number were admitted. The process of vetting these students was rigorous. Few could survive the onslaught of a dry esoteric doctrine. Those who persisted were revealed the hidden meaning (the baatin) behind the literal texts (the zaahir). They learned that the Quran was not meant to be read by novices—which meant ordinary Momins. A verse may have one obvious meaning for the masses, but its real import had to be learned from those authorized with the knowledge. In the absence of the Imam, Mowlana was that authority. He was the knower of the truth and the keeper of the faith. There were several levels to the halqa course; Shabbir had completed two levels.

Rukhsana asked him one evening, "What do you learn in your halqa?"

He told her one had to attend it to find out. "It is not a trifling matter that can be discussed in a casual conversation."

"But I'm serious, I really want to know."

"What I'm saying is that you cannot know just like that, and I cannot tell you just like that. We are taught sacred truths. Suffice it to say that without the purity of the heart one is incapable of understanding them."

"Maybe so. But why are these sacred truths kept under wraps? Why not reveal them to the world and let everybody benefit from them?"

"That would be like throwing pearls before swine."

"Well then, should one assume that these pearls have little value outside your charmed circle?"

"This reminds me of that old saying," Shabbir said, "what would a monkey know of the taste of ginger!"

"But the monkey wants to acquire that taste. Let's put it this way, how do these sacred truths profit the believers?"

"You have the wrong notion about the whole thing. We are talking about faith, not a balance sheet. There is no profit or loss here."

"Fair enough, but faith cannot be without purpose?"

"The purpose is the hereafter."

"So there is a benefit, then. And is the hereafter assured?"

"Hold on to the rope of Mowlana, and he will lead us to paradise."

"But that is not true, Shabbir," she said. "Nobody can guarantee paradise."

Shabbir looked at her with pity, but she knew that inside he was seething.

"You know, incomplete knowledge is a dangerous thing. In any case, there is no point talking with you on this."

Shabbir had gotten used to her line of argument which harped on Quranic teachings but completely ignored the Mowlana. He put this down to the typical myopia of the uninitiated. Her cussedness infuriated him, but he had found a way to give it back to her. And that gave him much satisfaction.

One Saturday on a warm summer day, Shabbir went to Lowe's and brought home a club hammer. Earlier that week

Mowlana had enunciated a new fatwa: get rid of Western toilets. The Indian-style squatting version—dubbed Noorani toilets—had found special favour with him. They were cleaner, he had decreed, and therefore the commodes everywhere must be demolished. In cities across the globe, local priests visited Momin homes with iconoclastic fervour, armed with a hammer, breaking down latrines. Rukhsana had tolerated many such pious absurdities, but this was the limit—she was furious when Shabbir took the hammer to all the toilets in the house.

"So how people shit is also Mowlana's business now," she wanted to say but held her tongue. She could not understand how an educated person who seemed so rational and practical in other matters could be so gullible. And he was not an exception. In the United States and Canada, many Momins, bright and brilliant doctors, engineers, and businessmen grovelled like imbeciles before the mullahs and were keen to do Mowlana's bidding no matter how ludicrous it happened to be.

When not consumed by his obsession, Shabbir was a loving father and as a family they would go to the movies and the parks on weekends. There were many community events, too, in the greater Boston area, to which they went. But Rukhsana had not been able to make friends with any of the Momin women. Their lives mostly revolved around ritual and ceremony which she did not mind but found it suffocating to be immersed in it all the time.

For her religion only mattered so far as it gave her a grounding, an identity. It was something she was born into and she took it as her cultural inheritance. She was not religious in a formal sense but observed important occasions such as Ramzan and Moharrum the way the girls of her generation were brought up to do. Growing up, Mowlana was a remote figure who lived in Bombay and did not impinge on their daily lives in any significant way. As she grew older she developed a deep sense of the sacred and found peace in praying namaz in the mornings. For her it was akin to meditation. During the month of fasting, she became very devout and followed all the tenets meticulously. When out with the congregation at the mosque or at religious gatherings she wore the hijab and blended in, performing all the rituals. Her sympathies remained with the Radicals. Like them, she thought that the cult of the Mowlana was against the very thing Islam stood for—idolatry. On the sly she had read the articles and books by Kaiser Ali Mistri and other progressive scholars of Islam, and had come to accept their points of view. Islam was not about personalities; it was about justice and doing good deeds; Allah had exhorted believers to read and to reason.

But for Shabbir, Mowlana was the living manifestation of Islam. With his halqa classes his faith only grew stronger. He started hosting religious ceremonies at home, and Rukhsana went along with grudging enthusiasm. The Momin world was the only social realm she knew, and the pressure to conform was not just from Shabbir but from others also. Every family tried to be holier than thou, wanting to outdo each other. Ironically, in Udaipur she did not have to attend every majlis and marsiya and had more freedom as long as her mother was able to shield her from her father. In Boston, she found herself steeped in orthodoxy, hosting and attending functions, running from one ceremony to another clad in hijab, pretending to be a devout Momin. Her own beliefs she kept to herself. Her conformity set in gradually and she did not realize when she had lost sight of the promise she had made to herself about charting her own path, about being her own self.

Even as she rued her vanishing individuality what troubled her more was that her two sons were being indoctrinated with the execrations of Mowlana-worship. She did not want them to become like their father. At dinnertime whenever Shabbir was out or when she drove them to school she would engage the boys in a discussion about religion and God and the meaning of life. She was determined to expose them to a world outside the orthodox circles. A year before she had developed friendship with a couple of Radical families from Udaipur. She had met Sharifa at the Farmland store in Woburn and recognized her as being from her hometown. They started talking and soon she had been calling upon them unbeknownst to Shabbir. Sometimes she would take the boys along with her and they would have a chance to see how "normal" Momin families lived.

At the local library, she had started volunteering in the mornings when the boys were in school. There she met housewives and working mothers and talked to them about books and children and careers. She met women who had gone back to college after raising their kids and had made successful careers for themselves. She envied them. She began to talk to people and made friends outside the confines of the community. Her social circle widened and became diverse, but deep down she remained lonely and sad. She sought different ways to fill her time and occupy her mind but none would give her the peace her heart craved.

At home with Shabbir and the boys her life had fallen into a domestic rhythm of a busy immigrant household. An uneasy peace existed between Shabbir and her. Yet there were lucid moments when she felt empathy for him and for his simple, uncomplicated faith. At the core, he was a decent person and could even be amiable as long as she kept her mouth shut about Mowlana. But then there were occasions when she would be provoked and get into an argument not caring about the consequences. Her artifices to dodge him didn't work all the time. Shabbir's retaliation would follow at night without fail like Newton's third law. She tried to curb his aggression by warning him that she would tell the boys, but he would just ignore her, knowing she would be too embarrassed to talk about it. At such moments, angry and desperate, she considered leaving him but she felt alone and helpless in the vast, alien country. She had no intimate friend to talk to, and even if she had she would never have divulged to them the horrid details, she would die of shame. One time she felt extremely depressed, and when she found no help and saw no hope she went to a psychiatrist who prescribed her anti-depressants which offered only temporary relief.

Her mother was wrong; patience was no panacea for one's problems. It makes one meek and powerless. She talked to her mother and sister on the phone once every few weeks, and sometimes poured her heart out. Zubaida had run out of words to comfort her. All she would say is, "This is our kismet, jaana. I had your father and you have Shabbir. I don't know what sins we have committed." And then she would start sobbing and Rukhsana would end up comforting her.

20

AKBAR'S FLIGHT FROM KUWAIT HAD landed at Ahmedabad airport in the morning, and he was on his way to Udaipur in a luxury Volvo bus, a type very much in vogue in India at the turn of the new millennium. He had never been to the Middle East before. Kaiser Ali had been invited to a conference there, and upon Moiz's urging Akbar had decided to accompany him and spend a couple of weeks with his cousin and make good on a promise made long ago.

He had found Kuwait clean, modern, and hot. The flashy cars and swanky malls impressed him much despite his Spartan proclivities. The Kuwait Tower by the sea was imposing and beautiful; tall office buildings rose proudly proclaiming the immense wealth the city state had found below ground. This obscure desert outpost had come a long way from its Bedouin past, though partly on the backs of foreign workers. It had pained Akbar to see Indian, Pakistani, and Bangladeshi labourers being treated like slaves, working long hours under the fierce desert sun, and housed in crowded and filthy labour camps, eight men to a room. But if you asked these men how they could endure such harsh conditions, they would reply that it was better here than back home; in India they were free but you can't feed children freedom.

On one occasion, he was caught in a sandstorm and had emerged from it bathed in dust. Moiz said it was their monsoon, in the desert it rained sand. Moiz seemed to have done well for himself. He owned a shop selling attar, traditional perfumes made from the extracts of flowers and herbs. He carried only high-quality, all-natural concentrates packed in small ornate bottles. He was satisfied with what he had accomplished. "Besides," he said wryly, "I am serving humanity by making the Bedouins smell better." The two cousins had a good time catching up. Udaipur came in the conversation many times and Akbar informed him that the Radicals were strong and committed to the struggle, and since they controlled and managed mosques and centres, the Loyalists had nowhere to go. Mowlana had done nothing for his faithful flock. Moiz was part of the Radical group in Kuwait, and they regularly collected funds to send to Udaipur for use in running schools and clinics.

The high-chassis Volvo with plush faux-leather seats and tinted windows was a bit of an oddity for the pot-holed Indian roads. He was aware that Gujarat's new chief minister, Narendra Modi, was serious about developing Gujarat, improving its infrastructure, particularly the roads, and taking its economy to new heights. Modi was also allowing violence against Muslims to be taken to new heights.

If a court date had not been set over a property that had belonged to his father and, unattended, had been occupied by a real-estate mafia, Akbar would not be travelling to Udaipur in this season of death. Akbar felt queasy and was only thinking about the state of the roads and the economy to distract his mind from the unspeakable blood-curdling carnage that had taken place a few days before. The immigration officer at Ahmedabad airport, on seeing his name in the passport, had sneered at him. "Why do *you* katelas come back to *our* country?" he had said, using a pejorative term, "cut-ones," meaning those who were circumcised. Slapping his passport on the counter, he hissed, "Why don't you stay with those fucking Arabs?" Akbar pursed his lips and swallowed his rage. What was an insult, he surmised, compared to the mayhem that was taking place?

On Kuwait Television's English channel he had heard the reports of women paraded naked and gang-raped. Many were molested in front of their families; men and women were tortured and quartered. Children were made to drink petrol and set on fire, pregnant women were raped, their foetuses gouged from their wombs. After every atrocity came the final one—burning the victims alive. The news anchor was moved to tears as she read the news. His stomach had turned. As in all sectarian violence, analysts wrote in the newspapers, the Gujarat pogrom was preplanned and aided and abetted by the police and the administration. A week before in Godhra, a city east of Ahmedabad, a train coach had been set on fire. Fifty-nine Hindus, including children, returning from Ayodhya, died in that dreadful incident. The tragedy was blamed on Muslims. The Ahmedabad massacre was the revenge. Modi, the chief minister, had allegedly instructed the state machinery to allow things to happen. Nearly two thousand people, mostly Muslims, were slain. Tens of thousands became homeless.

When Akbar emerged from the airport, he thought he smelled blood in the air. What a mind-numbing tableau of horror the city had staged against its Muslim denizens. *Could this ever happen in Udaipur? But then, why should it happen here, or anywhere else for that matter.* Two weeks out of India had given Akbar a new perspective, a detached way of looking at things. The distance made him fonder of his country but at the same time it also accentuated her flaws. It pained him to see right-wing Hindu groups adopting the worst aspects of organized, hide-bound Abrahamic religions. Militancy and fundamentalism had no place in Hinduism. Yet the virulent ideology of Hindu nationalism was driving ordinary people into extreme forms of bigotry. As for Muslims, and Islam itself, his interaction with Arabs had only confirmed his long-held suspicions. He found the Kuwaitis arrogant and spoilt. There was nothing Islamic about their behaviour—they were rich and wasteful, having taken their staggering privileges for granted. Treating foreigners with contempt was deeply ingrained in them; they called Indians *Hindi miskeen* (beggar Indians). And if you told them you were Muslim, they laughed in your face. "You Hindi have no business being Muslim. Islam was meant for Arabs," Yusuf Alyan, Moiz's business partner, once said in an argument with him. "Arabic, the language of the Quran, is not your language. Stop this pretence."

Recalling that exchange, Akbar felt a strange sense of uprootedness. Was his bond with the land of his birth defined solely by religion? Did the native air he had been breathing count for nothing? Did the soil of the land that roiled in his blood amount to nothing? His grandfather had told him that he had opted to stay in India at the time of the Partition even when his own brother and other friends chose to migrate to Pakistan. Did his grandfather's loyalty to the land count for nothing? But it was also true that the language, the history, the culture, the ethos and the other motley baggage that Islam carried was alien to the sensibilities of the land of his birth. Even though Muslims were of the same racial stock as other Indians, born and bred in India, and buried on its land for countless centuries, their faith marked them out as different in so many ways. Their holy places were in other lands, their prophets were from another culture. Their folklore was foreign, the stories they told their children were of unfamiliar people and places, the myths that gave meaning to their lives came from alien traditions. Their God spoke to them in a strange tongue. Even as they faced toward Makkah when they prayed, they seemed to be turning their backs on other things. In affirming something foreign, were they denying something indigenous, something natal? Their hearts and minds were rooted in India, but their faith harked back to a distant land. They lived on this land but revered another as holy, as sacred. *Is this why Muslims' loyalty is always questioned?*

But it was also true that Islam enjoined believers to be loyal to the country they lived in, and Muslims were as faithful to India as anyone else. And yet as a Muslim he had to prove his patriotism all the time; anything that he said or did which did not agree with a dominant "Indian" sentiment was viewed with suspicion. But a Hindu—even someone who assassinated Mahatma Gandhi—was always Indian by default, his patriotism never under question. People worshipped all sorts of gods with impunity, but the moment you brought Allah or Jesus or Moses into the equation, your Indianness became suspect.

Lost in these thoughts, Akbar suddenly realized that it had been an hour since he left Ahmedabad. He felt a little safer now that the epicentre of the carnage had been left far behind. He surveyed the bus to see if he could identify any Muslims. *Strange how religion is not written on one's forehead.* He looked again. And sure enough there he was, a man in Momin garb—topi, beard, and white kurta-pyjama—sitting across the aisle three rows behind. Was he from Udaipur? Akbar could not tell. *What is wrong with him, is this man stupid? Announcing his religion to the world. These are not normal times. You can't go around pretending everything is okay. No, everything is not okay, you stupid man.* He felt like going up to him and telling him to get rid of his topi, but how would that help? His beard and clothes were a dead giveaway.

Through his tinted-glass window Akbar could feel the warm March sun. He saw the passing green fields and trees. How indifferent nature was to human enterprise; a silent witness to their sorrow and happiness, to their enduring folly. A milestone zoomed past, announcing "Ratanpur 25 km." That dusty village was on the border of Gujarat and Rajasthan. *Once we cross into Rajasthan I will truly feel safe.* Just then the bus came to a screeching halt. He looked outside; it was not a bus station. There was no human habitation as far as he could see. What could it be? Perhaps it was a shepherd crossing the road with his herd, or a lazy stray cow blocking the path. Then he heard shouts. He stood up and craned his neck to look outside. He stopped breathing. Fear caught his throat, and his heart started pounding.

A number of men with saffron bandannas tied around their heads and crimson tilaks on their foreheads, shouting cries of "Jai Sia Ram!" were banging the sides of the bus with their hands and sticks. Some were armed with swords reflecting the bright sunlight menacingly off their naked blades. There was an insistent banging on the door. "Open the door, you bastard," came the shouts. As the conductor opened the door, two men got in. The first one, who appeared to be the leader, pushed the conductor with violent force, sending him reeling to the floor.

The leader was a swarthy, muscular man in a loose saffron shirt; he sported a full, luxuriant moustache twirled and arched at both ends; a crimson tilak looked like a gash on his forehead. He kicked the moaning conductor and told him to shut up. Then he came halfway down the aisle and cast his eyes at the back and front, studying passengers' faces. "If you are a Hindu," he said softly, "you have nothing to fear. But if you are a miyakda," he thundered, "I am your Yamraj. Consider it your last day, you Paki-loving renegades. Pray all you want, you bastards, your Allah will not come to save you today."

His sidekick, who stood near the door, brandished his sword up in the air, ripped an edge of the seat near him, and poked the weapon into the stuffing, causing it to spill out. The passenger on the seat recoiled in panic, disturbing the baby in the lap of the woman next to him. The baby started bawling. "Shut him up!" he yelled. Then, taking a step forward he announced, "Any katelas on this bus? You better stand up now! Or if we find you," he paused, "you will cry out for the many fathers whose illegitimate dog you are." He ran his eyes up and down the bus. The leader started moving towards the back of the bus. He held a cleaver in his hand. With its iron blade he raised the chin of an old man and guided his face sideways. "My name is Radhe Shayam, I'm a Hindu, brother," the man stuttered. "Please spare me." On his wrist were threads, red and yellow, talismans typical of a Hindu.

The leader let go of his chin. Then he raised the cleaver for everyone to see. "You know what this is?" he asked. "This is what miyakdas use to murder our cows, our sacred mother. Today I will use this to chop these haramis, these bastards, to pieces." Akbar caught him looking at him and lowered his gaze, muscles tensing in his neck. *This is the end.* He remembered Naseem, Farah, Mother. And Rukhsana, surprised that he should think of her, as well. He said a silent, quick, ardent prayer. The next moment he felt the cold metal blade under his chin. He looked up and was met with a sombre face, cold eyes.

He wore a silver ring in his right ear. His thick moustache covered his upper lip, and its hairs touched his broad yellow teeth when he opened his mouth. Akbar realized with relief that he was not wearing the attar Moiz had been dousing him with in Kuwait. Attar was a Muslim thing, and one could smell it from afar. The leader turned the sharp end of the blade under his chin and gave it a light jerk. "What is your name," he asked in a voice hard as steel.

"Ak . . . Ak."

"Tell me your name, bhenchod."

"Ak . . . Akaash."

Akbar closed his eyes. He didn't want to see, didn't want to know what was going to come next. A few moments passed. The pressure of metal on his chin eased. When he opened his eyes the leader had moved on towards the back. Akbar started breathing again. His thoughts immediately went to the Momin behind him, his brother in faith. He turned his head cautiously to look at him. Thankfully, he had removed his topi, but that might not be enough. It seemed the leader had noticed him already and was taking his time to get to him, increasing his agony with every passing second. Finally, he reached his seat and slapped him across the face. The sound of it rang through the bus.

"Madarchod, didn't I tell you miyakdas to stand up?"

The man stood up, a youngish fellow, his hair matted down and bearing the imprint of the cap he had been wearing. The white kurta hung loose on his lanky frame, as though from a scarecrow. Trembling with fear he said, "Brother, brother, I'm not Muslim."

The leader slapped him again, "Motherfucker, lying to me? Come out here." He caught him by the collar and dragged him out in the aisle. Outside, the mob continued the chant: "Jai Sia Ram, Jai Sia Ram!"

"You're not a miyabhai, ugh, what do you think I am, an idiot?"

"I'm a Momin, brother, not miyabhai."

"Momin? What the hell is that?" He turned to his sidekick and asked, "What is Momin?"

"They are Muslims all right, a different caste, just like we have Brahmins and Baniyas."

"You heard that, you . . . " the leader said and slapped the man again.

"Please, please, brother, don't hurt me. I'm—I'm going to get married," the man blurted out, his body trembling, eyes filled with fear, pyjama wet.

Akbar wished he could do something as he looked on helplessly.

"Oh, getting married, and then kuchi-kuchi," the leader moved his middle finger like a piston, and guffawed. "All the more reason to make mincemeat out of you, you *Momin*." He looked around the bus and grinned. "Actually, we will be doing Bharat Mata a favour. Fewer little Momin bastards running around. Didn't you termites get your separate fucking country? Why the fuck are you still here?"

"Please, brother, let me go."

Akbar cautiously looked around. The other passengers were too frightened even to breathe, let alone say anything to intervene, to stop this atrocity.

"Brother," a clear voice rose from a back seat.

The leader shoved his captive aside to see who had dared to speak.

"Brother, don't do this," said an old man. His head was

shaven. He wore a saffron robe and held a wooden staff in one hand, obviously a Hindu priest or a mendicant, a man of God. Akbar saw a ray of hope.

"You keep out of it, maharaj," the leader warned.

"Brother, this—this killing is not our culture."

"Not our culture? This is dharm yudh, holy war. Lord Krishna urged Arjuna to kill his own cousins, his brothers. But this," he said, pointing to the Momin, "this harami is the enemy."

"No, brother, no. Nobody is the enemy. We are all children of one Paramatama, one supreme being. Please let him go. Why kill an innocent man? Ours is the land of ahimsa. All life is sacred to us."

"Oh please, maharaj, don't you talk of ahimsa. All this mess we are in is due to that impotent Gandhi and his stupid philosophy."

"Please, brother, don't do it, I beg of you."

"Enough, maharaj, cut it out before I lose my temper."

The old man fell silent.

The leader pushed the Momin with his elbow. "Come on now, it's time to meet your Allah."

The man groveled. "Please brother, let me go."

The leader kept pushing him forward. Then he told him to stop. He caught the man by the collar and pulled him close to his face. "Say, Jai Sia Ram."

"Jai Sia Ram," the Momin said weakly.

"Louder, bastard."

"Jai Sia Ram," the Momin repeated, raising his timorous voice, almost crying in fear, hoping maybe this was his chance.

The leader pushed him forward towards the door. "Come on, come on, keep going."

The sidekick, who was blocking the door, made way for the Momin to pass and then placed the point of his scimitar on his back and pushed him hard. The man gave a sharp cry and stumbled out of the bus. Akbar closed his eyes and sent up a silent prayer.

21

"IT WAS A SIGHT TO BEHOLD," Shabbir said as he unpacked his bag and removed the dirty clothing to be washed. Rukhsana quietly listened as he enthusiastically related the details of his trip. He was trying to impress on her how large and genuine a following Mowlana commanded. "Have you seen the pictures of Makkah, Muslims doing the tawaf of Kaaba? The scene was similar to that. Thousands of Momins circumambulating Mowlana, with undivided devotion. It is not for nothing that Mowlana is called Haqiqi Kaaba—the Real Kaaba."

Rukhsana was in the kitchen sautéing onions for lamb curry, and was alarmed by the comparison he made but did not say anything. His naïveté, his childlike wonder was at once touching and pitiable.

"And you know what the highlight of the trip was? Mowlana shooting an elephant. I saw that with these very eyes. It's a once-in-a-lifetime privilege."

Shabbir had been away for three weeks, on a tour following Mowlana from Bombay to Dubai to Tanzania. Over the past several years Moharram had become a time for an annual gathering of Momins from around the world. Followers in various cities would plead with Mowlana to bless them with his presence, and then thousands would converge on the chosen city, while its Momins felt like they had won a spiritual lottery. The first ten days of Moharram for all Shias are a period of mourning for the martyrdom of Imam Hussain. For the Momins, though, it had now become a time of travel, sightseeing, and shopping. They were encouraged to close shops and take leave from schools in order to participate in the pilgrimage. That year in 2007 Mowlana had also added a hunting adventure in Tanzania.

———

The vast Tarangire National Park shimmered yellow and brown in the sun. The dry season had leeched the green out of the Tanzanian grassland; the majestic baobab trees dotted the endless acres that ran off the edge of the earth. Shabbir held a hunting rifle, it was heavy, and its polished wood and metal felt good in his hands. It was a .416 calibre Remington Magnum. He was on a game safari with Mowlana, a privilege only a few Momin could ever dream of. A Momin called Qasim Nurbhai had invited him to the expedition. Shabbir had befriended Qasim when he visited Boston some years before.

Qasim was about the same age as Shabbir but looked much older. Wide of girth and dark of skin he had distinguished himself as the most generous devotee of Mowlana south of the equator. Everybody knew him, and Shabbir was thrilled to have made his acquaintance. Prior to the hunting safari they were in Dubai, where thousands of Momins had congregated for Moharram ceremonies. From there a select group had followed Mowlana to Nairobi, Mombasa and then to Arusha, Qasim's hometown in Tanzania.

Shabbir had donned a flak jacket over his full community attire and was perspiring profusely. He was Mowlana's hunting caddy. The sun was blindingly hot and his palate was parched but he was in a state of ecstasy. He could not believe he was walking the same ground as Mowlana. But what had freaked him out was that Mowlana actually recognized him.

"How is it even possible," Shabbir exclaimed to Rukhsana. "Mowla told me 'Are you not the same child who dreamt of me and came to see me?' I was speechless. How does one respond to a miracle?"

Shabbir called his sons over to the kitchen table and resumed his story. They had camped not far from the Tarangire River and for three days roamed the grassland looking for game. The white safari guide, Jonathan, motored them around in a hatch-top safari jeep. Shabbir, standing up, his head popping through the roof, marvelled at the beauty and vastness of the savannah. Zebras and wildebeest tramped around in herds and at times were only a few feet from the vehicle. Giraffes, tall and lanky, with their odd languid gait had fascinated him endlessly. On the first day, when they came across a gang of buffalos, Mowlana shot one in the head and then posed for a photograph resting the butt of his rifle on the animal's head. Its great horns were magnificently curved. The second day was uneventful. They had returned to camp without incident. In the evening, a baby goat was roasted over a spit. The meat was soft and succulent and Mowlana was so pleased he sent his compliments to the cook. On the third day the Mowlana's son Mukammal Fakerudin sat in the back of the jeep. He complained about the heat, and admired how his father at ninety-five was fit as a fiddle.

Late afternoon Jonathan spotted a herd of elephants in the distance. He and his flunkies started preparing for the shoot. A bench-rest was set up for Mowlana and he trained his gun. Shabbir and Qasim and the rest of the entourage lay prone on the ground a few paces behind, holding their breath. The breeze whispered. The sun blazed. Jonathan adjusted Mowlana's gun, and several seconds passed. Then the shot rang. Shabbir saw

Mowlana recoil, as his assistant behind him cushioned him. Jonathan looked through his scope. He said the shot was on target. Then he fired several shots until the bull fell to the ground. The rest of the herd trotted off.

The hunting crew burst into jubilation and started high-fiving. Shabbir and Qasim ran towards Mowlana and kissed his hand and then fell to the ground at his feet. Others followed suit. They shouted victory slogans.

As the party drove towards the fallen animal, Qasim sat beside Jonathan in the front. "You know that elephant is blessed," Qasim said proudly, addressing Jonathan. "To be shot by our Mowlana is the highest honour any creature can aspire to. Its place in heaven is assured." Shabbir sitting beside him nodded, and when he looked at Jonathan he saw him stifle a snigger.

On reaching the dead elephant, everyone was awed by its size. They skittered around it excitedly, and then lined up behind the carcass for a photograph, some resting their feet on the torso. Jonathan clicked the picture.

Shabbir took out the photos from an envelope and placed them on the table. "Look," he said. Rukhsana walked over and nodded in appreciation. Taha and Taher exclaimed awesome, awesome as they riffled through the stack. "I want to enlarge this one and frame it," he said pointing to a photograph in which Mowlana stood smiling, rifle in hand, flanked by Qasim and him, the dead animal in front of them lying in a heap like an overturned mud hill.

Following the hunting success, Qasim had hosted Mowlana at his new home in the leafy suburbs of Njiro in Arusha. Qasim's family, the Nurbhais, had made their wealth from sisal. Momins and other trading communities had come to East Africa with a nose for business, seeking to make fortunes. Momins had done well for themselves. The Nurbhais were known for their philanthropy and had established schools and orphanages, not just for the benefit of Momins but for all communities.

Qasim's father, Qurban Hussain Nurbhai, was well-respected in Arusha and was a prominent Momin elder. The current Mowlana's father, Shatir Kaifudin, during his visit to East Africa in the fifties had ordered all the rich grandees to shut down their charity establishments. Overnight schools, orphanages, and endowment trusts were either disbanded or taken over by Mowlana. Qasim said that it was a masterstroke—Mowlana was consolidating charities everywhere so that they could be properly managed. Qasim's father had surrendered his establishments, but two prominent Momin families—the Karimjees and the Jivanjees—flatly refused. "Imagine, saying no to Mowlana. The lust for money can really go to one's head sometimes," Qasim remarked to Shabbir. "They were excommunicated; serves them right. And our people, even though they had benefited from these families, immediately cut ties with them, and cursed them." After a pause, he added, "Our people are the best. Their loyalty to Mowlana is like a rock."

Qasim had recently constructed a palatial mansion in Njiro and invited Mowlana to come and bless it. Mowlana arrived at the house in a procession with crowds lining up the street. Qasim helped Mowlana out of the car and led him to the plush living room, where a throne-like chair draped in silk counterpane was waiting to receive him. A red velvet pillow was placed as a footrest. When Mowlana was suitably ensconced, Qasim got down on his knees and kissed Mowlana's hands, knees, and feet. He then placed a Manila envelope on Mowlana's lap. "My

Master, please accept this pitiable gift from this pitiable slave."

The envelope contained the title deeds to the mansion. After the maghrib prayer, Mowlana was brought out to the pool-side where a chest-beating session was held. Men and women stood around the circular pool in concentric formations and thumped their chests. Beating the chest for the Shias is a ritual reserved for mourning the martyrdom of Imam Hussain, but Mowlana had proclaimed that every day was Ashura (the day of Imam Hussain's martyrdom), and so Momins had started beating their bosoms everyday on every occasion, happy or sad.

The banquet was held by the poolside. At one end of the pool stood a catering station and on the other Persian carpets had been laid for Mowlana. The floor and walls of the pool were made of golden and white tiles instead of the traditional blue. It was made to look like an upside-down Momin skullcap.

When Mowlana was seated for dinner, Qasim came and knelt down before him and kissed his hands and knees. Then he presented him with a bag containing fifty-two thousand American dollars. This gift was for blessing his humble abode and accepting to break bread with him. He sat beside Mowlana, feeling out of place, like a pauper among princes.

The lights had come on as dusk fell. Series of lights in primary colours had been strung everywhere and they danced and gyrated in a mad psychotic frenzy. When the dinner was announced, the servers waded through the pool from the other end, holding aloft platters of food. Their skullcaps were studded with glowing little lamps. They splashed through water back and forth causing much cheer and delight among the guests.

After Mowlana's departure, Shabbir had stayed back in Arusha at Qasim's for a few more days. He was not sure what impressed him more, his host's affluence or his readiness to part with his wealth for Mowlana. His money flowed like a stream, and Mowlana was the ocean with which it merged.

The morning after Mowlana left, the two friends faced towards Makkah and prayed and then pounded their chests for a few minutes. They took breakfast in the backyard under a mango tree. A cool morning breeze grazed the surface of the swimming pool, and the sun picked up the golden tiles on its walls, reflecting iridescent, blinding fractals. Shabbir blocked the glare with his arms and squinted. As they washed down mandazi and barazi with hot tea, Shabbir proposed the idea of doing a walk for the long life of Mowlana. People organized walks for all sorts of causes, for Momins what better cause could there be than Mowlana's health? Qasim jumped at the suggestion and it was decided that the following year on Mowlana's ninety-sixth birthday they would walk the distance between Udaipur and Bombay.

———

Taha and Taher were now into their teens; soccer and baseball and video games kept them busy outside of school and studies. They had completed the madrassa course, despite Rukhsana's cavilling, and were well-versed in the Momin faith and rituals, though they were not as enamoured of the Mowlana as Shabbir had hoped. Their mother had taught them Islam's core values of justice and peace, the fairness and simplicity of the Prophet, and had read to them Maula Ali's advice to the faithful, *Nahjul Balagha*. She had instilled into them the maxim that it is principles that matter, not personalities. The boys—otherwise typical American teenagers—began to understand their mother's point of view.

Rukhsana was satisfied about how they had turned out. When they were in middle school and did not need her caring all the time, she enrolled for a graduate course in Communications and Marketing at Bunker Hill College. Shabbir had at first said no, telling her that he was earning enough for all of them, and in any case women should not be working. But she had insisted and enlisted the help of her sons to make a case for her. Shabbir had relented. Taha and Taher were happy for their mother, and this little exercise in solidarity reminded her of her own early years when she and her sister and her mother would often convoke to win concessions from their father. What a stubborn man he had been and how he had crushed her heart. If she lacked confidence today it was because of her father. He had broken her spirit. Before that it had been Sister Amelia and before that, the trauma of circumcision. One after the other her spirit, her sense of self-worth had been under attack. And then for too long she had been confined to home and community in Boston, coping with Shabbir's erratic, mercurial behaviour.

When she started going to college she found herself woefully inadequate and timid compared to the other women, who were confident and self-possessed. She made friends with women of all backgrounds, and learned that sexual violence even within a marriage was a punishable offence; that there were many centres in the city which provided legal help and marriage counselling for the victims. This new knowledge gave her hope and courage. American society was progressive after all and had made laws to protect women. Emboldened, she was ready to confront Shabbir the next time he enacted his "play". And it so happened that the following week at breakfast he announced that he had planned a trip to India to walk for Mowlana's long life. The distance of five hundred miles would be quite a feat, he proudly added.

Taha, who was having his cereal, wondered how that would help Mowlana.

"It is like a prayer, an act of penance," Shabbir explained. "Allah hears the prayers of those who make themselves suffer."

Taha looked unconvinced. Rukhsana kept quiet, and when the boys had left for school, she told Shabbir not to go, that the idea seemed ridiculous. "Even the boys are questioning it."

"It's better we don't talk about this," Shabbir said with that hardness in his voice. Rukhsana knew what it meant.

That night he disrobed her and told her to lay on her stomach. And as he began to slap her, she quickly turned over and caught his hand. "Stop it Shabbir!" her voice was calm even though her heart was timorous. What she said next she had practiced all day, preparing herself for just this moment. She steeled herself, took a deep breath, "If you touch me I'll call the police."

"You . . . ," Shabbir trembled with rage.

"You thought, I did not know what your 'perking up things' was about?"

"So this is what they are teaching in college?" he said through gritted teeth.

Rukhsana ignored his comment, and mustering the last remnants of her courage said, "I just want you to know that you have been committing a crime against me for God knows how long. And it stops today, at this very moment."

Shabbir grabbed his pillow and went outside, and for several nights after slept on the couch in the living room. Rukhsana did not miss him. When he finally returned to bed he made it clear that she should not mistake this as a licence to do whatever she pleased; that Mowlana and the community were still integral parts of their lives. In his voice, she found the face-saving bravado of a man who knows he has lost control. Rukhsana left him alone, and ironically did not feel the need to challenge him on Mowlana, now that she had an upper hand. She continued to attend community events but now had become more discerning and would participate in only important ones like Moharram and Ramzan, the ones which gave her spiritual fulfillment.

Her social circle expanded further when she started working. On finishing college, she had found a job as a media associate at Nimbus Investment Group in downtown Boston. She became close friends with two co-workers, Sandra and Audrey, and would often go out with them on a girls' night and to an occasional spa in Cambridge. She started moving out and about beyond the Momin circles and began to regain her self-confidence, began to rediscover her old intrepid self that had been lost under the layers of fear and domesticity and despair. She observed the other women, how they held their own when dealing with men. She too began to assert herself, express her opinions. She picked up reading again with a vengeance and started reading widely. She learned how to cope with racism and proudly held forth on her culture and religion with her coworkers. She told Sandra and Audrey that although Islam had given women unprecedented rights the men had made sure to keep them under their thumb. One extreme example of it was female circumcision. Her friends were horrified to hear of it.

Rukhsana enjoyed going to work and applied herself with energy and dedication. Her hard work was rewarded and she began to climb the ranks. In a few years, she was promoted to the role of a media consultant and her duties took her to different cities across the country. When she was outside the mosque and her home, the Momin world seemed like an anachronism—distant, insignificant and backward.

———

As Rukhsana spread her wings, Shabbir regretted the decision of having allowed her to study and work. In her increasing independence, he only saw irreverence and defiance. Over the years he had tried the nightly "play" to control her but nothing seemed to have worked. On the contrary she had turned it around against him with legal threats. He would have considered himself fortunate if he had a wife who shared his piety and devotion. In that he had been unlucky. She had even poisoned the minds of the boys. They showed no particular passion for religion or for the Mowlana. All those countless Sunday trips to the madrassa had come to nothing. But even in her new defiance, he found something positive. It was a test of his faith. The more defiant she was, the more zealous he became. When he felt alone and besieged, he found strength in his beliefs. Hadn't he learned to hold tight to the rope of Mowlana? Hadn't he been made privy to the secrets of the Quran? Hadn't he been taught that common folk with their simple beliefs were ignorant of the inner truths of the faith? Didn't he know that Mowlana was the keeper of those truths and would surely lead the true believers to paradise? Above everything else, wasn't Mowlana his personal guide? This last intimate truth became the cornerstone of his impregnable faith.

On Mowlana's ninety-sixth birthday, Shabbir and Qasim

arrived in Udaipur for their walkathon. They started off with much fanfare, the local media in attendance. A ceremony was held on the dusty grounds of a sports arena. Local dignitaries were invited, and Loyalist Momins came in large numbers. The Noorani Guard band played regulation tunes, and white balloons, symbolizing peace, were released into a cloudless pale sky. A local businessman had arranged for fifty-two white doves to be released. They soared heavenward, heralding the message that the world was safe and secure under Mowlana's stewardship. Full-page ads were taken out in the morning papers, displaying pictures of Mowlana and informing readers that two NRIs (Non-Resident Indians) were undertaking an arduous walk for their spiritual father. Much was made of their foreign status. It was held out as a source of inspiration. If these well-heeled foreigners could come to India and walk for Mowlana, then it behooved the natives to do more.

When a reporter asked how this long trek would further prolong Mowlana's life, Qasim and Shabbir looked at each other, unable to comprehend.

"You have to have faith," Shabbir said, and that seemed to settle the question.

A large crowd followed the two men, the band playing ahead of them. Bystanders stared with puzzled amusement. Wearing brand-name sneakers with their traditional Momin garb of white kurta and pants, the two friends walked side by side. With garlands of jasmine and red roses around their necks, they could have been a gay couple in a marriage procession.

At Delhi Gate the traffic was stopped to allow the parade to pass. The crowd followed the two friends till Goverdhan Vilas, after which they were on their own, except for a Maruti car that followed them, carrying water, food, and other supplies.

———

Rukhsana was fairly active on Facebook and had gotten in touch with long-lost friends from school. One day she came across a comment by Akbar Zaki. She felt a little quake in her heart. It was *her* Akbar. She was surprised to be still claiming ownership over him after twenty-odd years; this one was in his forties and married with his own separate life. He was wishing happy birthday to a mutual "friend." His profile picture bathed in a shadow, showed only a part of his visage. He seemed to be holding back a smile. His hair were short and neatly combed. Should she message him and say hello? She toyed with the idea for a second and then decided against it. How he had faded away in the mist of time. Now he was there once again. A stranger.

Old memories—the haunted house, the daily hour of intimacy—came rushing back and with them bitterness and regret. If only she had not been such a coward. If only she had stood her ground. But she had feared her father. He could have done anything. Even killed her. She discovered that Akbar worked for a book publisher, and Khatun Auntie had married Kaiser Ali. She had no idea that he had advanced in his career; that he was chief editor and wrote for Indian journals, and had joined Kaiser Ali in the crusade against the clergy and wrote articles on Momin issues.

The literature put out by the Radicals was out of bounds for Loyalists; they were forbidden from reading anything that issued from the pens of the infidels. With the Internet, though, things had opened up. In the privacy of their homes, Loyalists could readily access the profane material on Radical websites. And Rukhsana avidly read Akbar's articles.

22

AFTER MUCH VACILLATION AKBAR DECIDED finally to write a book. One fine day he gathered his fears, his hangups, his sense of inadequacy, and his excuses and made a bonfire of them. He felt a new resolve, a new energy coursing through his veins. Possibly, he thought, he would break no new ground, maybe he had nothing new to say, but no one could say it the way he could. The uniqueness, the voice, the perspective would be his own. And that was reason enough to write. Perhaps not many people would read him, but he must write for himself, get it out of his system, unburden his soul.

Religious belief had always fascinated him. The moral teachings and philosophic heights of a religious faith were often undercut by faulty logic; its fantastic claims and inherent intellectual weaknesses were fodder for the unscrupulous and the cynics to manipulate them. More often than not a faith got hijacked by the dishonest and the crooked, who slandered its immortal message for power and profit. Then what was it about a religion that despite all vulnerabilities it still held such power over the minds of men and women?

Akbar took up on his friend Farid's advice and applied to various universities in the United States, pitching for a research grant so he could write his book. He made a case for the study of Islam and its particular weaknesses that lent themselves to exploitation. He outlined the themes of the book, the topics and angles he would cover, and the salient concerns that would guide his research. He would use the major libraries in the country, whose holdings were more extensive than any library in India. He was convinced that his work would make a significant contribution to the understanding of Islam in the current, post-9/11 period. He worked hard on the application, detailing the importance of the subject and its relevance to a world rocked by terror, where Western powers led by the US had laid waste to Afghanistan and Iraq. In reaction, Islamist terror groups were on the rise. Islam was being invoked by evildoers and do-gooders, and none was the wiser for it. Akbar proposed to sift through the morass and dispel the myths purveyed by both sides. He explained how the academia—not to mention the world at large—would benefit from his findings.

Despite the strong case he made for his project, all he received in reply were rejection letters. Some were curt, others encouraging but without offers. Finally, almost a year later when he had no hope left, there came an email from Columbia University in New York City awarding him a one-year grant. In exchange for a stipend and some standard benefits, he would have to work as a research assistant in the Department of Near Eastern Studies.

When he broke the news to Naseem, she was happy, but then the prospect of living without him dawned on her and she looked a bit dismayed.

"A year is a long time," she said.

"It will pass just like that, Nas, you won't even know it. You have your work, then there is yoga and your paintings."

"Yes, I know, but still, me and Farah alone."

"You're not alone. Mother is here. She can come and spend the weekends with you."

"Yes, yes, let's not decide all the logistics right away."

"I'm not deciding anything, it's just a suggestion."

"I know. I'm sure we will manage. Let's not spoil the good news with mundane matters. It is such a fantastic opportunity."

When Farah heard the news, she said she wanted to go, too.

"No, jaana, not now. Let me see how things work out," Akbar said. "Maybe you and Amma can come for a few weeks. I hear it's really nice there in the summer."

Farah, now all of fifteen, made a face and stomped out of the room. The two looked at each other and smiled the indulgent smile of parents who know when their child is acting out.

———

In early autumn the following year, Akbar landed at JFK airport in New York City. The sky was overcast, and an overnight chill still clung to the morning air. On his way to the campus he was stuck in traffic. Cars and concrete structures dominated the landscape. So this is America and these are the Americans. How is this different from any other busy city? Do these people have any idea what havoc their government and their corporations are wreaking around the world? How would they? Poor souls, they are too busy making ends meet. The media tells them that America is great and good and it needs to send out its armies to the four corners of the world to do good, to spread freedom and democracy. And they believe it. That's how people are everywhere, they believe the stories told to them in the name of their tribe or country or God. And if you have a different story to tell nobody will hear you, your voice will drown in the cacophony of lies.

It took Akbar a few weeks to adjust to a new life. The autumn cold reminded him of Udaipur, where temperatures could fall to a few degrees. In Bombay winter was a rumour, and he never felt the need to wear a sweater. He found Americans frank and friendly, as he had expected them to be. Things were systematic; people had civic sense, they cared for the places where they lived and worked. They actually threw garbage into trash bins. They were addicted to coffee. He missed his home-brewed tea. Dipping teabags in hot water was not the same thing. He had rented a studio apartment on 110th street. From his twentieth-floor window he had a commanding view of Central Park.

He found it odd at first that students addressed their teachers by their first names. And still odder when he saw parents being addressed similarly. In India these were sacred relationships that demanded respect, even reverence. But then this culture was not burdened with the formalities of traditional societies. Although he admitted that there was a certain charm in showing respect to your elders, he began to like the casual and democratic ways of the Americans. They implied equality. It wasn't that they did not respect their seniors; it was just that they expressed it differently, with a casualness free of pretences.

Akbar enjoyed his morning walk from his residence to Low Memorial Library, where he did his research and writing. It was time for self-reflection. He drew his gaze inward and tried to cut out the noise and scenery surrounding him. He would repeat to himself "I am," and the "I" was not this body, not this mind, it was the silent eternal witness. But invariably he would be distracted. The dogwood, honey locust, and ginkgo trees along the campus paths were aflame with colour. *How can consciousness not be caught up in such beauty?* Such vibrant hues he had seen only in calendars. He had never believed they were real. He chuckled at the memory, as he crushed the dry leaves under his new winter boots. His advisor, Adrian Jones, had told him to be prepared for the winter. "It carries a wallop," he said. "It will make you run back to India, but if you plan to stay and deal with it, buy a good jacket and a good pair of boots. It's worth the investment."

On Thanksgiving Day in late November, Akbar slept in late. He thought of Naseem and Farah; he had spoken to them the night before using a prepaid phone card. He told Naseem he was managing well foodwise cooking simple meals of daal, rice, chicken and vegetables; he hadn't found a good place to buy meat from. There was an Indian grocery half an hour's bus ride away in Lower Manhattan, though he preferred to walk there every two weeks. It was slovenly and unkempt, just the way it should be, reeking of back home. He bought vegetables and supplies, including loose tea and spices. He liked New York. "But I don't think I can live here," he said. "It's too bloody cold."

On her part, Naseem said it got lonely on weekends and that Farah was missing him.

"And you?" he asked.

"Me what?"

"Do you miss me?"

She said nothing, but he knew she was smiling at the other end. She was not the demonstrative type, but in the silence he fathomed a longing. He missed her. He missed the warmth of her body at night.

When he got out of bed it was past nine-thirty. He opened the curtains and what he saw took his breath away. It was snowing. White flakes were falling like confetti, unhurried, in languid grace. It was like love at first sight. Nature was putting up a spectacular show, and he didn't imagine he had seen anything more beautiful. He stood there for a long time transfixed, contemplating the miracle, trying to be one with it. It must have snowed all night. The earth below him was blanketed in white. This was another calendar picture from his childhood, now coming alive. He wanted to pinch himself.

He made a cup of tea and came and sat by the window. The aroma of the tea was soothing. His breath clouded the glass pane, and he drew a smiley face on it with his finger. He blew on it and it vanished. *Rukhsana lives in Boston. It must be snowing there, too. It's not far from here.* The other day he had sent her a "friend request" on Facebook. He had done it on an impulse. Since he was here, it made sense to connect. Maybe they could meet. They had their own lives, but couldn't they be in touch as friends? She had not responded to the request. Perhaps she didn't see it the same way, and rightly so. How would she react if she knew he was in her neck of the woods? Does she even remember him?

He logged on to Facebook on his laptop and she hadn't replied. He wished he hadn't sent the request.

———

Rukhsana's heart leapt to her throat when she saw Akbar's message. She wanted to accept it immediately, but then stopped herself. Where could it lead to. Why was he reaching out? It was a long time since they last saw each other, when he returned home after his father's death. And suddenly now, out of the blue, why? What was his intention? What to do? Four days passed in anxiety and indecision. She went through the motions at work and at home, those same questions nagging her. If this was her condition now, she feared to imagine what it would be like if she actually chatted with him online.

Another thought kept assailing her mind. Hadn't she hurt him already? Why hurt him again by ignoring him? *And it is Akbar, for God's sake, the person without whom life was once unimaginable. Oh, that night under the stars.* That seems like another life. He did not deserve her indifference. But at the same time, she should not read too much into his overture. Perhaps she was overthinking it, there was nothing to it after all. Following the Thanksgiving long weekend and after a nerve-wracking internal debate, she went to the office on Monday, opened Facebook on her computer and pressed the Accept button.

She waited nervously for his next move. She checked out Akbar's Facebook page again. His "wall" had links to his articles and a few pictures of himself. She stared at his family picture for a long time. She knew Naseem; they had been in the same school, she was one year her senior. She felt a pang of envy. Their daughter looked lovely, she detected hints of his features in her face. The picture was probably a few years old. And there he was, smiling without showing his teeth as was his habit. He had put on a little weight, and his hair was not the thick mop it used to be; streaks of grey peeked here and there. The same religious impasse still separated them, she thought, recalling how he had come to the rescue of her mother in Sadikot. They were so close to realizing their dream. Then suddenly it was all over.

———

Was it her proximity? Why was he obsessing about Rukhsana after all these years? Her silence did not bode well. What did he expect. Maybe she had not seen the request. She must be busy.

He had spent the entire weekend by himself. He went for long walks in the afternoons, the snow having been cleared from the sidewalks. It was cold, and it was quiet. What a contrast to the clamour of Bombay streets. Here one could hear oneself think. And the thought that rattled in his brain was, *why is she not responding?* With every passing moment hope melted away. The pristine white beauty around him was now tinged with melancholy. The world couldn't get colder.

Monday morning, he walked to the library, carefully step-ping over slush and puddles. It was a warm day, the sun was out, and the gloom of his mood had lifted. He was glad to be out. Seeing humans cheered him. In India people were in your face all the time, but here you had to go looking for them. India had an abundance of all the wrong things: pollution, noise, people, corruption. Among all its ills, population was the big-gest. Just too many people. And India was the country whose attitude toward sex was anything but promiscuous. How could so much prudery result in so much fecundity? He smiled at the thought. Yet it was the land of Kamasutra and the Khajuraho. *Oh, the eternal contradictions of my dear motherland!*

His student Megan saw him from across the street and waved at him. He waved back cheerfully. It's a new day with new possibilities, he said to himself. After all, the world doesn't turn on its axis for nothing.

The Low Library reminded Akbar of the Central Library in South Bombay. They had a similar colonnaded structure out front and evoked the same old-time grandeur. Inside, Akbar sat in his usual carrel by the window, soaking up the warm glow of the sun. He turned on his laptop. She had accepted his "friend" request. Suddenly he felt uneasy. What next? He messaged her: "Hey, long time no see. Just to let you know that I'm in New York City, at Columbia University on a one-year fellowship."

He waited. No response for ten minutes, although he noticed that she was still "online." On her page he saw her pictures: with family at gatherings, with friends, at birthday parties. In some she wore the Momin hijab. She still looked the same after all these years. America had been treating her well. Shabbir in his beard and traditional outfit looked older than his age. His arm was around her shoulder. He felt a vague sense of envy.

———

Akbar in New York? She was not sure she had read it correctly. My God, is this a joke or what? Nervous and excited, she felt dizzy. The office around her became a blur. When the information sank in, she got up and walked to the kitchen to get a drink of water. Her eyes glazed over, the office seemed to be in a whirl, and she held the countertop to steady herself.

Audrey, her friend, asked, "Are you okay?"

"Ugh!" She appeared confused. "I'm fine," she said listlessly. If only Audrey knew how her past was suddenly cartwheeling back to her; the person whom she had taken a long time and a great distance to forget was once again knocking at her door, stirring up the memories and dreams that had long been embalmed and buried.

She went back to her desk and told herself to breathe calmly. "What a surprise, can't believe you are in America," she texted. They chatted for a few minutes, catching up on family, parents, life back in Bombay, Udaipur. Their past sat between them like a live, dormant animal. Both could feel its presence, and both tried their best not to touch it.

The next day and most of the time thereafter he initiated the chats, each time questioning, wondering if he was imposing himself. She responded dutifully. Over time they fell into a routine, chatting three or four times a week during her lunch hour. They talked about his American experience, his research, her work, her boys. When he asked about her life, she responded with a "rolling eyes" smiley. He did not press further. The conversation was teetering close to disturbing the hibernating creature. And it soon did, when a few days later he couldn't hold himself back from asking, "Are you happy?" After a pause she said, "I could have been happier." He thought he understood what she meant. It was clever of her to answer in such a vague and open-ended way.

When Rukhsana posed the same question to him, he could not lie. He said he was happy. Naseem and Farah meant the world to him. Naseem was a good partner, a good friend, they had their ups and downs, but who didn't? Still, he admitted to a void. He couldn't put a finger on it, but there was something lacking. The syntax of his life was near perfect, words in right places, well-punctuated, grammar proper, sentences nicely structured. But somehow in the reading of it, the inflection was ever so slightly off-key.

Rukhsana was amused when she read that. It was typical of Akbar, hiding behind verbosity. That's what he used to do when he was not sure of himself. He could have just said, like her, that he could be happier. It wasn't that he was not content with his lot, but deep down, unconsciously, he must yearn for her. The life he had missed. That was the emptiness he struggled with, but he could not bring himself to articulate it. After all, what was the point? Life had created solid, immovable walls around them. They were not the only people denied their dream.

Despite the caution and reservation in their chats, an intimacy became implicit, an affection harking back to the old times, to the haunted house, to the easy rapport, to the dreams they had nurtured. The intervening years and their separate lives had kept them apart and adrift, but as they chatted the old affinity eased in and along with it the sense of ownership they once felt. They began to claim each other, solid realities not-withstanding. Rukhsana, as she had feared, found herself more vulnerable partly because of her guilt. She had always blamed herself for their breakup. When she confessed how weak and submissive she had been, how she failed to stand up to her father, Akbar tried to console her. As a daughter to a fanatical, callous man she could have done nothing.

She opened her heart to him, telling him how she had been trapped in the community merry-go-round for the longest time and how she had struggled to stay afloat. Things are much better now that she had started working, still, keeping her sanity was a constant challenge. Akbar admired her resilience to have made it so far. But he had no idea how badly she was affected. How she had grappled with loneliness and depression. How she had been punished for speaking her mind. God knows what he would make of it if he found out. She would die of shame. She would never tell him.

———

After his Tanzania trip with Mowlana, Shabbir's devotion had acquired a sharper edge, hobnobbing with Mowlana had inflated his ego, made him more supercilious. Rukhsana had long given up on calling him out on his absurdities. As long as he did not harm her she did not care. And that suited him just fine, for he too had given up on her. They lived under the same roof but inhabited different worlds. As a family they had never taken a vacation, had never had a fun outing in a long time. Work and friends filled her time, kept her occupied and distracted but none gave her the satisfaction, the contentment that comes from deep within. There were always random moments of depression and she could never figure out what triggered them. Her sons were now big boys on the verge of going to university. They gave her a tenuous fingerhold to her life's meaning and worth. But such moments were fleetingly short and rare. The boys would soon have their own lives to live. A gloom had gathered inside her. Until Akbar came back.

———

One day as they chatted she told Akbar she wanted to meet him at least once before he returned to Bombay. She said she had forgotten how he looked, how he sounded. "I want to meet you" became a constant refrain. "You're so close, only a few hours' drive, surely we can meet. We must meet," she said. "I travel often for work. I can use that as a pretext to get away for a few days. Let's go to Berkshire Hills. It is beautiful out there in the spring. You can drive up north. You have an international driver's licence, don't you?"

"Yes, I have. I've driven quite a few times, but of course not in the city. The traffic here scares me, pedestrians and cyclists all over, even though it is a lot more disciplined compared to the chaos of Bombay. But back home you get used to the madness, there's a method to it. Everyone takes care of themselves and you learn to operate on that principle. Traffic in our country is free and democratic. And just like in all fake democracies, those who wield power—the cars in this case—ride roughshod over all the rest."

Rukhsana imagined the chaos and smiled at the memory. It had not taken long for them to settle into an easy, unselfconscious familiarity they had left behind. The jokes, the taunts, the playfulness came back unbidden. Their chats began to be peppered with name-calling and in equal measure were salted with declarations of love. There was an undercurrent of intense yearning—said and unsaid—that pulled them closer. His physical distance from home and her emotional distance from her husband encased them in a bubble, a meta-life detached from circumstance.

Before long they started talking on the phone, since online chatting, they both agreed, was too impersonal. She longed to hear his voice. She wanted to know all about his life after they had been separated. She told him how she had discovered his articles on the internet and read them surreptitiously. She felt a vague pride in reading them, even though she would often disagree with his point of view, his stubborn socialist tendencies, and oh, his biting, unbearable cynicism about everything.

"Has anyone told you how pessimistic your writing is?" she asked.

"No, not until today."

"Well, now you know. Where does all this negativity come from? You offer no hope—nothing ever makes you happy."

"Maybe I expect too much of the world. Wherever I look, it falls short of the way it should be. Take a close look at our cookie-cutter lives. We think the same thoughts, speak the same phrases, laugh at the same jokes, our dreams are the same, and so are our prayers. We are being steamrolled into flat and one-dimensional beings. It's disturbing, this terrible sameness of things."

Rukhsana could relate to it all too well. She had seen it in her own lifetime how Momins, once a diverse and variegated people, had been cloned to look and behave like robots. She had been living and breathing in the terrible sameness of things. And if that banality was not enough, she had had more than her share of the weird and the violent too. But she had never felt angry at the world. Maybe at Mowlana, but in the end, she had come to accept her fate as a will of God.

Now with Akbar again on the horizon she wondered if this were another divine signal. She was thrilled to be in touch with him again but she knew it would not last long. His commitment and his life were elsewhere. And who is to know if he were still the same Akbar of twenty years ago. He moves in a different world, his concerns are literary, intellectual; there's little that's common between them except their past. Had they been married she would have been more like him, or perhaps more like her real self, bubbly and cheerful and full of vim. How much she had changed. And how she had allowed herself to change. A regret coursed through her body like a spasm.

"Do you ever think of the old times?" she asked wistfully.

"Yes, of late. Beautiful memories they are. It happened such a long time ago that you wonder if they were real at all."

"Yup, time plays tricks on your mind, but . . . "

"But what?" Akbar asked.

"But I would rather have the reality than just memories, no matter how beautiful."

Akbar remained silent.

Then after a pause she asked, "What happened to all *our* poems? I mean your poems. You could have at least mailed them to me."

"Well, you know how it all ended so suddenly. And I didn't see the point."

"Hmm, I want to read them. Hope you have not thrown them away."

"I wish I had. They were quite juvenile, if you ask me. They should never see the light of day."

"I'm saying I want to read them. You will bring them when we meet. Okay?"

23

In the communal kitchen at a meditation centre, a couple of old women residents were methodically preparing breakfast. One of them knocked over a box of walnuts, spilling them on the floor. Akbar rose to help her clean up, but Rukhsana motioned him to stay put. They watched her as she swept them into a dustpan and threw them in the garbage. The two of them, brought together by a mysterious quirk of fate, sat at a corner table and sipped tea.

They had met the previous evening at the retreat in Glastonbury after months of yearning; so much trepidation, hesitation, and guilt had gone into that decision. He had arrived before her. It was a beautiful spring day, sunny and bright. In the early evening the grounds were enveloped in silence, sprawling into the woods. He could hear a stream running nearby. He walked around in eager anticipation, trying not to imagine what it would be like to meet her after such a long time. *When did I last see her? Twenty years?*

She was running late, she texted. He sat by the stream, taking in the sun, listening to the unhurried water dancing over rocks and pebbles. Squirrels scurried up and down the trees. He spotted a cardinal on a branch chirping, apparently calling out to his mate. Then he saw her walking toward him. They smiled. He rose and walked a few steps to meet her. They held each other's hands. Her hands were warm and not as soft as he had expected. He pulled her ever so lightly to hug her but she resisted. So many months of wasted sighs had at last found culmination in that moment. She wore a white linen shirt and blue jeans. Her shoulder-length hair was loose, swept carelessly; a few streaks of grey peeked rudely here and there. She looked stylish with the sunglasses. She always had a sense of fashion, he recalled. She had put on a little weight, but was still attractive, and desirable, after all these years.

He removed her glasses and looked into her eyes. She met his gaze and smiled. Her eyes were moist, with faint shadows under them. He mumbled something about the impossibility of them meeting again, trying to be poetic and profound.

She was more down-to-earth: "After all these years, haan!" She put her hand on his belly.

"What is this?"

"A sign of prosperity," he said.

They laughed. In the distance to the east were guest cottages. The sky was clear and blue and the sun was waning, deepening the calm around them. Except for the trees and invisible birds and an indifferent stream nearby, nobody witnessed their hesitant, awkward reunion.

She held his hands close and looked at them as if she had not seen a man's hands before. They walked aimlessly in the woods, lost in conversation and bewilderment, not believing their luck. When the twilight began to creep in, they decided to drive to a nearby town and get something to eat. It was Sunday evening, but the main street was still abuzz with activity.

After dinner at a pizza joint, when they came out night had fallen. The weather was balmy, pleasantly warm with a gentle breeze caressing their faces. She took his hand and they walked to the far end of the street. They crossed over to the other side and sat on a stone bench at a street-side park. It was a typical small-town garden with a cenotaph dedicated to war heroes.

There was a large gazebo behind them, and a fountain on one side and a huge tree on the other, the branches of which reached out and formed a canopy over the entire park. "What tree is this?" he asked.

She looked closely at the leaves and said, "Oak."

He pulled her closer and wrapped his arm around her waist, feeling the supple warmth of her body under her shirt. She smelled exquisite; her perfume had delicate undertones of heaven. He gave her a light peck on her lips. "Please don't," she said. He did not press, but held her close. They sat there for a long while watching the street at the far end and talking softly. She rested her head on his shoulder. "I can't tell you how happy I am to see you," she said. "You haven't changed that much except . . . gained some fat and lost some hair," she smiled and ruffled his hair.

"And you have become more charming," he said.

"Flattery will get you nowhere, Mister," she retorted.

Back at the retreat their room had two single beds. He sat on one of them and watched her going about her things—taking out the toiletries and clothes from her carry-on bag and preparing for the night. She went outside to the common bathroom and returned wearing a printed knee-length nightie. They had not talked about how they would spend the night and his heart thrummed with trepidation, guilt and excitement. She had spurned his advances all evening, and it was just as well. Naseem was tugging at his conscience. He gathered his things and went out to take a shower. He came wearing pyjamas, drying his hair with a towel. She was sitting propped up against a pillow on the bed reading a book, a white bedsheet covering her legs. She closed the book when he entered. "It's late," she said "and I am tired." She had started early that day, worked till lunch time and then had driven for three hours. To Shabbir and the boys she had said she was going to Albany on business.

Akbar said he too had a long day and would like to turn in. He stood next to her bed and looked at her, then he leaned, took her face in his hands and kissed her on the forehead and said good night. He opened the window and a breeze wafted in carrying a scent of jasmine. A nightstand separated the two beds. He switched off the table lamp. The two lay quietly with a distance of three feet between them. "I can't believe we're here," she whispered. They turned on their sides facing each other and talked. Akbar holding back the urge to get up and cuddle her. He felt restless torn between love and loyalty, yet he talked calmly and haltingly not betraying his emotions.

Rukhsana wanted to reach out and hold his hand. She had not encouraged him earlier that evening and was not feeling good about it. But how could it be otherwise. They were both married with children. She thought of his wife and his daughter and wanted to do right by them. Besides, it was just wrong. Her religion had condemned it as a sin. But despite all the inhibitions the desire was strong and she was battling it determinedly. She had loved nobody else. The affinity that she shared with him was special and exclusive. Sex with Shabbir was a chore and many a time a punishment. She had never known real physical, sensuous love which she had imagined she could only find with Akbar. And here he was, just a hand-stretch away.

Soon Akbar nodded off and started snoring and she listened intently to the wheezing and whistling of his breath. For a long time she lay awake caught between her heart and her scruples. So much was at stake. She did not realize when she slid into slumber. When she awoke it was still dark and for a split second she could not tell where she was. Akbar was still sleeping. She quietly traipsed to the bathroom to relieve herself. Upon her return, she stood between the two beds for a moment contemplating, then she lay down beside Akbar. He stirred and scooted a bit to make room for her. He wrapped his arms around her and sighed. "Come closer," he said. She moved. "Closer still." She tightened the embrace. They did not stir for what seemed like an eternity. Their breaths mingling, their bodies fusing, their hearts pounding.

He grazed his lips over hers, softly, teasingly. Then he kissed. First gently and then gradually tongued his way inside. She responded with purpose, pushing her tongue into his mouth, taking him by surprise. They kissed hungrily—passionate, and sloppy at times. As he kissed her face, he was generous with the tongue, leaving a patina of saliva. She lunged back and protested. He smiled, half embarrassed, half amused. In his defence he extolled the virtues of the tongue and its uses. "A woman," he said, "can work wonders with her tongue—when she is not chattering, that is." That was a deliberate salvo to rile her. She did not take the bait but laughed instead.

In that mirth all their guilt and hesitation melted away. His hands and lips probed, she submitted gratefully, responding to his every touch, every gesture, moulding herself as though she was clay and he a potter. In a cramped bed, in a pre-dawn stillness with the stars spying on them through the window they made love for the first time. Then they slept foetus-like in each other's arms. When he awoke the room was bright with sunlight. She was beside him, eyes closed, sweet and vulnerable, breathing deeply. Slowly she stirred, and they kissed languidly. Their mornings had never been sweeter. Neither of them had opened their eyes to so much joy. She said she could hardly sleep, first out of anxiety and then out of joy.

The intimacies of the night still clung to their bodies as they drove up north to Greenville, a sleepy village in the Berkshire hills, where they had rented an apartment to spend the next two days. Neither of them wanted to think how far they had come, what impossible boundaries they had crossed. Their being together was at once an act of subversion, love, betrayal. Despite their good sense, here they were, blessed and cursed by fate, destined to be happy and sad. They made no mention of what had come to pass. The earth should have shaken, but it did not. How natural and organic it had seemed. As if they had been gravitating towards each other just for that purpose, just for that moment of singularity. That it was always meant to be.

But their new-found bliss was not without blemish. A deep sense of guilt nagged them. Akbar would suddenly fall silent for long moments, his conscience weighing him down. Every time he thought of Naseem he felt like a cad. He had fewer reasons than Rukhsana, in fact, no reason at all to be betraying his wife. When he had sent a "friend" request to Rukhsana, he had not imagined that it would culminate into this crisis of conscience. He had always thought of himself as an upstanding, responsible, and moral person. He bristled at the injustices of the world. Now here he was, cheating on his wife. He was ashamed of himself, yet he felt powerless.

Rukhsana drove, and he would navigate, fumbling with printed directions, losing them on one occasion at a grocery store, creating a minor panic. Far from Udaipur, in the middle of an American countryside, the unlikeliest of places, they were living out the dream they had cobbled together as teenagers. They could not kiss and touch each other enough. He would play with her gold bangle, feeling its unadorned smooth texture, and she would take his hands, caress them, and push back the cuticles of his nails.

The country road was scenic; spring foliage was in full bloom. Occasionally a car would zoom past from the opposite direction, and he would caution her not to speed. She said she had always imagined that when they met, she would start a big fight, just to see how he would reconcile. "Making up after a fight," she said, "is the sweetest thing between lovers. But there is no time for all that." Life had not given them that luxury. With what little time they had, they did not need a falling-out to bring them closer. He reached out to touch her neck with the back of his hand and played with her dangling earring.

"Why are you so desirable?" he said.

She gave him a look a man could die for.

A ramshackle car, stripped to the chassis, lay on the side of the road with a "for sale" sign on the windshield. The villages they were passing through seemed poor and forgotten. Some of the houses had certainly seen better days, paint peeling off from the sidings, roofs weather-beaten, yards unkempt, junk scattered all over. Faded plastic toys, broken swings, abandoned half-torn tires, rusting bicycles—remnants of lives crushed by the march of time and a heavy-footed economy.

"This is the underbelly of America the world does not see," Akbar said. Before the conversation could turn into an argument about the rich and poor, about personal responsibility and public policy, they reached a quaint little town and he started fumbling with the directions.

It was time to do some grocery-shopping for the evening and have lunch. She pulled up into a parking lot in front of a supermarket with a sign saying "Kelly's Super Mart" in big bold red letters framed by a yellow border. They were greeted by heat and humidity as they stepped out of the car.

"It never used to get so stuffy in the spring before," she said, adjusting her sunglasses.

"Thanks to global warming," he said knowingly and detachedly, like he knew exactly who to blame, and he certainly was not one of them.

They bought salmon, mushrooms, a green pepper, and shallots. The salmon didn't look too fresh in the Styrofoam-plastic wrapping, and he wondered if it would keep until they put it in the fridge later that afternoon. He also added some fruit and a six-pack of beer to the cart.

"I won't drink that," she said. "Maybe a sip of wine."

"In India," he said, "nobody much cares for wine." Beer and whiskey were preferred libations. In Momin homes, though, Radical or otherwise, alcohol was anathema. With her friends Sandra and Audrey, she had tried a red a couple of times. She didn't take to it with any degree of enthusiasm. More than the taste she liked the idea of drinking it. It gave her a certain thrill, a sense of defiance against Shabbir and his exaggerated pieties.

"Alcohol is not good for you," Akbar teased. "It makes you age faster."

"Oh, you should take your own advice then," pat came her reply. They were in the checkout line, he carried the grocery basket. In it was a bottle of wine instead of the beer. "You know," she confided, "before we got in touch again, I used to think life was too long, and actually I did not mind dying, if death came quietly, painlessly. But now I have a reason to live, I don't want to die." She nuzzled her face into his shoulder.

Out in the parking lot, the midday sun was sharp and so bright that it hurt their eyes. They drove around the main street and found a restaurant to have lunch. It was large and spacious, tables set apart offering privacy. The furniture was unremarkable; the red-and-white chequered tablecloth stood out. The waitress was young and pretty, and he eyed her. Rukhsana glared at him in turn.

On the road again, he turned on a ghazal CD on the car stereo.

"You still into ghazals?" she asked.

"What do you mean *still*? Can one ever tire of ghazals? I bet no romantic love can be complete without ghazals. No other language can be sweeter than Urdu."

"Right, it is known to cause diabetes, doctors are advising against it," she mocked, and then reached out to take his hand, as he smiled shaking his head in pretend disbelief.

Their destination was still one and a half hours away, and they were in no hurry to reach anywhere. The two-lane country road once again opened up to a scenic landscape. Open glades and farmlands alternated with thick wooded patches. For long stretches the road was lined with trees on either side, with a thick undergrowth of fern, clover and wildflowers. They seemed to be the only ones on the road. Suddenly she swerved the steering wheel, giving the car a violent jolt, and then smiled at his shocked, annoyed look. "You are so childish," he protested. She laughed.

"Will you miss me?" she asked. "Once you're gone, what would become of me, have you thought of that?" she said half-accusingly, her voice sad and wistful. "You're cool as a cucumber, nothing affects you. You tell me nothing, what's on your mind, what's in your heart."

Akbar took her hand and gave it a gentle squeeze. "You think it would be any easier for me?" But he knew he was being disingenuous.

"There's a world of difference between our circumstances, you know that." She peered out, removing her sunglasses to determine the house number. "But why worry about that *now*? Here we are!" Her voice brightened up, even as she fluttered her eyelids to hide the tears.

They pulled up in an unpaved empty space adjacent to a two-storey building, its white paint peeling off, on the windows black shutters rickety, glass panes dusty and loose in their frames. The ground floor once housed a telegraph office and was now a makeshift museum displaying artifacts from its not-so-eventful past. It was four in the afternoon, and the sun was still beating down hard. Musty air assailed them as they entered through the main door. The apartment on the second floor was large and clean, and had a tacky, homestead-like feel about it.

A combination of the heat, a large meal and a long drive had made them languorous. After taking in the apartment and giving it their general approval, they went to the bedroom, removed the white covers and crashed. He took her in his arms, pulled her closer, and they kissed until he dozed off. She could not sleep for a long time. She propped her head on her hand, elbow digging into her pillow, and watched him sleeping. His breath rising and falling, the shape of his eyebrows, his nose, his lips, his hair greying in places, and his body at rest, completely lost to the world. She looked at him and wondered, *What am I doing here? This strange village, this apartment, this bed and Akbar and I in it, together.* Something was so right and also so wrong with this picture. She knew all too well what was wrong. The wrongness, the stupidity, the idiocy, the preposterousness, the outrageousness of this whole crazy thing had been haunting her. In moments when she was not occupied by his presence, enthralled by his closeness, a mixture of guilt and doubt had been tormenting her. A million times she had questioned herself, and a million times she could not bring herself to do the right thing.

Except for the sound of his heavy breathing and the noise inside her head, it was quiet. The window by the bed was wide open, light and breeze floating in. In the lawn across she stared at a huge elm, sturdy and proud, its branches spreading out to claim the whole village. A swing tied to a lower branch rocked. The joy of being here, with him, alone, overwhelmed her. She knew it was ephemeral, and wanted to live in the moment, and wanted to keep the real world out, the moral world out, banished, as long it lasted. Soon she too dozed off.

When he awoke, he found her by his side, looking at him. "Didn't you sleep?" he asked.

"Not much," she said. "You were snoring, it disturbed me."

"I snore?" he asked in mock surprise.

"Let's go for a walk and explore the village," she suggested. Greenville seemed like a ghost town, silent and deserted. They sat on a parapet overlooking a canal, the water flowing lazily. The setting was vaguely redolent of Fateh Sagar back home, he thought. How the entire population converged upon it every Sunday evening! There were other lakes and parks and attractions, but there was something special about Fateh Sagar. It nestled in the lap of the Aravali Hills like a protected jewel. In the middle of the lake was the island park, Nehru Garden, teasingly, elusively beautiful. Fateh Sagar drew people again and again, like lovers who could not have enough of each other. On a full moon night, the view made poets out of men. When the rain came, it became tumescent with possibilities, compelling every heart to seek the beloved.

Side by side, holding hands, they pretended they were at Fateh Sagar, something they were never able to do. They reminisced about the haunted house, the time they spent there. He told her how he had gone there and waited for her after she came visiting upon his father's death. "If you had come, our lives would have been so different."

Her eyes teared up, then she suddenly laughed. "Well, we are here now."

They decided to visit the hideout together someday to pay homage. They talked and laughed without a care in the world, suspended in time, nowhere to go, nothing to do except to be together and drink happiness out of every passing moment. Akbar told her about the incident on the bus from Ahmedabad to Udaipur; how he had come this close to death, and he pinched his forefinger and thumb to demonstrate, and how a lie had saved his life. "I am lucky to be alive. When I think about it my hairs stand on end." Rukhsana cuddled up to him and hugged him tight, as though to protect him.

On the way back to the apartment they walked through the village. It was a typical rural hamlet, a bit run-down but well-endowed with trees. Akbar took in deep breaths of the fresh air. He liked trees. He had the habit of touching a tree trunk whenever he got a chance, his way of connecting to its ancient energy.

Against a pigeon-grey sky, reds and purples were drawn in wild streaks across the firmament. The sun's rays escaped from the edges of gathering clouds. They stood and looked in awe. "Another day gone," Rukhsana said with a sigh.

24

A COSY, WARM FEELING WASHED over her as she sat by the table lamp in the living room and watched him prepare dinner—a conjugal scene she had so often fantasized was unfolding before her eyes. She was not sure whether to exult in it or rue the rarity of this scene. He spoke across from the kitchen, asking her not to stare at him. She walked over and sat at the kitchen table. "I need a better view," she said.

When dinner was ready, he brought the food to the table and before they could start eating she asked him to wait. "I want to say a prayer." She closed her eyes and took his hand in hers. After a few seconds, she opened her eyes, "Our first cooked meal together." They ate in silence, words unnecessary in the serenity of the moment.

She insisted on doing the dishes, but he wouldn't let her. When they retired to the bedroom, he played ghazals on the CD player. He changed and brushed and came out of the bathroom carrying a brown paper bag and a naughty smile. "What is that?" she asked from the bed. Without answering, he put his hand in the bag, scooped a fistful of flowers, and threw them at her. "Jasmine," she exclaimed. He proceeded to spread the blossoms all over the bed. He had plucked them from a bush earlier that morning at the retreat and put them away in his haversack. She took a bunch in her hand and inhaled. "Oh, how I love the smell." They slipped under the white, crisp cotton sheet. He asked her to move closer. "Closer still," he said. Before long they drifted into a realm of fragrant ghazals and singing jasmine.

In the morning when he awoke, she was still sleeping. The white sheet pulled up to her shoulders, soft morning light falling on her face like a blessing, jasmine tangled in her hair, head slightly tilted towards him, chest rising and falling. He mumbled a silent prayer of gratitude. It seemed as though life had distilled all the nectar into this moment. She must have sensed him looking at her; she opened her eyes and smiled. "You know, I dreamed of you," she whispered, her voice still not fully awake. In the past few months she would often complain how he had consumed her whole life. Her daily routine had gone haywire. Many of her tasks remained unfinished, and she had become listless at work. She went through the motions, her mind could not be without thoughts of him. She neglected calling her mother and sister and friends. They had started complaining. Even in their wildest imagination, they could not have guessed *where* she might be.

She was at a place where dream and reality intersected. She hoped that time would stop, that this slice of meta-life would remain frozen, free from all the physical and moral laws that order and limit and stifle this world. But she knew time would not submit to the heart's plea. It was slipping away like sand through the fingers, relentlessly. She slid closer to him and buried her head in his chest with a deep sigh.

"I'm hungry. Let's have breakfast," he said.

She held him tight. "Don't go. You know I've never slept naked in my life," she whispered.

He held her close for a while and then went to the kitchen to put on some tea, and she lay in the bed looking out the window. She was thrilled at the prospect of spending another day with him. Jumping out of bed, she let out a big yawn. She stretched, fingers interlaced, her head delicately tilted to one side. It was a posture Urdu poets had waxed lyrical over for centuries, investing it with supreme feminine charm. If they were to see her, they would have collapsed in one big collective swoon. Unmindful of her own sensuality and the effect she was having on unseen eyes, she started looking for her nightie under the sheets. She recalled how deftly he had removed it. And oh, the jasmine.

In the kitchen, he had started chopping shallots for omelettes. "The slices are too big," she said. He took a certain pride in his culinary skills, and although making omelettes did not call for exceptional talent, he didn't like being critiqued on his shallot-cutting ability. He smiled. "Oh, is it, then why don't you do the honours?"

"My, my, somebody's touchy," she said and gave him a peck on the cheek.

As he cracked an egg, he jokingly asked, "How would you like your eggs—fertilized?"

"Yeah, by you." She was quick on the take, surprising him with her alacrity.

A bright, delightful day greeted them as they stepped out. They drove around the countryside and found a public park to make a picnic. The well-trimmed lawn was hemmed in by white palisades, like a row of stakes. Two women sat on a bench by the curb, talking and eating sandwiches. Akbar and Rukhsana strolled around the park, and by the time they returned, the women had left. Now they were alone. They walked hand in hand, talking about nothing in particular.

"Let's walk barefoot," he said. "Let our feet touch the bare ground, the earth. Let's feel the vibes of nature."

She smiled knowingly. His homilies, his throwaway philosophic one-liners did not surprise her. From their book discussions all those years ago, she remembered how pedantic he used to be and how she would challenge his rhetoric. But now she just indulged him.

They removed their slippers, left them under a tree, and walked barefoot. The grass was soft to the touch and surprisingly a little moist; it tickled her soles for the first few steps. She liked the feel of the cushioned, accepting earth beneath her feet.

When they had walked a few loops, they sat under the tree where they had left the slippers. She lay on the ground with her head in his lap. Looking up, she saw his face from that odd angle, the tree arching above it, the leaves dancing in the wind, scattering the sunlight. He ran his fingers over her lips, her hair, and caressed her cheek and neck with the back of his hand. She could have died of joy.

In his eyes she saw a look of admiration and a tinge of regret too. She had always been conscious of her good looks but without him they seemed irrelevant. None of it mattered when she was wracked with hopelessness, when Shabbir used and abused her body, and when she had ended up taking anti-depressants. Now she realized more than ever that love—Akbar—was the cure of all her troubles. And for her this was not a trifling matter. She knew what the price was, what was at stake, and yet she had risked it all.

She pulled his head toward her and kissed him. After a while he also lay down. Side by side, they looked up at the sky, the tree, the unseen goldfinches and robins chirping and the breeze humming. "Remember the Big Night when we lay under the stars?" he asked.

"How can I not. You know, I cannot look at the night sky without thinking of that night."

"I remember your dupatta, you looked so lovely in it," he said. "That reminds me, I haven't got anything for you. I wanted to buy you a scarf."

"That's not necessary. I love scarves, though."

Back at the apartment, he poured wine into two goblets. She took a sip and smacked her lips, trying to dispel the taste of tannin. The night descended, bringing with it the smell of rain. A thunder rumbled in the distance. They sat in silence, close and intimate. He could hear her heart beating.

Rukhsana walked to the window and stood there watching the rain. But she could only hear it; it was too dark to see anything. Another day had gone by; she did not want to think about it, still less talk about it. When the rain stopped, she said, "Let's go for a walk."

It was close to midnight. He hesitated for a moment then got up and looked for the key. Outside it was cool. Light from a street lamp looked dim and hesitant, reluctant to shatter the settled darkness of the night. It reminded him of the light bulb in the murky entranceway of his Udaipur house. It was so weak that Moiz used to joke about it: "This damn light, when you turn it on, it spreads more darkness."

Hand in hand, they walked like two lost souls in a ghost town, in their hearts seeking a way to be together like this, in this dream state, forever. How many times and how ardently she must have wished that somehow, by some miracle, by some divine ploy this might become possible. But she knew it could never happen without hurting other people, without devastating other lives. And that neither of them wanted or even dared to contemplate.

On reaching the end of the street they turned and headed

back. The clouds had cleared and the deep inky sky was stippled with stars. In bed she read his old poems aloud from yellowing pages clipped to a plastic binder. He had asked Naseem to send them over. As she read, he squirmed in embarrassment, pleading with her to stop.

"Okay, enough of that. Now come here." And he pulled her close, flinging the binder away. He buried his face in her breasts and sighed.

Soon he was snoring. Sleep would not come to her again, and she stared at the ceiling. First it was the anticipation of meeting him that kept her awake. Now it was the anxiety of separation. In the morning when he awoke, she had fallen asleep. Presently she opened her eyes. She looked around at the room, her eyes pausing at every detail, trying to burn the scene onto her mind. She knew she would come back to this picture again and again. After taking their showers they packed their bags and departed. She wondered if she would ever see this place again.

A fierce sun was at its zenith, and tall, lush trees provided welcome shade. The world was as it should be: ordered and predictable. In the car, as they turned around a bend, she looked back one final time at the main street, their apartment building, and mouthed goodbye.

She drove quietly, lost in thought, not in the mood for any tomfoolery. He looked at her and took her hand and squeezed it gently. They were heading back to the retreat where his car was parked. For long stretches they sat in silence, her right hand in his hands. Every few minutes she looked at him with an expression he had never seen before: pinched nose and mouth, puckered eyes—a look at once sad and loving.

The past three days were bliss, and now the world was closing in on them. It was not just that soon they would go their separate ways; the thought that occupied her mind was, what would become of her? Now that she had lived with him, how could she live *without* him? She could feel her heart shrinking in anguish. The drive back home and the days ahead she did not want to contemplate. She could see desolation at the other end, waiting to embrace her in its frigid arms. She had been tough and sure-footed in so many other ways—despite the difficult marriage, she had kept a brave front. Those who knew her would vouch for her pragmatism, that she had had it all together, that she was not the one to be swayed by romantic fripperies. She never imagined that she had it in her to be swept off her feet again after all those years. She still couldn't figure out how it happened, or how on earth she had *allowed* it to happen.

She parked the car outside the retreat where they had met two days before; they came out and stood looking around. The early afternoon sun sieved softly through the trees, a breeze playing with the leaves. Not a soul was in sight. They took each other in their arms and hugged for a long time, then kissed goodbye.

"Let me know when you reach home," she said. There were tears in her eyes.

He nodded.

At home that night she waited to hear from him. He should have reached before her, but hadn't texted yet. As the minutes passed her anxiety mounted. The ten o'clock *Newshour* was on, and still no news of him. She had already texted him umpteen times but could see that he had not seen the messages. Fear and anxiety exhausted her, nightmare began to creep in.

In the morning, bleary-eyed and heavy-headed, she checked

her phone. Still no news from him. First she was angry. *How can he be so careless?* Then scared, *What if he had an accident? He was tired and we did have a late night. What if . . . ? No, God, no.* A cold shiver ran down her body.

She went to the kitchen and started preparing breakfast. The boys came in and had their toast and cereal. She made eggs for Shabbir.

"How was your trip? Where did you go, Albany?"

"It was the usual. Yes, Albany."

That was the extent of the conversation that morning. It felt like she was two people: the physical quotidian self that went about the chores mechanically, and the inner self completely detached from the world around her, consumed by anxiety. In the bathroom, she called him on his cell, her throat dry, her heart aquiver. She was not sure if she would be able to find her voice if he answered the phone. The phone rang. He did not pick up.

She did not know how she reached her office. On the way she had tried to block out all the bad things that could have happened to him. The more she tried, the more she thought of them. *How can I contact him?* From her desk she called Columbia University. She asked for Akbar Zaki who worked in the Near Eastern Studies Department. After fifteen minutes of dealing with automated messages and clueless humans, she reached Adrian Jones, Akbar's advisor.

"It's good to know there's a soul here who knows him," he said, sounding relieved.

"Where is he? What happened to him?"

"He's in the hospital. Had an accident."

What the professor said next, Rukhsana could barely register.

25

Soon after Akbar departed for the United States, Naseem had started volunteering at an arts NGO, where on weekday evenings she taught painting to children from poor homes. She had set up her own private studio in the back corner of the classroom. She worked on her painting whenever she could snatch a few moments of time. She had finished one canvas. It depicted a rain-lashed street of Bombay: a taxi, black and yellow, ploughing through the water, people hurrying along, some exposed to the torrential rain, others trying to shelter themselves with their inadequate umbrellas. The painting was grey, with little colour; the tops of tall buildings in the background disappeared into the clouds. On one side of the canvas in the foreground, a beggar sat on a stool perhaps, which was submerged, holding a broken umbrella. It seemed as if he were floating on water.

Currently she was working on a vertical canvas of Times Square. Akbar had sent her a selfie with him posing in front of the iconic, garish billboards that dominate that intersection. The shot was of early evening, the lights had come on. She had got the photo printed. He was smiling, his head tilted ever so slightly to one side. That was how he always posed for pictures. She had not remembered to ask whom he had gone there with.

Naseem was finishing the curved strokes on the Coke logo on one of the billboards in her painting of the Square, when her cell phone rang. An American number. She was puzzled. This is not Akbar, who could this be?

Professor Jones was on the other end. Akbar had told her about his advisor and how he had helped him settle down in New York. When the professor informed her about Akbar's accident, she listened in silence and barely managed to say goodbye. The brush had fallen from her hand, the red paint splotching her white salwar. She thought of calling Khatun, who was visiting her that weekend, and on Naseem's insistence had agreed to stay over for the rest of the week. Kaiser Ali was away at a conference.

It didn't seem appropriate to talk about the accident on the phone. *Amma will have a heart attack.* She took a taxi home. Farah was out at a students' rally in Azad Maidan in south Bombay. Khatun was in the kitchen cutting gavar beans for dinner. Onions were peeled and soaked in a bowl of water. She rang the doorbell.

"You're early today," Khatun said in surprise, upon seeing her. "Everything all right?"

"I've bad news, Amma. Akbar is in hospital. He met with an accident."

"Who—what? What are you saying?"

"He's in stable condition, though. His professor called. He was driving on the highway, was hit by a minivan. His car went off the road and hit the guardrails. He has injuries on the arms, maybe a fracture or two. Some injuries on the head too, possibly a concussion but they don't know yet."

"Ya Ali. Oh my jaana . . . " Khatun choked on her words. "What are the doctors saying? Is he okay, will he be fine?"

"He is going to be fine, Amma. The professor is saying that his condition is stable. It will be a couple of months before he recovers completely."

Khatun, who was holding a knife, put it on the dining table

and stepped over to give Naseem a hug. "Oh jaana. I hope he recovers fast. But my boy is alone in a foreign land, nobody to take care of him."

"Amma, you think I should go, be with him . . . but how? The tickets are so expensive and I will have to get a visa also."

"Don't worry about the cost, beta, I've some savings. Why don't you apply for an emergency visa?"

"Okay, let's do that. But going to the US embassy is such a nightmare. Let me call Bela, maybe she knows of an agent who can help."

"Yes, and we must do sadqah, must feed the poor," Khatun said as she sat down at the dining table, losing the will to cook.

"Yes, Amma, we will. The professor said that the university will take care of the medical bills. And will perhaps extend his stay."

———

Rukhsana slumped in her chair, dropping the receiver. It beeped annoyingly, like a dirge. She had caught this much, that he was fine. She left the office and at a coffee shop downstairs ordered a latte and sat there for what seemed like hours, dazed. She blamed herself for drawing him out, for insisting on meeting. *Now see how the universe, our ally, our enabler that brought us together has stabbed us in the back. That's our comeuppance.* And how swiftly it came about, she could not believe. Upon regaining her composure, she called the professor. Akbar was at the Presbyterian Hospital in New York City. He said that his injuries were not serious, and that he had informed his family in Bombay. The next morning she was by his bedside, having made excuses at work and lied to Shabbir about a client in New York.

Akbar attempted a smile on seeing her but instead winced in pain.

He looked a wreck. His head was wrapped in a bandage, the face and chin had dressings, one of his arms was in a cast. A nurse was tending to him and she informed Rukhsana that the elbow was dislocated and there was a minor fracture on the shoulder blade. Doctors had put temporary cast, and a surgery was scheduled for tomorrow. He was on oxycodone to keep his pain in check. His lower jaw was swollen and it would be out of commission for a couple of weeks.

And the professor said it was not serious, Rukhsana thought.

"I'm sorry, janum," she said as she took the chair beside the bed. "It's all my fault."

Akbar glared at her.

She said it again. She didn't know what else to say. Seeing him in that state made her feel guilty. *Is it all worth it?* Life had devised a different plan for them so why not accept it, be content with it? That he had come to America was a coincidence, not some divine design. All this talk of the universe conspiring in their favour was so much self-serving nonsense. *What gullible fools we have been.* She questioned every excuse, every artifice they had employed to rationalize their relationship. She looked at him looking at her and couldn't help her heart from breaking.

But then the accident might itself be a random coincidence. He could have slipped down the stairs and injured himself. Maybe she was reading too much into it. Maybe it had to happen, one way or another. Her reverie was broken as the doctor entered the room. She rose from the chair on seeing him.

"I'm Anil Menon," he said, and turning to Akbar, "So how is

Akbar the Great doing this morning?"

Rukhsana introduced herself, saying she was Akbar's friend from Udaipur.

"Oh, you guys are from Udaipur? We went for our honeymoon there. The Lake Palace Hotel. What a beautiful city, out of this world."

Rukhsana smiled proudly.

"I must declare my bias upfront now," Dr Menon said. "Since you're from my favourite city I must take extra care of you, Akbar saab."

"Doctor, his bones will heal completely, won't they?" Rukhsana asked, her voice begging for assurance.

"Absolutely, and I make no bones about that," he smiled. Then turning to Akbar as he made for the door, "You hang in there, Akbar saab, tomorrow is a big day."

Rukhsana resumed the seat and gently patted on his bandaged head. "I'll stay with you for the next few days. I'm in the city on work," she confided with a smile.

The phone on the bedside table rang, startling them both. Rukhsana looked at Akbar, eyebrows raised. Must be from the nurses' station. *How inconsiderate of them. Don't they know the patient is no state to answer the phone?* She picked it up on the fourth ring, ready to give the caller a piece of her mind.

"Hello, can I speak to Akbar Zaki," a female voice asked. It was not the nurse.

"May I know who is calling?" Rukhsana said.

"I'm his wife Naseem, from Bombay."

Rukhsana froze.

"Hello, hello," Naseem repeated eagerly.

Rukhsana considered the voice, its clear and steady timbre now sagging with anxiety.

"Yes, sorry . . . uh, I'm Rukhsana. You may not know me, I'm a family friend from Udaipur."

"Oh, Rukhsana." It took a moment for the name to register. Naseem had known about their affair but she and Akbar never talked about it, except on occasions when she would tease him, complaining that she was only his second love. The allegation scratched an old wound, and he would just smile in response. And in his silence she saw an affirmation of her charge. Both understood, though, that all this was in the past, safely fossilized under layers of accumulated years, petrified under the weight of entrenched Momin politics.

"Oh, I didn't expect you to be there," Naseem said. After a few seconds when Rukhsana did not respond, she asked, "Is Akbar there?"

"Yes, yes! He is doing fine. He can't talk. His jaw is swollen. Some injuries on the hand and the shoulder," Rukhsana tried to mitigate the extent of damage so as not to alarm her. "They have given him painkillers, and the surgery is tomorrow. The doctors are positive he will be all right."

"Rukhsana, I'm so glad you are with him," Naseem said, hoping she would supply the reason for her being there. "Amma and I were so worried."

"Not at all, Naseem. I got the news from his professor and so came down to see him."

Maybe she was getting ahead of herself, Naseem thought. Still, why was she there? Why would the professor inform her? She expected Rukhsana to tell her but she did not oblige. And Naseem could not bring herself to ask, thinking it might be impolite to do so. Yet, she did not want to speculate. Being a woman and a wife, her mind raced in all directions to make sense of it. It was a good thing she had applied for the visa. She should know the outcome in a day or so. In any case, Akbar would soon be back in India, she rationalized, and Rukhsana would be back where she belonged, out of their life.

Khatun overheard them talking from where she sat on the couch. She had turned down the television volume to catch the conversation. When Rukhsana's name was mentioned, she felt a strange sense of relief. *Oh, there is somebody with my jaana.* The doubts plaguing Naseem didn't even occur to her. She was happy that good old Rukhsana—of all people—was there to look after Akbar. The two of them might have had a history, but they had moved on. That the two could be up to something would be unthinkable for her. Her upbringing, her moral certainties, her mother's implicit belief in the goodness of her son had not equipped her to suspect anything untoward. Even if she were told the truth, she would have brushed it aside as preposterous. "How can such a thing even be possible?" she would have said with a look of puzzled incredulity.

When Naseem hung up, Khatun asked what happened, pretending not to have overheard. Naseem gave her the details: the painkillers, the surgery, and Rukhsana.

"Rukhsana? Who, my Zubaida's Rukhsana?"

"Yes."

"I'm so happy she is there to take care of him."

"Amma, there are nurses to take care of him," Naseem said impatiently.

"Of course, of course. I didn't mean it that way," Khatun said. "You know at such times it is always good to have someone . . . ," she wanted to add "close to you" but stopped short, seeing how Naseem had snapped. "Someone for moral support, someone to talk to."

"Yes, Amma, yes, you're right." Naseem said, a little morti-fied at being cross with her. "Tomorrow I'll give alms to the beggars outside the Sidhivinayak temple."

———

At the hospital in New York, Rukhsana bit her lip as she put down the phone and emitted a deep sigh. She placed the back of her hand on Akbar's neck as though checking for fever. "It was Naseem," she said. "Sorry, I had to tell her who I was. It happened so suddenly, I didn't have time to think."

Akbar smiled weakly. What Rukhsana thought and what Naseem understood . . . what a mess he'd gotten into! If he had not tempted fate, none of this would have happened. He looked at Rukhsana sitting by his side, worry lining her beautiful face. Look at her, how can one not be tempted?

But what if I were dead? Would that be such a bad thing? He could count on the fingers of one hand the people who would be directly affected. What did that say about him, his place in the world? For the first time he considered his smallness, his insignificance. All the four women in his life—Khatun, Naseem, Farah, and Rukhsana—would be inconsolable at first, but time they say—and how he hated that cliché—is a great healer. It was just as well that life would go on. Hadn't he and his mother come to terms with his father's death? Life has a way to force itself upon you. And death is the square root of life. It is a mathematical certainty. At the time of the accident, in a fleeting moment when he had teetered between life and death, something fundamental had shifted in him. For the second time in life he had been this close to death.

Post-surgery, Rukhsana sat by his side for two days, talking

to him, reading to him, watching TV. After that, she did not
visit him again. Work kept her busy and away from home most
of the time. She chatted with him on the phone when he had
recovered sufficiently and was able to talk. She sensed that he
was not the same as before. His puns, his play with words, his
spontaneity had gone. He seemed distant, lingered over her
questions, and answered them vaguely. The subject of them
meeting again did not come up. She put his reticence down to
trauma. As it was, he was always quick to question their relationship, and now this accident, she feared, would give him the
justification to cut her loose.

No, her heart screamed. She had lost him once and was not
prepared to lose him again. How her world had brightened up
ever since he came back into her life, how the shadows had
retreated into the background. Every morning she awoke to a
new day, to a life which had meaning. Even now, despite the
brooding gloom he brought to their conversations, she was
content just talking to him. She did not want to question too
much his aloofness, lest her eager probing break the tenuous
thread that still linked them. And she knew how fragile it was.
For no matter how many times and how ardently they might
express their love for each other, in the eyes of society their
relationship had no legitimacy. This is the thing with love. It is
like a waif, an orphan, an outcast, frail and vulnerable; except
for the place in the heart, it has no home. Celebrated by poets,
condemned by puritans. It has no standing, no validity, and it
can be shut out in an instant, just like that. Nobody to cry over
it, nobody to commiserate its passing. Yet, it is all there is.

At no time did Rukhsana feel the helplessness at the hands of
love as she did now. He did not belong to her. He had his family,
his life. If their relationship had any meaning, it existed in their

private, secret world. After the haunted house, Greenville was the only tangible core of that world. Its solidity could not be denied. But its memory now seemed distant, far away, like it had never happened. The more she thought about Greenville, the deeper she buried its memory inside her secret vault where time and forgetting wouldn't reach it. It was a piece of heaven they had snatched from the gods and embellished it with their love and foolish courage. It was tainted by betrayal. It was their love child, so to speak, beautiful and flawed, and needed protecting because it was beautiful, and especially because it was flawed.

She knew she would cherish Akbar's second coming till the day she died. The memory would give her solace when she was alone, old and abandoned. Although his departure was still some six months away, she had already begun to dread it. She could already sense a distance between them after the accident. Their relationship, its illicit nature, had always made him uneasy. Not that she was any less concerned about her own disloyalty, but for her the choice had always been clear. Marriage had given her only grief. She had the right to be happy even if it meant violating the moral and religious codes she so valued. She wanted Akbar in her life—in whatever way possible. Even if the relationship was long-distance and digital, it was alright with her. Some nights she would wake up from a nightmare, in a cold sweat: abandoned, stranded on an unknown planet where vicious, vulpine creatures chased her to the galactic edge. Beyond which a dense nothingness howled to suck her in. She wants to shout but her voice dies in her throat. Akbar grabs her hand as she falls over the precipice, then the grasp loosens, and . . .

———

In two and a half months Akbar had recuperated sufficiently to get back to work, and was busy with research and teaching. He had been cold toward Rukhsana. The impossibility and untenability of their situation had come in stark relief after the accident. In the hospital, he had had time to think. How all these years his love for Rukhsana had lingered deep in his consciousness, and how it had come to the fore like an air bubble in amber released from its ancient trap. How they had exulted in declaring that love triumphs all. That it was divine grace, when it will strike you, who is to know? And when it does, it is like a flash flood that in its mindless fury destroys everything in its path. Both of them had tacitly accepted the transient nature of their coming together, and had somehow found in that transitoriness a reason to quell their conscience. But now he was not so sure, he wanted to end this madness.

On another level, the accident brought him face-to-face with mortality. As he lay in bed, his pain dulled by medication, he would often close his eyes and meditate. After a while he would feel his body coming alive, every cell inside him aware and awake. As he slid deeper into his inner self, his conscious mind, his thoughts subsided. There were moments when Akbar felt completely detached from the body. His inner reality, the "I am", came within his grasp for a split second. The "I am" is nothing but *you*, as you are now, at this very moment. There is no need to seek it. He recalled the teachings of Nisargadatta Maharaj, the self-realized guru, whose talks he used to attend in Bombay. The guru's refrain was, "the seeker is the sought." Those five words, if understood, he used to say, explained the mystery of existence.

The accident and the meditations reinforced his belief that the only truth is the realization of the inner self. He could feel it when he went deep into silence, into the stillness of his bones. In that stillness this life, this world, its laws, its religions, its struggles held no meaning; the ego lay dissolved; he experienced himself as an amorphous presence seeing the world in childlike wonder. The idea that God existed outside of ones' self was hard to comprehend, and even more incomprehensible was the notion that God prescribes rules that believers must follow to earn His pleasure. Oh, what trickeries men have conjured up to fool themselves and one another!

26

ONE LATE AUGUST MORNING AKBAR sat on the steps of the Low Memorial Library, taking in the sun. He was reading the book *A Modern Approach to Islam* by A A A Fyzee and occasionally lifted his head and looked blankly into space, mulling over what he had just read. It had rained last night, but the trees, the buildings, the steps didn't look any tidier than they were the previous day. Everything was always so clean. In India people wait for the rains to wash their cities. Monsoons were celebrated with exuberance—they brought renewal, life, and relief from the blazing, merciless sun. These past years it hadn't rained much in Udaipur. Fateh Sagar had gone bone-dry; not a drop this year either, his mother told him when he called her yesterday, she was in Udaipur on a visit. Akbar couldn't picture it—didn't want to picture it. A dry Fateh Sagar could not be imagined.

Rukhsana would call him any minute now. She called him twice a week and did most of the talking. She talked without guile, eager to share all that was happening in her life. He listened. He loved to listen to her voice, its underlying melody. At times he just focused on the cadence, the lisping, the rising and falling octaves. He knew when she would pause and clear her throat. At times he would be unable to recall what she had said and she would protest, "Do you ever pay attention to what I say?"

As he turned the page of the book, his phone rang. He quickly placed a bookmark in it and shut it. She said hello, her voice warm with happiness. Her younger son Taher had been selected to go to Geneva for a WHO conference. "You know," she said, "I haven't done much for the boys, never been after them, pestering them to do their homework. They managed on their own. I don't even know how. Maybe they are bright, like their mother." She laughed.

"Hmm, that's a bit of a stretch."

"Shut up," Rukhsana said.

Over the weeks as they talked, Akbar's post-accident reserve slowly began to dissolve. Rukhsana had been patient with him, giving him space. On occasions when he wanted to talk about their situation, their future, she tactfully steered the conversation to something else. She knew what was on his mind and which direction it was going to lead to. She didn't want to go there. Instead, she talked about everything else in the world. Things at home, her voluntary work, office, and her friends. Akbar saw through her little game but let her go on with it.

At one point, in the hospital, after intense introspection, he had arrived at a decision. It was time for the inevitable, to put a stop to their relationship. But when she called next, on hearing her voice, he could not find his. As days passed he began to lose the will to talk about it. The matter now lay in abeyance between them, like a landmine. But when overcome by a troubled conscience—remembering Naseem—he just wanted to be done with it.

Naseem had been denied the visa. She had called him to inform; the immigration officer at the embassy was rude and said the United States government did not trust that she would return to India. And that was that. You just can't argue with them. She had felt terrible and small. "How does the US government know my mind?" she was puzzled. Akbar had asked her not to come, saying it was not necessary and wasn't worth all the expense. Naseem thought he was trying to keep her away for other reasons. She was disappointed when the visa fell through and spent her days in anxiety even though during her subsequent phone calls she had discovered from the nurse that no woman had been visiting him.

The university had extended the research grant by three months, up to the end of December. "That's fantastic," Rukhsana said on the phone. She suggested he go up north to New Hampshire and see the fall colours. "It is an experience you won't easily forget."

Akbar looked at the sugar maple across the library lawn; some of its leaves were already bleeding red. Why do Americans call autumn fall? Autumn was such a beautiful word, it had a nice ring to it. Fall, on the other hand, was so prosaic, flat, so to the point, and so devoid of romance. In his mind it conjured up the biblical idea of fall from grace, of which autumn was the complete antithesis.

By mid-October, the trees around the campus began to ooze colour, as if mischievous goblins were secretly watering them with pails of paint under the cover of darkness. As pumpkins and jack-o-lanterns dotted the landscape, the trees blossomed into full-blown finery as though ready for the last wild rave before winter skulked in and turned off the lights. In Udaipur they had just two seasons, summer and winter, and the monsoon, if the rain gods obliged. But here the successive equinoxes opened up curtains on a new scenery every four months. Peoples' moods changed, fashions changed. The seasons broke the monotony. Akbar noticed that after the autumnal equinox the darkness had begun to eat into chunks of daylight, and there was a nip in the breeze.

Sitting at a bistro *al fresco* in his cashmere sweater, Akbar sipped a cappuccino and mused about the class he'd just given on Shia theology. He had explained that the belief in the infallibility of the Imam was based on faith, not evidence. The same was true of the belief in the immaculate conception or, for that matter, the free market or socialism. Faith was a function of conditioning, of propaganda. An animated discussion had followed. The students wanted to know why the Imam, instead of guiding the faithful, was in seclusion for hundreds of years. He had told them that mullahs were very inventive in explaining it away. That an absent Imam was more useful to them than a present one, just like a dead elephant was more valuable than a living one. He did not tell them that he came from a Shia tradition where the Imam was missing in action and represented by a leader called the Mowlana, who considered himself infallible. And he and his priests used infallibility like a bludgeon. He had so dumbed down his flock that once when he casually mentioned not to waste food, armies of boys were recruited overnight, and after community meals they were seen literally licking plates of food for every last fleck of leftover.

He took a sip from his cup and a bite from his chocolate chip cookie. The sweetness elicited a sharp pain in his molars. He tongued the offending tooth. Sitting outside the Artopolis Café—his favourite retreat recently—surrounded by the sights and sounds of the modern metropolis, the quadrangle of a great university on the other side of the busy street, the talk of the Imams and the Mowlana seemed so fantastic, like a tale from the *Arabian Nights*.

———

On the last Saturday of October, Akbar drove up north on Interstate 91 toward New Hampshire to see the autumn colours. He could have gone via Boston but didn't want to tempt fate, yet again. Eyes glued to the road, he paid close attention to the traffic, constantly checking the rear-view and side mirrors, only too aware of his mishap in the summer. In a month's time he would be flying back to Bombay; his ticket was booked. He planned to finish the first draft of his book before leaving and would give it to Adrian Jones for review.

With the windows rolled down the breeze battered his face and a percussive blast filled the car, drowning out the ghazal singer Mehdi Hasan's deep rasp on the stereo. The sky was overcast, and moisture in the air whispered of rain. Soon he would exit the freeway and take the country road. He glanced at the empty passenger seat and wished he had asked her to come. It started drizzling, he rolled up the window and turned on the wipers. The ghazal now had his full attention. He started singing along. The poet was lamenting about sitting by the river and still going thirsty. Akbar felt like crying.

He exited the freeway. On the country road a vivid panorama opened up before him; the trees were aflame with reds and yellows and oranges and the rain it seemed was battling to douse the fire. Akbar pulled up on the side of the road, cut the engine, and sat still, awestruck. The flash of lightning and the crack of thunder chased each other in some kind of celestial game. The wind was strong and furious, and the tall trees swayed from side to side like drunken dervishes. Sheets of water hammered down, threatening to drown him in his dinky little car. For an instant, he was scared. His soul sufficiently stirred, he beseeched Mother Nature to cut out the drama.

Later that afternoon, he drove up to Mount Washington, stood before the summit sign, and took a selfie. The rain had ended. The sky was still dense with clouds, and the air felt cold and sparse. He walked around, breathing deeply, and then went inside the café and ordered a hot coffee and a turkey sandwich. It was warm inside and crowded. The smell of food, mainly of burning fat, and the animal warmth of humans were reassuring.

Driving downhill from Mount Washington along the winding road, Akbar feasted on the panorama of natural beauty like he alone was privy to it. The clouds had broken up, and the setting sun, as if to outdo the autumn kaleidoscope, had emptied its own cornucopia of colours across the firmament. The earth and the sky melded into a seamless canvas. For the second time in one day Akbar was spellbound by nature. First it was its fury, now its finery.

By the time he checked into The Lodge in Jackson, night had fallen. It was a two-storey colonial building with green-gabled roofing and pale yellow sidings. The room smelled of wood. The walls were wainscoted, and the pine furniture and bold plaid drapery exuded a typical New England charm. The bed looked inviting. He had no plans for the evening; he thought he would go out and eat something and then come back and curl up with a book. He took a quick shower and changed into a fresh set of clothes. As he fastened the horn buttons on his cardigan, there was a knock on the door.

27

BEFORE HE CAME TO THE United States, Akbar had promised Naseem and Farah that he would call them over for a visit in the summer. But the accident had put paid to the plan. By the time he was out of the hospital, a new school year had begun in India. Naseem was not keen at all. The thought of America and Akbar in it made her uncomfortable. All she wanted was Akbar to come home. She immersed herself in her work: school, yoga, and painting. Still, at night in bed she missed him. Exhausted, with the day's busyness behind her, she could not keep her mind from thinking about him and what he might be up to. They had been talking on the phone regularly.

He would invariably call and would ask her about every little detail—even what she was wearing and how she had done her hair. He joked in his typical way, alternating between puns and pedantry. He would tell her about life in New York, the university, and how ridiculously expensive education was; campus life was like a self-contained world unto itself; libraries were vast and the books and resources endless. What he liked most were the students, they were a diverse bunch and were aware and articulate and it was such a pleasure to talk to them. He told her about his walks and about the changing seasons, the autumn colours—their glory and beauty—were to be seen to be believed. The photos just cannot do justice.

In his talk and in his voice, Naseem tried to look for clues of whether he might be meeting with Rukhsana. The thought was always at the back of her mind like a dull niggling unease that would not go away. She looked in the mirror and imagined how she compared with Rukhsana. She had never regarded herself as a stunner, but she thought, vainly, that she did not look bad for her age. Rukhsana wasn't young either. The skin around the corners of her mouth was showing a little sag, the crinkles under her eyes were hinting at crow's feet, grey hairs had begun to appear, but overall at forty-two she had the feminine allure to keep her man. More importantly, she had the legal and social claims on him. But deep down she knew that none of these things—talent, education, marriage, sense of superiority—mattered. What mattered was the flame in one's heart. All the conventions in the world cannot put out that fire.

One evening she confided her fears to her friend Bela, who listened attentively, and although Naseem spoke matter-of-factly, there was a touch of anxiety lurking in her tone.

"Don't you trust Akbar?" Bela asked.

"I do, but there is always a doubt. You have no idea how close they were at one time," Naseem said.

"That is all in the past, a long time ago. They have their own lives now. People do not remain the same. Marriage and children, that is the social ballast, it keeps them grounded."

"I know, Bela, but when has all that grounding stopped anyone from doing what the heart desires?"

"Why don't you ask him whether he is seeing her?"

"Don't be crazy."

"Why not? She was there in the hospital room. You talked to her. So he knows that you know. It wouldn't be so odd to ask. Okay, not directly, but perhaps casually, like, 'How's Rukhsana, it was good to talk to her the other day', something to that effect."

"No, no, I can't do that. That would mean I'm expecting him

to be seeing her."

"What would you have done if you were in her place?"

"What do you mean?"

"If you were in Rukhsana's place. Wouldn't have you gone to see him after the accident?"

"I really don't know. Maybe I would have—and probably would never have left him after that," Naseem said, surprising herself with that admission. "But that's not the point," she continued. "What's eating me up is how they got in touch again and why?"

"Oh, Naseem, don't be naïve. With social media people are unearthing their long-dead friends. Finding an old flame is not a big deal."

After a pause, Bela said, "You know what! You should have an affair of your own."

"Bela, you know that's not funny."

"Just kidding, calm down."

The next day when Akbar called, she was on the verge of asking him about Rukhsana but thought the better of it. Why stir up something that would have no relevance in less than a month's time? She knew, even understood, how he must feel toward Rukhsana; but that is in the past, now he had her and Farah. And from what she knew of him, he did care about them. But distance and loneliness can affect the best of us. Especially men, they could be tempted.

———

When Akbar opened the door, he saw Rukhsana beaming at him.

"You?"

"I thought you would be pleased to see me."

"Pleased? I cannot contain my joy."

"Can I come in?"

"Oh, yes of course."

He shut the door behind him, then turned and took her in his arms.

"Five months," Rukhsana said, "it's been five months and seven days since I touched you."

Akbar tightened the embrace.

"Were you expecting me?"

"I was, to tell you the truth. I gave you the details for a reason."

"I know, but you were too proud to ask."

"No, not proud. Just circumspect, considering what happened last time."

"Even though this was the last chance for us to meet? Don't I know you? You are a ditherer, an idiot."

"And for an idiot you've come all this way?"

"Had to take matters into my own hands, as always," Rukhsana said.

"In that case," he said, smiling stupidly, "it's my turn to take matters into my own hands," and he pulled her closer and crushed her lips with his.

"Easy does it, Romeo," she said, wriggling in his arms.

The night was warm and humid. She wore a loose white tunic over black slacks and red pumps. Her large hoop earrings danced with every gesture she made, her hair was swept back, held by a barrette. Hand in hand they ambled to a quaint little tavern by the Ellis River. They sat at a corner table talking quietly amidst a hum of chatter. The solid oak tables and benches were bare and polished to a high sheen. Brown paper sheets served as placemats. Akbar took a fork in his hand and considered its heft and was satisfied with its gravitas. Rukhsana said she was famished and ordered a steak. He settled for a salad and a pasta and prawn dish. It came lathered in a mushroom cream sauce and basil. Something bland. He was not in the mood for spicy food, even so the American fare did not live up to the standards of pungency he was used to.

"I thought you didn't like red meat," Akbar said.

"Yeah, but today I feel like a steak. I'm so hungry, I could eat a horse."

"And a pig too, I suppose."

"Yes, will get to you after."

They laughed, and he glanced around and noticed the convivial scene, the happy, warm faces brought together by such ordinary and mundane things as food and drink.

"There was no way I could let you go without seeing you again," she said wistfully. "I had to see you for the last time." She paused. "If this is the last time, that is." Her voice dipped a bit, and she looked away from him. Then she dabbed her eyes with the paper napkin, smiled broadly, revealing her teeth. The playful glint in her eyes had returned in an instant. A lick of her hair fell across her left cheek. In the glow of the candle she looked edible. Akbar was seized by delight and regret.

"What the heck," she said, "I'm not going to waste time moping about the future. What matters is *now*, that you are with me, that we are together." She took his hand and pressed it. "Remember Greenville?" she said.

Akbar nodded.

"Did it really happen? Or was it a dream? I keep thinking about it. I've never been so happy in my life. I mean it."

"Yes, it seems surreal."

"Why do people who can give each other so much happiness can't be together? It is so unfair."

"If I can be philosophical, life can't arrange for everyone's happiness. In any case, don't you think it is better to have met again than not at all?"

"Yes, but it all sounds so easy to say it. Separation is staring me in the face, and I've to live with it, live and breathe every moment and think how different, how wonderful things could have been. But I know you. You will get busy with your books and your work, and your family. Not that I grudge you any of that. On the contrary I'm always feeling guilty more because of Naseem and Farah than Shabbir. Never thought I'd be that other woman, stealing somebody's man. I hate myself for it, feel like a bitch, but at the same time I feel so helpless. You can never imagine how much this brief reunion means to me."

Akbar did not say anything.

"In a way I'm happy that you'd soon be back with your family. And my conscience would be at ease. But then I will be here alone and miserable—the boys will soon be gone, and then what? Life would be long and lonely. For all his faults Shabbir is at least loyal. One up on me. But his loyalty doesn't add up to much. It doesn't make you want to be with him, to like him. His obsession with Mowlana keeps us apart and . . . " she checked herself.

"And?"

"Nothing," she paused. "Just that I've never seen a man who is so brainy and so stupid at the same time. He is brilliant at his work, a beautiful analytical mind, and is valued at his office for his algorithm genius. What I don't understand is the algorithm that underpins his fanaticism."

Akbar looked at her intently, feeling helpless, not sure what to say that would comfort her.

"You know," she said, changing tack, "of late the Momins have been running around with tiffin carriers—the steel lunch boxes."

"What do you mean?" Akbar asked.

"You are so out of touch," Rukhsana protested. "Mowlana has named his son Mukammal Fakerudin as successor. They say he is quite a character—his speeches are pure bombast, always scolding his congregation and always ready to send you Radicals to hellfire. Soon after he was declared the successor, Mukammal comes up with this idea of delivering food to people's homes."

"Isn't that a good thing?" Akbar said. "Freeing women from kitchen work."

"Yes, that would be great if that were the intention. But Mukammal doesn't want women to work. He wants them inside homes—serve their husbands, make topis and sew hijabs and do other womanly things. When women go out to work they come into contact with other men and then, he famously said, *you never know what can happen.*"

"Well, patriarchy is the staple of priests."

"He is dragging us back to the caves. He is the missing link evolutionary scientists have been looking for. Somebody should tell them to stop the search. This royal effing family is the bane of my life," she said as she dug the fork into the table.

"Please don't do that." Akbar had never seen her so full of anger, so foul of mouth.

"They are the reason we are in this situation, don't you get that? And they are the reason why my life has been a . . . My husband, that cretin, never tires of licking their backsides. And it was fine by me as long he kept it to himself. I had learned to live with it. But then he wanted me to quit my job because Mukammal Fakerudin issued that fatwa."

"What?"

"He told me that Mukammal doesn't want women to work, for they are the jewel of a man's home, they must remain indoors, look after the family. He insisted I quit working. I told him that was not going to happen. I reminded him we had agreed upon that before marriage. He said that that deal was off the table. With Mukammal we have to start with a clean slate. That made me mad. I told him what to do with his clean slate."

Akbar had never realized Shabbir was so antiquated, and felt less bad about hating him. He stroked her hand wishing to caress her troubles away. "Can't he think for himself?" he said.

"Tell me about it," she said. "I'm so tired, please take me away from this, this . . . " Her voice trailed off. She took a sip of water, emptying the glass, looked around, aware of Akbar's gaze on her. She did not want him to feel sorry for her.

"Well," she said, forcing a smile, "I came here to forget my troubles, not to talk about them."

"I wish I could help," he said.

"Yes, you can," she said and then, leaning forward, squeezed his hand and whispered, "Let's run away."

After dinner they walked by the river. Local artisans had set up stands selling paintings, hand-made jewellery and all kinds of hokey trinkets. He bought silver ear-studs for Naseem and a mother-of-pearls wrist band for Farah. At one stall Akbar spotted scarves, a bunch of them hanging from a huge metal ring, knotted on it like neckties. While Rukhsana was trying on some bracelets, he quickly went over and picked up a silk scarf. It was indigo, with red-and-white dots, and secured at both ends by tassels. Having paid for it, he folded it into a tight wad, he shoved it into his back pocket, and pulled his cardigan over it to hide the bulge.

The moisture from the day's rain still hung in the air. The birds had retired for the day, delegating to the breeze the task of making music for the night. The leaves in the trees trilled, their vibrant colours muted by darkness. The two of them sat on a soaked bench facing the river, which now in spate was gushing urgently, eager to meet its beloved. Rukhsana closed her eyes and tilted her head back. She felt time rushing past her, like the river. How she wished she could stop the Earth from turning; scoop out this moment from this incessant churn and set it free on a hot-air balloon to nowhere, to notime. She took a deep breath and kissed the back of Akbar's hand. The last time they were together, she at least had the hope of meeting him again. Today there was no such hope.

Back at the hotel, they settled down in bed. She read his newer poems he had penned in his diary. Some of the poems recounted their spring rendezvous—the time and place they had named as their second piece of heaven, the haunted house redux. It was lodged in their memory like a honey-tipped thorn. When a thought touched it, it emanated sweet anguish. She reread the lines from a poem:

> The directions laid out on paper, a sad collection of
> Words and markings, but when seen through a prism
> Of tears, it looks like a territory where white hot love
> Breaks into a colourful spectrum of pain, each ray
> A path to the dreams that end at a cliff and then a thud.
> Turn left, then right, and then left again, no matter
> How many turns you take, how far you go you always

Arrive at the same place, the place where all things end

"Beautiful," she said.

He smiled and pulled her over onto him, and there they lay for a long time, talking. "Come closer," he said. Then he remembered and reached for the scarf under the pillow where he had hidden it. She opened up like a flower on seeing it. "I love it," she said. They made love, and she cried. Drained by tears and sadness, she slept wearing just the scarf. He saw her face in the murky light of the bedside lamp. The brightness was adjustable; he had turned it down to the lowest setting. She looked vulnerable and ever so luscious. He gave her a peck on her cheek, tuned off the lamp and turned in.

In the morning, half-awake, eyes still shut, he groped for her and found warmth in the hollow of the bed where she lay. He moved his hand to the pillow and stopped where his fingers felt a dampness. It was completely quiet; he felt an arctic chill traversing his body. He called out to her in a voice that could hardly carry the syllables to completion. Her name remained half-spoken.

28

THE STREET SEEMED TO HAVE shrunk with age. The house too looked unremarkable, it's old grandeur faded by the passage of time. Dust had settled on the building in layers, even the rains had failed to wash away the caked grime. The monsoon had returned to Udaipur, and lakes were full again, water licking the shore. Akbar longed to go to Fateh Sagar and spend an evening there, all by himself. But that would have to wait. He had come to Udaipur after ten years, and it had changed so much, and yet nothing had changed.

His ancestral home where he grew up was not just old and flaky, it was falling apart. The front door where his cousins, Farzana and Zainab, had stood nightly to sadistically tempt neighbourhood Lotharios looked forlorn. Few passed through its portals anymore. In the passage leading to the courtyard he could hear the faint echoes of him and Moiz chasing each other, and in their wake the censorious admonitions of Fizza Chachi. On the wall he saw the charcoal scrawl of a bird flying away from a cage. The drawing had faded and was written over with other doodles by other hands. That it had survived for so long surprised Akbar. He had drawn it to symbolize freedom, but what inspired it he could not recall. He must have been too young to appreciate its political connotations. It was such a long time ago.

It had been two years since Akbar returned from the States. There was never a day when Akbar had not thought of Rukhsana. She had disappeared from the hotel as quietly as she had come. Her arrival was a surprise, and so was her departure. It was just as well. Their brief interlude had given him a taste of how things might have been. In its brevity was the sweetness. If only she was content. Content in the sense of having a decent, normal life. Like his. For her there was no joy, not even a possibility of it. Her sadness, her loneliness, the complete absence of affinity with her husband made him sad. He left the United States carrying the weight of her misery in his heart.

He had not been in touch with Rukhsana. They had agreed not to communicate, though Rukhsana did so reluctantly. Still she texted him a couple of times. Her messages were sombre. She said it was hard to get through the day, that she missed him very much. He replied trying to cheer her up, offering platitudes. Beyond that he could do little. He felt utterly helpless. There was too much distance of everything between them. And although their "piece of heaven" still perfumed his lonely moments, its memory was increasingly swamped by the tidal force of life and responsibility.

Back in Bombay, facing Naseem had grated his conscience. He had never imagined he would be at such a crossroads, straddling love and betrayal. He had no idea how he would look her in the eye and not feel like a despicable human being; how he would touch her and not feel as if he was violating her. He had broken her trust, the bedrock on which relationships are built. For all his high-minded pretensions and sanctimonious preaching, he had turned out to be a shameless, cheating Janus-faced fraud. As often as he remembered Rukhsana, he also secretly begged for Naseem's forgiveness. Admitting that he had wronged her greatly, that he would forever be her sinner, and that there was nothing he could do to absolve himself, that there was nothing in God's awfully beautiful universe that would forgive him. Maybe the pleadings were to comfort his conscience, but he believed in their sincerity. She was the last person on earth he would have wanted to hurt knowingly, and he had done just that. His conscience was a festering wound that could not be healed. He had found love but had lost so much for it. Deep down he knew he was less of a man, less of a human being.

Yet no matter how troubled he felt, Rukhsana never left him. He suffered silently for her love and suffered more for her suffering. In Udaipur, when he heard rumours that Shabbir would settle back in India, alone, Akbar felt relieved that at least she would now be at peace. That the thorn would at last be extricated. He counted on her resilience, on her innate cheerful nature to pull herself back.

Akbar was visiting Udaipur to settle his mother back in her native hometown. Her failing health had not allowed her to keep pace with the hectic Bombay life. Dealing with the crowds on buses and trains was not easy at her age. She felt isolated in the suburbs. Akbar wanted her and Kaiser Ali to come live with them, but she did not want to be a burden. Kaiser Ali was also getting on in years; his public engagements had dwindled to one or two a month. Travels had completely stopped. He spent most of his days reading and writing. He would not mind settling down in Udaipur and looked forward to working with the Radicals.

And the Radicals could do with a bit of rejuvenation. The fervour of the early years had fizzled out; the hot-blooded activists like Luqman and his gang had settled into middle-aged complacency. The reform struggle trundled along but had achieved little after those initial years. Sidelined and devoid of hope, they indulged in nostalgia, telling their children the stories of their confrontation with the powerful clergy, their sacrifices and their hardships. They would point to the abject servility of the Momins and remind their youngsters that the freedoms they were enjoying had been hard won. The Radicals prided themselves in having created a template for the transformation of the community but they did not possess the wherewithal or the vision to take it forward. The clergy had outmaneuvered them and rendered them irrelevant.

The separation between the Loyalists and the Radicals in Udaipur had become permanent, with excommunication still in force, but things were not as water-tight as before. Loyalists had begun to meet friends and relatives from across the fence but only in private and unofficial capacities. Each other's mosques and functions were still out of bounds. Intermarriages between the two camps happened now and then and would often result in confusion as to which side would officiate the nikah, where the functions would be held, who should be invited etc. But often the boy's side would settle the matter for patriarchy gave them an upper hand; if not, then patriarchy's good old friend, class—wealth and prestige—would weigh in.

Even as the clergy turned a blind eye to the Loyalists playing footsie with the Radicals in Udaipur, it had masterfully reined in the Momins everywhere else, suppressing dissent and creating a cult-like adulation for the person of the Mowlana. The threat of excommunication still dangled over them, keeping them in line and on their toes, making sure another Udaipur never happened again. More than ever before Momins were kept busy with ritual and ceremony, and had become like Plato's cave men, believing the shadows to be real. The Radicals were reporting to them that there was a world outside the cave, that they had seen the sun, but Momins, too enthralled to the shadows, dismissed them as crazies. Mowlana was their sun, their god of small things, and big things. Everything.

———

Khatun had expected that settling back in Udaipur would be easy. It was her home after all, but she had not accounted for the intervening twenty years. The Udaipur she returned to had metastasized haphazardly and operated on a cadence different from the quaint, little town she remembered. Her friends had moved on; they too were older with their own priorities; they nursed illnesses, and she did not get their jokes, she was not clued in to their gossip and politics. Her relationships with them had wilted out of neglect. She would need time to catch up, to tune in. Akbar was uncomfortable leaving her behind in Udaipur, although Kaiser Ali would soon join her. He was wrapping things up in Bombay. For him the transition would be far more onerous. But they would be fine, Akbar surmised. Life like water seeks its own level.

The Zanana Wing, the women's movement that Khatun once spearheaded, had become a caricature of its old self. Instructing girls in religious knowledge had become its solitary occupation. Female circumcision and iddat—the isolation of widows—were still practiced, the former as secretly and the latter as flagrantly as before. The controversies of old had been forgotten. When she brought up the subject with her former sisters-in-arms she was met with a weary shrug of the shoulders. The Radicals may have given the boot to the Mowlana all those years ago but were unable or unwilling to break free of the orthodoxy they had inherited.

This pained Khatun much. She dusted the room in her old

house with great determination, taking to the cobwebs as the social ills she wanted expunged. Her head was swaddled in dupatta with only her eyes showing. This is what she would look like if she were to wear the niqab, Akbar, who was watching her, thought with a shiver.

"Amma, are you sure you can live here?" he asked. "Looks like time has stood still in this place."

"Open the windows," Khatun said. "Let the fresh air in. That's what this place needs. And not just this house!"

Akbar went to open the windows. They were stuck. He struggled with the latches, pulled at them. If he tried to yank them any harder he was afraid he would break their heads.

"I'll get pliers from Bherulal," he said to his mother. "Or maybe some lubricant if he has any."

Bherulal, his childhood buddy, lived across the street. Akbar hadn't seen him in years, and a queasy sense of nostalgia crept up at the prospect of meeting him. Bherulal knew about Rukhsana, and he remembered how he had commiserated with him over the breakup, gave him words of encouragement and held forth on the fickle nature of love.

The young man sitting in the doorway across the street saw Akbar coming over but did not recognize him. Akbar asked for Bherulal. The young man, in cheap faded jeans and a checked, body-fitting shirt, said he might be inside.

"Is he your father?" Akbar asked.

"No, my uncle," the fellow said, smoothing his hair back with his fingers. Akbar noticed encrusted grit in his nails. A bracelet made of entwined brass twines adorned his wrist.

"What is your name?"

"Sohan."

"So, Sohan you're Shamu's son, then?"

"Yes."

"I am Akbar. We used to live there," Akbar said, pointing to his house. "Your father and uncle, we were good friends."

"Yes, I know," Sohan said, "I've heard stories."

"Oh, have you?"

Inside they had now built a labyrinth of rooms, crowding out the open space as Akbar remembered it. He could not tell which was Bherulal's room. He went back outside to find Sohan, but he had left. Akbar saw him turn the corner at the end of the street. Back inside, he knocked on a door. A woman opened it cautiously, holding it ajar enough to show her head. An edge of her marigold sari hiding her eyes. A large nose ring flirted with her lips. She pointed him to Bherulal's quarters.

Bherulal was eating supper, seated on the ground, a thali before him, containing two chapattis, a portion of beans and potatoes, and a small steel bowl filled with daal. On the side, a generous splotch of mango pickle spiced up the meagre victuals; the oil from the pickle had made its way to the chapattis, staining the bottom one. In nearly forty years the food on the plate hadn't changed much, Akbar noticed. Nor the time of supper. It was early evening, and they were still in the habit of finishing their meal before sunset. Akbar recalled how people in his household used to make fun of them. Fizza Chachi used to say, "These villagers, they are so backward, they eat their dinner while it is still so bright outside." If she were alive today, she would have seen that their so-called modern world was slowly turning back the clock to traditional, simpler ways.

Bherulal did not recognize Akbar immediately. But when it dawned on him, he shot up.

"Oh, Akbar, it's you, what a surprise," he said and hugged

him, making sure his dirty right hand did not touch Akbar's clothes. In the press of their bodies Akbar felt time collapsing, the old kindred affinity returning.

Bherulal was balding, and the remnant fringe of hair on the sides and back was greying. His moustache, thicker and greyer, made up for his caved-in cheeks. He beamed, displaying the extensive damage tobacco-chewing had done to his teeth.

"Good to see you," Bherulal said.

"Yes, it's been a long time," Akbar said.

His three daughters, now all married, lived in different cities. "You know," Bherulal said, "we don't marry our daughters in the same town, in the same *gotre* (sect)." He said he was still into carpentry. "Once a carpenter, always a carpenter." He smiled. "Work is good, I do more contracting these days. Don't have to dirty my hands anymore. How about you? How is life in Bombay?"

Bherulal's was a family of hardworking artisans. Life was tough and basic. While children from rich families like Akbar's went to school, boys like Bherulal had worked to supplement their family income. Akbar had seen him chiselling wood or pulling the plane with his older brother. He often used to go to their house to get sackfuls of wood shavings for his mother; she used them as kindling to start a fire for making chapattis.

Bherulal was not entirely illiterate; he had learned to read and write, enough to ply his trade. He talked about his family and his modest achievements with an easy, unconscious pride, without trying to impress anyone that he had done quite well for himself, despite life's disadvantages. With Akbar, his old friend, there was no need to show sneering contempt for the rich. He had made sure, he said, that his daughters got an education. And no, he did not go for a fourth one in pursuit of a son. "Daughters are more loyal," he said. "Also, I did not want to be blamed for the population explosion." He laughed heartily.

His wife came into the room from the adjoining kitchen bearing a cup of tea and Krackjack biscuits on a plate. The cup and saucer looked newer, rarely used, reserved for a special guest like him. She had overheard the conversation and must have sensed who had come and skipped the formality of asking whether the guest would have tea. Akbar was touched by the gesture. He had long come to understand that people who were hard done by, made hardy by misfortune, were instinctively generous. Their hospitality was genuine, radiating a warmth that people of his class had lost in their cold, calculating snobbery. The simple act of how a guest was treated, he thought, revealed so much about a people, about the temperature of their hearts.

"Oh, thank you, but there was no need for this," he said, mindful of not protesting too much.

"No formality, Akbar," Bherulal said, consciously eschewing the playful "Akbaria" he had used before. "Come eat roti with me?" he offered.

"No, thank you," Akbar said, placing his hand on his chest. "I came to . . . "

"Okay, never mind, have tea. Tell me, how's life treating you?"

Akbar said Bombay was no different from Udaipur, people were always busy, always rushing, and then there was the chaos of traffic, and all the pollution, and the madness of commuting. "It is a daily struggle."

"I miss Udaipur," he added.

"But you will see Udaipur has changed, too," Bherulal said.

"It is not a big city but pretends like it is. It has acquired all the bad habits of a metro. We even have malls now, can you believe it? There are more vehicles than people. Cows and cars fight for parking space." Bherulal chuckled as he licked the pickle with his forefinger.

———

Back in the house, the dust had settled from Khatun's furious cleaning spree. With the windows flung open, the festering air was swept away by the warm evening breeze. Khatun sat down on the bed to catch her breath. Arthritis in the knees didn't allow her to be on her feet too long. She asked for a drink of water. Akbar filled a glass from the flask they had brought with them.

"Would you like some tea?" he asked, and when she nodded, he went out to get some from the teashop.

The owner was a familiar face, now furrowed with deep lines and sagging skin and crusty eyes. Sitting beside a bubbling cauldron of oil, he was frying samosas for the evening clientele. Two stores down, a cluster of men stood around the *paan* shop, burdened with the affairs of the world. Each of them had the solution to set the world right, but unfortunately nobody would consult them. Their frustrations were plastered on the wall beside the *paan* shop. The colour of the wall was dark burgundy from the spat betel juice. For their targets, a local wag had sketched the likeness of politicians on the wall. Through the layers of red spit the outlines of the rogues' gallery were still recognizable: Sonia Gandhi, L K Advani, Narendra Modi, Mayawati, and Laloo Prasad Yadav. Quite a non-partisan spitting wall, Akbar thought, and public ire was surprisingly indiscriminate.

The politicians' caricatures brought to mind the blood-curdling 2002 riots in Ahmedabad. To him the episode of the young Momin man on the bus which he had taken from Ahmedabad to Udaipur summed up Narendra Modi's dubious achievements; he had been chief minister of Gujarat and was alleged to have encouraged the pogrom. He came to be known as the "Butcher of Gujarat", and his animus against Muslims was further underlined when he referred to the refugee camps of displaced victims as "baby-making factories". His political stars were on the ascendant and he was being touted to become the next prime minister of India. The Hindutava project, Akbar realized, was similar to that of Momin clergy's. They wanted to do to India what Mowlana had done to the Momins: turn a diverse vibrant people into a pliant, brainwashed citizenry with one religion, one language, one purpose, genuflecting to the great leader. And Akbar noted with alarm how rapidly they were achieving their goal.

The Momin man who had been taken away by the thugs, Akbar later discovered, was a relative of Shabbir. His remains were never found, and the news of his murder appeared as a small item buried in the back pages of the local Udaipur papers. Akbar had written an eyewitness account of the incident, but no editor in Udaipur would touch it. Later, when the story was published in *India Weekly*, it hardly stirred a conscience. So many had died and with such brutality and with such frequency that an isolated killing here and there perversely came as a relief.

As Akbar took the two cups of tea and went back to his mother he recalled that the man on the bus was not the only Momin victim. During the carnage in Ahmedabad dozens of Momins had to flee for safety as their homes and shops were

attacked and gutted. Mowlana had done nothing to rehabili-
tate the affected families and instead, as if to rub salt into their
wounds, had later felicitated Modi, inviting him in the mosque
and showering him with honour and honorariums.

29

SHABBIR FLEW TO BOMBAY ON a whim one January morning. He told Rukhsana he had a premonition; or was it a dream? He was certain, though, that something momentous was going to happen, and Bombay beckoned him. In his sleep, he sensed an apparition of Mowlana, a faint hovering image like a distant mirage, waving to him, saying goodbye. He woke up that morning sweating, his mind ill at ease, his head spinning. Some inner force was impelling him towards Bombay. He had to go.

Whenever Shabbir departed for his junkets, Rukhsana was happy to have him out of her hair, but when she heard the reason for his trip this time, she poured scorn over him. Although she had long decided not to interfere in his affairs, of late she had become short of temper, and lashed out at him on one pretext or the other. He responded to her with silence. That would make her angrier.

The two boys were away. Taher was a sophomore in Berkeley, and Taha was in New York, looking for a job after having graduated from Boston University. Rukhsana had now become manager of media relations, and work occupied her to an extent, but Akbar's departure and the possibility of never seeing him again had created an unease in her mind. Shabbir's obsession with all things Mowlana was a constant irritant. His antics, which she had learned to ignore before, now raised her hackles. She challenged him often and would ridicule him for his beard, the way he looked, the way he dressed. She nagged him about how he neglected his family and how he was running all the time after his Mowlana like a puppy. She told him if he was so besotted with the guru, he shouldn't have married and ruined her life.

Cantankerous, irritable and obnoxious. She was becoming a person she did not like, a person she did not recognize. Akbar would definitely not approve of that person. For his sake, she wanted to be sane. She would always care about what he thought of her, although she had completely lost touch with him. She texted him a few times, in desperation. He was kind enough to reply, but he did not encourage her either.

A bleakness descended upon her, and everything seemed pointless. As a wife she considered herself both a failure and a victim and as a lover unbelievably unlucky. She was back to a place where she had been in the early years of her marriage. Wracked by hopelessness and despair, she began to see the psychiatrist again who prescribed a slew of multicoloured capsules to calm her nerves. She woke up every morning as though from a hangover.

All through this she kept in touch with her mother. Her father had passed away some years before following a sudden stroke. Zubaida said he had made some bad business decisions and had piled up debts. None of Mowlana's blessings helped. Stress and shame got to him in the end, Zubaida said. She was now old and not keeping well. Her husband's financial ruin had left her in penury, alone in a rented house. Their house which Qamar had renovated with such messianic joy for Mowlana and from which he had so callously banished Rukhsana had been sold to pay the creditors. Rukhsana sent her mother money to help her get by. Her brothers would visit her every few days, bring her groceries, and take her out for fresh air if she was up to it. Zubaida had mentioned that Khatun had come to visit her and that she, Khatun, was planning to move back to Udaipur. Rukhsana asked about Akbar, whether he was moving, too. Zubaida said she did not know.

Rehana, her younger sister, was settled in Singapore, with her engineer husband. When she talked to Rehana or her mother, she would relate Shabbir's latest shenanigans. Zubaida had stopped cursing their fate. Instead, her new refrain was that she was responsible for Rukhsana's misery; that she should have stood up to that pig-headed man. Rukhsana felt for her mother, she too had suffered but had finally learned to deal with her bully. Her mother was not so lucky. She never uttered a word to her mother about the abuse or about her battle with depression. She made no mention of Akbar, how he had come back into her life, all too briefly, illumined it, and had then fallen away like a shooting star. How could she tell her what demons had possessed her since.

———

After the Sadikot incident, the Radicals had threatened unrest if Mowlana stepped into their city. The infallible, absolute leader did not come to Udaipur for twenty-five years. When he finally did come, the Radicals had become complacent, their numbers had dwindled.

Like the jubilees of olden times when slaves and prisoners were freed, the Mowlana prior to his visit to Udaipur lifted the excommunication fatwa. The slaves were suddenly allowed to meet their friends and relations—those whom they had shunned for a generation. Qamar had been excited by this news. He came home and announced, "Mowlana says we can meet the infidels and is urging us to make special effort to reconnect with friends and relatives. Why don't you call your family and your friend Khatun and talk to them?" He had no shame when he said that. She reminded him about Rukhsana and Akbar. "That means we destroyed their lives for nothing?" Then Zubaida let out a litany of pent up complaints: "We broke relationships with our people for nothing? I could not be with my family to mourn my mother's death; I could not attend my nephews and nieces' weddings. On countless occasions, happy and sad, we could not be with our loved ones. All that was for nothing?" To which Qamar simply said, "Mowlana knows best."

A few years later, Mowlana excommunicated the Radicals again, because they would not return to the fold without their grievances being addressed. Once again an embargo on relationships was imposed. Qamar conveyed the news and ordered Zubaida not to have any truck with the infidels. Zubaida was furious. "Don't you have a mind of your own? Dancing like a puppet on Mowlana's strings. You and that fool Shabbir and his dimwit father, you all should wear bangles?"

To question his manhood and associate that with Mowlana was the ultimate insult. Qamar could not believe his ears when she said that. He waited for a few seconds, fuming, and began trembling like a reed in the wind, and then he let his hands fly. Zubaida covered her face with her arms but was not afraid, and she did not ask him to stop or move away. Nothing could be worse than the pain of her girl's suffering. Perhaps, she deserved this. A punishment was in order. Ever since Rukhsana was sent packing all those years ago to her aunt's place, she had been breathing regret. And whenever Rukhsana narrated Shabbir's misdeeds on the phone, she wept silently, wishing the ground would open up under her. For this dithering Mowlana and this spineless husband she had crushed her daughter's heart, ruined her life.

———

Shabbir was convinced that Rukhsana was faking her depression; she was being a drama queen. She lacked faith and purpose, and his single-minded devotion made her jealous. She was a lost soul, and her hatred for Mowlana had made her mean and evil. That's what happens to people who have nothing to believe in. America was the shining example of a society where a lack of faith leads people astray into infidelity, promiscuity, incest and other sins. It was little wonder that half the marriages in America failed. Then they called it depression.

If she had held on to the rope of Mowlana she wouldn't be so deranged. And by God, he had been very tolerant of her. Even when he was forced to mete out punishment it was out of good conscience; it was for her own good. He was duty-bound to quell her heresies, to instill faith in her. And he always took care not to overdo it because he was mindful of the Quranic ruling which prescribed only light beating, and which according to some commentators meant no more than patting with a feather. But Shabbir disagreed with that interpretation. If he could disown his mother for the sake of Mowlana he could damn well teach his wife a lesson or two. But she had proven to be incorrigible. He would have long divorced her but he did not want his boys to suffer a fate similar to his. A broken home would have deprived them of proper care and love and stability. He had seen enough broken families in America and did not want to be like those selfish parents who only think of themselves. Besides, he had a good standing among Boston Momins and did not want to be seen as the man of faith who could not control his wife. The tolerance and self-restraint he had shown her all these years now turned into pity. And he had run out of patience with her.

That morning, after the liminal urging of Mowlana in his sleep, he took a flight to Bombay. The day after he arrived, Mowlana passed away. Thousands gathered outside Kaifee Mahal in south Bombay for the funeral. The coffin was draped in the Indian tricolour, an honour reserved for national heroes. That gesture did not go down well with overseas Momins, especially those of Pakistan. They could not imagine why their spiritual master, whose followers lived all over the world and belonged to different nationalities, should identify with Indian nationalism in death, and in so public a manner. Shouldn't he have been covered with the sacred verses of the Quran? But wonder was all they were capable of. The same Mowlana had trained them to keep their opinions to themselves. And perhaps, like everything else, there was hidden wisdom in this, too.

Shabbir was heartbroken. Sad beyond words, beyond consolation. He felt vindicated that his premonition had been correct. Mowlana had personally called him out here, and that too with enough notice. He felt blessed, he felt like the chosen one, Mowlana had singled him out for beatification. The accretions of his acts of devotion had at last culminated in this miracle. His faith had become hard and beautiful, like a diamond, and now the glint from that rock-solid devotion illuminated another divine face on the horizon: Mowlana Mukammal Fakerudin, the son and successor. He was the new master.

Shabbir met Qasim, his friend from Arusha, at the funeral. Qasim reminded him of their trek from Udaipur to Bombay, the arduous journey they undertook for the long life of Mowlana, who despite the prayers and peregrinations of a million Momins was now dead, six feet below ground. He told Qasim perhaps the walk was not long enough. They should have circled the globe. But he found solace in his special connection to him. He did not tell Qasim about the miracle that brought him to Bombay. That would amount to bragging. If anything, it was a sign to rededicate himself with equal zest to the new Mowlana.

———

The following year, Mukammal Fakerudin visited the United States in a whirlwind tour of the cities where his flock lived. Shabbir followed him wherever he went. The supplicant's posture—joined hands and the mantra of "Mowlana Mowlana" on his lips—had become his second nature as it had in all the devotees. Mowlana Mukammal had a special penchant for palanquins, and it became his preferred mode of conveyance. He would arrive at a mosque in a luxury car, and then would be immediately transferred to a palanquin and carried around the precincts of the mosque. He enjoyed the ride with a muted smile, wearing his smirk like a nose ring while devotees shelled out hard cash for the honour of lending shoulder to his royal weight.

Shabbir paid five hundred dollars for five steps. He would have gone for more, but he wanted to spread out the privilege, and also take his benedictions in small doses. Mowlana visited nine cities, and in every city Shabbir carried his palanquin for five steps. Every step seemed like a pilgrimage. For Mowlana was, the believers were always told, the *Haqiqi Kaaba* (the Real Kaaba) and *Quran-e-Natiq* (the Speaking Quran). In the presence of Mowlana, the tenets of Islam stood abrogated. The Quran, the Sharia, the Kaaba were meant for ordinary Muslims. Momins had their Mowlana who completed their religion.

Among them, Shabbir felt he was the chosen one. He now

carried three passport-size photos in his wallet of the new Mowlana, his father, and his father's father. Large portraits of them encased in elaborate gilt frames occupied the length of his living room wall above the fireplace. The three pairs of eyes presided over every mote of dust that floated in the room; nothing escaped their scrutiny. Rukhsana thought they followed her every move, and she always sat with her back to the three portraits, their collective gaze burning into her. Once she caught them looking at each other and smirking under their straggly white beards as Shabbir lay prostrate before them. He prayed facing the altar. He had been delighted by the coincidence that the portraits and the Kaaba were in the same direction. When he had hung up the pictures, he said that it was not for nothing that his faith in Mowlanas was aligned with that of Allah. All the heavenly bodies were perfectly lined up. If any proof of the correctness of his belief were needed, here it was.

———

Shabbir went to JFK airport to bid adieu to Mowlana. He waited outside in the parking lot until he saw the aircraft taking off. It was an Emirates flight, and he saw the logo. He closed his eyes, joined his hands, and prayed for a safe flight for his Mowlana. Then he bent forward towards the prayer beads hanging from the rear-view mirror and gently pulled them towards his mouth to kiss them. The pendant bore the photo of Mowlana. The string of beads snapped, and he was left holding the pendant as the beads slithered and scattered all over. This was a bad omen, for sure. But since the pendant with the photo was secure in his hands, he knew Mowlana was safe.

The next day, his boss, Joe Abigail, called him to his office, looked up at him over black-rimmed square glasses, and gave him the pink slip. "I'm doing this with great reluctance, Shaybier" he said. "We value your work, you know that, but we have no patience for negligence. I gave you enough time, more than I should have, more than I was allowed to, but it seems you are not interested in your work any longer. I'm sorry."

Shabbir couldn't care less. He was given two weeks' notice, but he said he would rather quit immediately. He packed his things and left. This setback was foretold, and he was relieved that it was just this, a minor blip, nothing more calamitous. He went home, and the first thing he did was send an email request to Mowlana wanting to know what to do next. Two days later he got the reply asking him to come meet the lord. He took the evening flight to Bombay, and the following day he was sitting at the feet of his master in Kaifee Mahal.

Before he was allowed audience with Mowlana, a handler at the door asked Shabbir how much was in "there."

"In where?" Shabbir asked.

"In the envelope, for the salam."

"Seven hundred US dollars."

"Not enough, a thousand for a private one-on-one."

Shabbir dug around in his pockets but could manage only another ninety.

"That will not do," the handler said, shaking his lean, bony face from which sparse strands of white down swayed under his breath as he spoke.

"That's all I have."

The handler pointed at Shabbir's fingers with his eyes.

"What?" Shabbir asked.

The handler bobbed his head again and pointed at his finger.

"What, this?" Shabbir raised his ring finger. It was a solid gold band with a delicate lattice design engraved on it.

Rukhsana's father had bought it from Zaveri Bazaar during a special trip to Bombay for her wedding shopping. Shabbir hesitated for a moment then quickly removed the ring and put it in the envelope. As Shabbir was pocketing his ninety dollars, the handler motioned him to put that in too.

At the far end of a large, carpeted hall, Mowlana Fakerudin sat in an ornate cushioned chair, the type used at wedding receptions. He looked forlorn, like an abandoned groom—there was no one else in the hall. Shabbir walked toward him obsequiously, bent double and feeling terrified. When Shabbir kissed his feet, Mowlana nudged Shabbir's face with his left foot, signalling him to stop. Shabbir lifted his head and sat on his knees before him with joined hands, tears in his eyes, unable to speak. He could still feel the brush of Mowlana's foot on his cheek.

"What brings you here," Mowlana asked.

Shabbir told him. He also told him about his wife's stubborn lack of faith and how unhappy his life was.

Mowlana listened to him, expressionless, and remained quiet for a long time. Shabbir sat staring at Mowlana's feet with their silk socks. Tears had dried up on his face, which was still contorted in an expression of tragedy.

"What is missing in your life," Mowlana said suddenly, startling Shabbir, "is the roti of love."

Shabbir lifted his head, puzzled.

"Ask your wife to make roti—chapatti—you also make chapatti with her. Everything that you do in life must be about roti. This is how you will attract love back into your life—love of your wife, of God and, of course, me."

"But she will not listen to me, Mowlana."

"You are a man. Must I teach you how to deal with a woman?

Don't you know what is to be done with disobedient wives?" Mowlana said, and dismissed him with a supercilious motion of the hand.

———

One year later, Shabbir was on the phone finalizing a business deal. He was sitting in his air-conditioned glass-walled cabin in his new factory in Udaipur, from where he had an unobstructed view of the shop floor.

The wheel of a lathe spun furiously, and sawdust flew from it as a worker expertly shaped a piece of wood. Towards the front of the factory, by the large sliding door through which the sun came rushing in, an aluminum pane as big as a bedsheet was being fed into a roller and emerged with small circles cut into it. The screech of metal cutting metal rent the air. At the back of the factory a section was portioned off where female workers were hunched over sewing machines. The women were stitching hijabs, attaching lace trims, giving the finishing touches. The master tailor stood at a bench, cutting a pattern out of a pink dotted cotton cloth. Bolts of colourful fabrics were stacked on one side of the shack. Hijab-clad Momin women were ridiculed as "penguins" when this outfit was first introduced, but now, a generation later, the dress had become a fixture of Momin identity. Girls began to wear them as they came of age. There was a captive market for the hijab and Shabbir was keen to cash in on it.

A dusty, tin-roofed factory in the outskirts of Udaipur was a far cry from his swanky, carpeted former office in Boston. Trained as a software engineer who built algorithm models for actuarial risk assessment, he was now sourcing materials for toys and hijabs. He did not regret this new status, did not see it as a slide down the social ladder. He felt blessed. If not for the new Mowlana, he wouldn't be back in his native land, serving his people, serving his master. With the previous Mowlana's blessing and instruction, he had travelled across the seven seas to a foreign land to make a living and raise a family. And now after three decades Mukammal had commanded him to uproot his life in the US and return home. Shabbir had not questioned the Mowlana then and had less reason to question this one now. It was not for him to reason why.

He sat amidst the clang and clutter of his factory in Udaipur, producing toy rolling pins, roti boards, skillets, lumps of white playdough and stoves. The roti-making set was packed in cellophane and tied off with a red ribbon. The ends of the ribbon were twirled into spirals for effect. Shabbir insisted on this flourish. He found a hungry market for these toy sets which had become *de rigueur* as return gifts at children's parties. His high-end products were in even greater demand. Handmade rolling pins were carved out of soapstone and marble and sandalwood. They had Mowlana's name engraved on them. They came in different sizes and soon began to adorn the showcases and mantles of Momin homes. Some of the premium rolling pins were studded with semiprecious stones. Mowlana had made the rolling pin the emblem of his realm. The Momins were rediscovering the roti and roti-making all over again. They took to it as if Mowlana had invented bread, and after having invented it had then the wisdom and generosity to infuse it with his spiritual aura. That bread being the cardinal link between their body and their soul came to be treated as a revealed truth.

Shabbir had worked the rolling pin into the logo of his company, Mukammal Art Emporium. The name stood in bold relief across the sign board, painted in red and green above the entrance of the retail outlet in Bapu Bazaar where he sold his products. The business flourished, making not only roti sets but all kinds of trinkets and gift items in which the rolling pin motif appeared in one form or another. He shipped all across India where Momins were settled, and orders had begun to come in from the Gulf countries as well.

But success had not been easy. At one point he had almost given up, faced with the sullen bureaucracy, the endless greasing of palms, the labour tantrums and the run-around for a million other things. But the faith in Mowlana kept him going. He had become so busy that he hardly remembered Boston—or that it had been a part of his life. The only thing he did religiously—no matter how preoccupied he was—was to speak to Taha and Taher weekly. In their talks, though, he never asked them about their mother. He did think about her but only with a sense of relief, like a man who had been freed of a great burden. He felt lighter, and happier and was ever grateful to the Mowlana. He had blessed the divorce, as his father had blessed the marriage.

30

On the drive back to Woburn from Logan Airport, Rukhsana was crawling on I-93 going north. Home was just thirty minutes away, but now caught in the rush hour traffic there was no knowing when she would reach. She was not eager to get home. It was empty. Taher, who had been with her for four months in the summer, was off to Berkeley. She had just dropped him off at the airport. Having him around had kept her mind anchored. For one week during the summer, his older brother Taha had come visiting. Rukhsana's joy had no bounds. She cooked their favourite foods—mutton samosas, daal chawal palidu and butter chicken. Over dinner they would have long chats, and the boys would inform her what their father was up to in Udaipur. Rukhsana would make no comment and listen quietly. The boys had long known the estranged relationship between their parents, and although they had a soft corner for their mother, they had begun to understand their father's dedication to his faith. They did not approve of it but were able to appreciate that he was different and wanted to colour his world differently. And that was okay. This, they tried to explain to Rukhsana, and it gladdened her heart to see that her boys had an open mind and could empathise with different points of view, with different ways of being.

But how could she tell them that there was more to Shabbir's fanaticism than what they knew. How could she tell them that she too had desired to colour her world differently? How could she tell them that many a time, out of humiliation and pain, she had wanted to chuck it all away and go back to her mother in India? But she stayed put because of them. They kept her going. If she was able to get through life thus far, it was because they were the reason for her to live. All other men had been less than faithful. The three of them together made a good team and understood each other without context, without having to refer to the specifics of life's vicissitudes.

So far life had had purpose. Now the boys had flown the nest for good. She had given them the best a mother could. She knew she could not hold their hand and guide them every step of the way; she had told them to follow their desires, what pitfalls to watch out for, to be good people and not to give up on their dreams. Ultimately they had to be on their own, that was the way of the world. Much as it pained her to admit it, she knew they would fall and stumble and learn life's harsh, unforgiving lessons. They would laugh and cry, they would find joy and love, they would be pummelled by sorrow, and they would be beaten by defeat. Life would hand them their share of happiness and heartbreak, but in the end, she knew, they would do fine. She started crying. Tears flowed from a mythical place as ancient as a mother's heart. But it gave her great satisfaction that they would always be there for her. In a few years' time they would marry and have families and she would have grandchildren. There was something to look forward to but for now she was all alone and perhaps always would be.

On reaching home, she felt an end-of-the-world sadness that she had not experienced since she had left Akbar sleeping in the hotel room in New Hampshire two years ago. She shut the door behind her, flung her bag and keys on the side table, crashed on the couch, buried her face in her hands, and sobbed. Just as she had wept quietly in that hotel room. She had stared at him for a long time as he slept. She wanted to kiss him goodbye but was afraid she might wake him up. There was nothing left to say. Their last night together, just like their first, she could not sleep. They lay entwined, enveloped in a silence that comes before the end of things. He was to go back to Bombay in a few weeks, and that would be that. But she would have memories to cherish. Akbar had given her a happiness she had never known or ever expected. How could she have, given the odds? It came as a surprise, out of nowhere when she was not looking. And it was worth every moment while it lasted, and worth every tear now that it had ended. How she had cried all the way home after leaving him that morning; how she was seized by the desire to turn back at every freeway exit on the way.

In the two years since they parted, a darkness had seeped into her soul despite the meaning and purpose her sons gave her. She felt restless. She could feel bits of her *self* dissolving; a breach had occurred, her personhood, her sense of being was leaking and she was powerless to plug the levee. Every bout with depression would end in tears. She missed her mother whom she had not seen in years. How she yearned to bury her face in her mother's lap, the only place in the world where she knew she would find peace. Security.

As she wiped her tears, she felt like she were rising in a graveyard among a miasma of rotting corpses. Her back ached, and she could sense the end was nigh. She was tired, tired of being herself, tired of being alone, tired of being lonely. Her head was splitting. *I should make some tea.* She went to the kitchen and put on the kettle. She watched as the blue flame leapt up, and then returned to the living room and stood before the triumvirate of Mowlanas on the wall and stared at them. This was Shabbir's holy wall. *Why didn't the fool take his gods back with him?* Three pairs of eyes stared back at her, mocking.

Here was the unholy trinity responsible for all that was wrong with her life. She reached out for the middle portrait and yanked it off the wall in one quick jerk. This one had even robbed her of her name. *Who actually does that?* The frame was heavier than she thought, and she slightly lunged forward to keep her balance. She heaved the frame above her head and brought it down with as much force as she could muster on the coffee table. Glass shattered on solid oak. The frame held, and she brought it down again. It split into pieces. She turned the portrait face up, placed it on the table, and beat it with a side of the frame like a washerwoman beating clothes at Fateh Sagar. The stick broke, and she was left with a sharp stump in her hand. She stabbed the portrait. Pockmarked and gashed, the face, she felt, was still contorted in a sneer. She spat on it and ripped it into pieces, paying special attention to the eyes and the mouth. Exhausted, she slumped on the couch and studied the remaining two portraits. The kettle started whistling insistently. She got up as though waiting for the signal and went after the remaining two portraits with renewed rage.

When she had finished, she stood in the middle of the mayhem like a warrior queen who had slain the demons. The whistling of the kettle had died down. The sole of her right foot bled from a gash, and she was hot and sweaty. Throat dry. She looked around, eyes cold, face blank, body strangely calm. She gave a light shove at the coffee table with the injured foot and shrieked in pain. She threw herself on the couch, looking up, hands and legs spread-eagled.

Shabbir should have been a witness to this, she thought, surveying the room. She should have staged this desecration for his benefit, the day they had their last fight. On returning from

Bombay after his meeting with Mowlana, he was a changed man, aggressive and impatient like he used to be before. He did not tell her that he had lost his job, but declared that they must move back to India, settle in Udaipur, start all over. She had said she was not going anywhere.

"My boys are here, my job is here, my life is here."

"But my Mowlana is not here," he said.

"What do you mean?"

"Nothing. I've made up my mind. We've got to move."

"I'm not going anywhere."

Rukhsana would have yielded, if he had broken the news to her gently and kept Mowlana out of it. But he was too gung-ho, too pumped up to have any use for tact. He was in no mood to cajole a nutcase and saw no need to win her favour. He was tired of her, of her nagging, of her cussedness.

"You can stay here if that's what you want. I'm leaving."

It had been a year now since Shabbir left. Before he departed, she had made sure that all the loose ends were tied up: the house was transferred to her name; the remainder of the mortgage, for another five or six years, was his to pay; he would see Taher through university; he would foot the bills till they were formally divorced, after which he would be on the hook for alimony. He had no savings, no investment. A better part of his income had been squandered on Mowlana.

———

Rukhsana looked at her foot. The blood had clotted around the cut. She wiggled her toes and winced as pain shot up from the wound. Thinking of Shabbir depressed her more. Her life could have been so different. Even after Akbar's second coming, and going. For the first few months after his departure she had managed fine, then she didn't know what happened. *Maybe I've sinned in the eyes of the world. But I'll do it again and again, a thousand times over. I've the right to be happy. Too bad if my happiness does not sit well with the morality of the world. To hell with the whole lot of them. And what do I care? And what is left to care for? Look at me, alone and abandoned.* She did not attempt to wipe her tears and felt the burning sensation on her cheeks.

She surveyed the living room and felt completely detached from the scene, feeling like an alien who had suddenly landed in a strange, unknown place. *What am I to do?* Tears rolled afresh, wails emerging from unfathomable depths. She felt the devastation around her assuming a shape, like a beast, baring its fangs, slowly creeping toward her, ready to swallow her whole. She reached for the TV remote lying on the armrest and threw it at the menacing apparition. The remote hit the cabinet across the room and crashed to the floor. She bawled again. *Oh my boys, my darlings, I love you so much.* She kept repeating their names as she wept.

Night had fallen. The neighbours' kids could be heard playing outside on the driveway. She was impervious to their shrill cries. She sat in the dark for a long time, hungry and thirsty and defeated. She had heard the kettle crack and sputter but paid no heed to it. *Let this house burn down for all I care. Let this world end.* She got up suddenly. She tramped carelessly on the debris and headed to the walk-in closet in the bedroom, slid the door open, and pushed the hangers aside; she reached for the clothes, threw them down. Then she went for the chest of drawers of a dresser, flung out makeup kits and cosmetic knick-knacks and vials in careless fury.

There it was, in the bottom drawer beneath Akbar's plastic

folder of poems, which she had kept hidden. It was the scarf he had given her. His parting gift, his only gift. She took it to the living room. She did not bother to turn the lights on. She felt her way to the foyer and looked up at the ceiling fan; the street light from the high window in the side wall fell on it. She climbed up the stairs, clutching the banister, scarf in hand. She flung one end of the scarf around the stem of the fan trying to lasso it. After several unsuccessful attempts, she felt exhausted. She went down to the kitchen and brought a step-stool. Securing one end of the scarf to the fan, she tied the other around her neck. She stood there contemplating. *Life is too long to keep living without you.* Then the faces of her sons flashed into her mind.

———

The day before returning to Bombay, having settled his mother in Udaipur, Akbar went up to the terrace, to revisit his child-hood haunt. He was dejected at what he saw. The plants which had brightened up the terrace were long dead and gone. The concrete planters that Dadaji had got built into the wall lay bare. The deep red paint on them, once bright and brilliant, was eaten away by the rain and the sun, exposing the grey under-belly like ugly, naked truth. The cement grille along the front railing through which Moiz and his friends spied on women taking baths on the opposite terrace was broken in places, given to gaping holes, no longer capable of shielding voyeurs.

Akbar stood at the spot where he used to sleep in the summer months. The floor was hot from the afternoon sun and covered with a patina of fine dust. He lay down on the ground, palms cushioning his head. The sky was clear, a bleached blue ceiling of a late summer afternoon. At night the stars would come out. Many must have fallen like autumn leaves since he and Rukhsana last saw them, and many more must have been dimmed by the city lights.

Few slept on rooftops in summertime now. Progress and prosperity had driven people indoors to air-conditioned rooms. The moon and the stars continued to put on their nocturnal show, their magic wasted on humans. He recalled the sepia giggles of the young cousins as they teased each other and played the fool before their mothers hushed them down and told them to go to sleep. He recalled a time when he awoke in the middle of the night and was stunned by the star-studded heavens. That was perhaps his first moment of epiphany: a pair of eyes, a beating heart, and the indescribable grandeur that hung over him. He had felt small and insignificant yet seemed strangely connected to the infinite.

He got up and dusted his clothes and took another flight of stairs up to the next terrace. This was his kite-flying arena. Here his many dreams had foundered as his kites were defeated and cut away. He had wanted to excel at kite-flying, like Moiz, but had no innate talent for it, and his efforts never amounted to much. He walked around the railing surveying the city; everything he remembered looked broken and old. In the distance, though, on the horizon in the north of the city, tall, new apartment buildings had risen up. Traditional joint families were breaking down and moving into single-family flats. Progress had distanced not only people from Nature, but also from each other.

He looked at the "tower top", the topmost terrace. It seemed so tiny. How he used to scramble up to it. Now he should be able to scale it in one swift pull-up, and he did just that. He stood in the centre, not daring to go to the edge. It was indeed so tiny. He couldn't imagine how he was allowed to climb up here unsupervised. What motivated him? Rukhsana? Had this been his attempt to impress her? He took a step forward and looked down, and the same dizziness that seized him all those years ago returned.

He turned his glance to Rukhsana's house. It lay abandoned. He had learned that it was sold to repay a debt. Her father had passed away. His fortunes had declined despite Mowlana's blessings, and he died a poor man, buried in debt. Few turned up for his funeral. The Mowlana, to whom he had devoted his life and for whose sake he had broken his daughter's heart, had denied him the "passport to paradise," because an indigent Zubaida could not afford to pay for it. He was buried without any guarantee of heaven.

What an absurd end to a life of unflinching faith. Something knotted up in his stomach. A father's folly and a daughter's ruin. How innocent lives were trapped in blind worship and wasted. He felt sad and desolate, as he had felt on that awful night in prison. The shrieks of Moiz and his friends had become a metronome of pain in his memory. It reminded him of loss, of loneliness, of everything that was bad and horrible in the world.

It started drizzling, and the bone-dry earth emanated a scent of happiness. Soon the drizzle turned into a steady downpour, drenching the thirsty world. Akbar felt grateful for the rain. From which unknown skies it had come to touch him, soak him, to wash away the debris of wasted dreams, of wasted hopes.

The parrot-green doors on the balcony were shut. His eyes were fixed on them, and through the mist of rain the scene looked surreal. He willed the doors to fling open, and Rukhsana to emerge like a resplendent seraphim, tearing through the scrim of stubborn, persistent reality. *Oh Rukhsana!* A wave of *saudade* swept over him. His knees felt weak. He slumped down on the floor and sobbed. The tears mingled with the rain. He sat there for a long time, his arms hugging his legs. The Monsoon Palace on the hill behind him was shrouded in the clouds. A deafening thunder rumbled overhead and he waited for the lightning to claim him. Some things are just not meant to be.

Glossary

aapa   elder sister
ahimsa   nonviolence
akni   meat broth
aakhirat   the hereafter
aleph, bey, tey   first three letters of the Urdu alphabet
baniyas   a Hindu community or caste of traders
barazi   East African breakfast dish (pigeon peas simmered in coconut milk)
bhenchod   sister-fucker
beta   son
bhabhi   sister-in-law
bhai   brother
bhajias   savoury fritters made with chickpea
bindi   round dots Hindu women wear on their foreheads
biryani   rice cooked with meat and spices
chacha   paternal uncle
chachi   paternal uncle's wife
daal   lentil soup/curry
dada/dadaji   paternal grandfather
dupatta   scarf usually worn with shalwar-kameez
Eid ul-Fitr   Islamic festival celebrated after Ramzan
Eidie   cash gifts received/given on Eid
Fajr namaz   morning prayer
Fatiha   opening chapter of the Quran
gora   fair—slang for a white man
Haj   the pilgrimage to Mecca
halqa   group, class
haq   truth, right
harami   bastard

houri   angel

iddat   period of mourning

Inqalab zindabad   Long live the revolution

Insha'allah   God willing

jaana/janum   dearest

Jai Sia Ram   Hail Lord Rama

Janab   Sir

kaamwali bai   slang for domestic help, woman servant

kaffir   unbeliever

kajal   kohl

Karbala   the place of the martyrdom of Imam Hussain in Iraq

keema   curry made from ground meat

khameer naan   flat bread made with a rising agent (khameer)

Khamma Mowlana   Welcome Mowlana.

Kurta-pyjama   loose long-sleeved tunic and pants

lanat   curse with divine reprobation

lehnga   long skirt reaching up to the ankles

madarchod   motherfucker

Maghrib   West in Arabic, also time for evening prayer

maharaj   honorific for a king or priest

majlis   religious gathering

marsiya   hymn or elegiac poetry, its recital

mandazi   East African fried sweet bread

matam   beating of chest in memory of Imam Hussain

Miyakda/Miyabhai   Slang/derogatory term for Muslims

mohalla   neighbourhood

Moharram   The first month of Islamic calendar; its first ten days are commemorated by the Shia in honour of Imam Hussain and the tragedy of Karbala

muddai   infidel, accused

mullah   muslim priest

munafiq   hypocrite

Nahajul Balagha   The Way of Eloquence—collection of sermons, letters by Iman Ali

namaz   ritual prayer Muslims perform five times a day

nani   maternal grandmother

nankatai   Indian-style shortbread

nihari   curry made of boneless beef, cooked overnight on a slow fire

nikah   marriage ceremony

niqab   veil that covers the entire head and face except the eyes

Noor   Divine light

paan   betel leaf concoction which usually includes diluted lime paste, catechu paste and tobacco

pagdi   a turban

Paramatama   Supreme Being

paratha   flat bread

paya   goat trotters

pheta   hard round hat golden in colour

pilla   puppy

Qayamat   The Day of Judgement

qazi   judge or cleric

Ramzan   also Ramadan, month of abstinence and fasting

rogan josh   meat dish

Saab, Saheb, Sahib   Sir

sabr   patience

sadqah   charity

salam   greeting of peace, also in Momin parlance the act of greeting and giving money to the priest

salwar-kameez   slacks and tunic worn by women

shaheed   martyr

Shariah, Shariat   Islamic law

shahzada   prince

sheer-khurma   a sweet dish—vermicelli sautéed in ghee, and boiled in milk, sugar and dates, and garnished with nuts and saffron

sherwani   long overcoat similar to Nehru jacket

Sunnah   practices of Prophet Muhammad

surah   verse of the Quran

tawaf   circumambulation (around the Kaaba)

tasbih   rosary

thaal   large metal platter around which people sit and eat

tilak   dash of vermilion on the forehead

topi   skullcap

Urdu   a language of the northern Indian subcontinent closely related to Hindi

Yamaraj   the god of death in Hinduism

zanana   of or belonging to women

Ziyarat   to visit, pay respects at a gravesite

Author's note

I owe a debt of gratitude to many people without whose inspiration and support this book would not have been written and published.

The first draft of the novel was long and rambling and I'm grateful to Lubaina Fidaali, Sriram Sirinivasan, Razia Sanwari and Saeeda Quaisar for ploughing through it and giving their thoughtful comments and suggestions. I must thank Allister Thomson for editing one of the many early versions. Farzana Doctor was always generous with her time and advice, guiding this rookie author through the intricacies of the publishing world.

I am indebted to Nurjehan Aziz and MG Vassanji for seeing promise in the book and believing in the importance of the story I wanted to tell. It was an honour to have my work edited by Mr Vassanji. He pointed out many gaps and inconsistencies in the manuscript and helped me put this novel into shape. With his keen editorial eye and sharp focus on the story, he kept my wayward fancies in check. But, alas, not always successfully. The shortcomings and lapses that might still remain are entirely of my own doing.

Lastly, I wish to thank my wife Shahnaz for her unwavering support. She indulged my mad desire to write and was one of the first readers and critics.

This book is a work of fiction. Resemblances to people and events are either coincidental or have been fictionalized. The story spans many years during which time Bombay becomes Mumbai, but I have stuck to using "Bombay" throughout to be consistent and to avoid confusion.

I dedicate this book to all the brave men and women who have dared to challenge religious tyranny and continue to fight for their freedom of conscience and self-dignity. It is a story that needed to be told, and what a privilege it is to be able to tell it. I feel humbled and grateful.